HELLSING 8

平野耕太
KOHTA HIRANO

translation
DUANE JOHNSON

lettering
WILBERT LACUNA

DARK HORSE MANGA

DMP
Digital Manga Publishing

publishers
MIKE RICHARDSON and HIKARU SASAHARA

editors
TIM ERVIN and FRED LUI

collection designer
DAVID NESTELLE

T 251341

English-language version produced by
DARK HORSE COMICS and DIGITAL MANGA PUBLISHING.

HELLSING VOLUME 8

published by
Dark Horse Manga
a division of Dark Horse Comics, Inc.
10956 SE Main Street
Milwaukie, OR 97222

darkhorse.com

Digital Manga Publishing
1487 W. 178th St. Ste. 300
Gardena, CA 90248

dmpbooks.com

To find a comics shop in your area, call the
Comic Shop Locator Service toll-free at 1-888-266-4226

First edition: June 2007
ISBN-10: 1-59307-780-7
ISBN-13: 978-1-59307-780-8

1 3 5 7 9 10 8 6 4 2
Printed in Canada

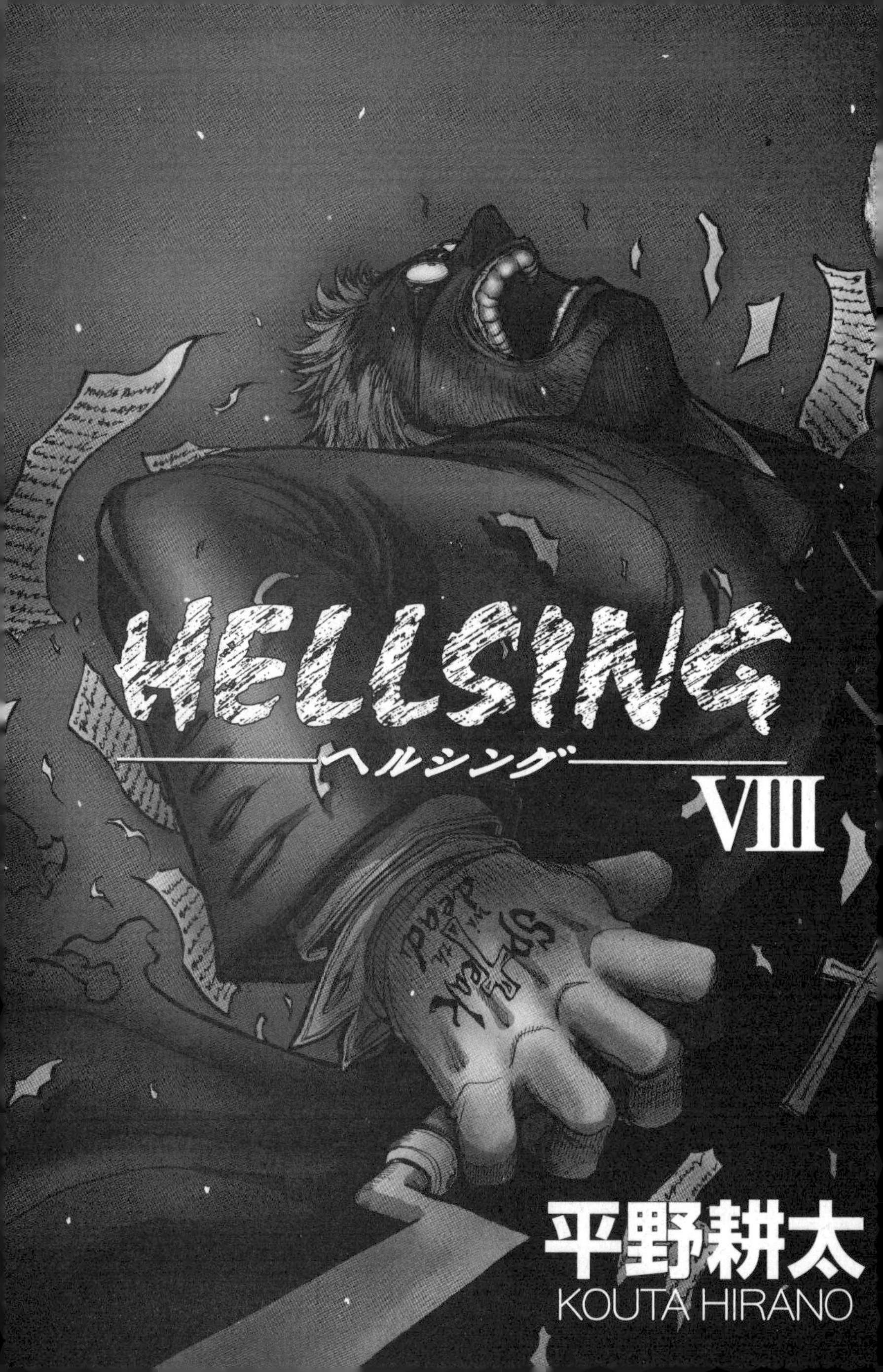
HELLSING
ヘルシング
VIII
平野耕太
KOUTA HIRANO

HELLSING⑧

ORDER 1

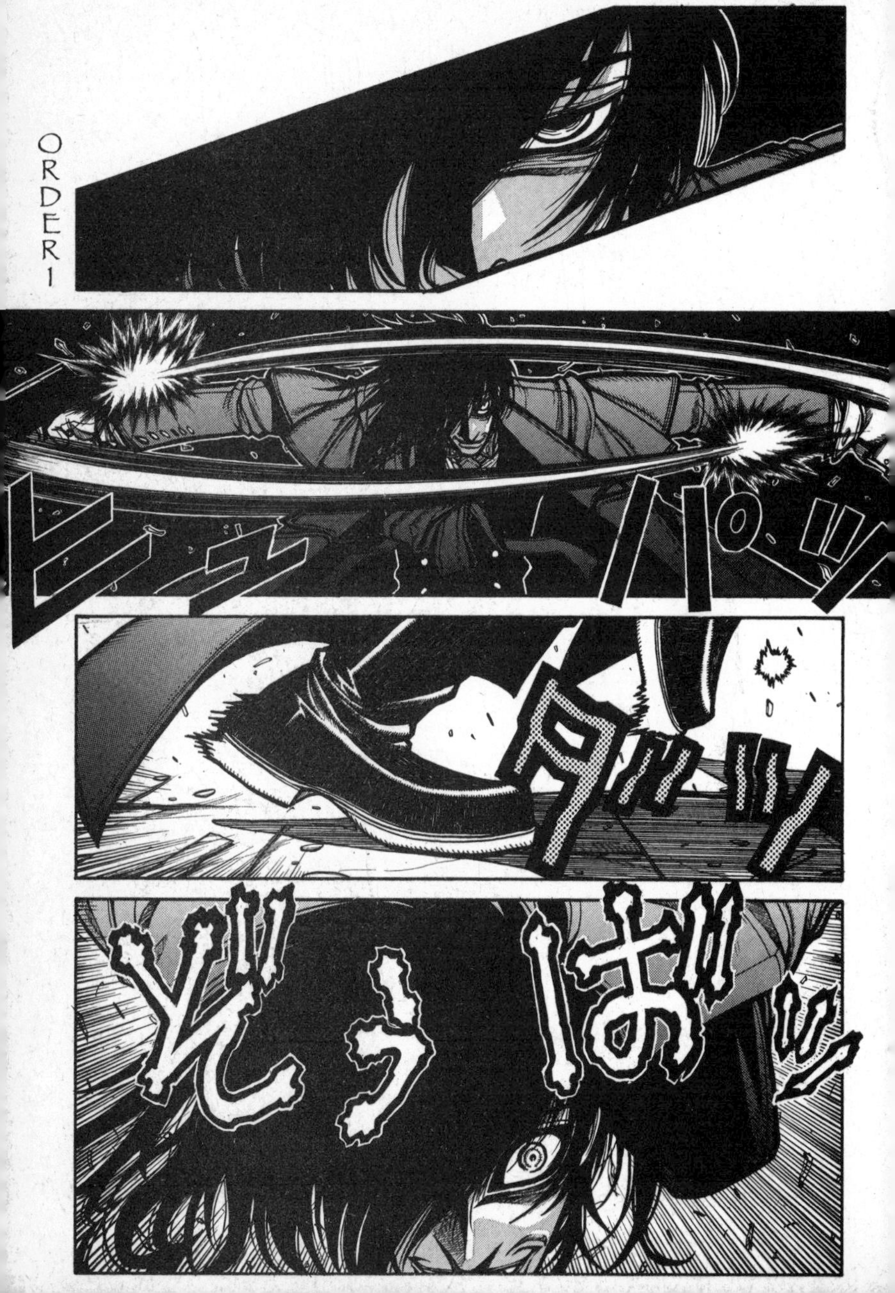

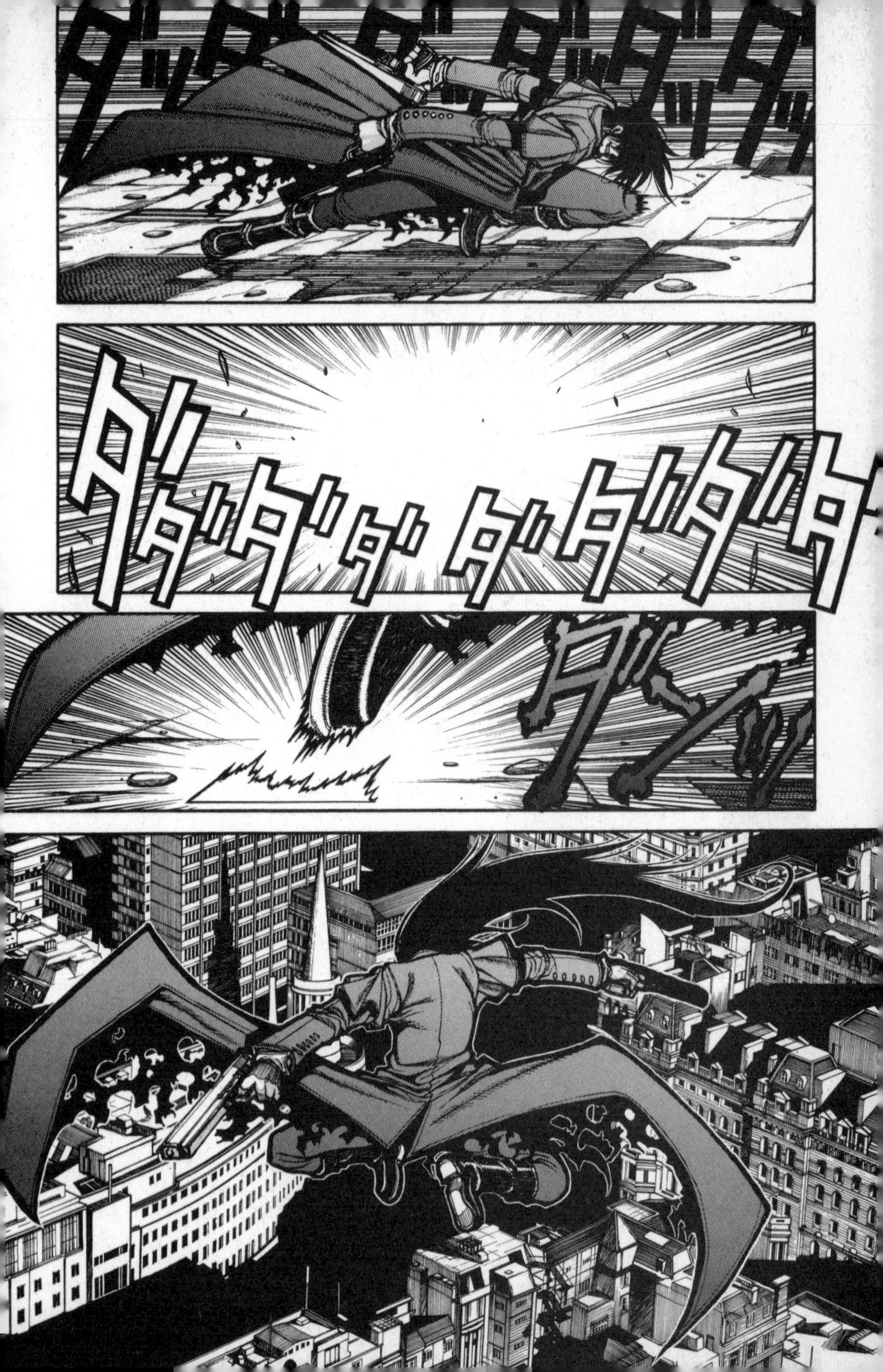
ダッ

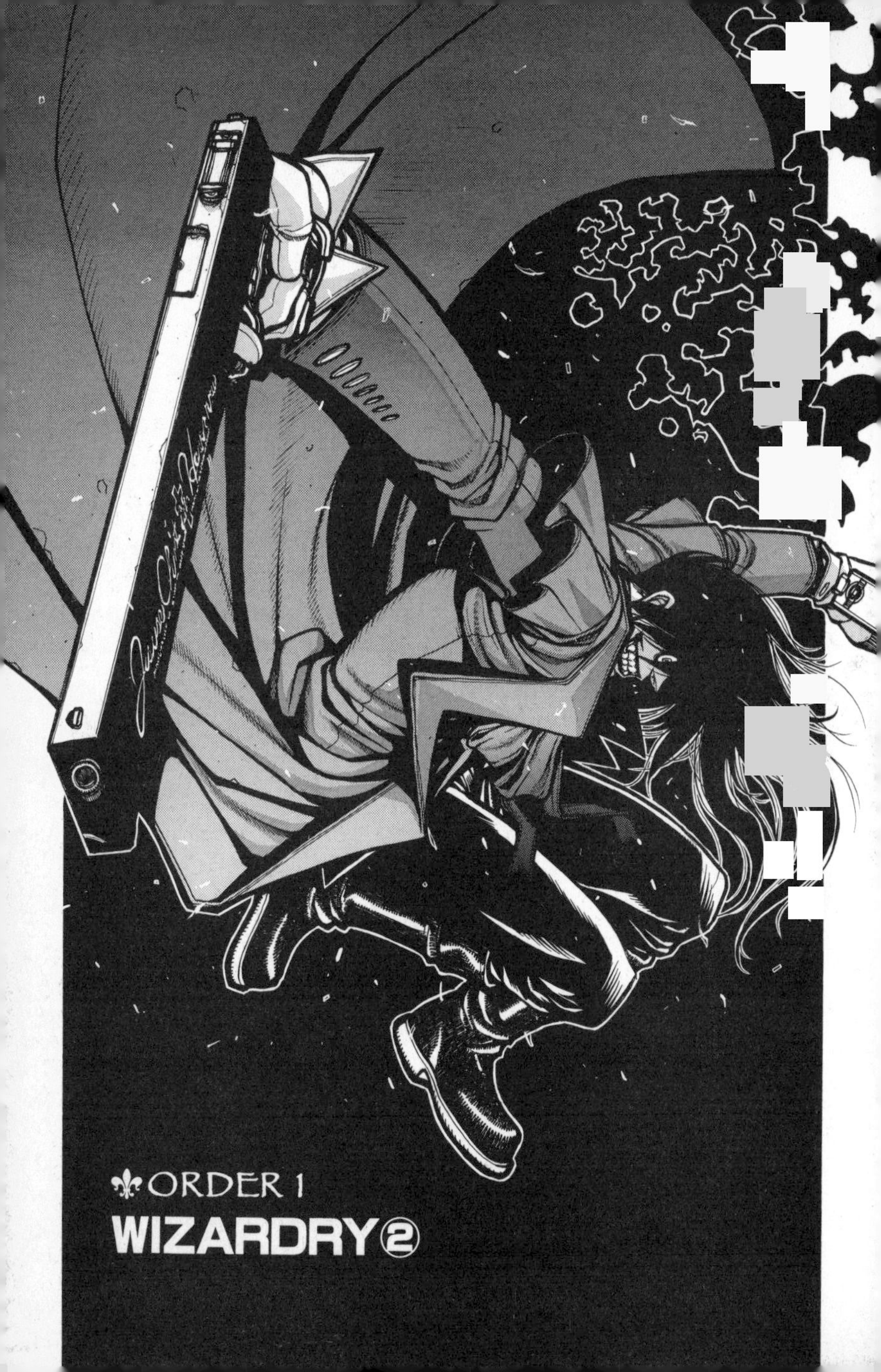
ORDER 1
WIZARDRY 2

ズズズズズズ
ズズズズズズ・・

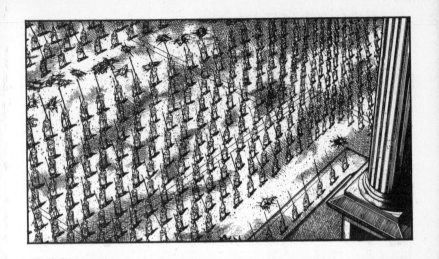

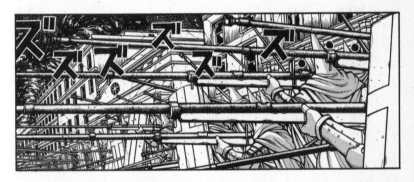

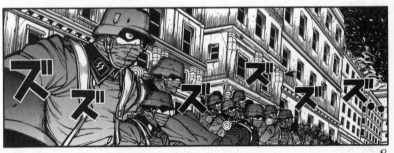

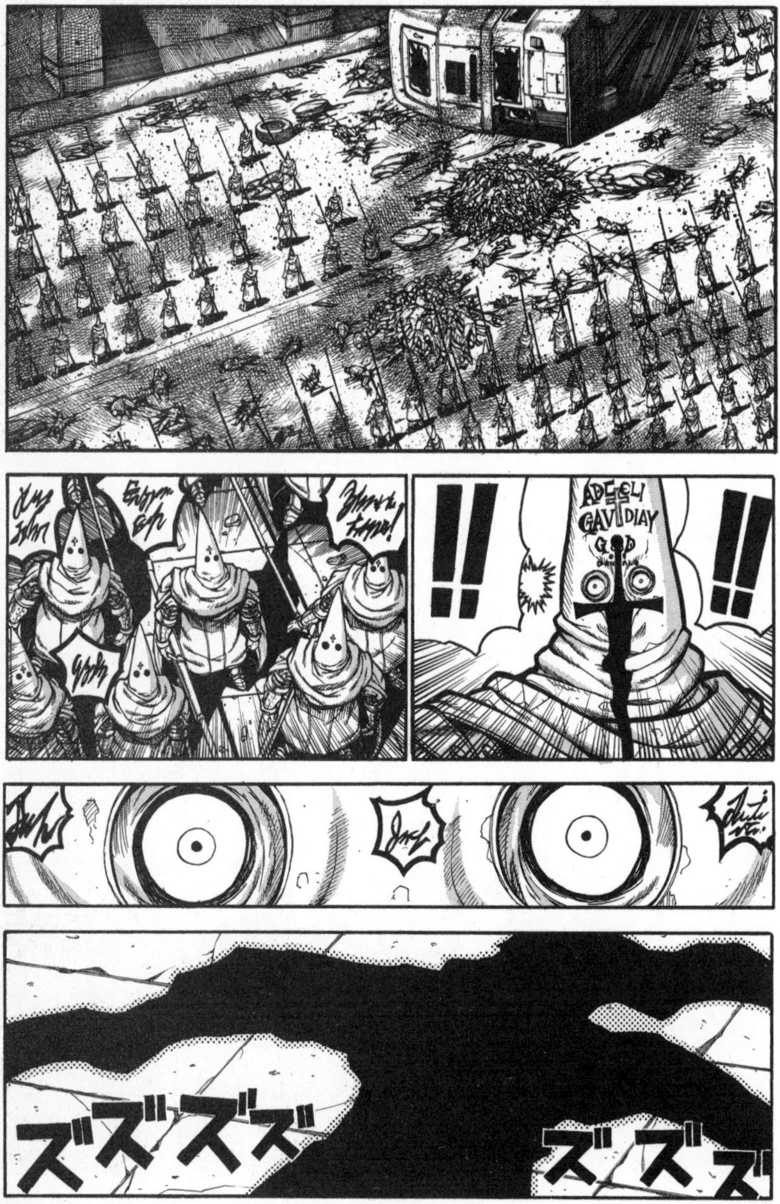
ズズズ
ズズズズ

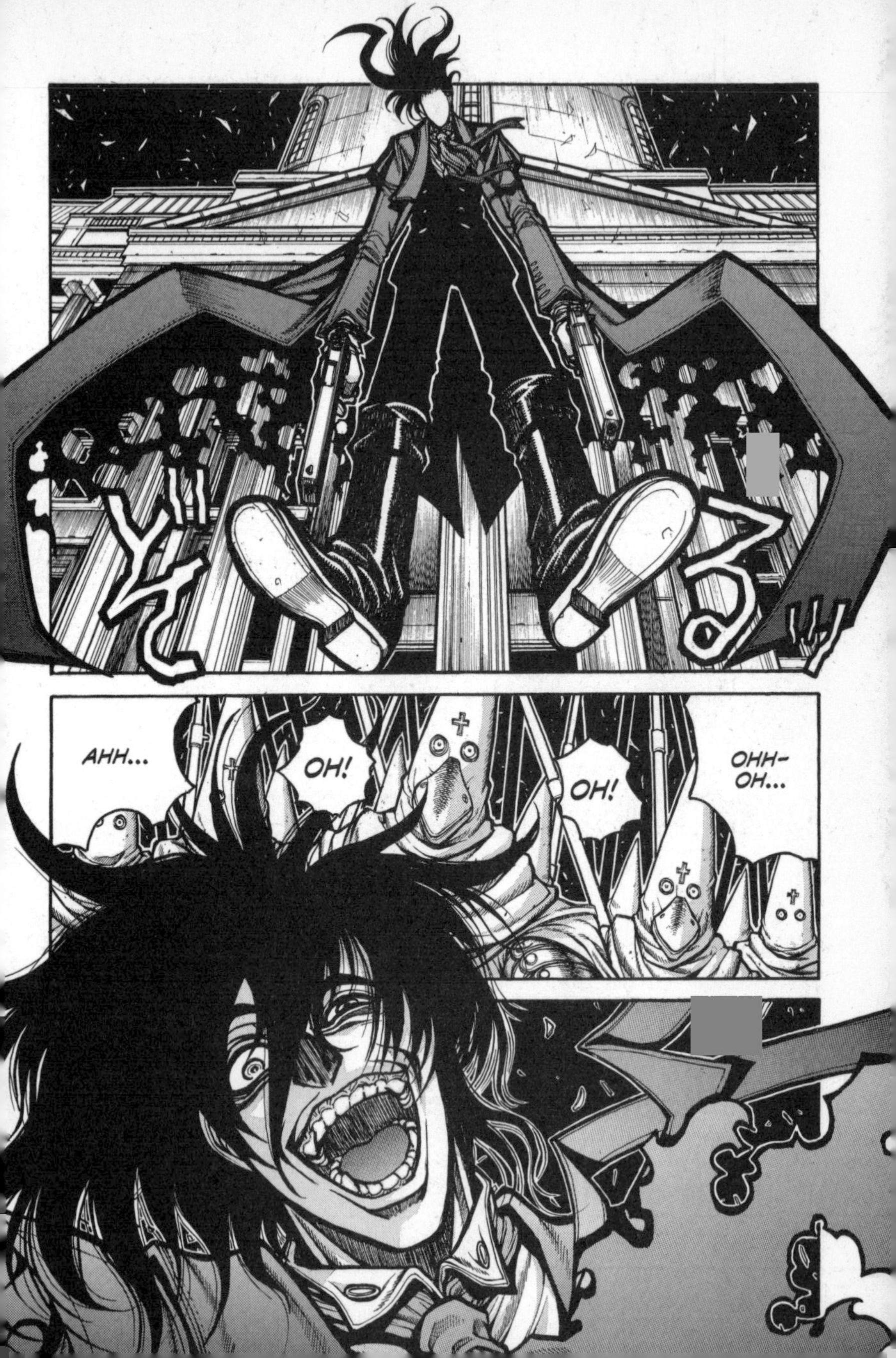
OHH-
OH...
OH!
OH!
AHH...

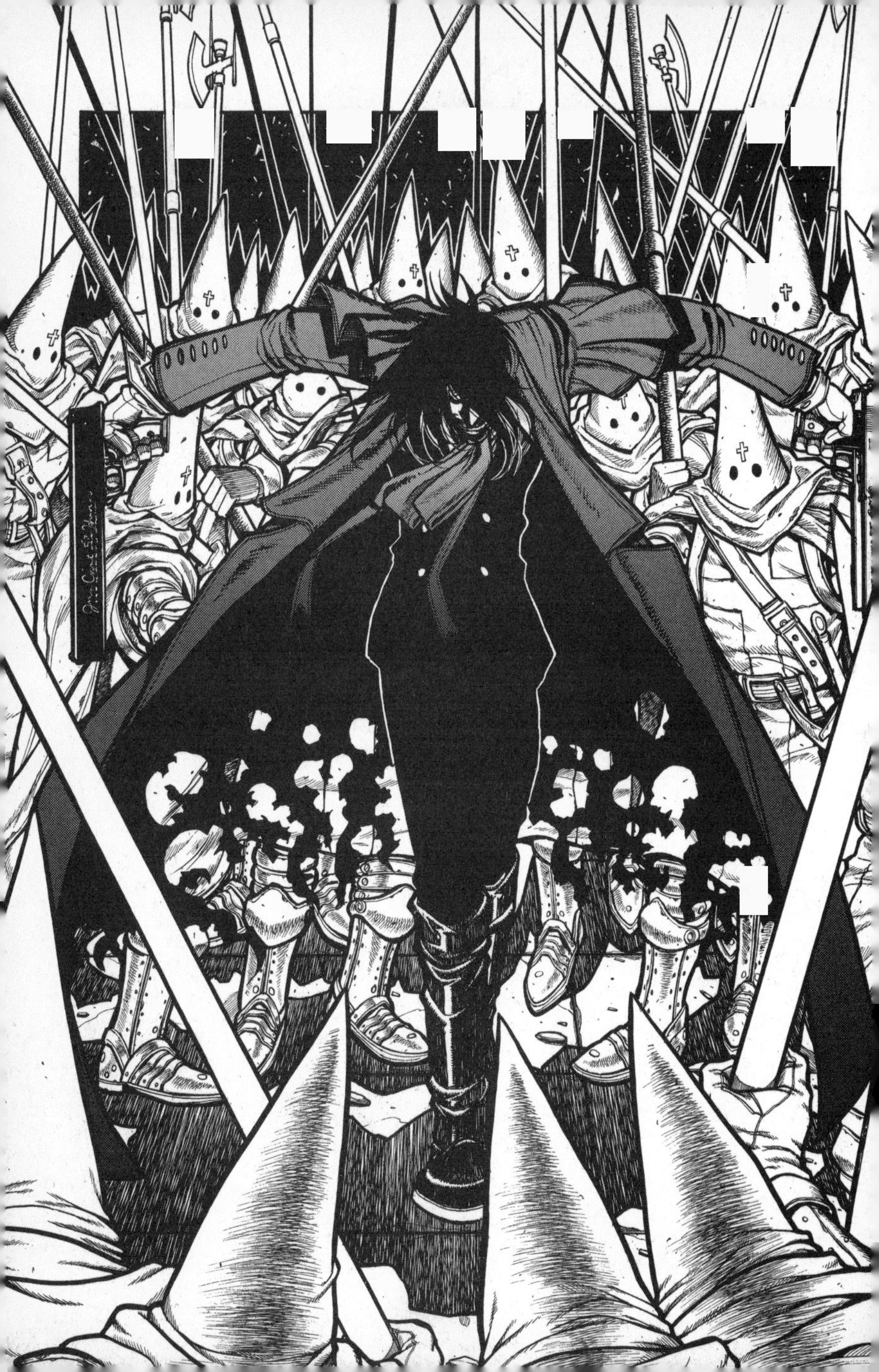

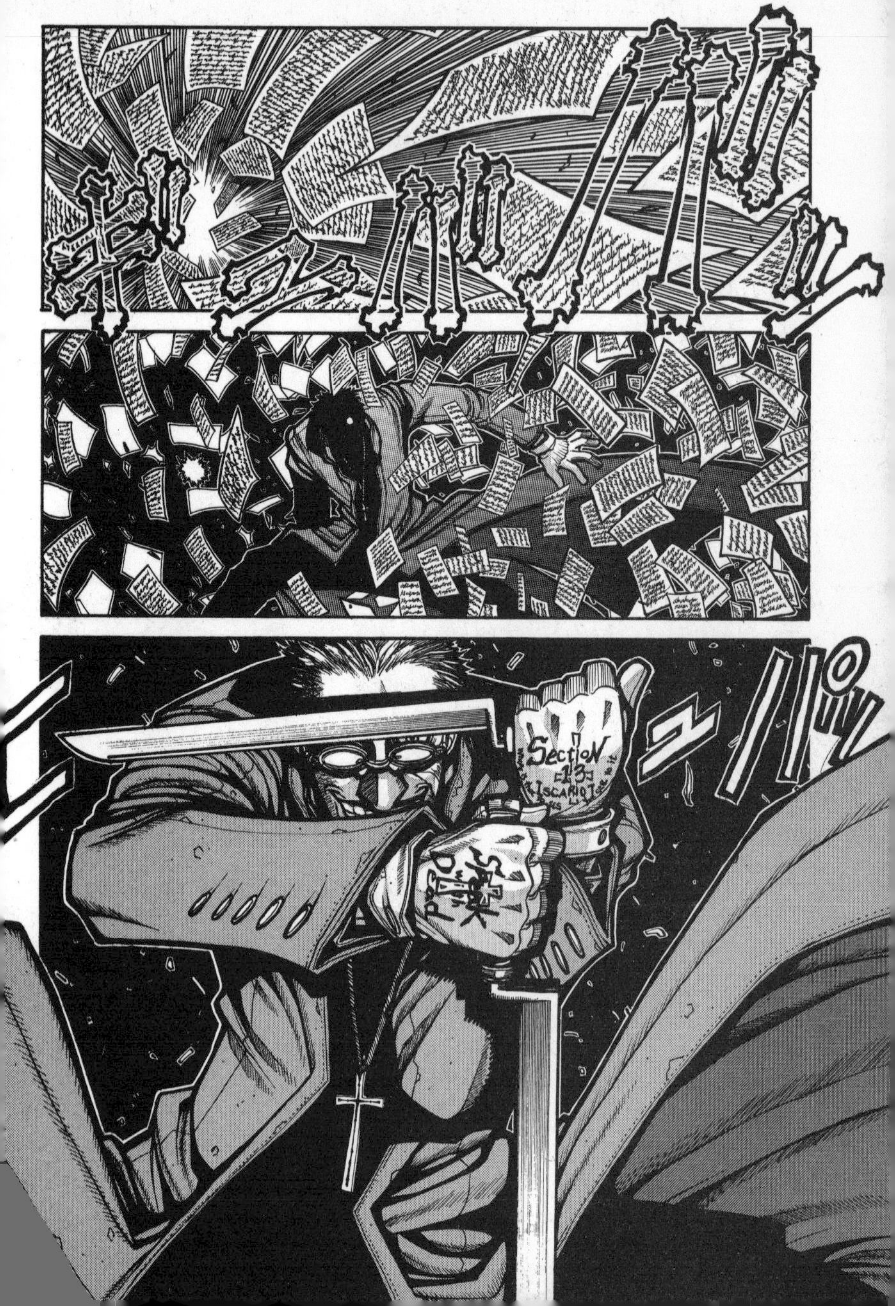
Section
13
ISCARIO

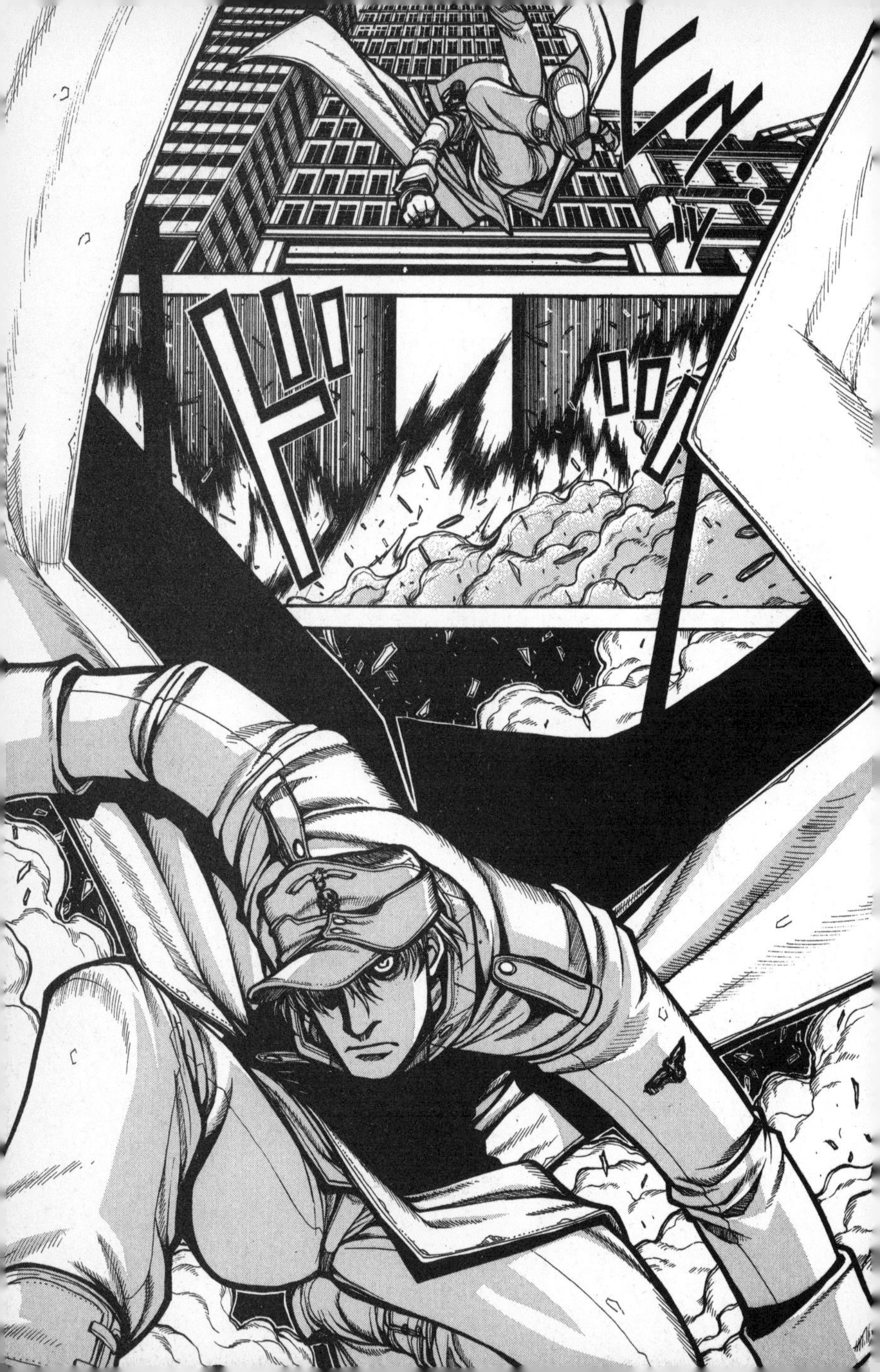

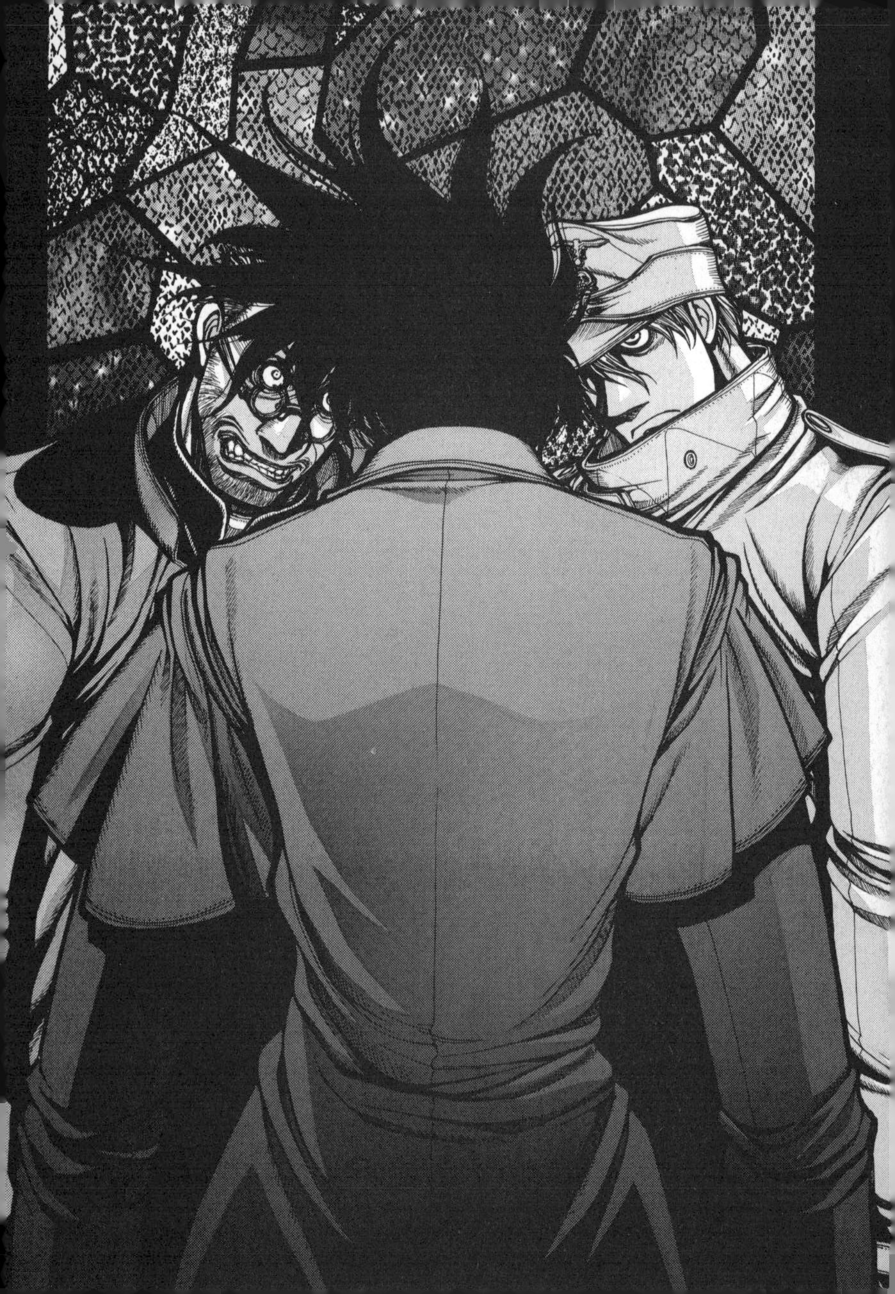

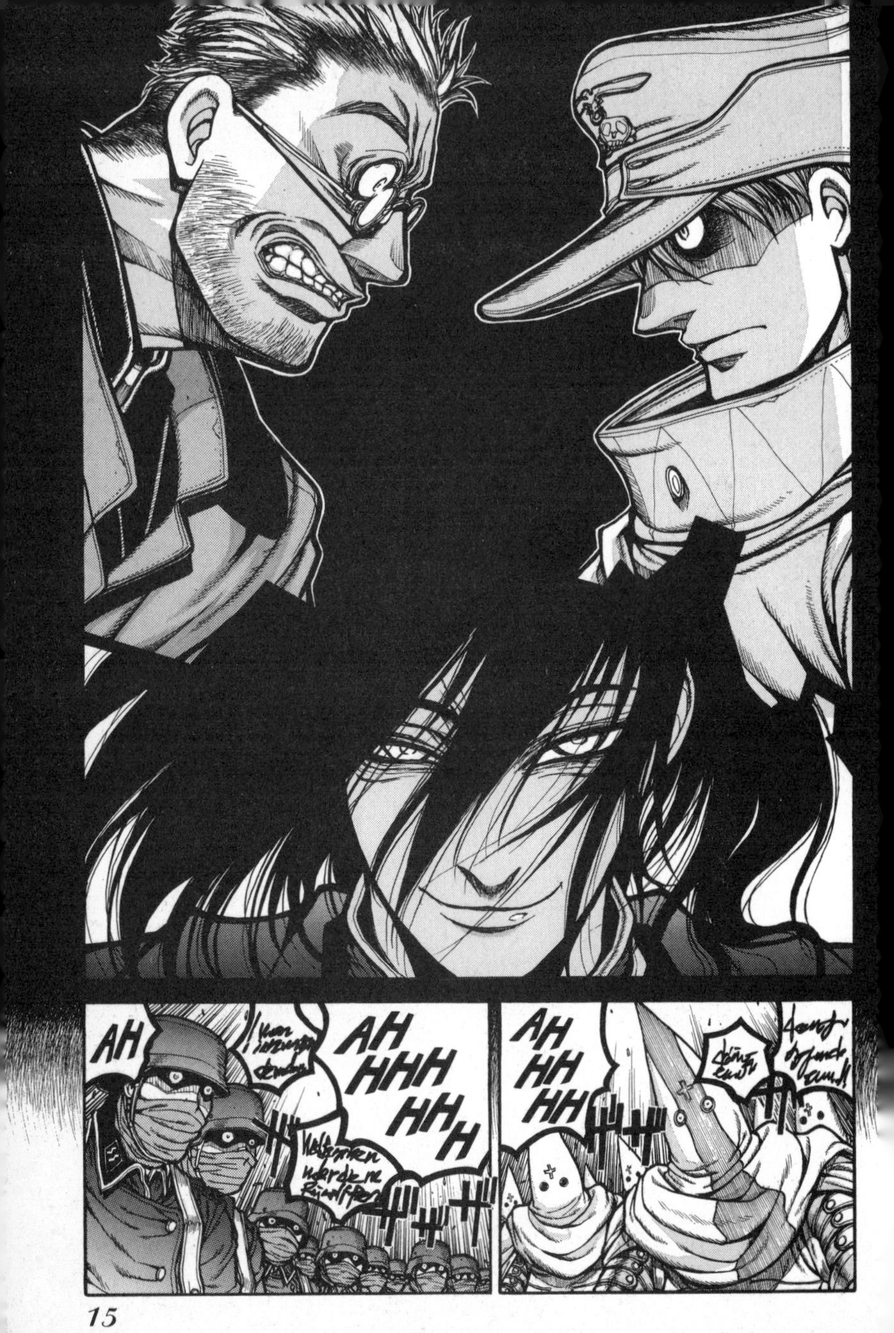
AH
HH
HH
AH
HHH
HHH
H
AH

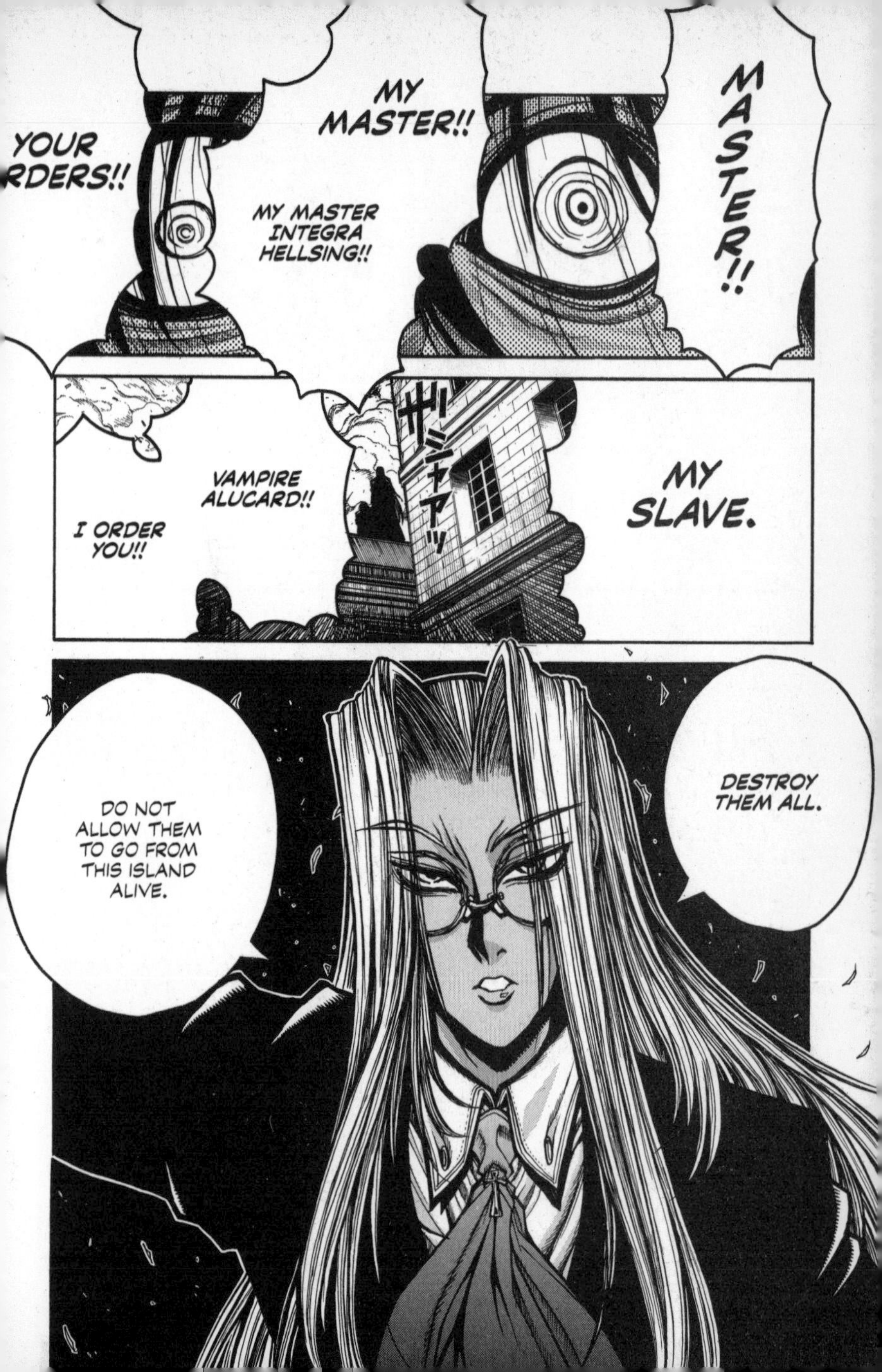
MASTER!!
MY MASTER!!
MY MASTER INTEGRA HELLSING!!
YOUR
RDERS!!
MY SLAVE.
ザシャアッ
VAMPIRE ALUCARD!!
I ORDER YOU!!
DESTROY THEM ALL.
DO NOT ALLOW THEM TO GO FROM THIS ISLAND ALIVE.

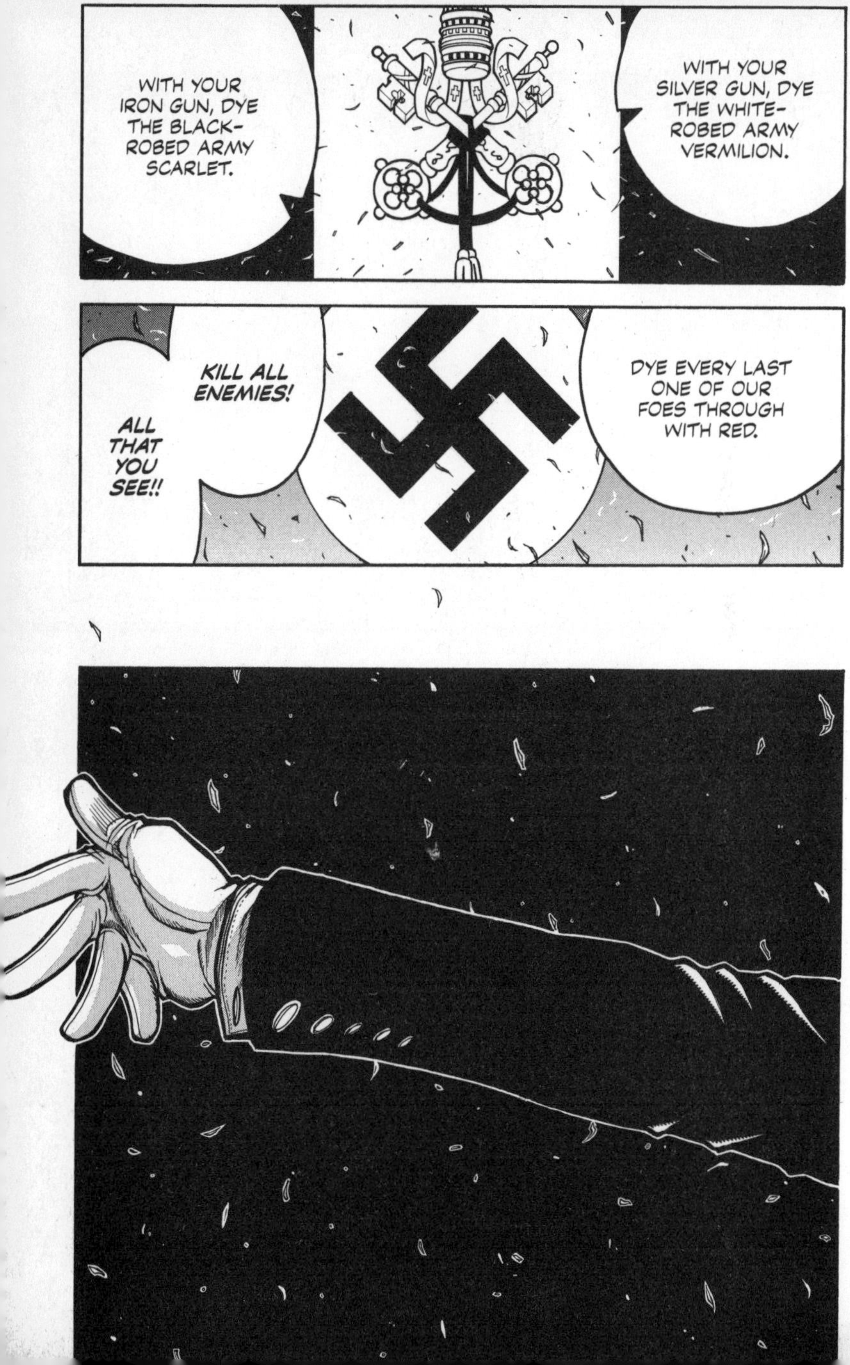
WITH YOUR SILVER GUN, DYE THE WHITE-ROBED ARMY VERMILION.
WITH YOUR IRON GUN, DYE THE BLACK-ROBED ARMY SCARLET.
DYE EVERY LAST ONE OF OUR FOES THROUGH WITH RED.
KILL ALL ENEMIES!
ALL THAT YOU SEE!!

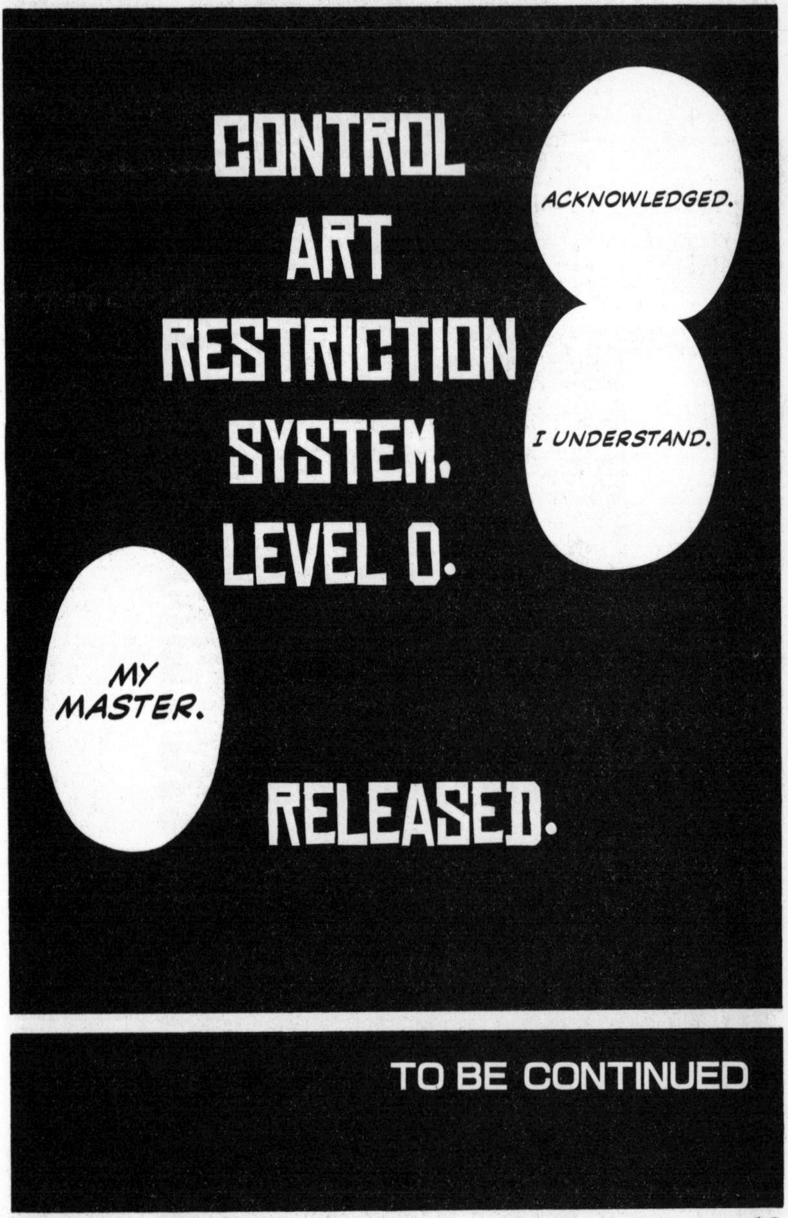
ACKNOWLEDGED.
I UNDERSTAND.
CONTROL ART RESTRICTION SYSTEM. LEVEL 0.
MY MASTER.
RELEASED.
TO BE CONTINUED

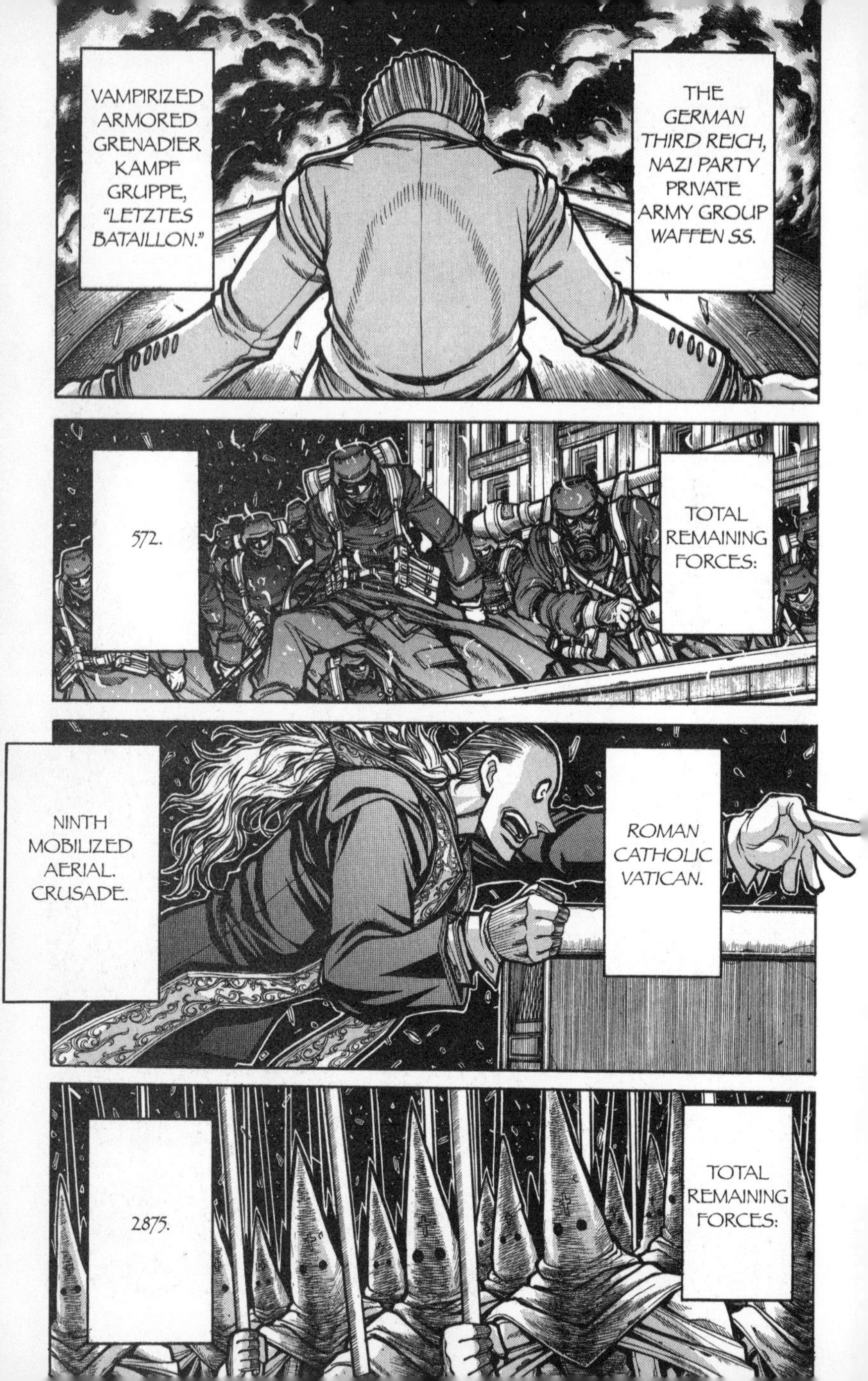
THE GERMAN THIRD REICH, NAZI PARTY PRIVATE ARMY GROUP WAFFEN SS.
VAMPIRIZED ARMORED GRENADIER KAMPF GRUPPE, "LETZTES BATAILLON."
TOTAL REMAINING FORCES:
572.
ROMAN CATHOLIC VATICAN.
NINTH MOBILIZED AERIAL. CRUSADE.
TOTAL REMAINING FORCES:
2875.

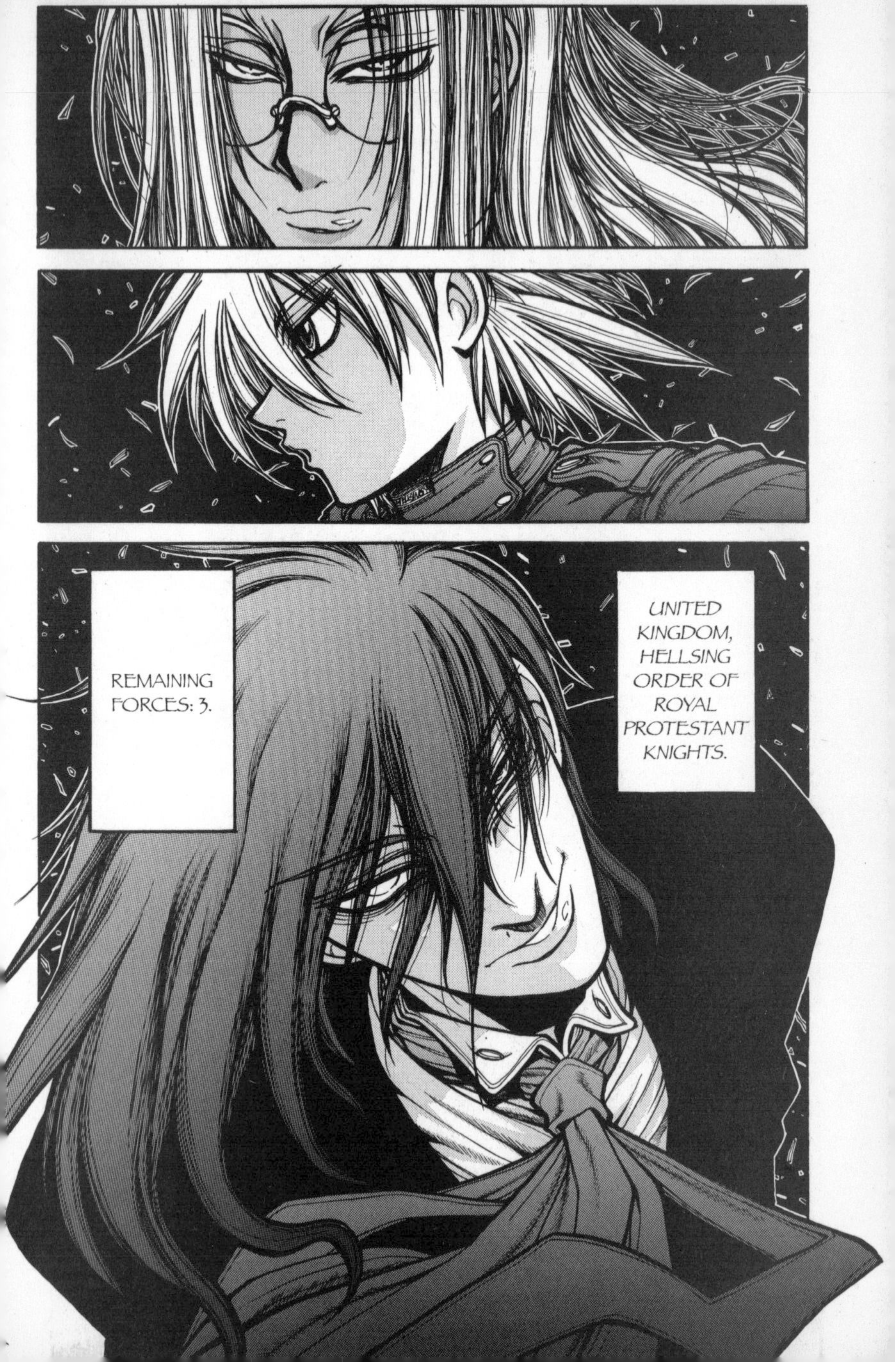
UNITED KINGDOM, HELLSING ORDER OF ROYAL PROTESTANT KNIGHTS.
REMAINING FORCES: 3.

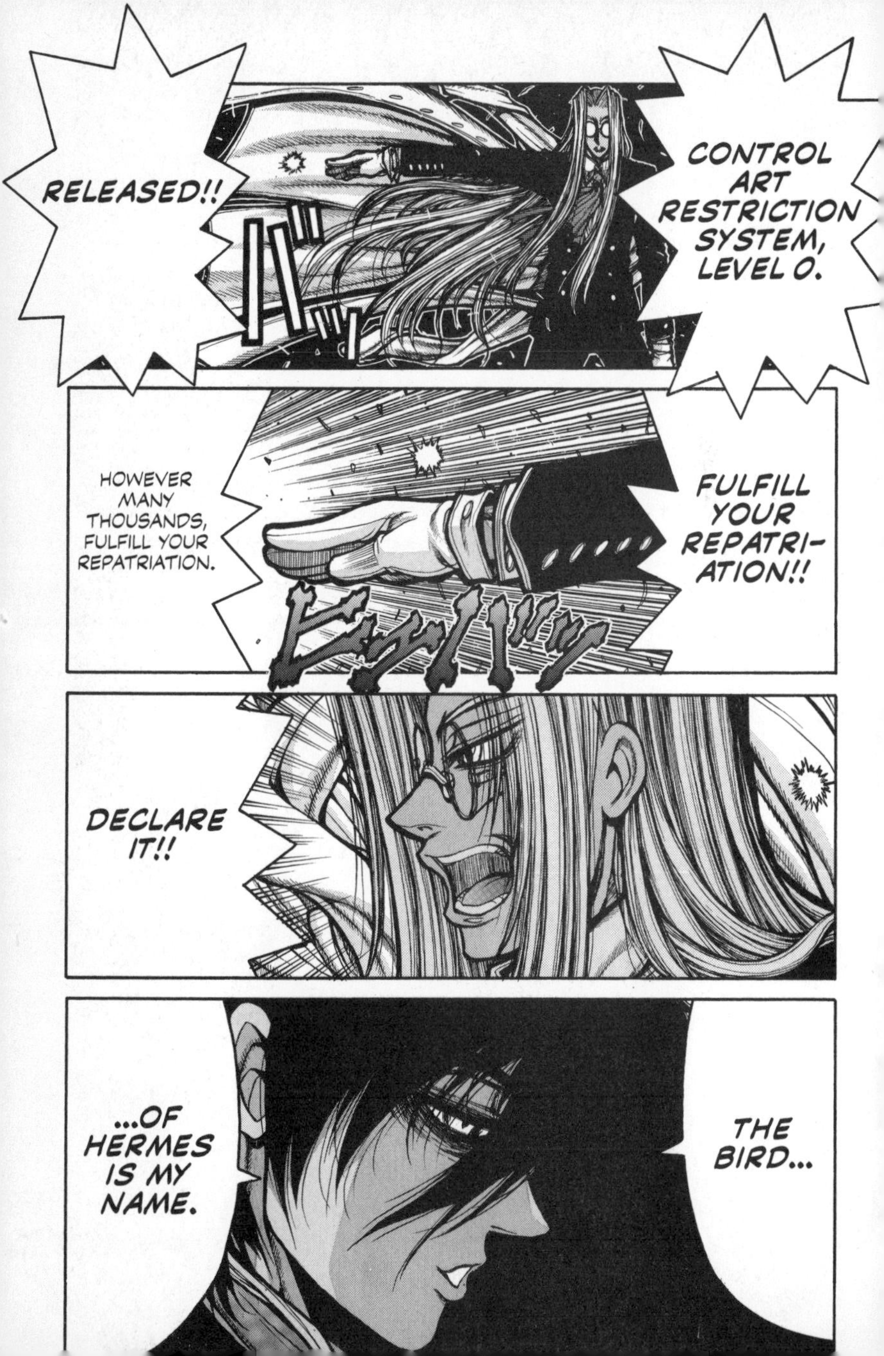
CONTROL ART RESTRICTION SYSTEM, LEVEL 0.
RELEASED!!
FULFILL YOUR REPATRI-ATION!!
HOWEVER MANY THOUSANDS, FULFILL YOUR REPATRIATION.
DECLARE IT!!
THE BIRD...
...OF HERMES IS MY NAME.

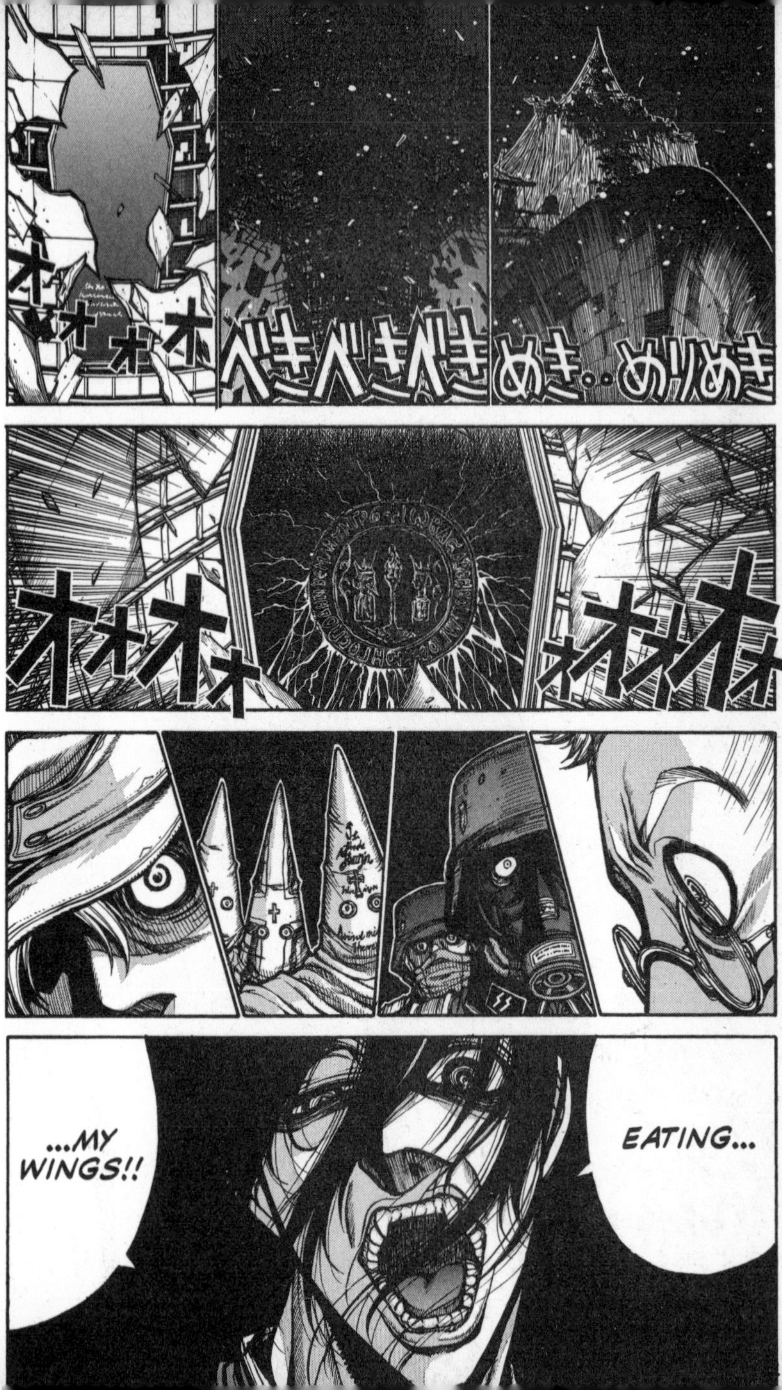
めき‥めりめき
べきべきべき
オォオォオ
オォオオォ
オォオオォ
EATING...
...MY WINGS!!

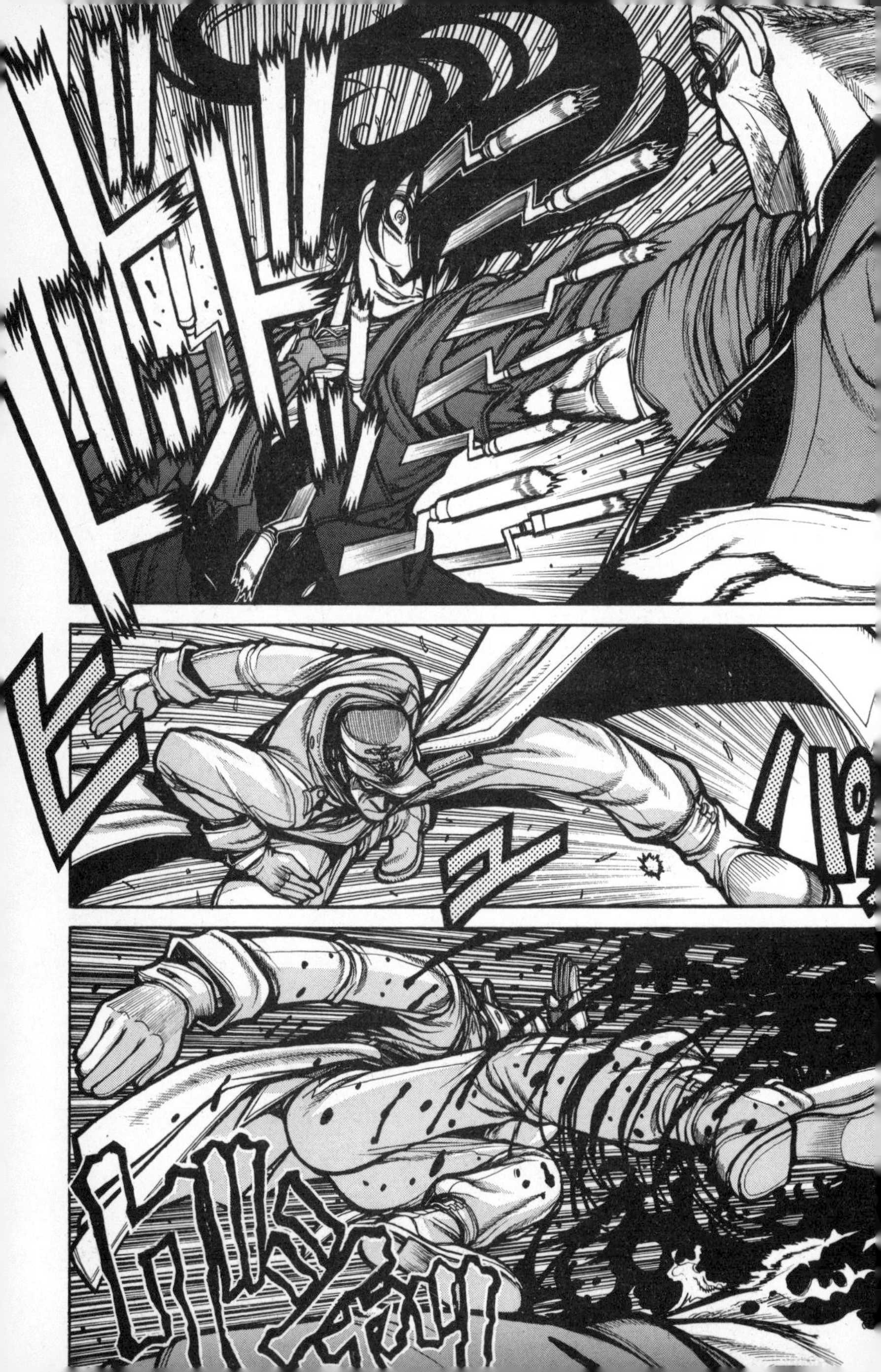

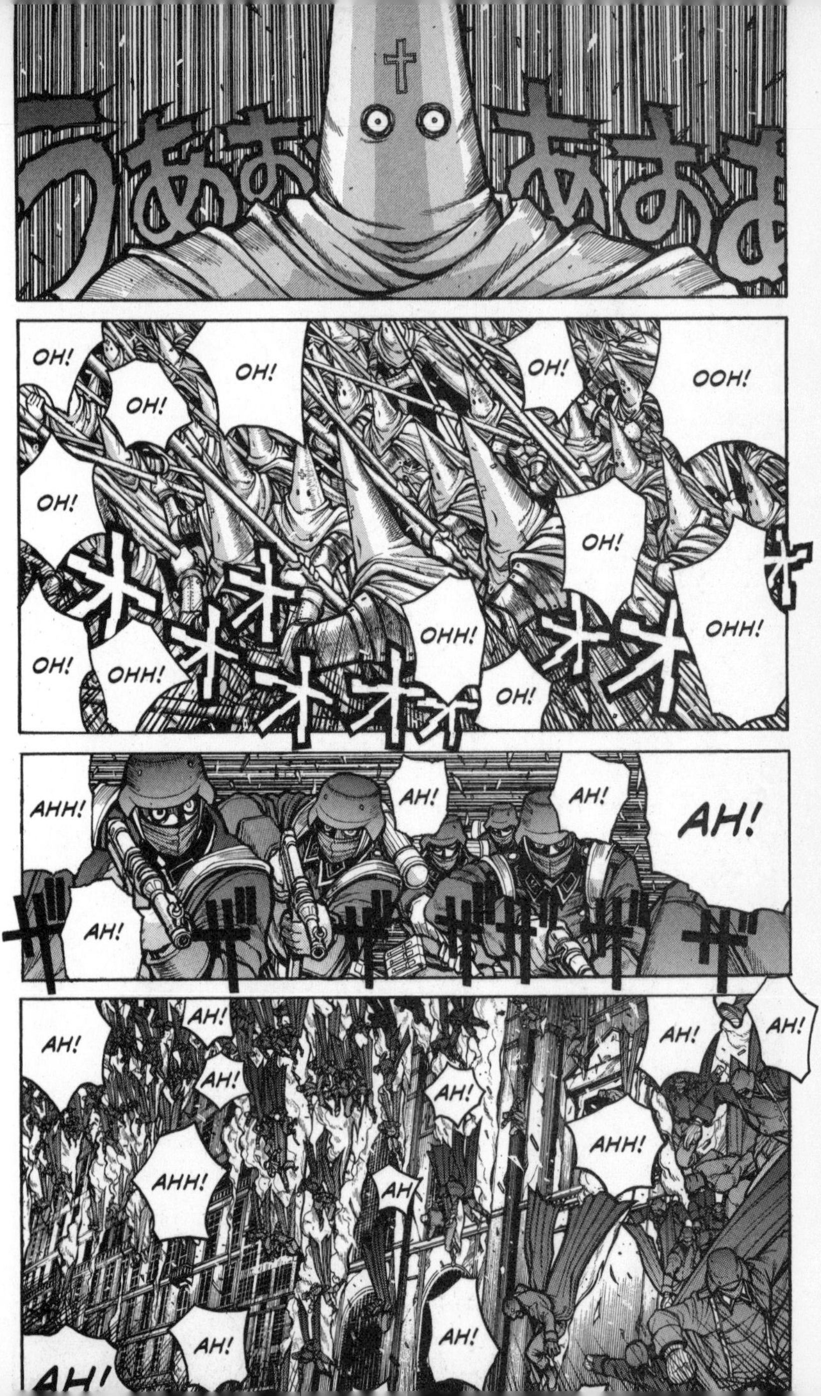
OOH!
OH!
OH!
OH!
OH!
OH!
OHH!
OH!
OHH!
OHH!
OH!
OH!
AH!
AH!
AH!
AHH!
AH!
AH!
AH!
AH!
AHH!
AH!
AH!
AH!
AHH!
AH
AH!
AH!
AH!

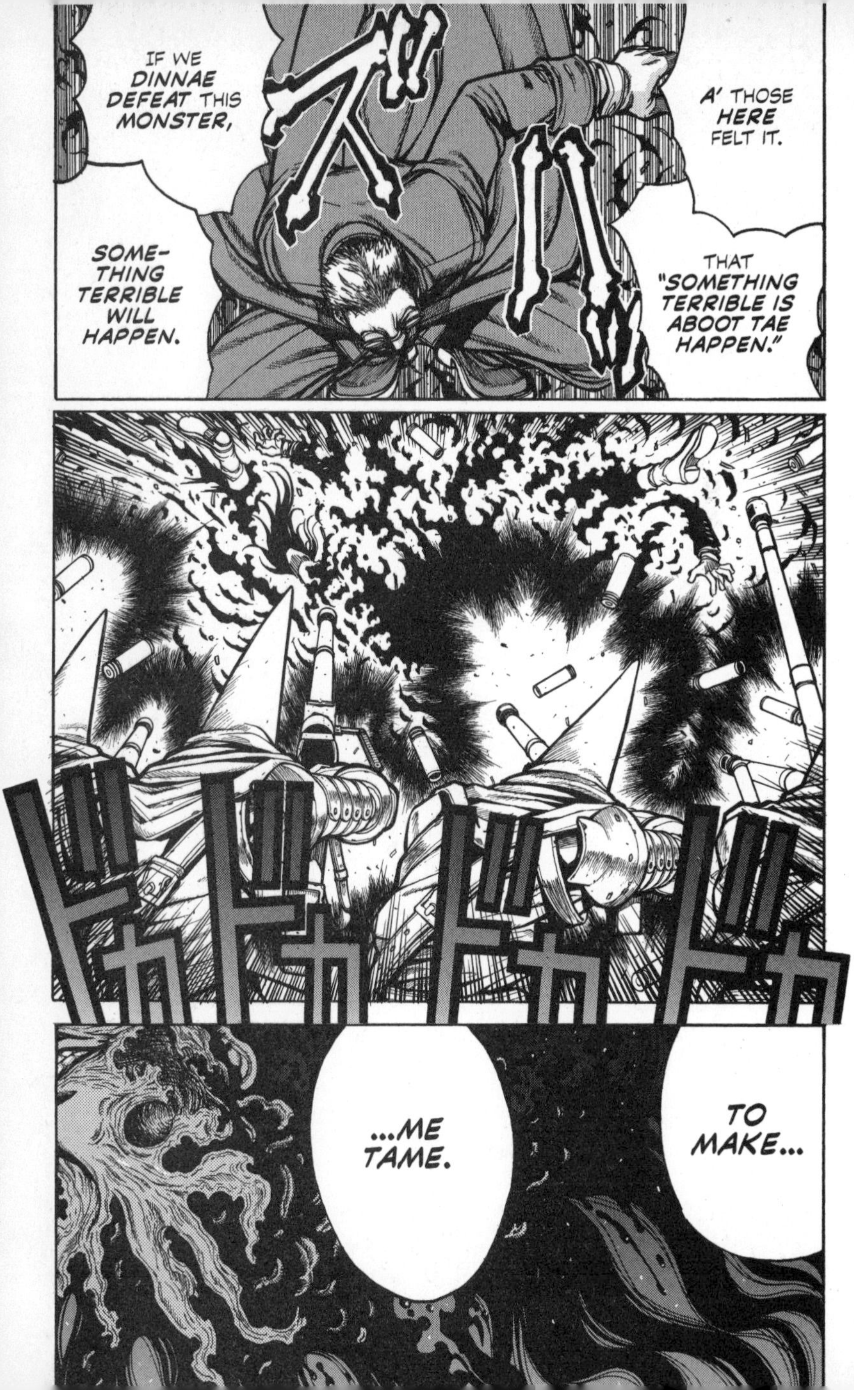
A' THOSE HERE FELT IT.
THAT "SOMETHING TERRIBLE IS ABOOT TAE HAPPEN."
IF WE DINNAE DEFEAT THIS MONSTER,
SOME-THING TERRIBLE WILL HAPPEN.
ドォドォドォドォ
TO MAKE...
...ME TAME.

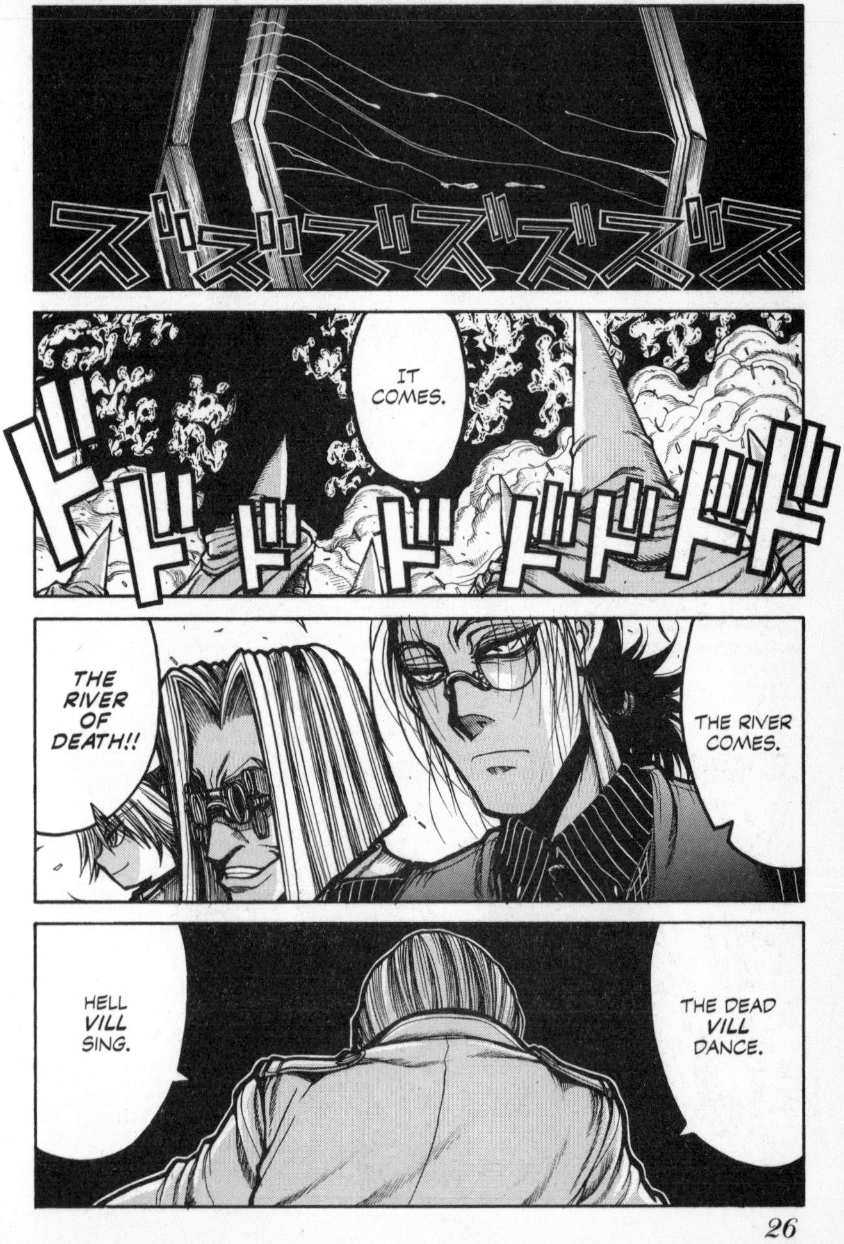
ズズズズズズス
IT COMES.
ドドドドドドドド
THE RIVER COMES.
THE RIVER OF DEATH!!
THE DEAD *VILL* DANCE.
HELL *VILL* SING.

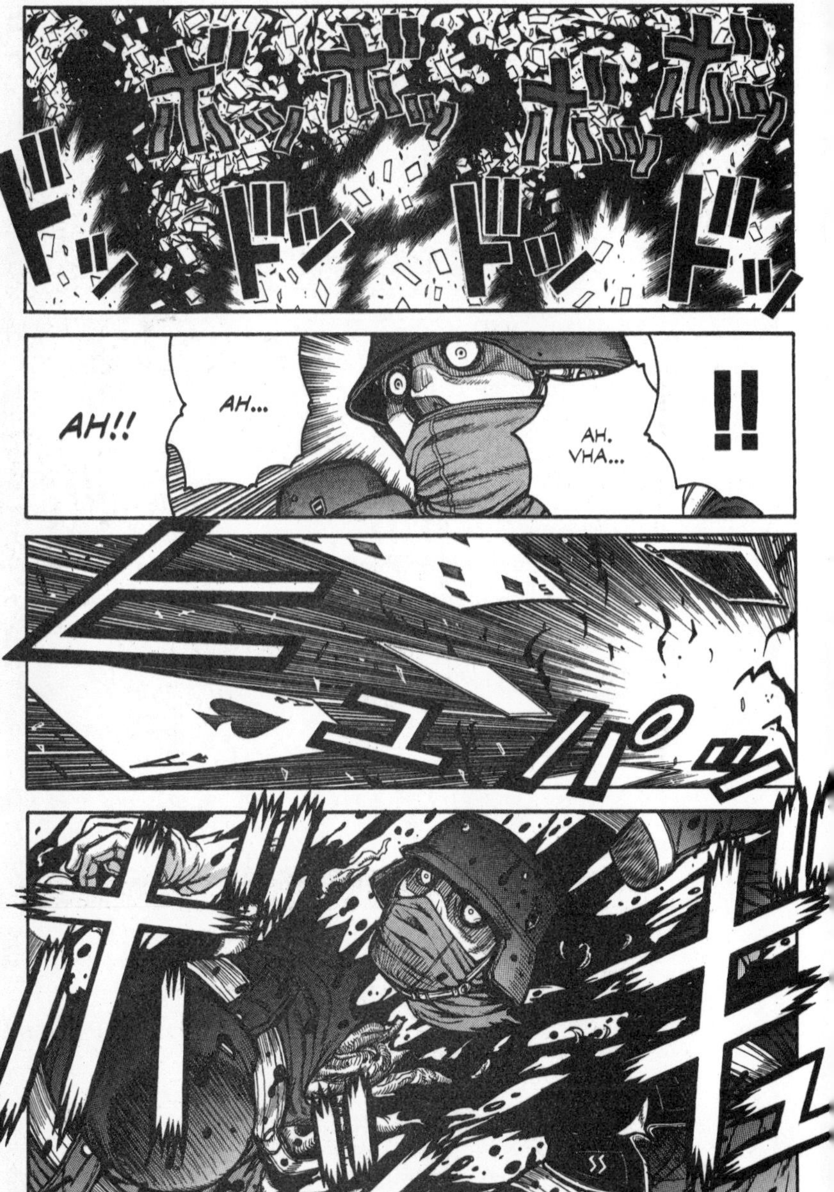
ボッ ボッ ボッ ボッ
ドッ ドッ ドッ ドッ
!!
AH. VHA...
AH...
AH!!

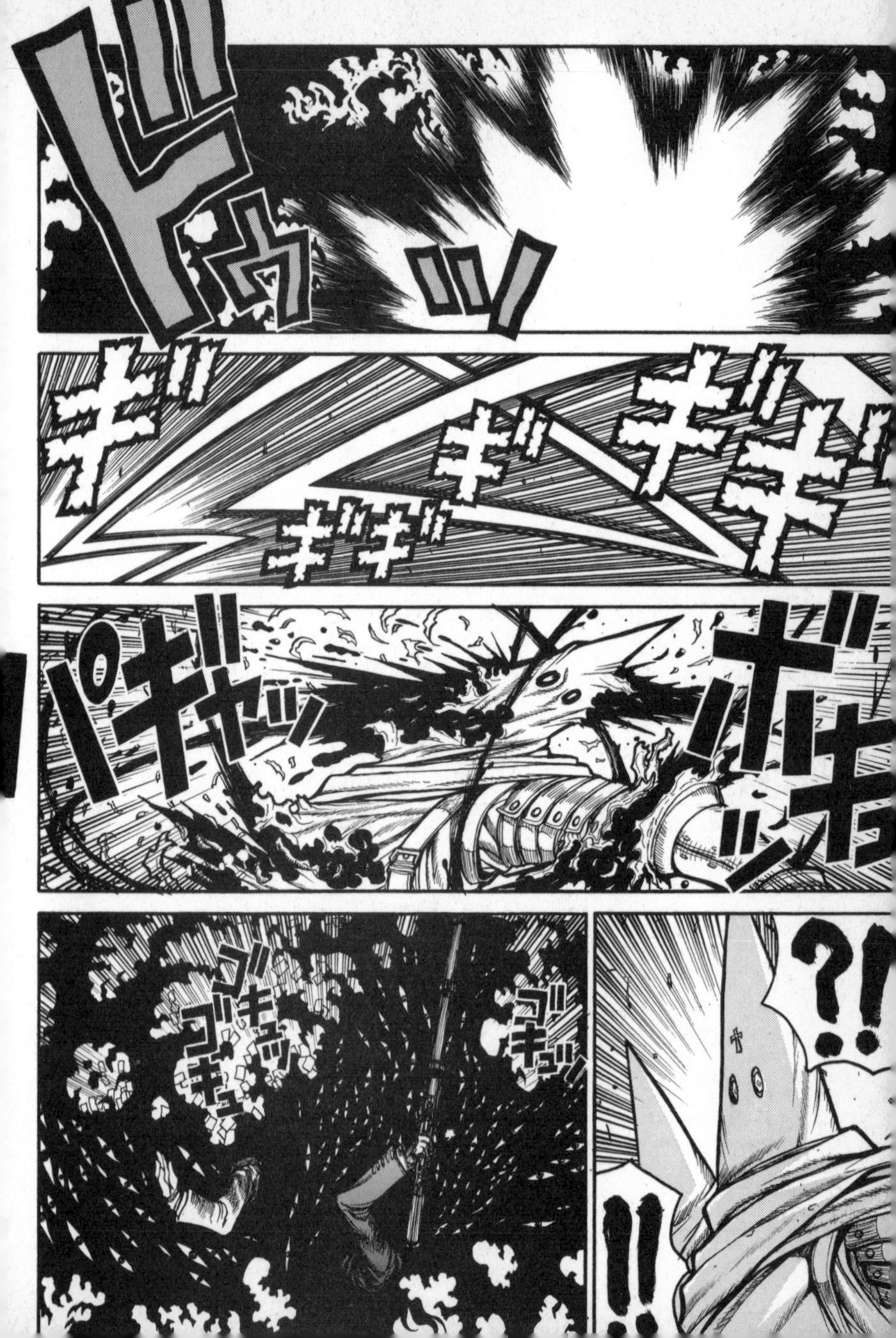
ドゥッ
ギギ
ギギ
ギ
ギ
ボギッ
パギャッ
?!
!!
ゴキッ
ゴキッ
ゴキュ

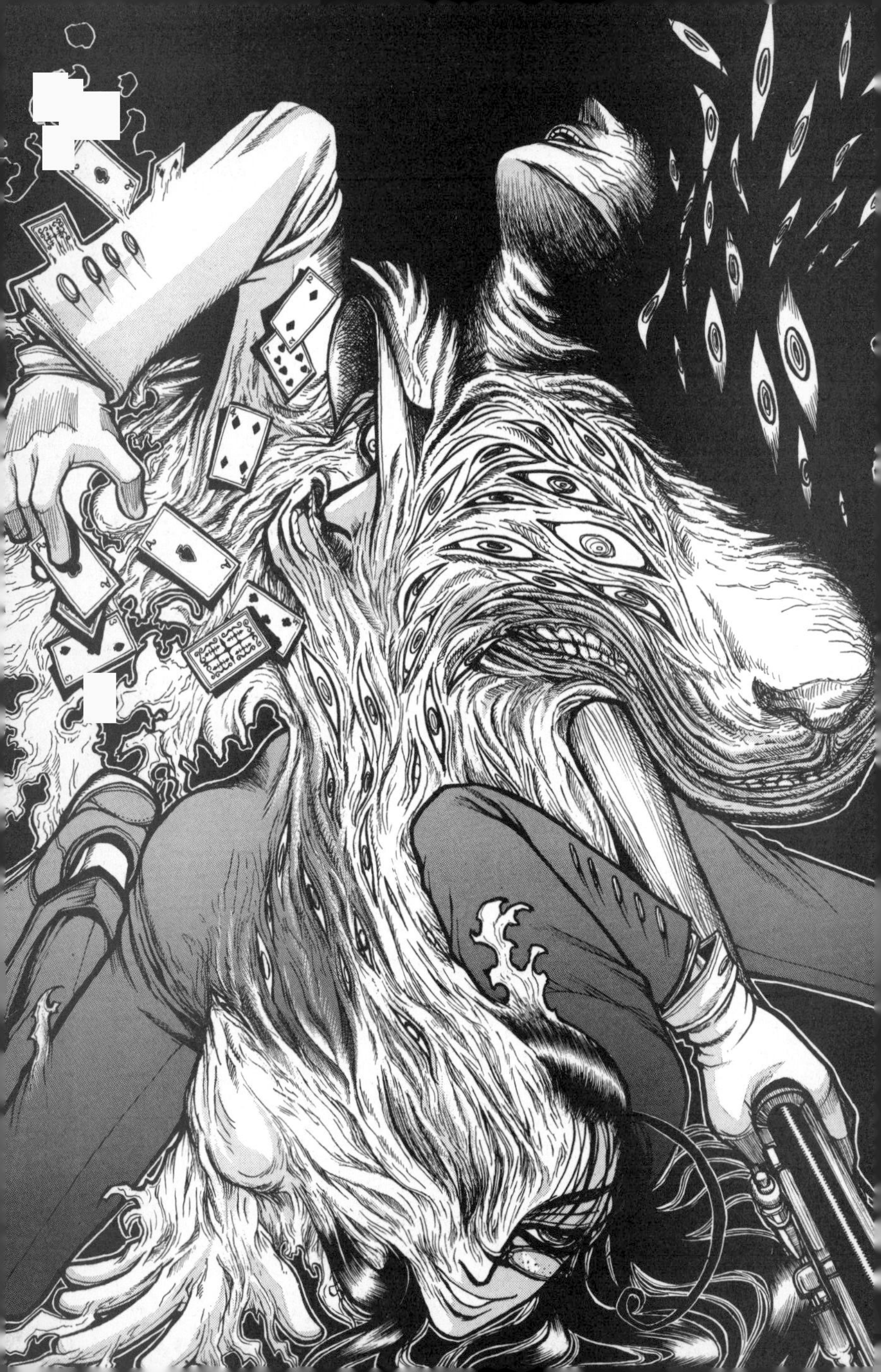

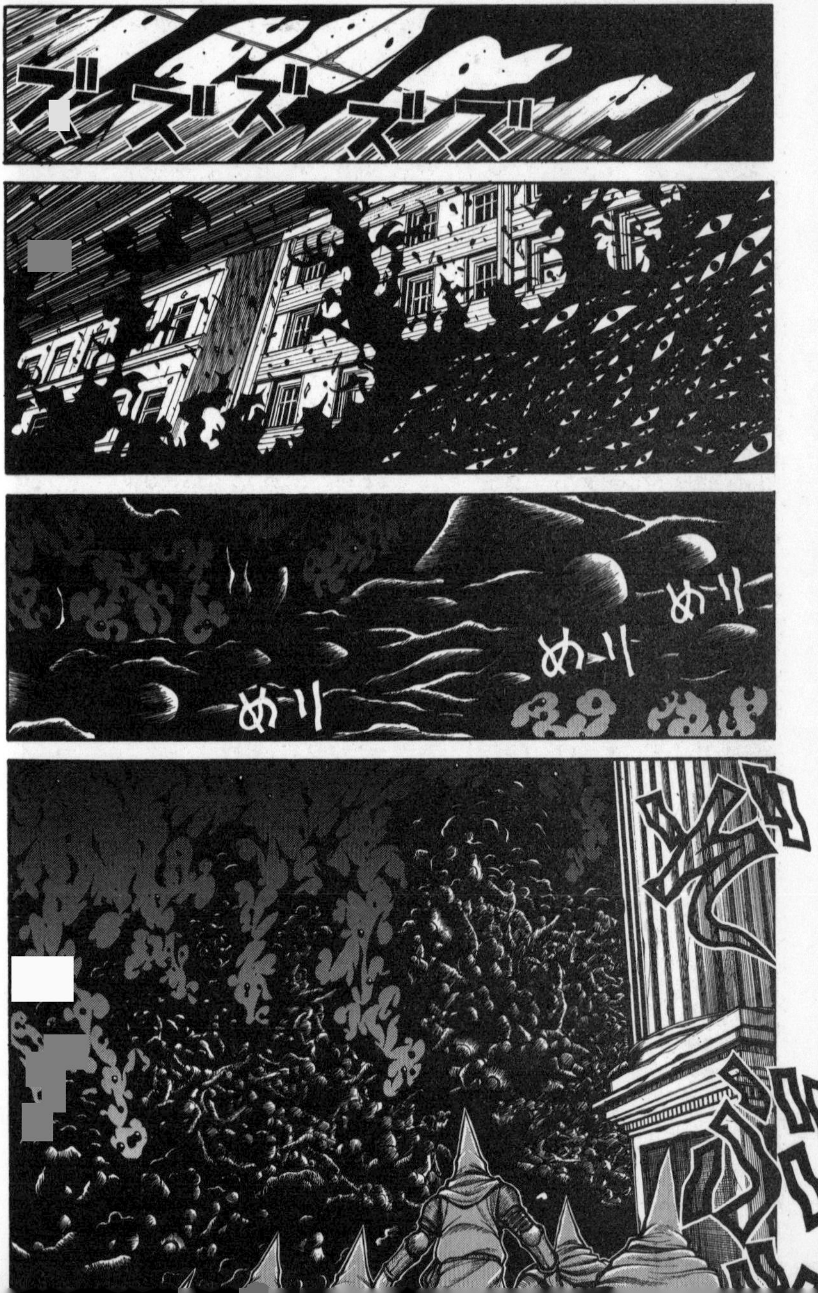
ズズズズズ
めり
めり
めり

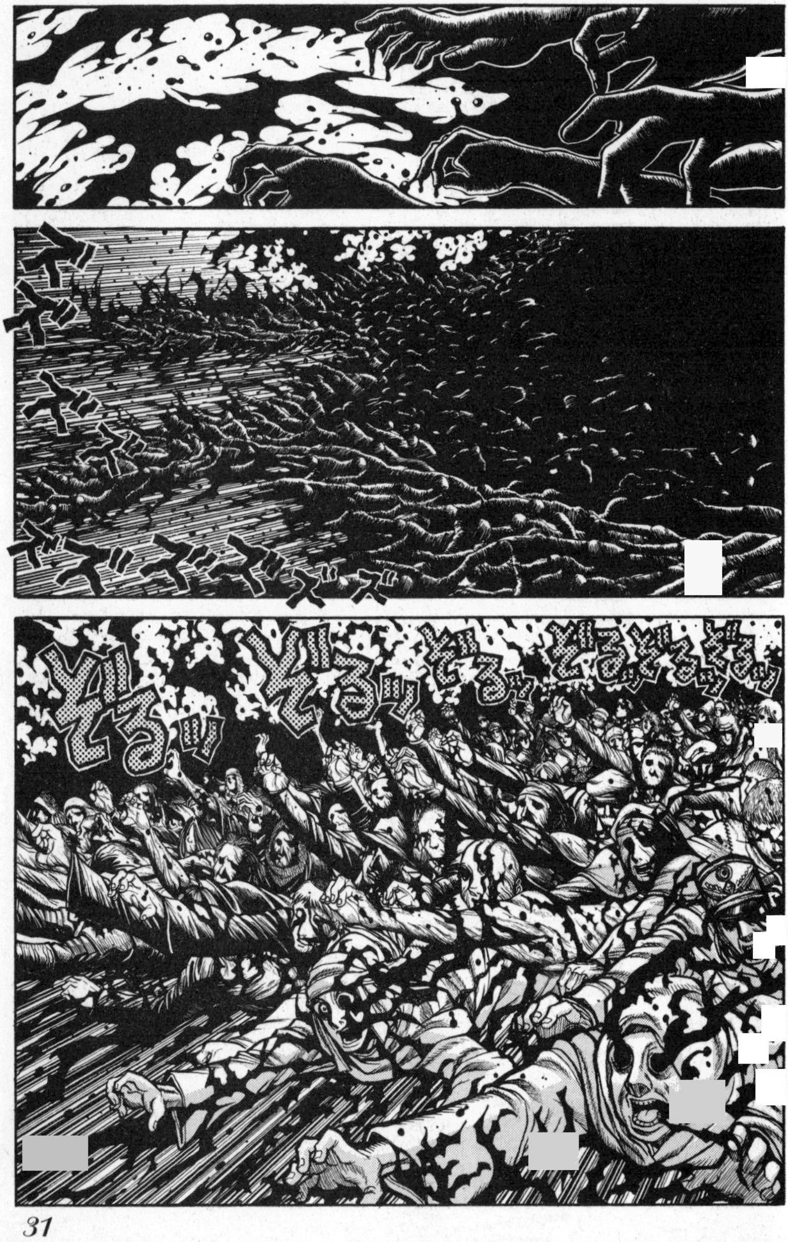
ズズズズ
ズズズズズズ
ぞるっ ぞるっ ぞるっ ぞるっぞるっぞるっ

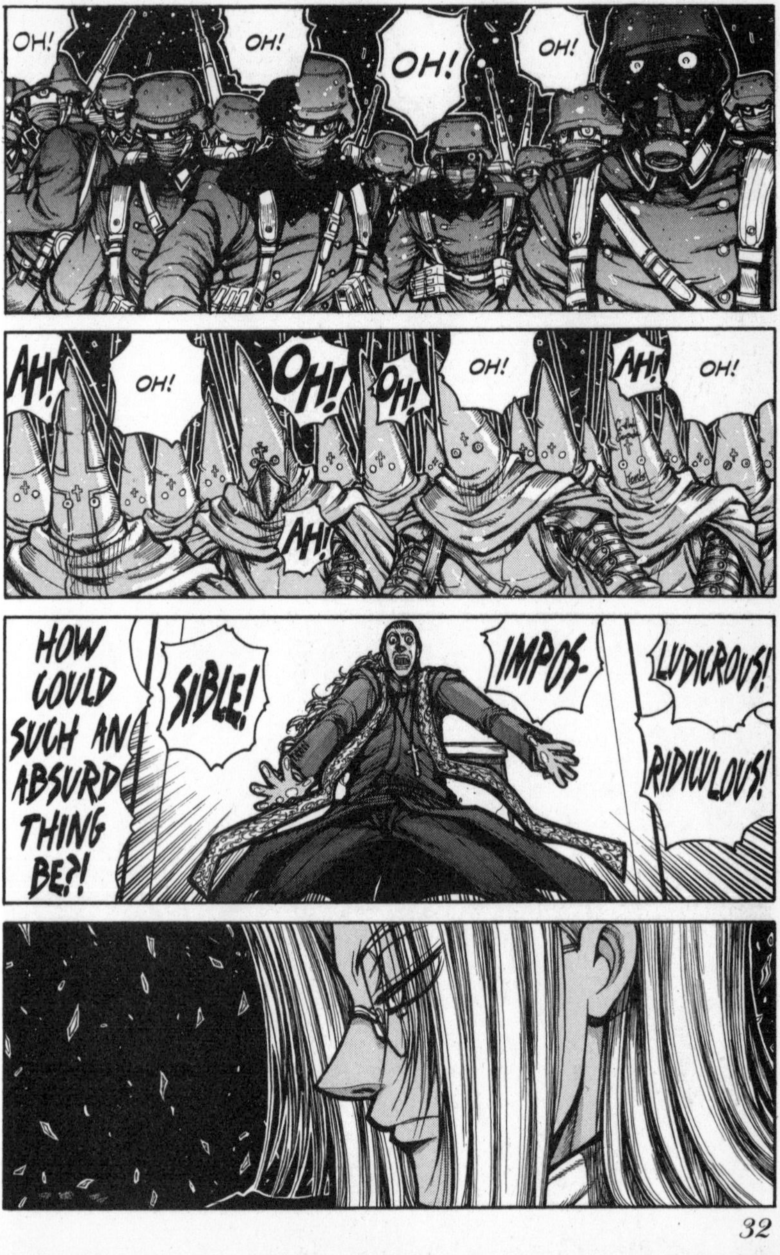
OH!
OH!
OH!
OH!
OH!
AH!
OH!
OH!
OH!
AH!
OH!
AH!
LUDICROUS!
RIDICULOUS!
IMPOS-
SIBLE!
HOW COULD SUCH AN ABSURD THING BE?!

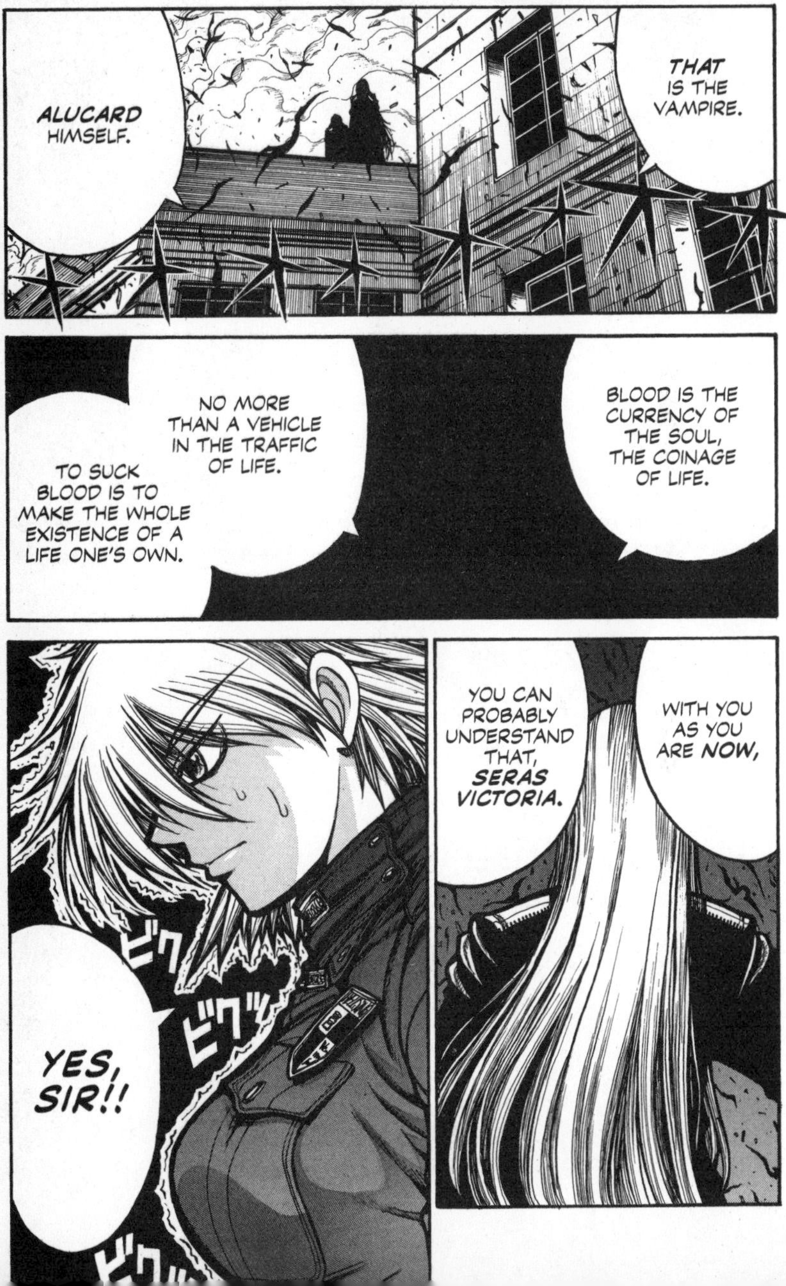
THAT IS THE VAMPIRE.
ALUCARD HIMSELF.
BLOOD IS THE CURRENCY OF THE SOUL, THE COINAGE OF LIFE.
NO MORE THAN A VEHICLE IN THE TRAFFIC OF LIFE.
TO SUCK BLOOD IS TO MAKE THE WHOLE EXISTENCE OF A LIFE ONE'S OWN.
WITH YOU AS YOU ARE NOW,
YOU CAN PROBABLY UNDERSTAND THAT, SERAS VICTORIA.
ビク
ビクッ
YES, SIR!!

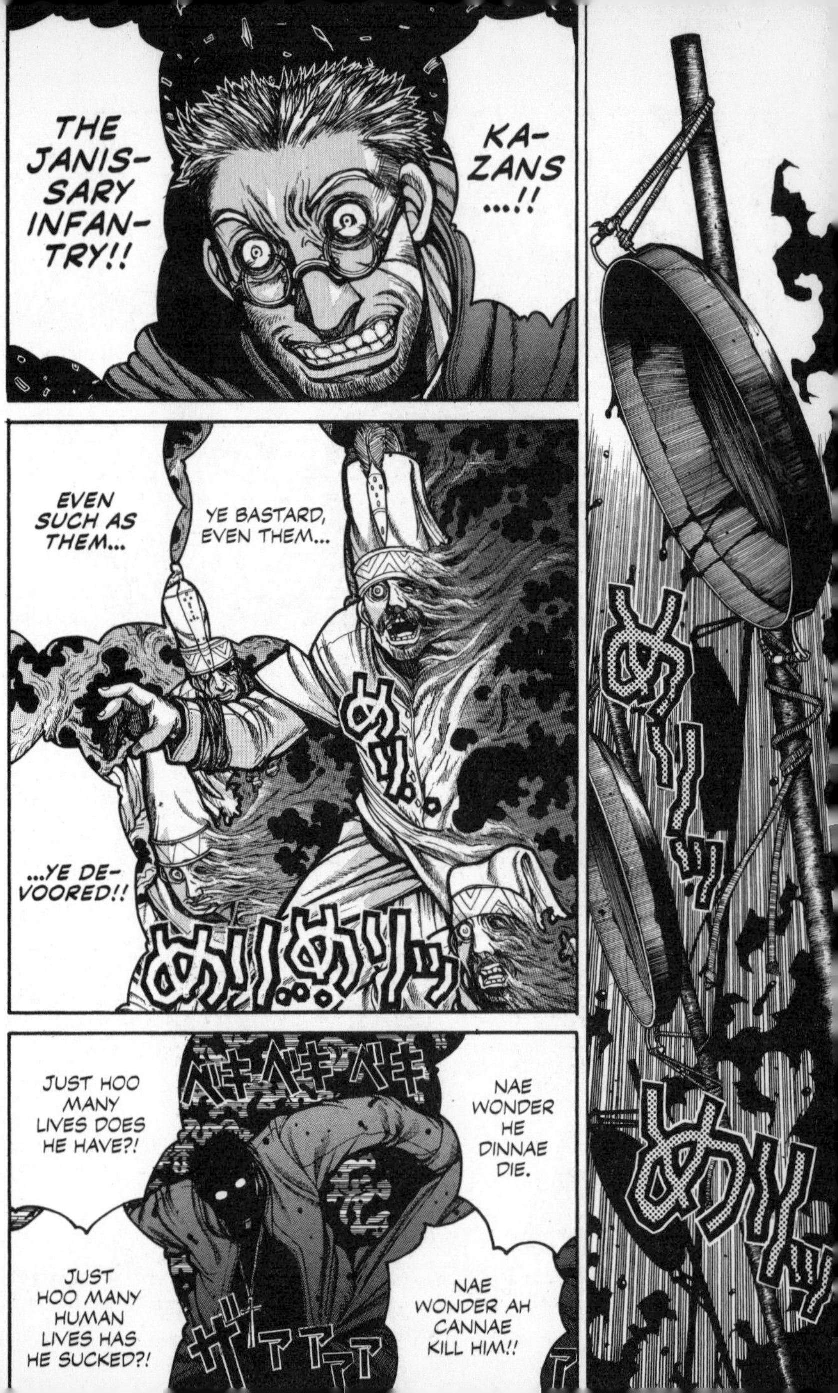
KA-ZANS...!!
THE JANIS-SARY INFAN-TRY!!
YE BASTARD, EVEN THEM...
EVEN SUCH AS THEM...
...YE DE-VOORED!!
NAE WONDER HE DINNAE DIE.
JUST HOO MANY LIVES DOES HE HAVE?!
NAE WONDER AH CANNAE KILL HIM!!
JUST HOO MANY HUMAN LIVES HAS HE SUCKED?!

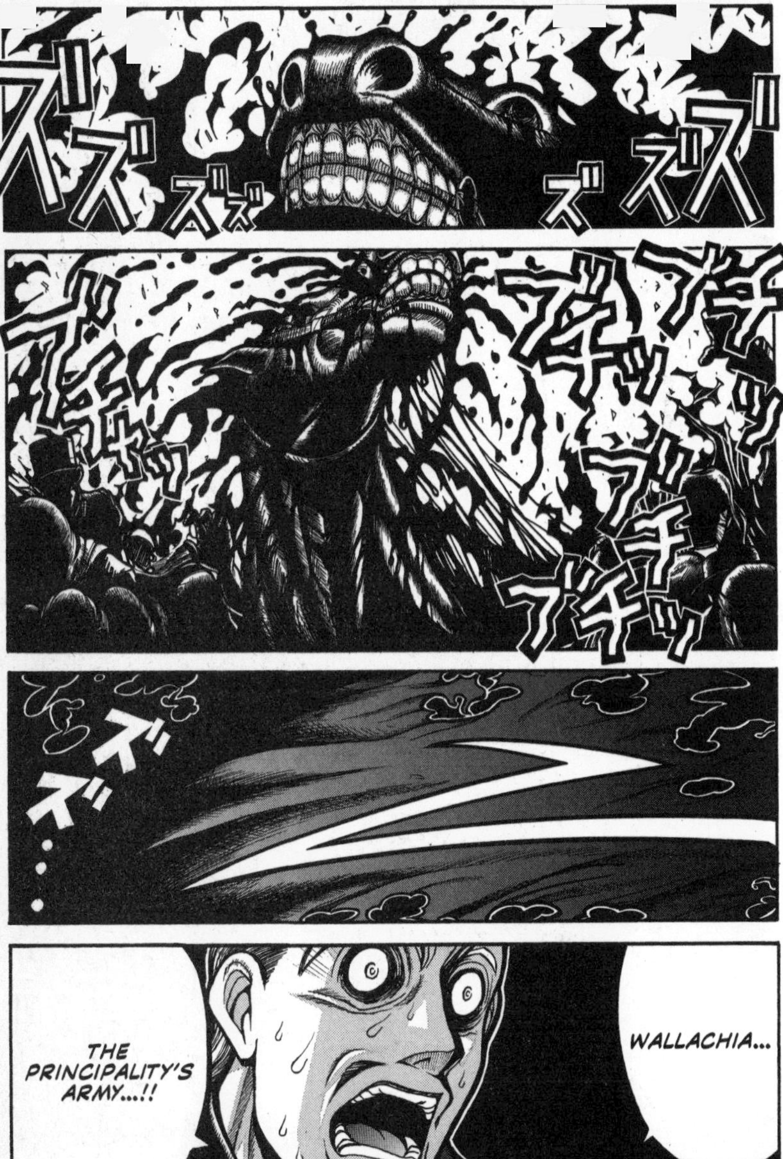
ズズ…
WALLACHIA...
THE PRINCIPALITY'S ARMY...!!

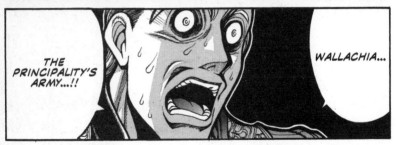

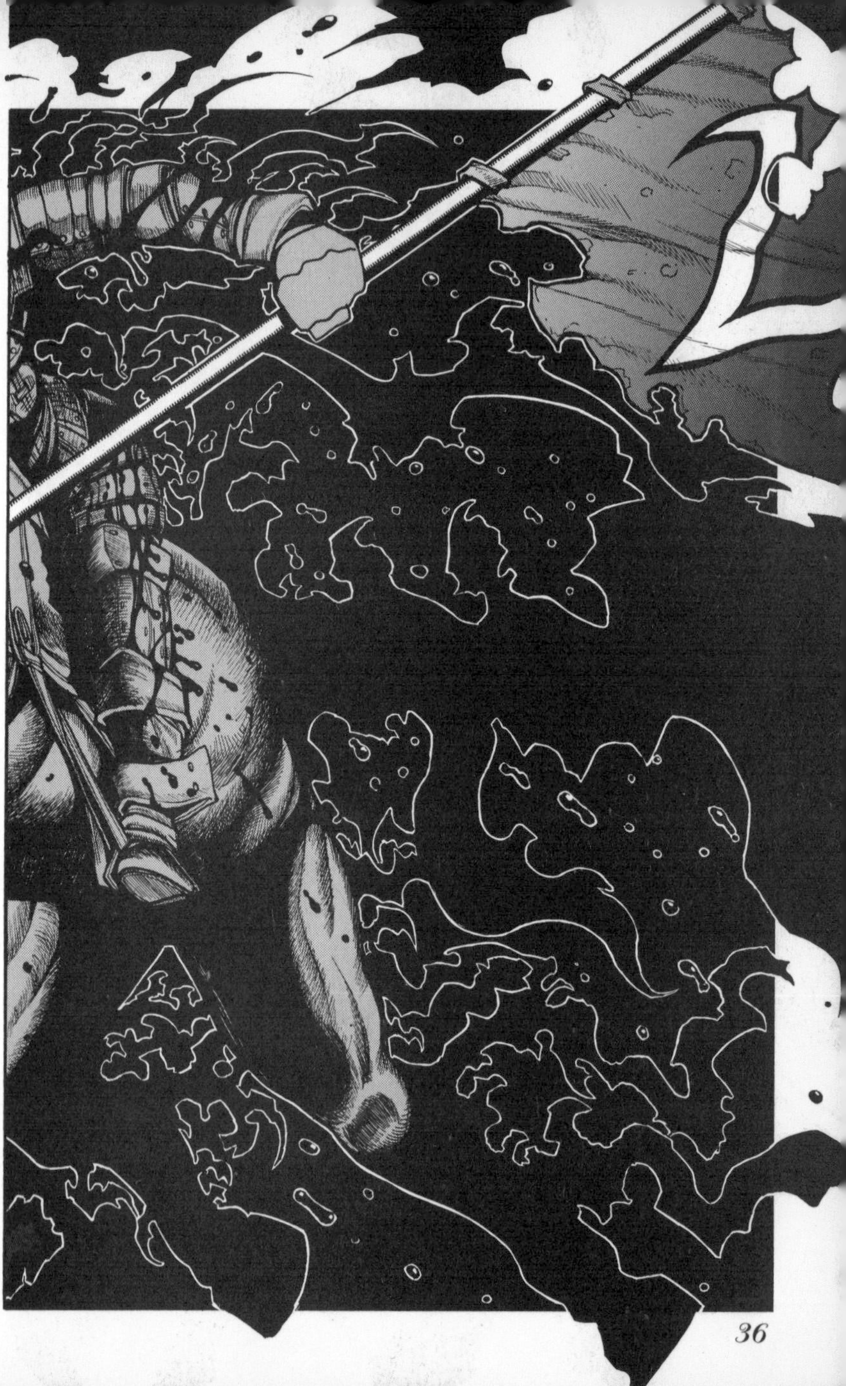

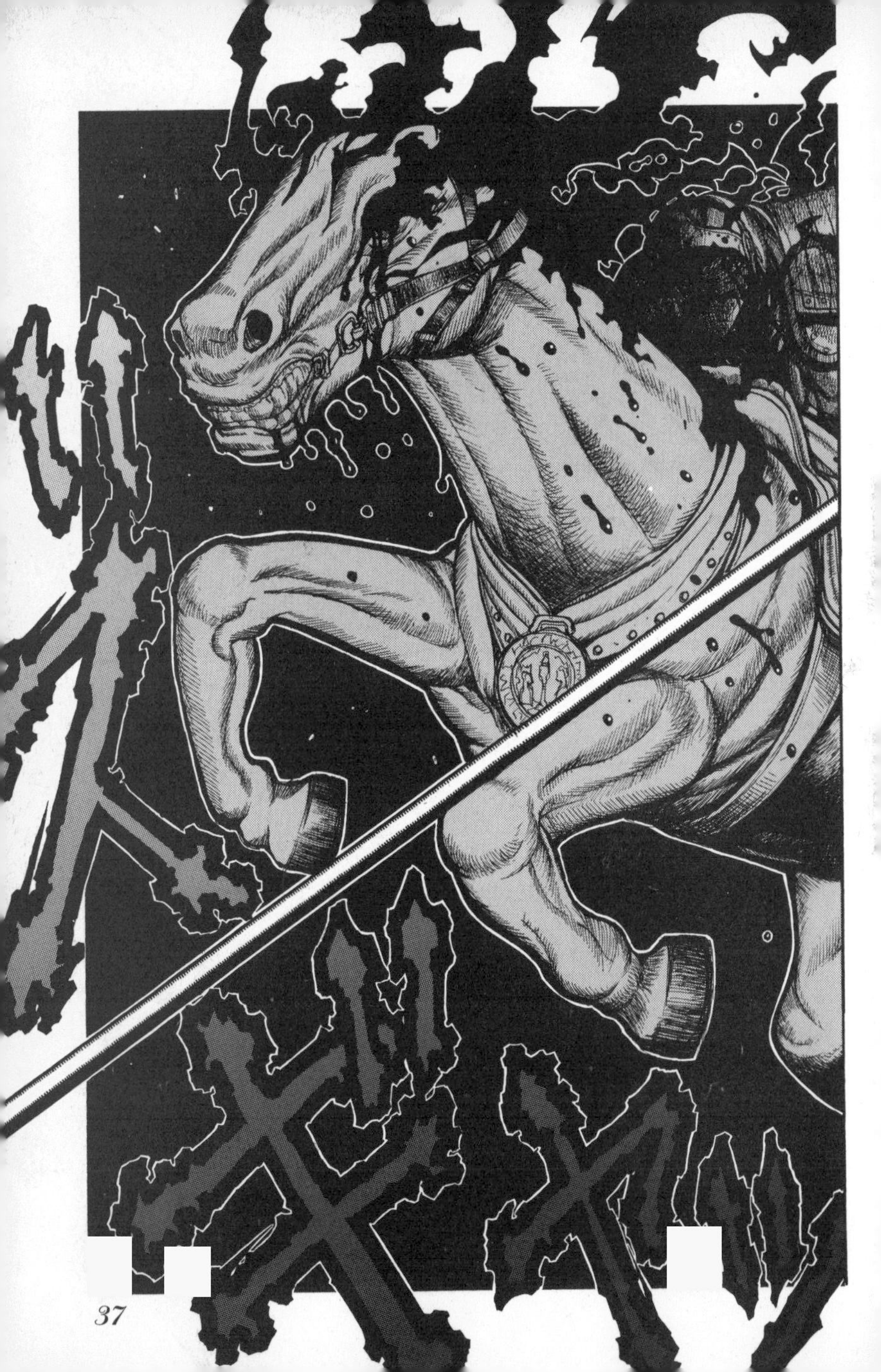

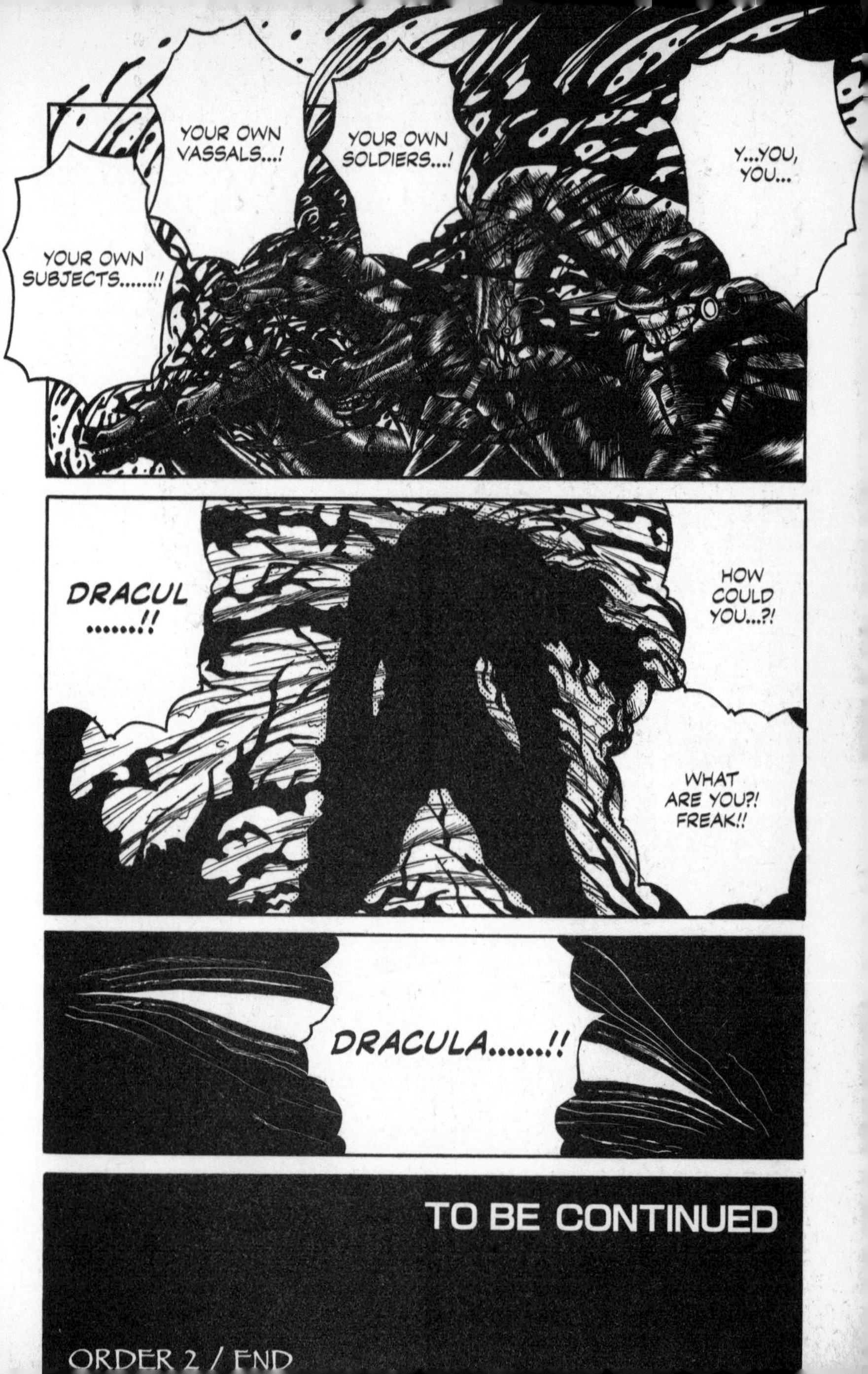
Y...YOU, YOU...
YOUR OWN SOLDIERS...!
YOUR OWN VASSALS...!
YOUR OWN SUBJECTS.......!!
HOW COULD YOU...?!
WHAT ARE YOU?! FREAK!!
DRACUL ....!!
DRACULA.......!!
TO BE CONTINUED
ORDER 2 / END

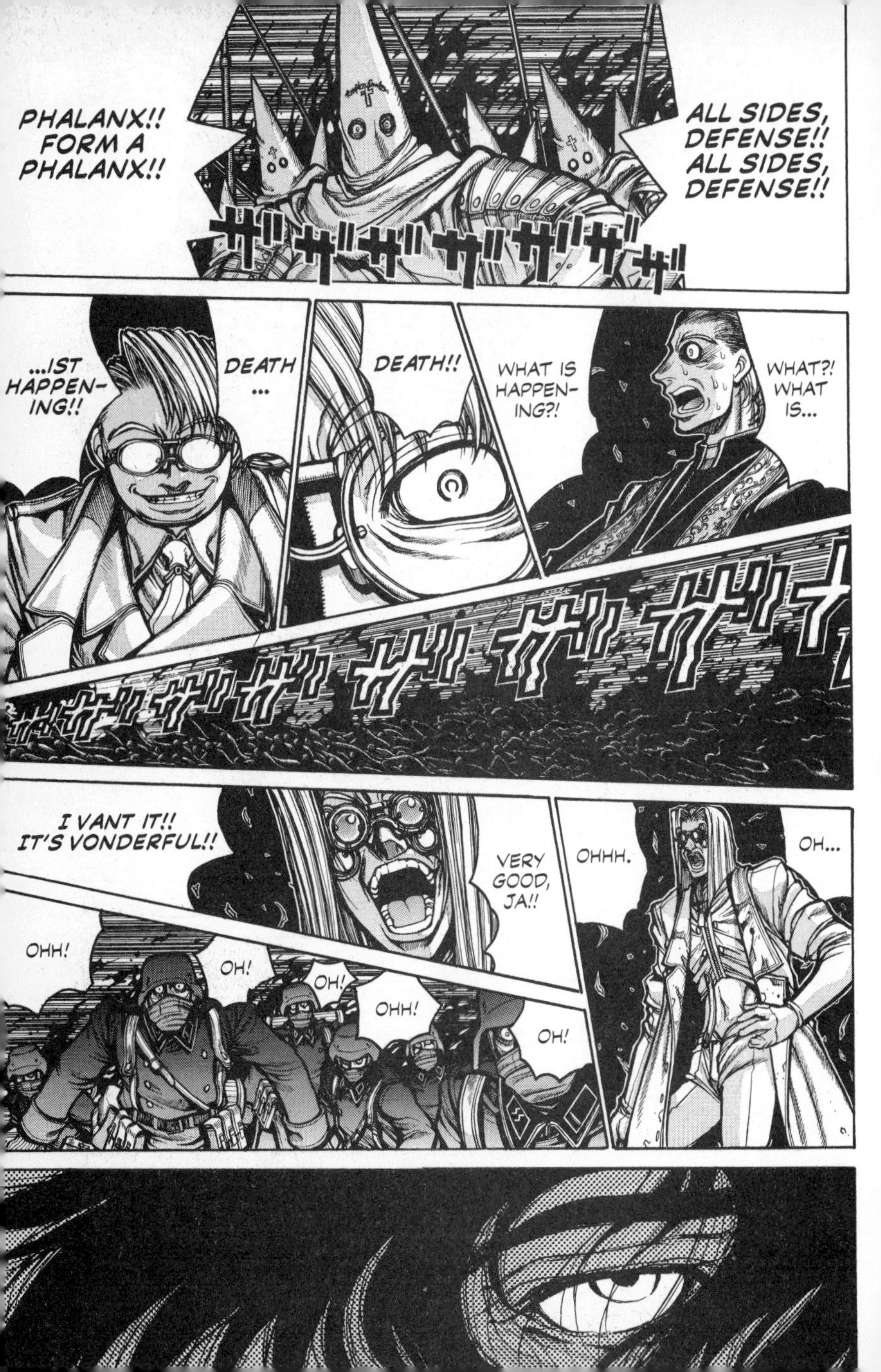
ALL SIDES, DEFENSE!! ALL SIDES, DEFENSE!!
PHALANX!! FORM A PHALANX!!
WHAT?! WHAT IS...
WHAT IS HAPPEN-ING?!
DEATH!!
DEATH ...
...IST HAPPEN-ING!!
OH...
OHHH.
VERY GOOD, JA!!
I VANT IT!! IT'S VONDERFUL!!
OH!
OHH!
OH!
OH!
OHH!

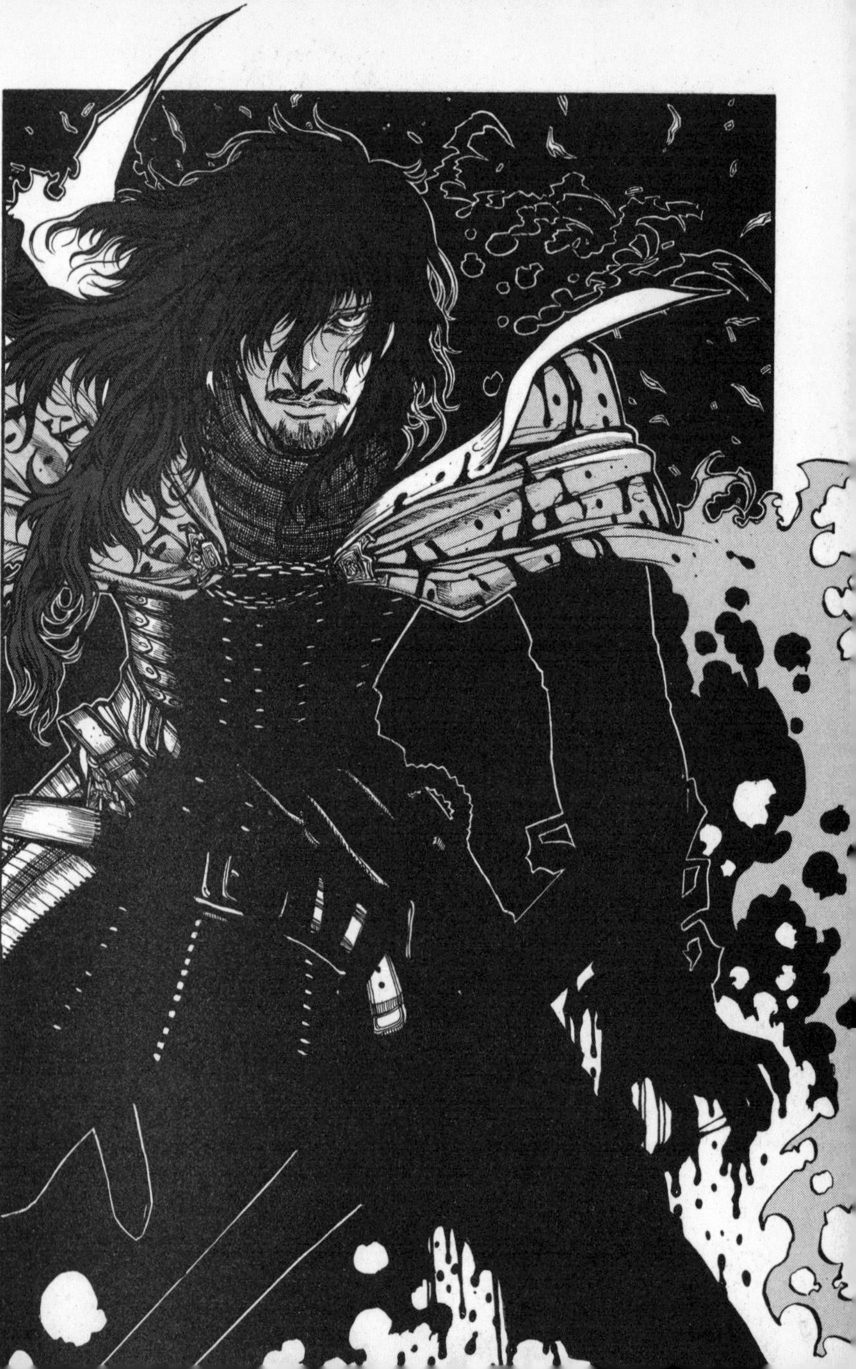

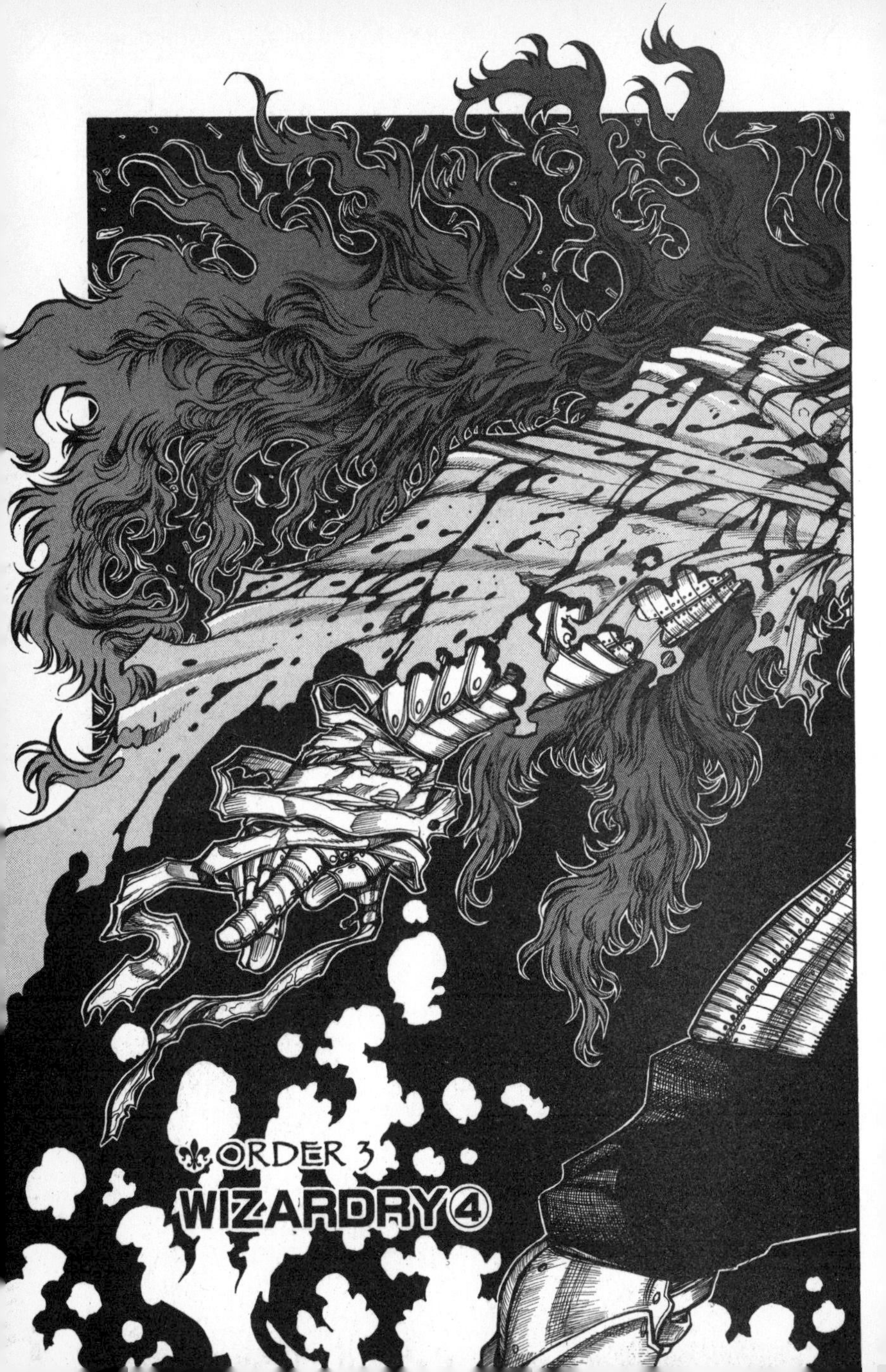
ORDER 3
WIZARDRY ④

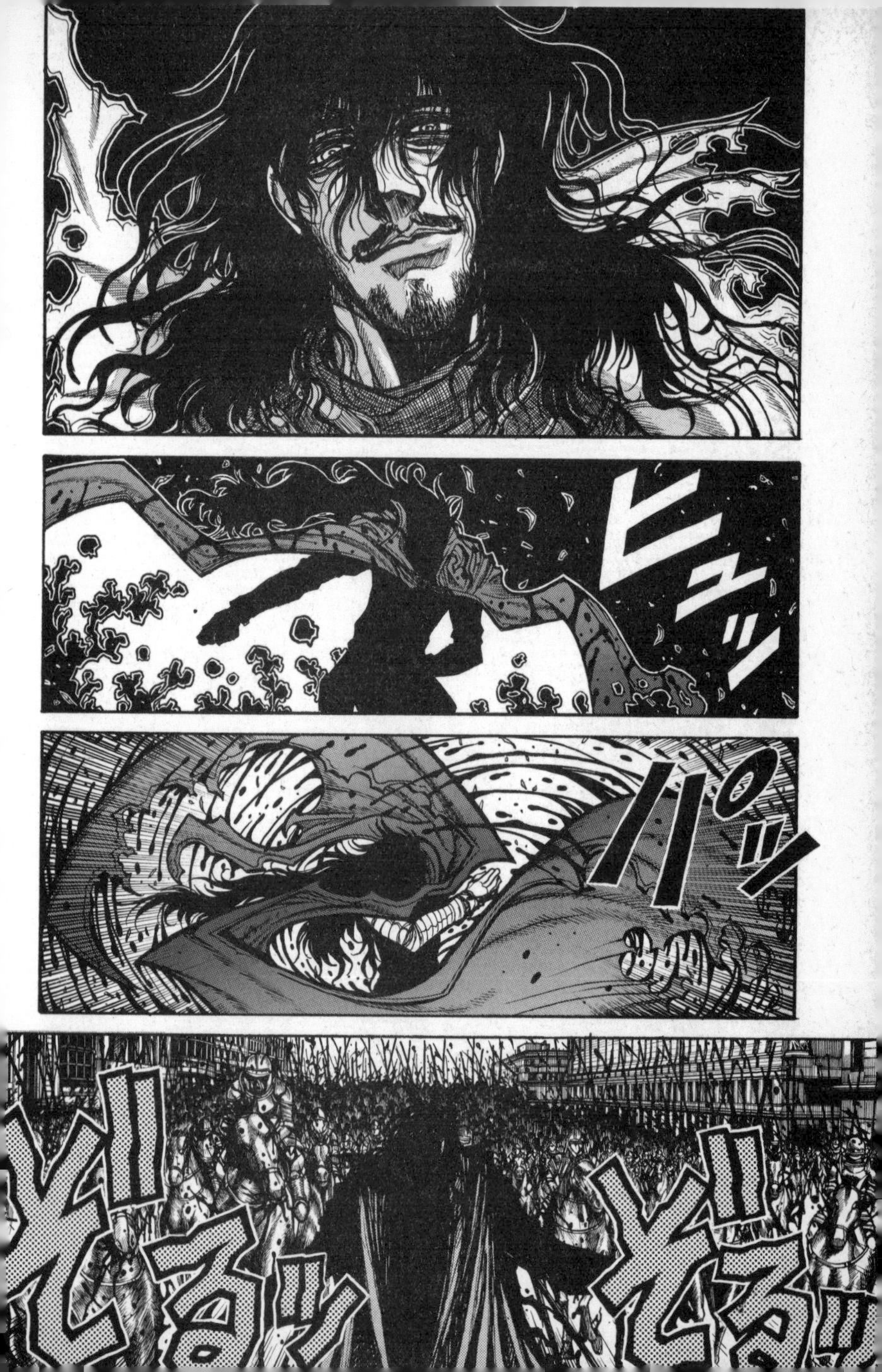
ヒュッ
パッ

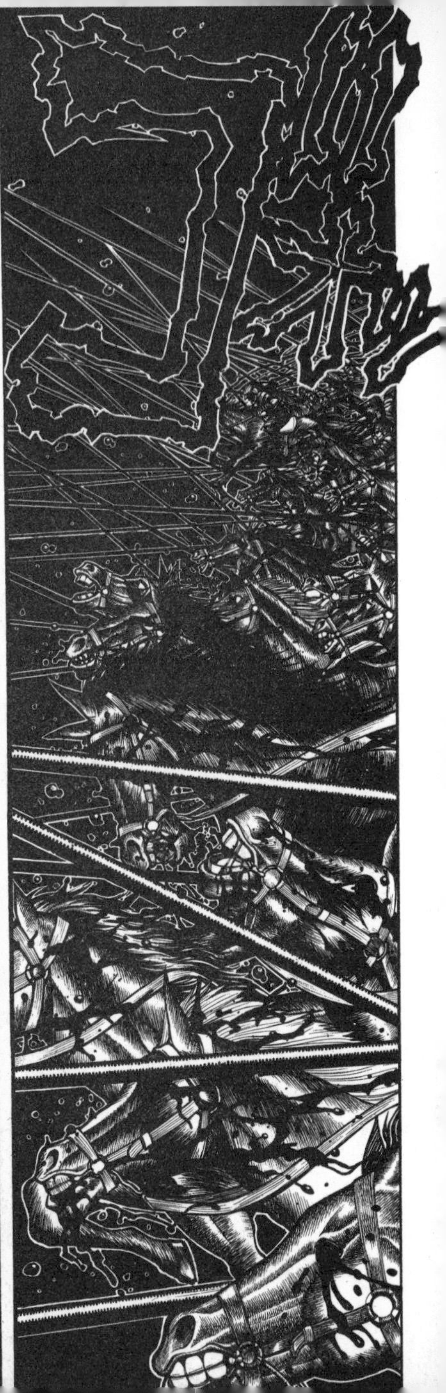
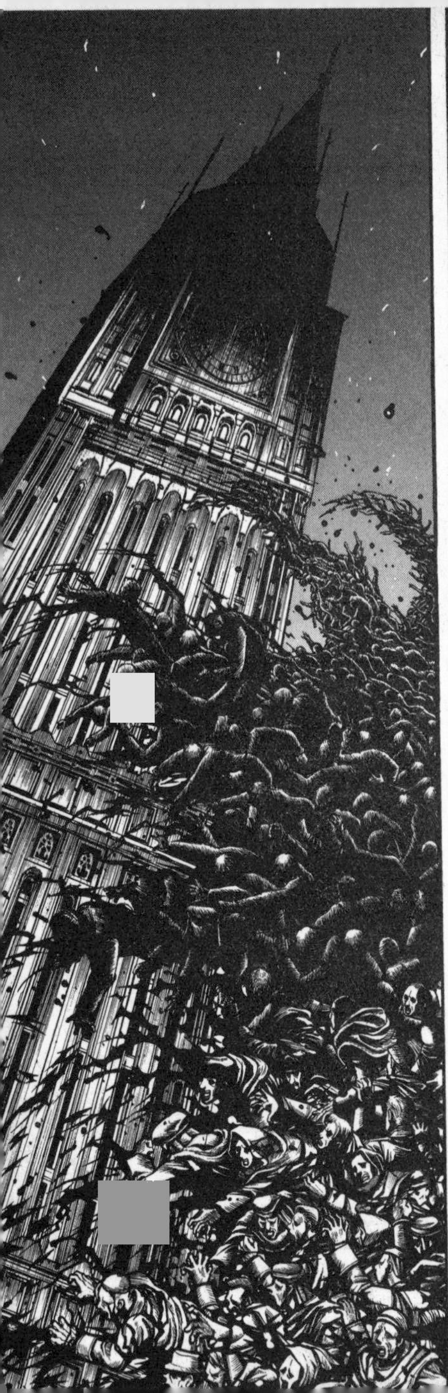

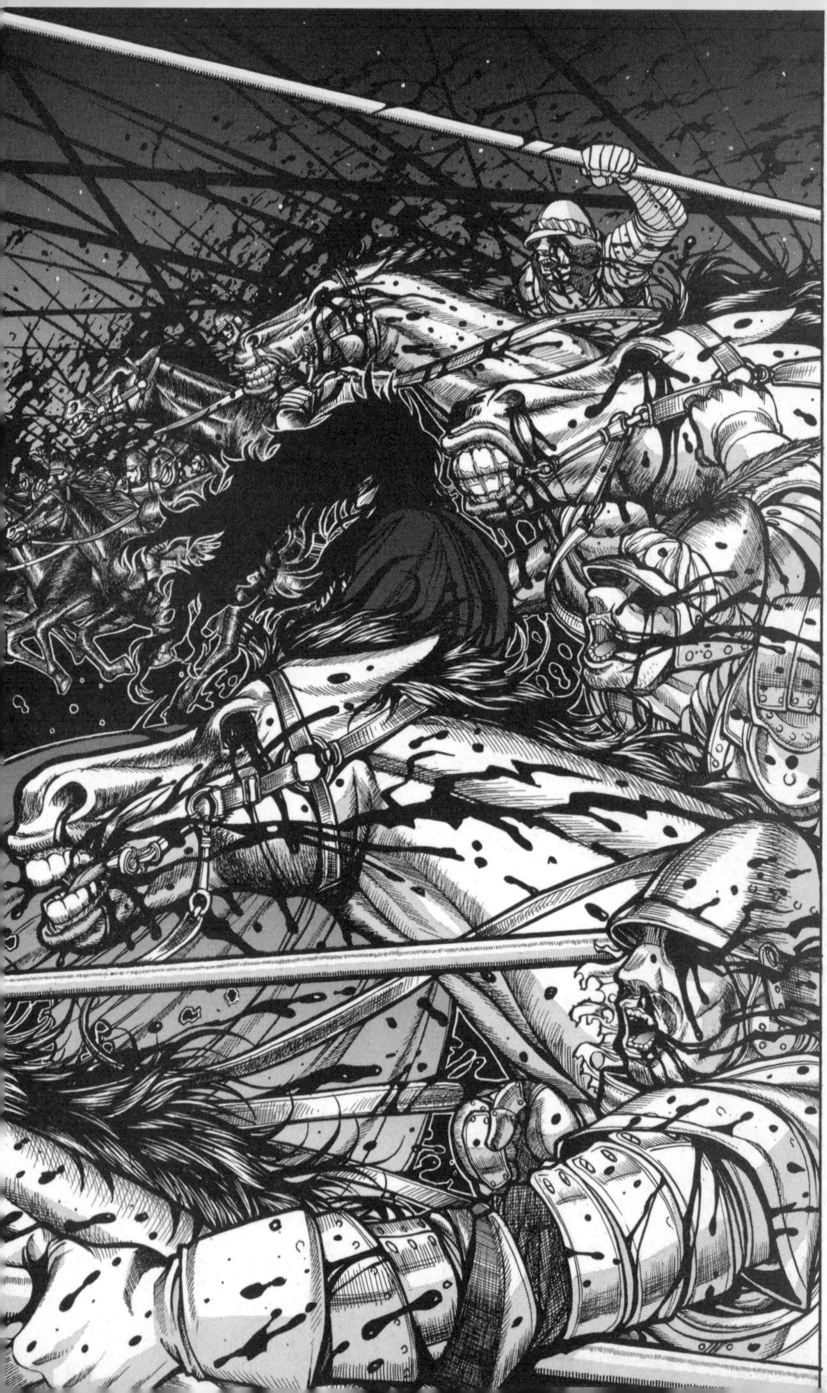

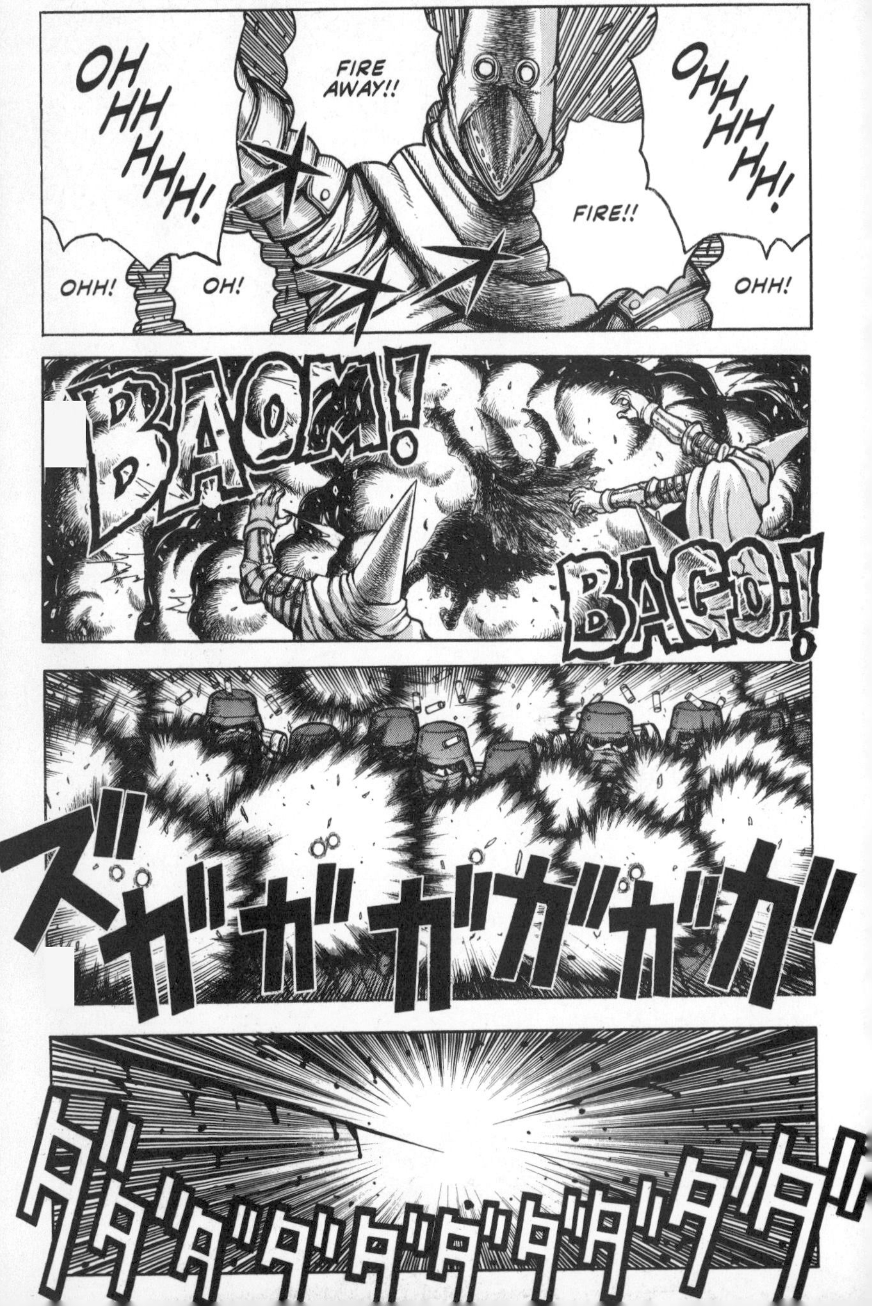
OHHHHHHH!
FIRE!!
OHH!
FIRE AWAY!!
OH!
OHHHHHHH!
OHH!
BAGOH!
BAOM!
ズガガガガガ
ダダダダダダダダダダダダ

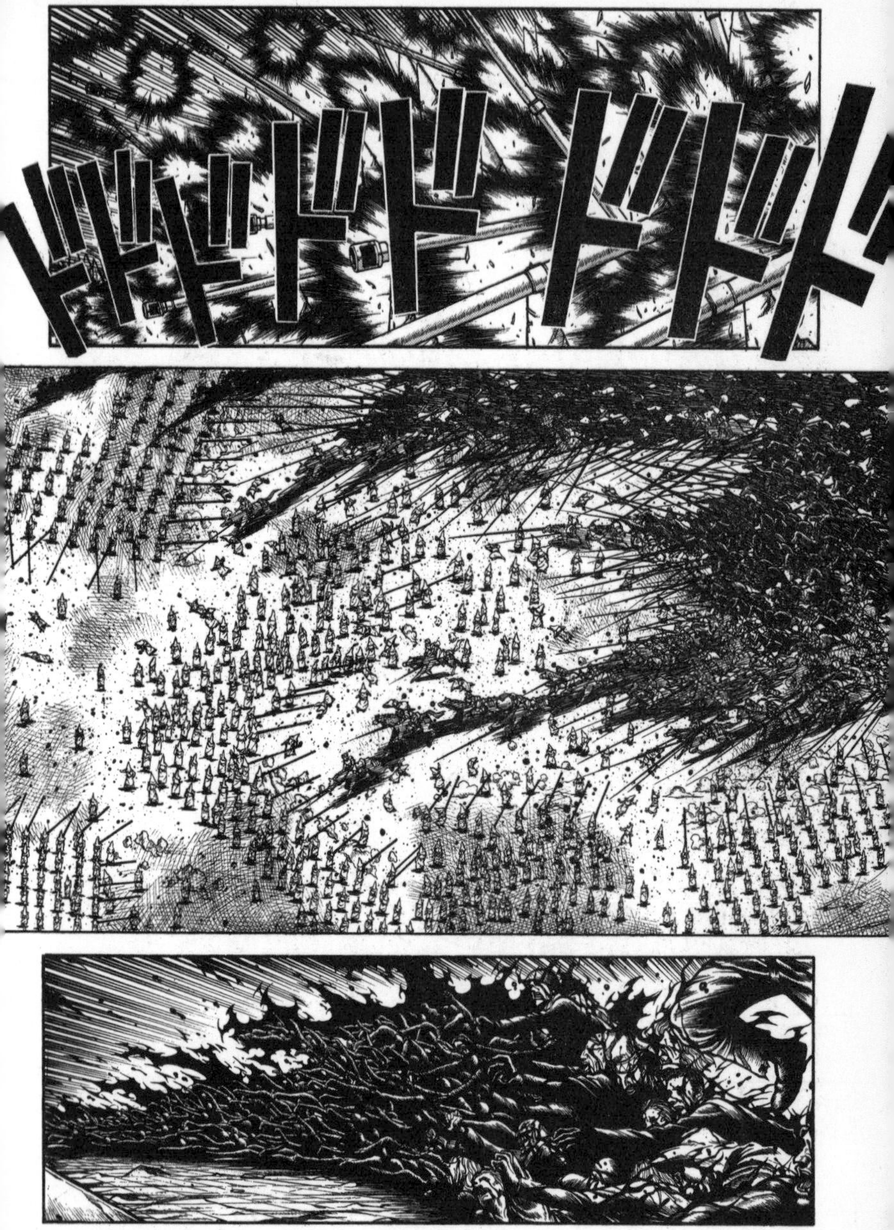
ドドドドドドドド

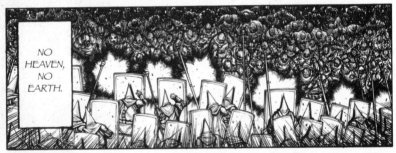

NO HEAVEN, NO EARTH.

MEN SPRINT, BEASTS BELLOW AT THEM.

AS IF THEIR ENTIRE UNIVERSE HAS BEGUN TO ROAR.

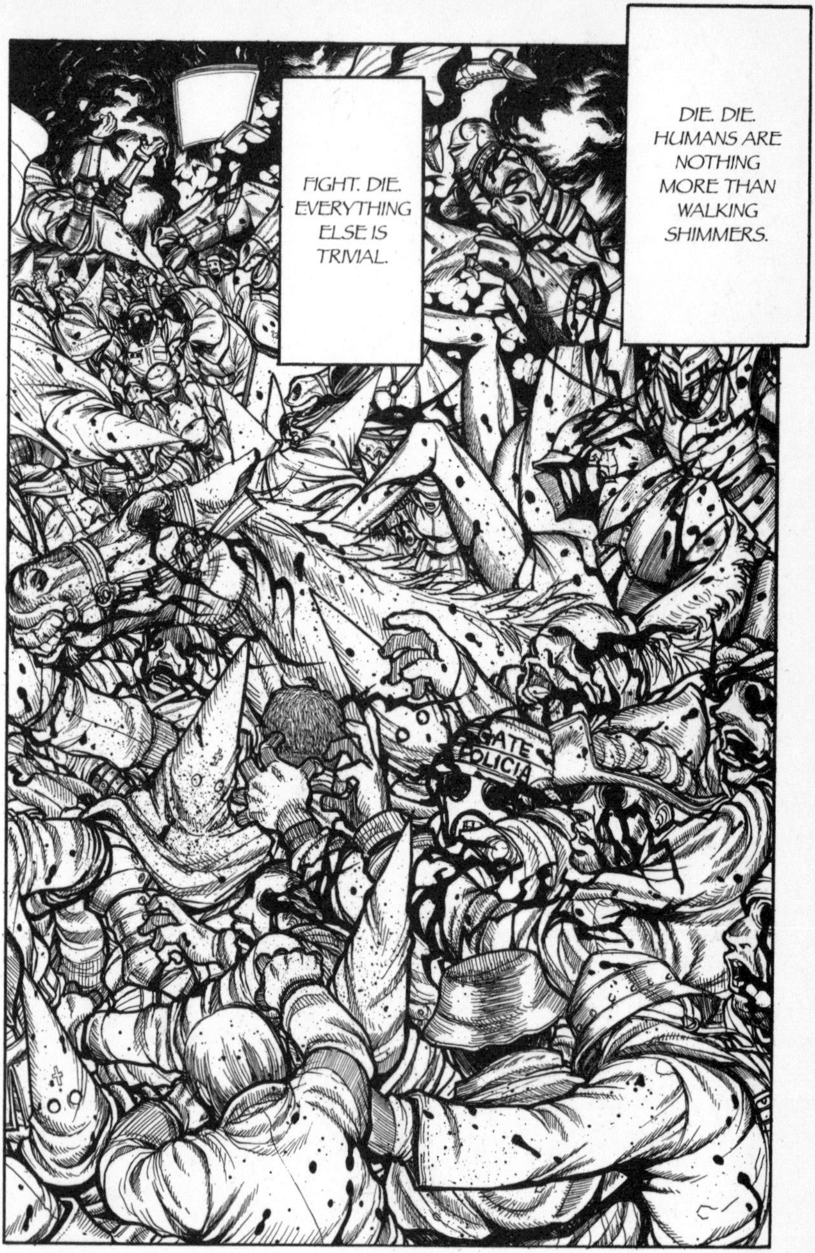
DIE. DIE. HUMANS ARE NOTHING MORE THAN WALKING SHIMMERS.
FIGHT. DIE. EVERYTHING ELSE IS TRIVIAL.
POLICIA

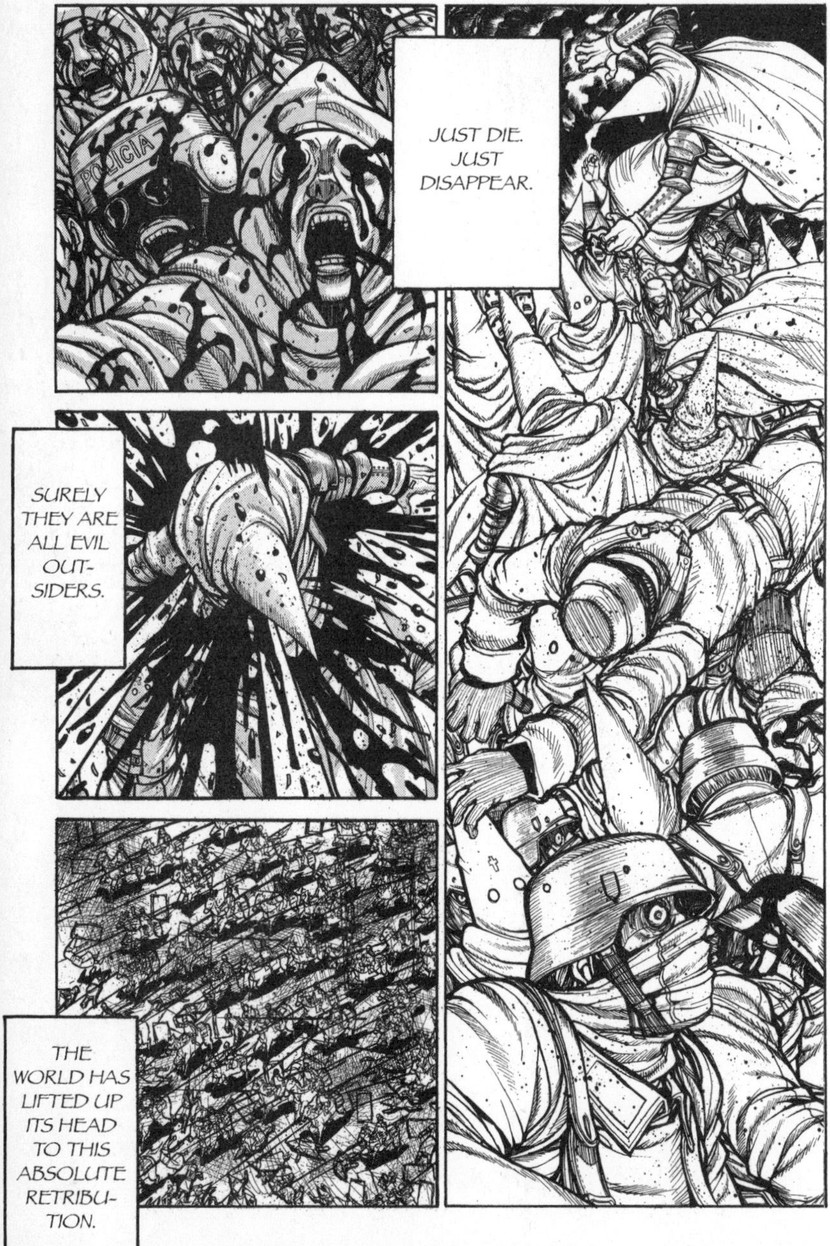
JUST DIE. JUST DISAPPEAR.
POLICIA
SURELY THEY ARE ALL EVIL OUT-SIDERS.
THE WORLD HAS LIFTED UP ITS HEAD TO THIS ABSOLUTE RETRIBU-TION.

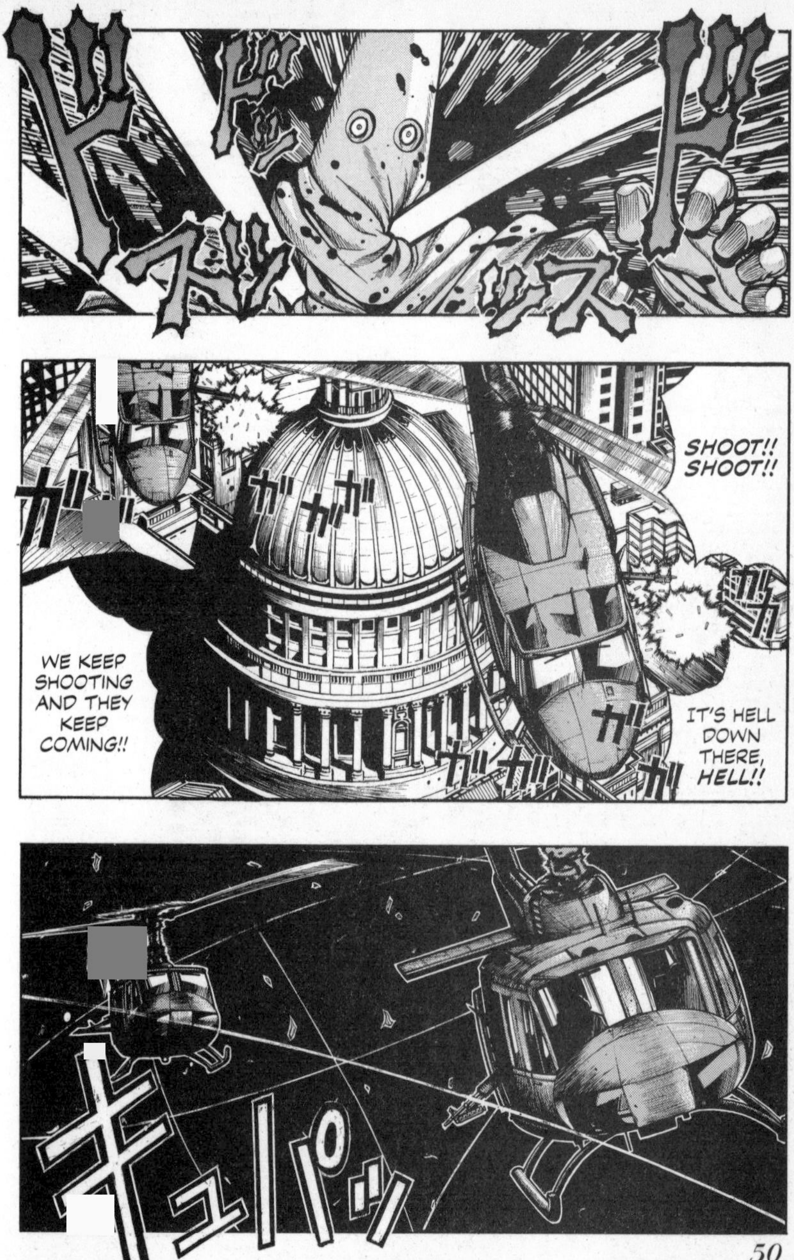
SHOOT!! SHOOT!!
IT'S HELL DOWN THERE, HELL!!
WE KEEP SHOOTING AND THEY KEEP COMING!!
ギュパッ

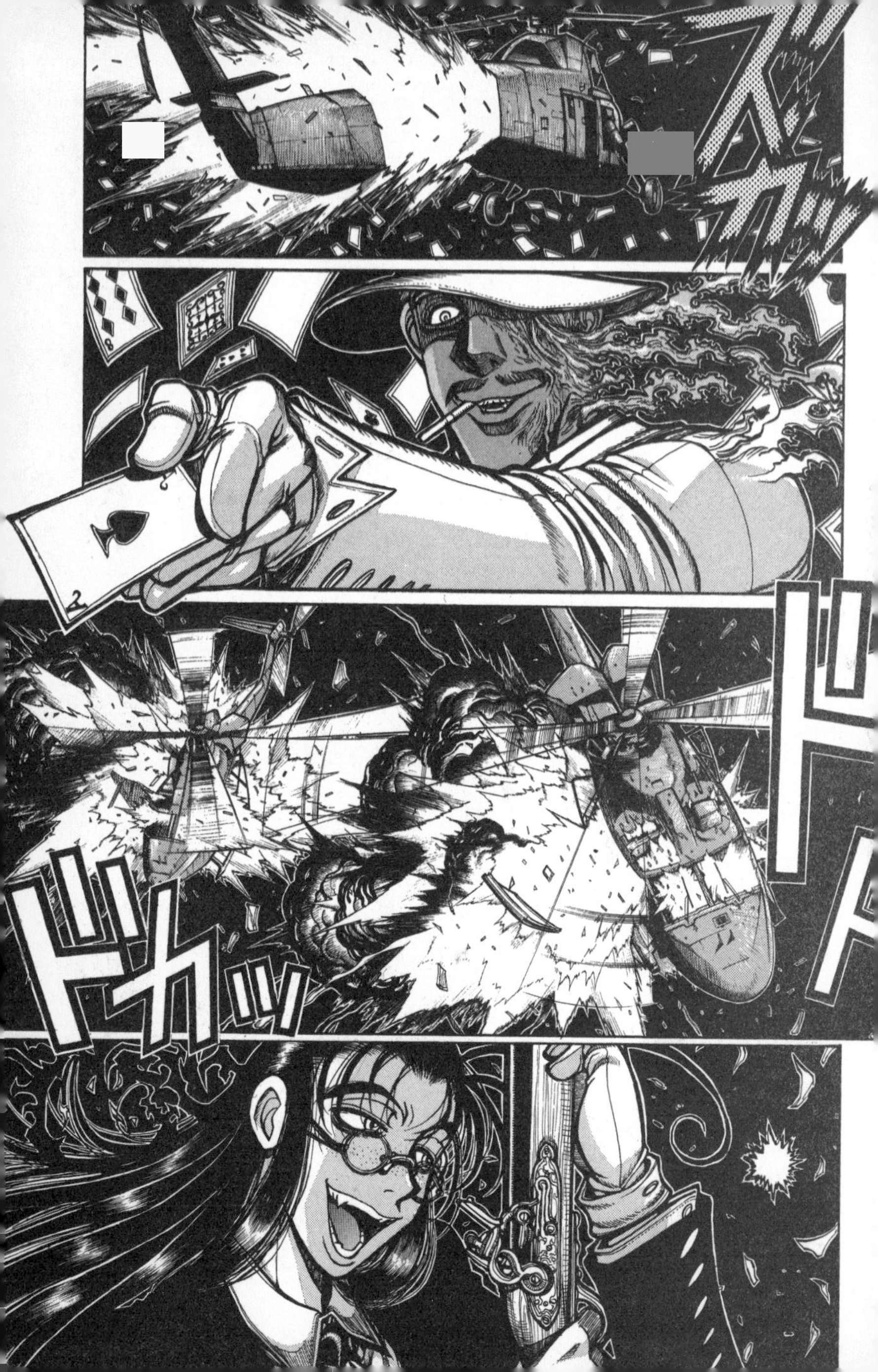
ドド
ドカッ

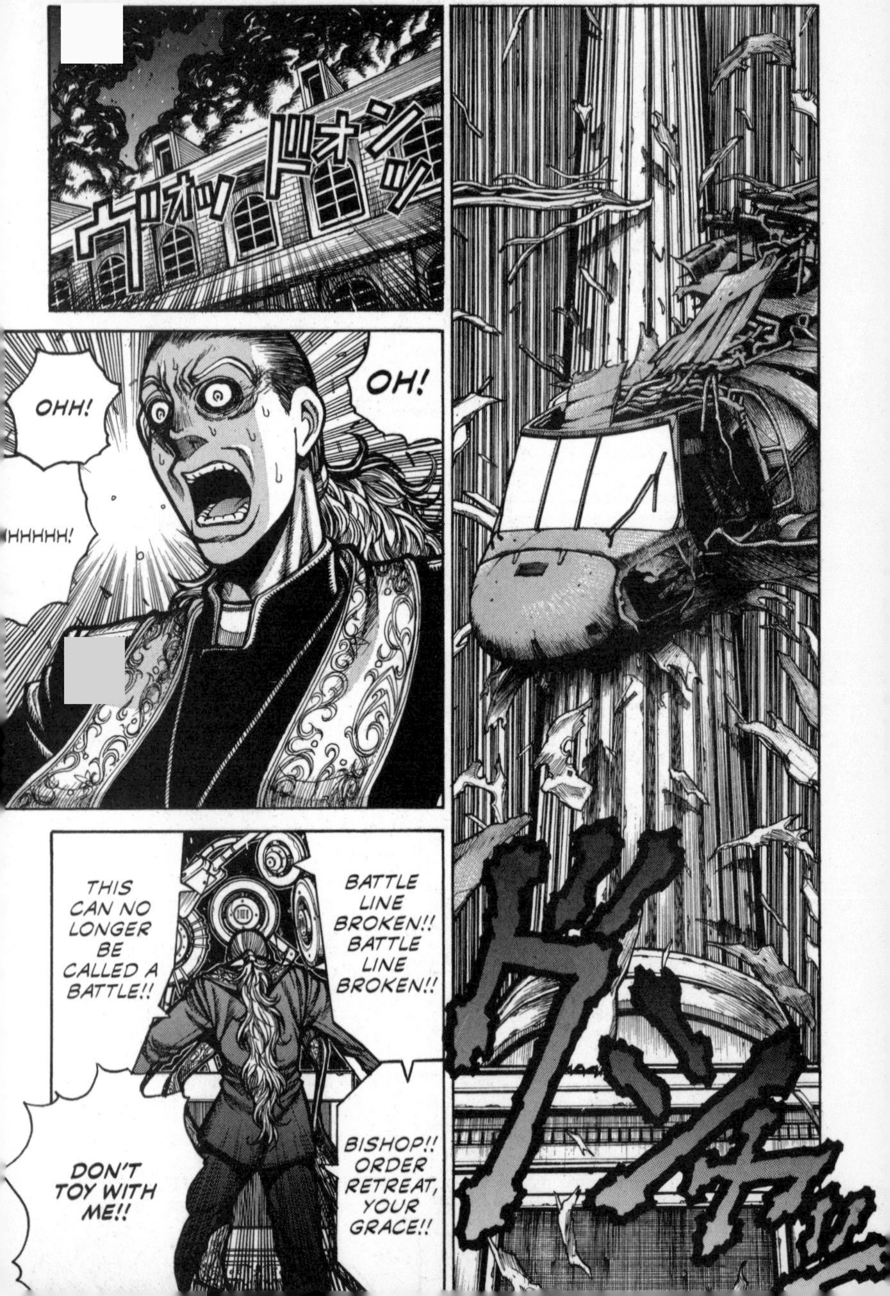
OH!
OHH!
HHHHH!
BATTLE LINE BROKEN!! BATTLE LINE BROKEN!!
THIS CAN NO LONGER BE CALLED A BATTLE!!
BISHOP!! ORDER RETREAT, YOUR GRACE!!
DON'T TOY WITH ME!!

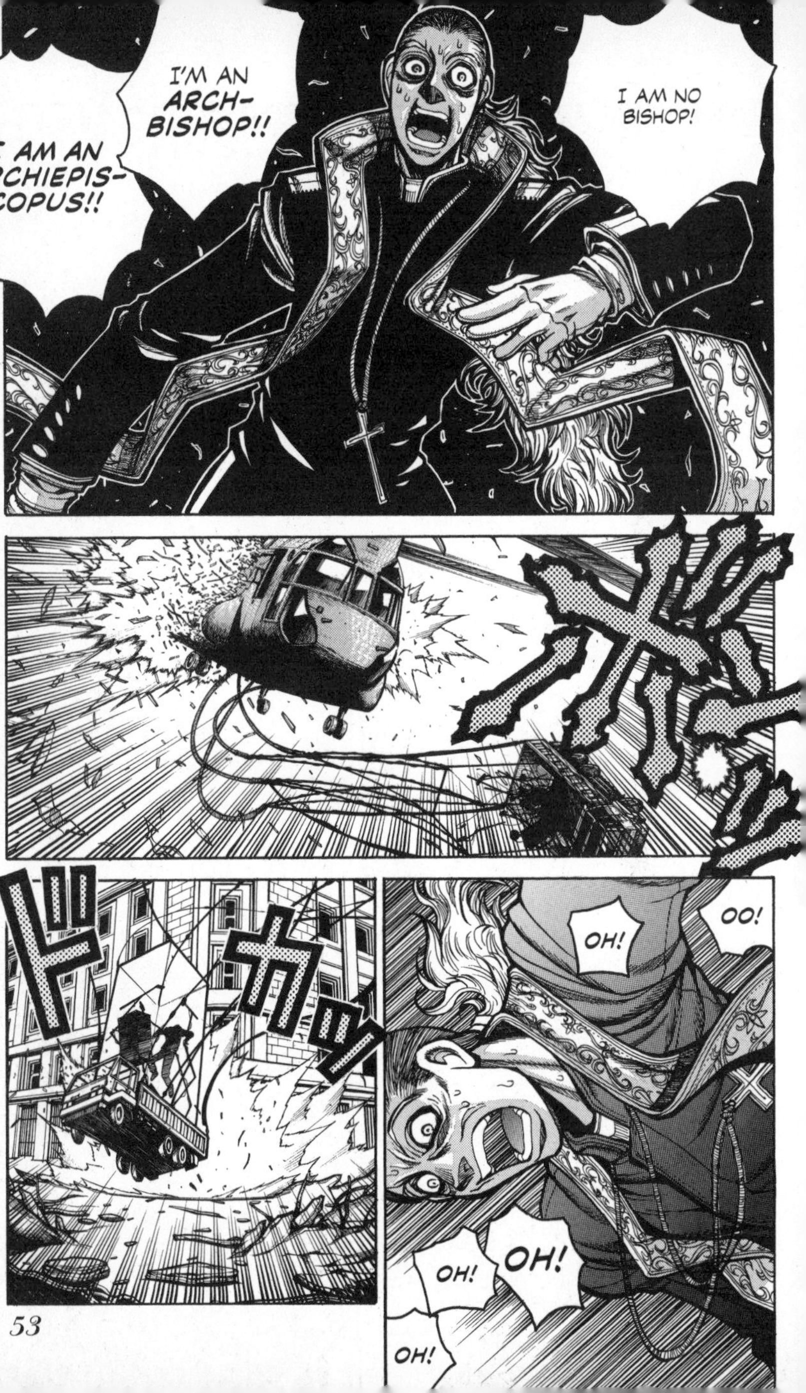
I AM NO BISHOP!
I'M AN ARCH-BISHOP!!
I AM AN ARCHIEPIS-COPUS!!
OO!
OH!
OH!
OH!
OH!
ドカッ

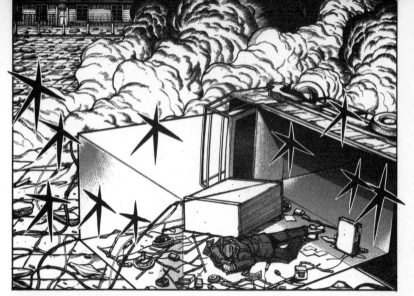

!!

UGH...

GUH...

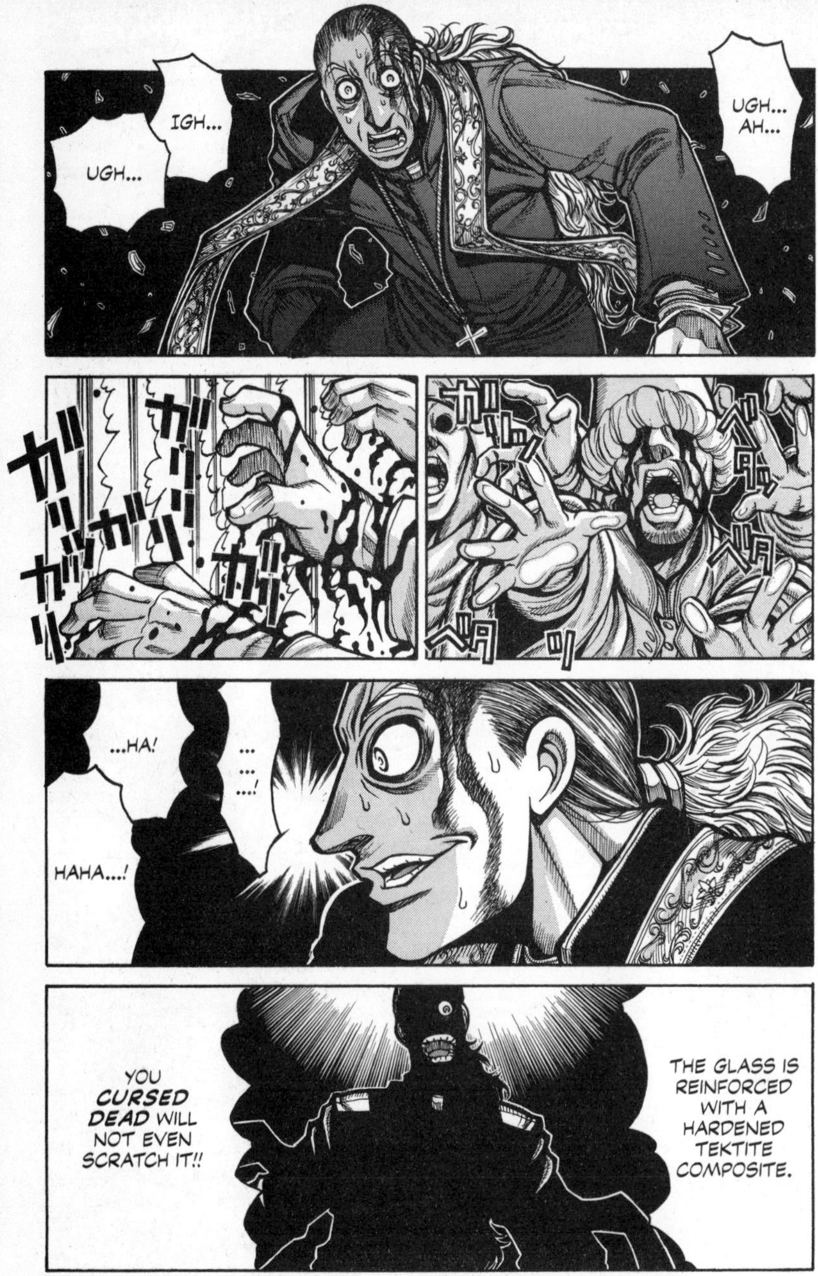
UGH... AH...
IGH...
UGH...
...
...
...!
...HA!
HAHA...!
THE GLASS IS REINFORCED WITH A HARDENED TEKTITE COMPOSITE.
YOU **CURSED DEAD** WILL NOT EVEN SCRATCH IT!!

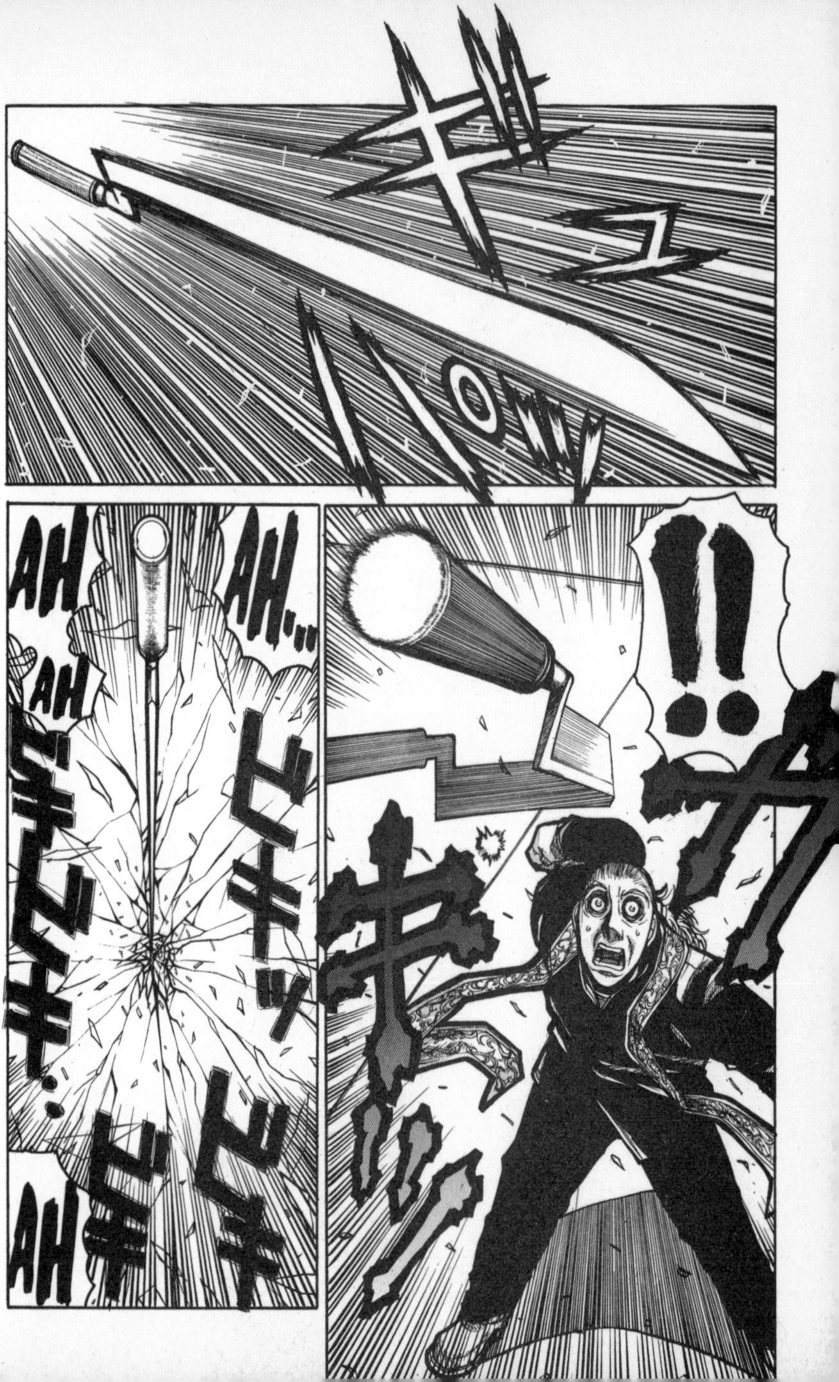

!!
AH...
AH
AH
AH

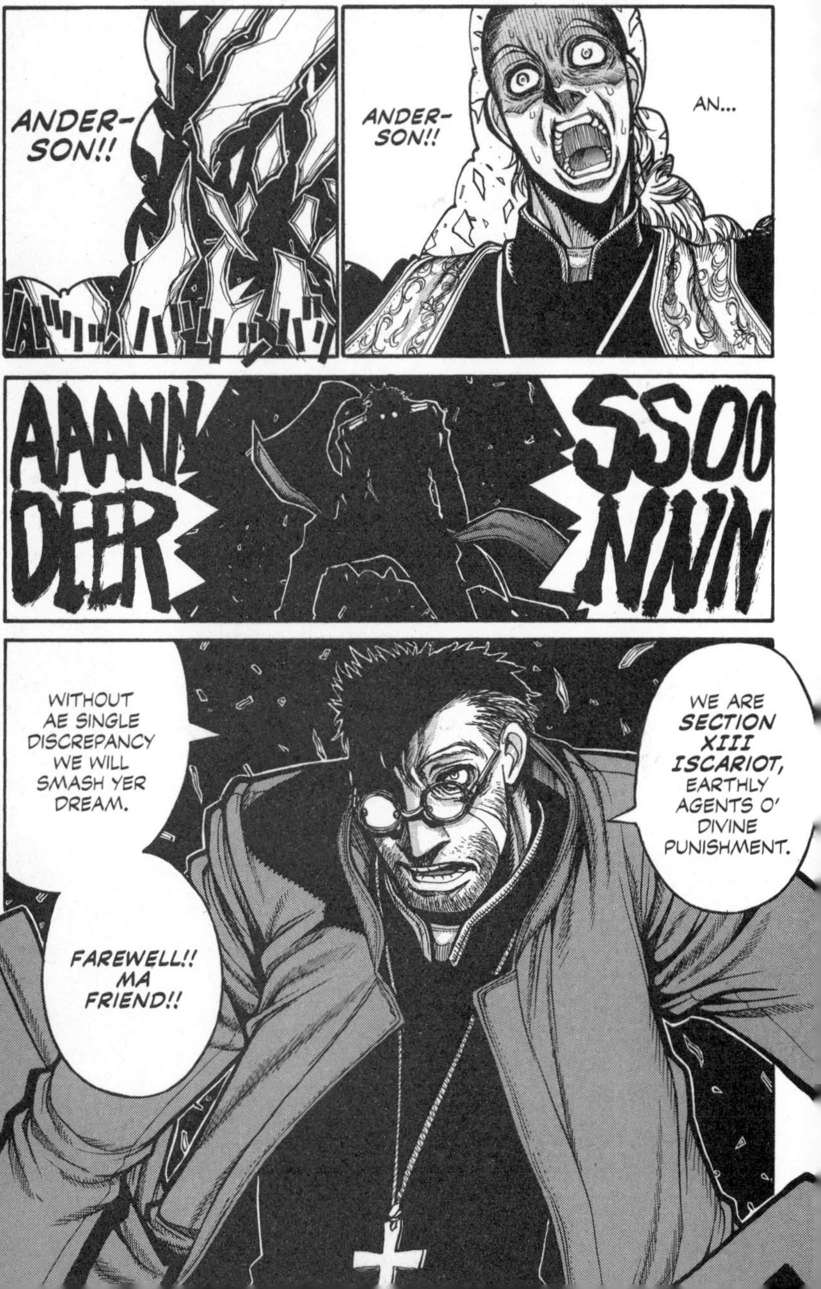
AN...
ANDER-SON!!
ANDER-SON!!
AAANN DEER
SSOO NNN
WE ARE SECTION XIII ISCARIOT, EARTHLY AGENTS O' DIVINE PUNISHMENT.
WITHOUT AE SINGLE DISCREPANCY WE WILL SMASH YER DREAM.
FAREWELL!! MA FRIEND!!

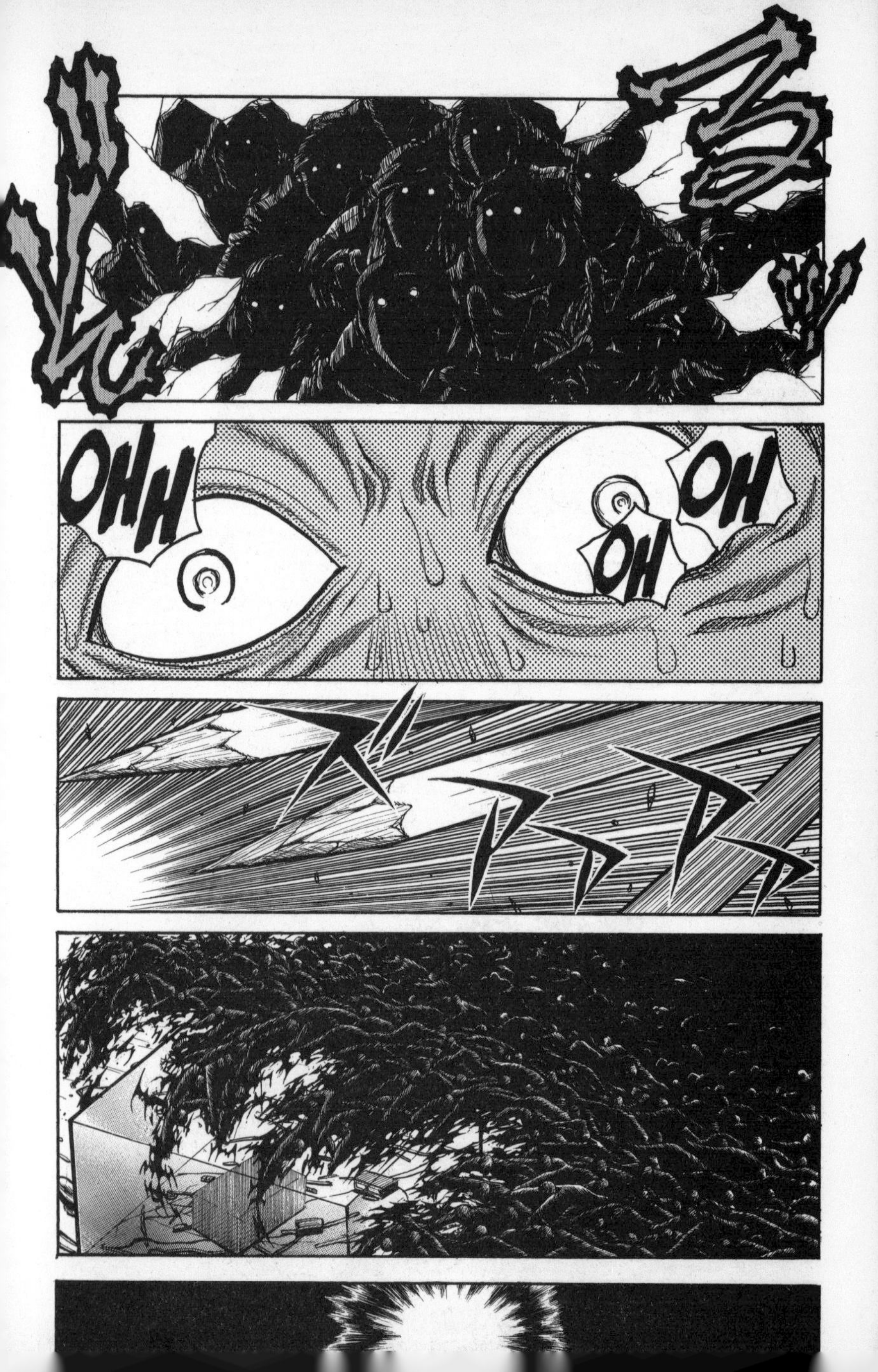
OH
OH
OHH

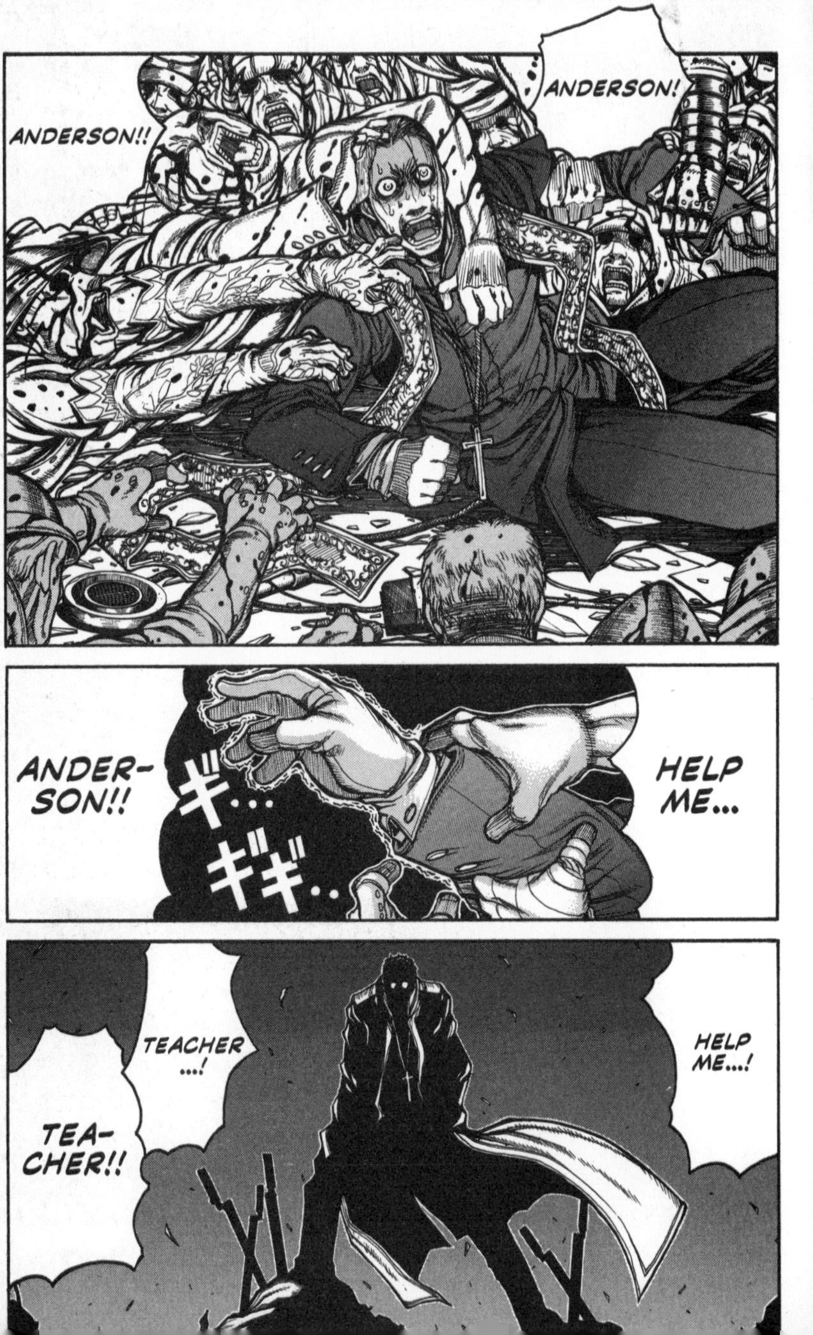
ANDERSON!
ANDERSON!!
HELP ME...
ギ... ギギ..
ANDER-SON!!
HELP ME...!
TEACHER...!
TEA-CHER!!

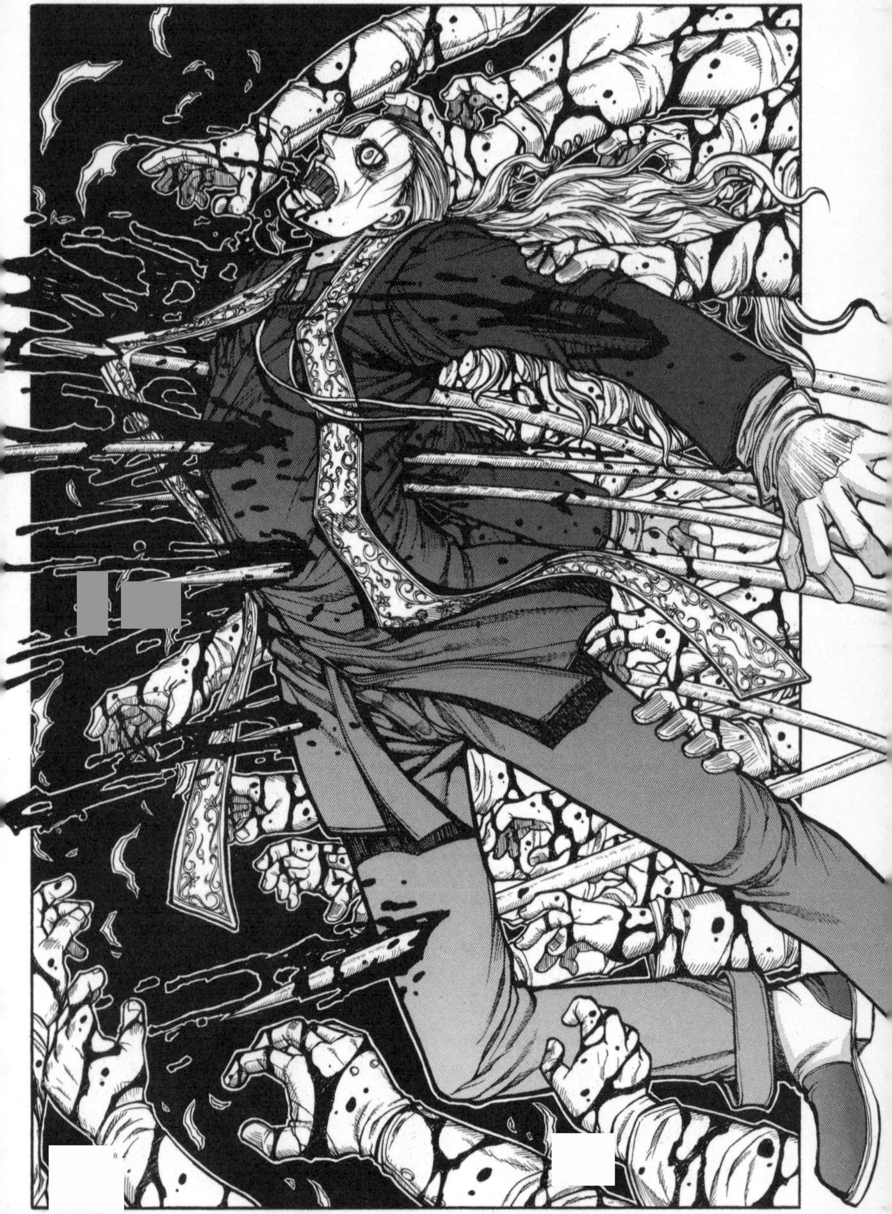

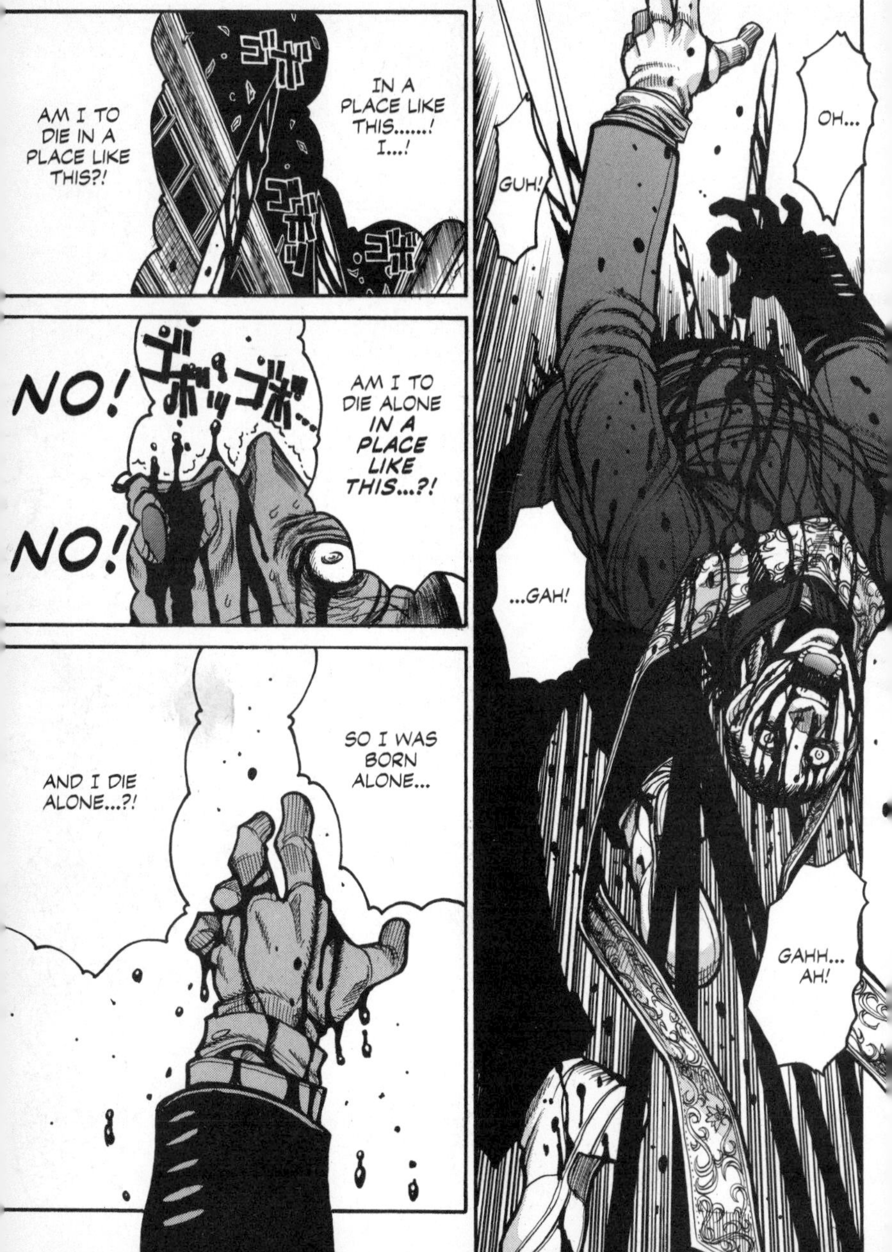
OH...
GUH!
...GAH!
GAHH... AH!
IN A PLACE LIKE THIS......! I...!
AM I TO DIE IN A PLACE LIKE THIS?!
AM I TO DIE ALONE *IN A PLACE LIKE THIS...?!*
ゴボッゴボ...
NO!
NO!
SO I WAS BORN ALONE...
AND I DIE ALONE...?!

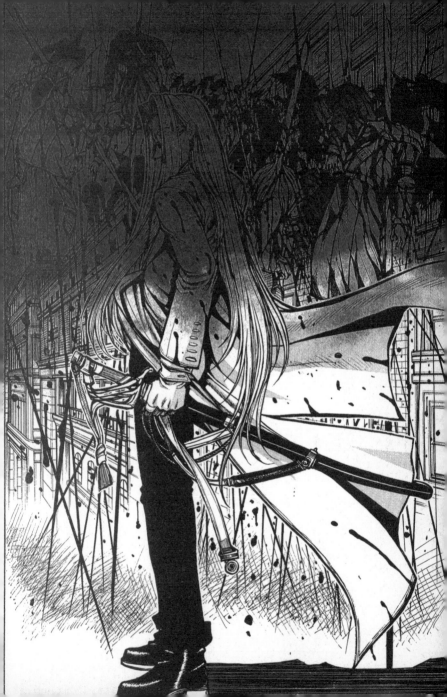

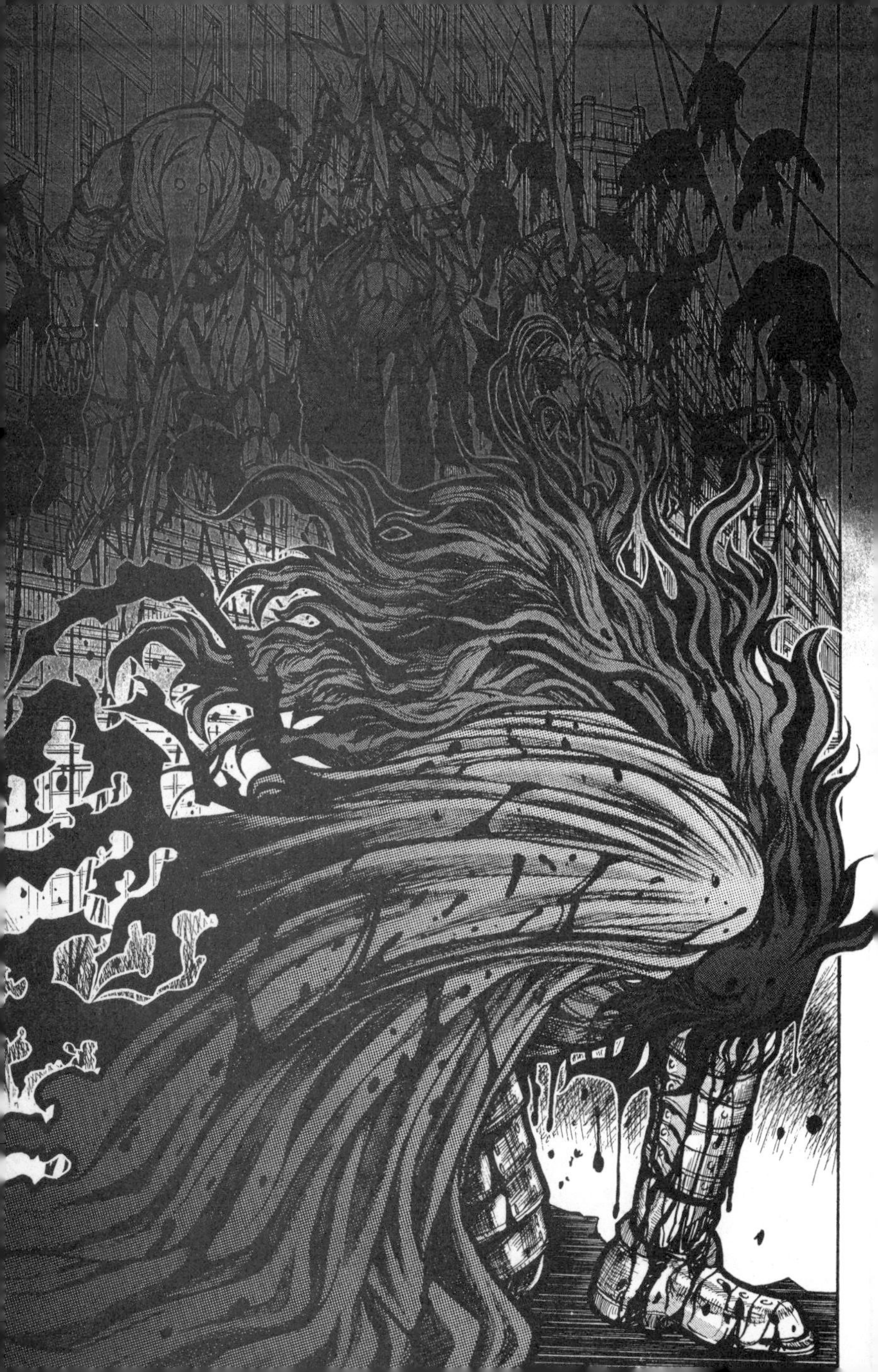

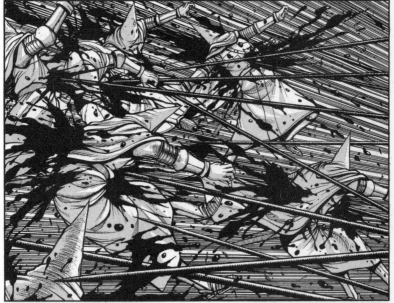

JEEESUS...!

ORDER 3 / END

TO BE CONTINUED

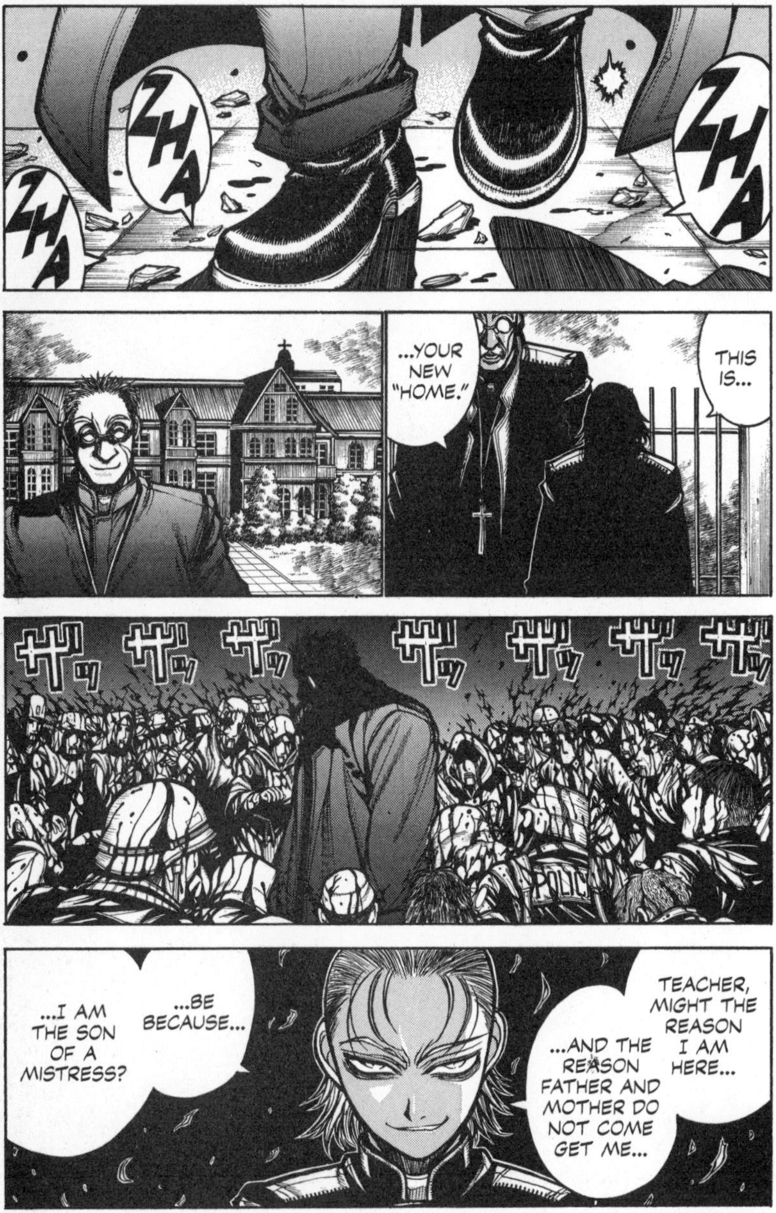
ZHA
ZHA
ZHA
THIS IS...
...YOUR NEW "HOME."
ザッ
ザッ
ザッ
ザッ
ザッ
ザッ
ザッ
TEACHER, MIGHT THE REASON I AM HERE...
...AND THE REASON FATHER AND MOTHER DO NOT COME GET ME...
...BE BECAUSE...
...I AM THE SON OF A MISTRESS?

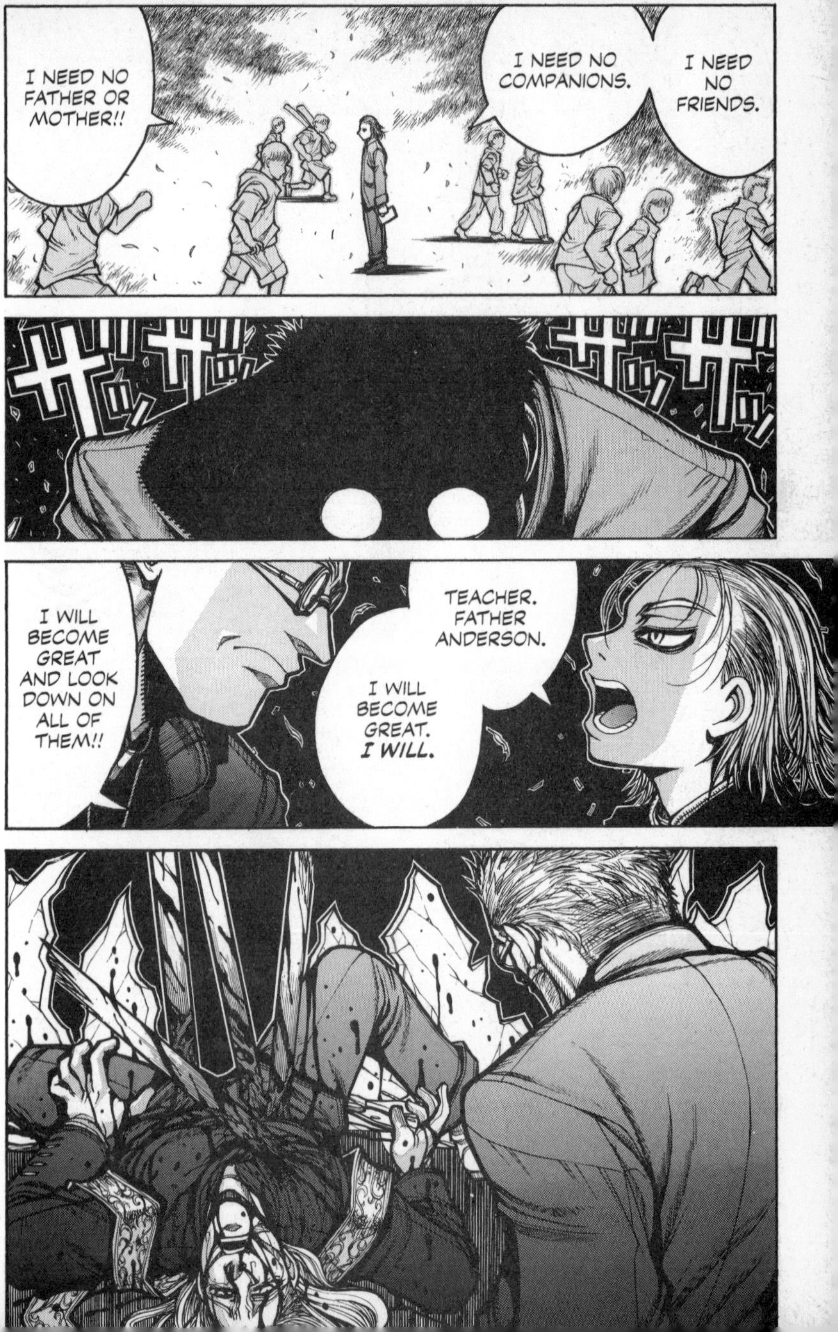
I NEED NO FRIENDS.
I NEED NO COMPANIONS.
I NEED NO FATHER OR MOTHER!!
ザッ
ザッ
ザッ
ザッ
TEACHER. FATHER ANDERSON.
I WILL BECOME GREAT. ***I WILL.***
I WILL BECOME GREAT AND LOOK DOWN ON ALL OF THEM!!

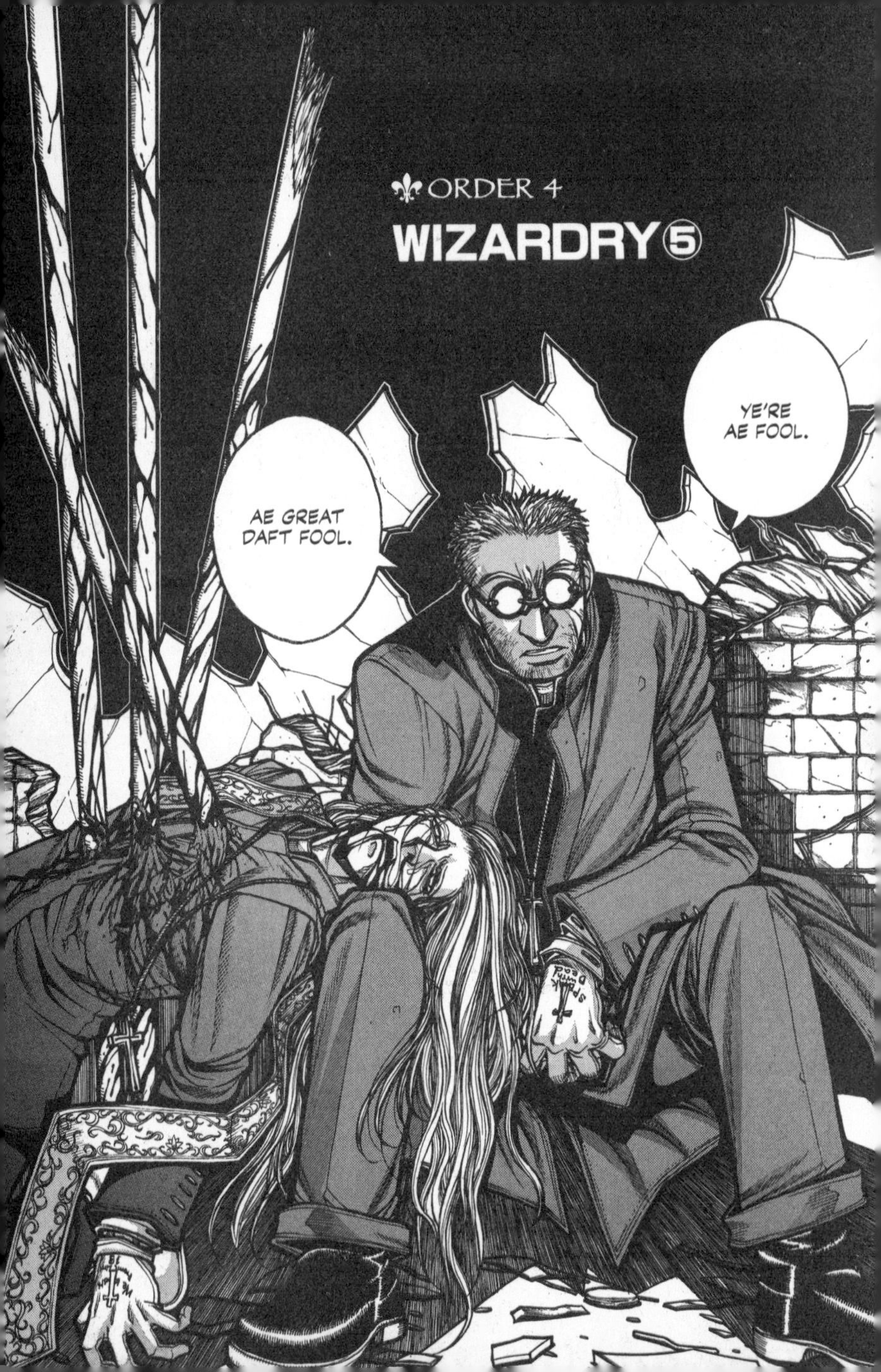
ORDER 4
WIZARDRY ⑤
YE'RE AE FOOL.
AE GREAT DAFT FOOL.

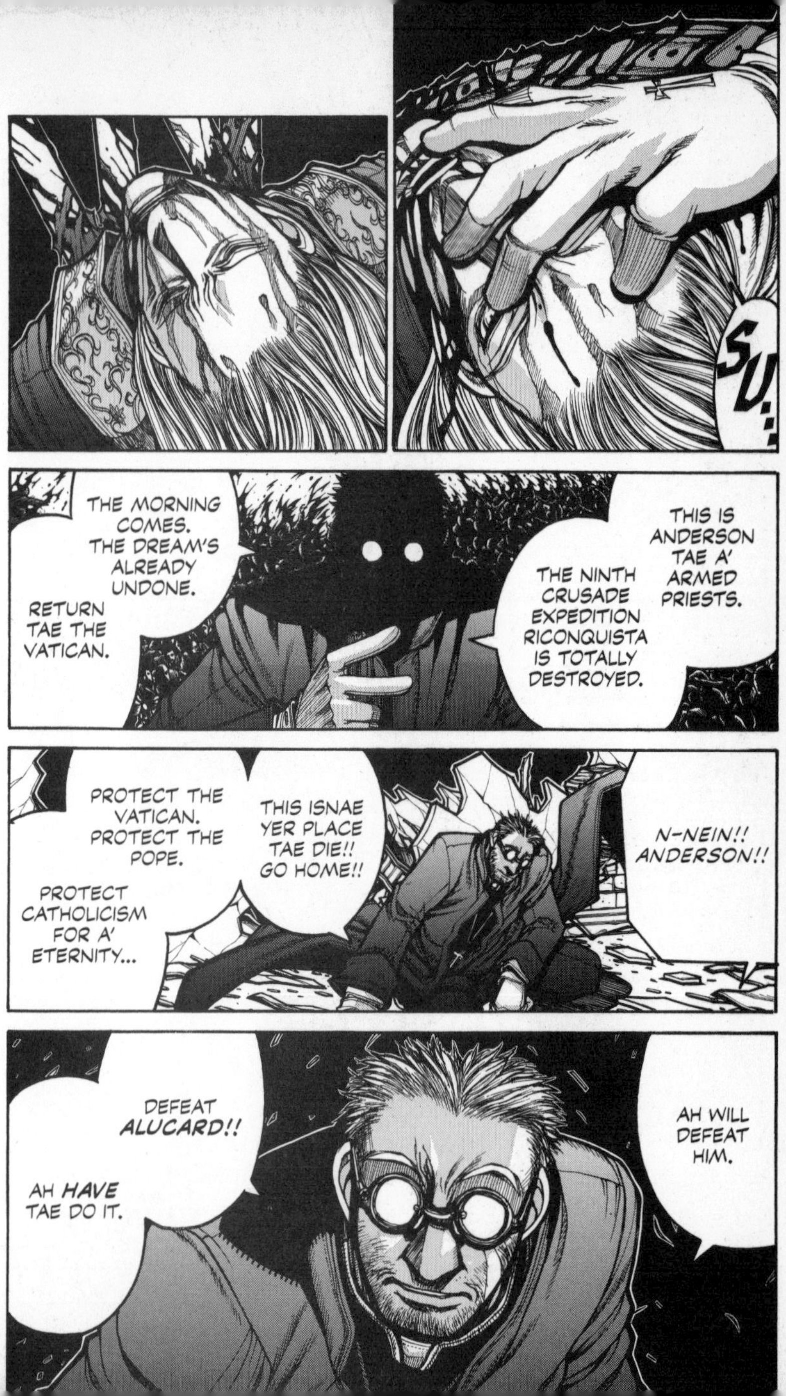
SU...
THIS IS ANDERSON TAE A' ARMED PRIESTS.
THE NINTH CRUSADE EXPEDITION RICONQUISTA IS TOTALLY DESTROYED.
THE MORNING COMES. THE DREAM'S ALREADY UNDONE.
RETURN TAE THE VATICAN.
N-NEIN!! ANDERSON!!
THIS ISNAE YER PLACE TAE DIE!! GO HOME!!
PROTECT THE VATICAN. PROTECT THE POPE.
PROTECT CATHOLICISM FOR A' ETERNITY...
AH WILL DEFEAT HIM.
DEFEAT **ALUCARD!!**
AH **HAVE** TAE DO IT.

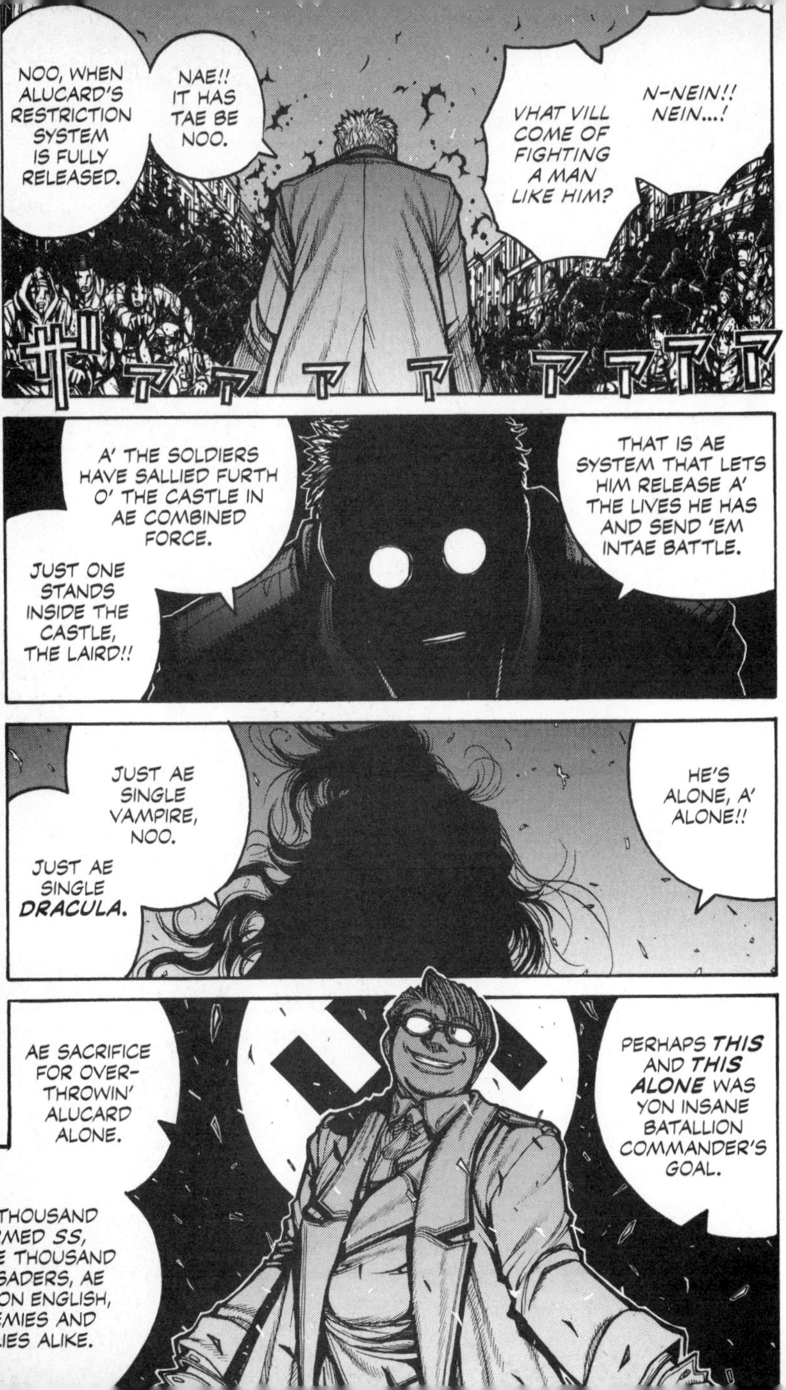
N-NEIN!! NEIN...!
VHAT VILL COME OF FIGHTING A MAN LIKE HIM?
NAE!! IT HAS TAE BE NOO.
NOO, WHEN ALUCARD'S RESTRICTION SYSTEM IS FULLY RELEASED.
THAT IS AE SYSTEM THAT LETS HIM RELEASE A' THE LIVES HE HAS AND SEND 'EM INTAE BATTLE.
A' THE SOLDIERS HAVE SALLIED FURTH O' THE CASTLE IN AE COMBINED FORCE.
JUST ONE STANDS INSIDE THE CASTLE, THE LAIRD!!
HE'S ALONE, A' ALONE!!
JUST AE SINGLE VAMPIRE, NOO.
JUST AE SINGLE ***DRACULA***.
PERHAPS ***THIS*** AND ***THIS ALONE*** WAS YON INSANE BATALLION COMMANDER'S GOAL.
AE SACRIFICE FOR OVER-THROWIN' ALUCARD ALONE.
AE THOUSAND ARMED *SS*, THREE THOUSAND CRUSADERS, AE MILLION ENGLISH, ENEMIES AND ALLIES ALIKE.

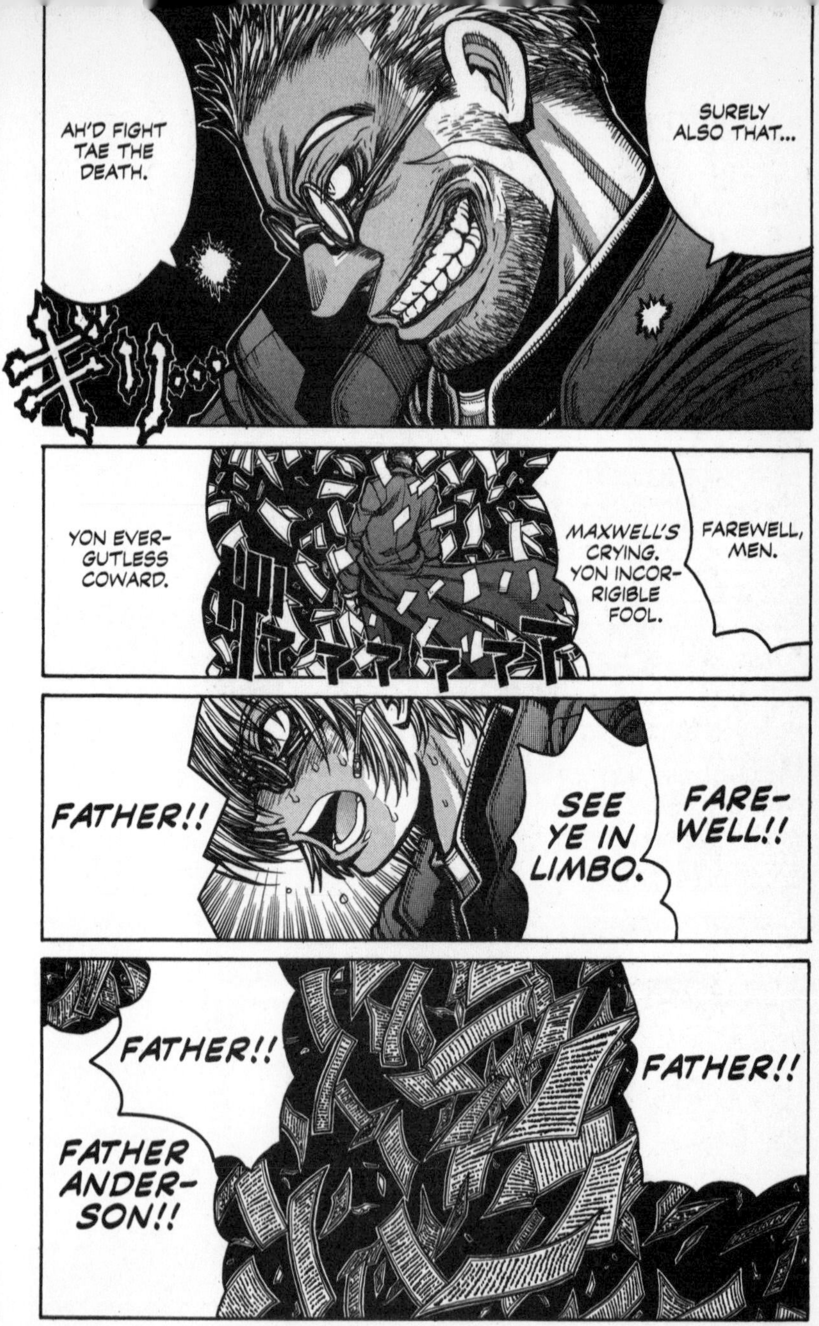
SURELY ALSO THAT...
AH'D FIGHT TAE THE DEATH.
FAREWELL, MEN.
MAXWELL'S CRYING. YON INCORRIGIBLE FOOL.
YON EVER-GUTLESS COWARD.
FARE-WELL!!
SEE YE IN LIMBO.
FATHER!!
FATHER!!
FATHER!!
FATHER ANDERSON!!

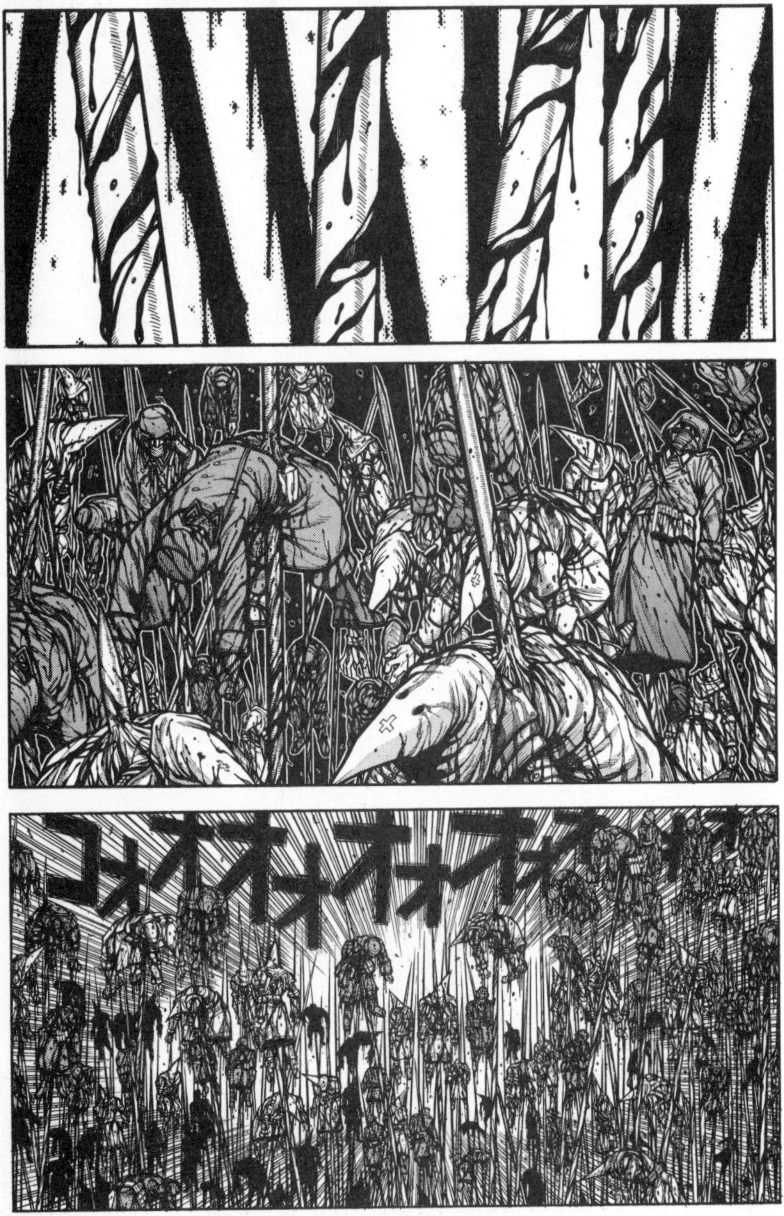
コォオォオォオォオ

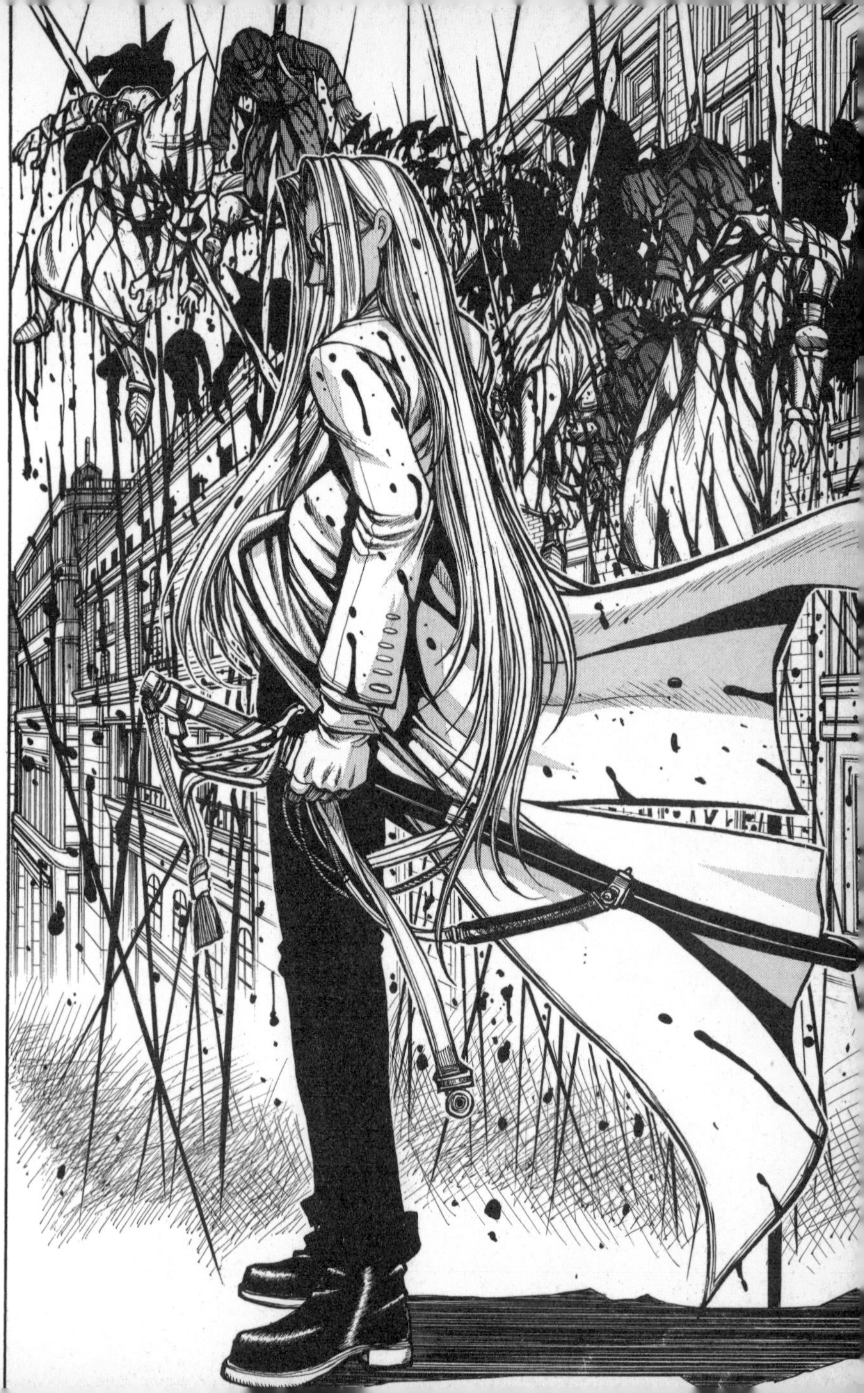

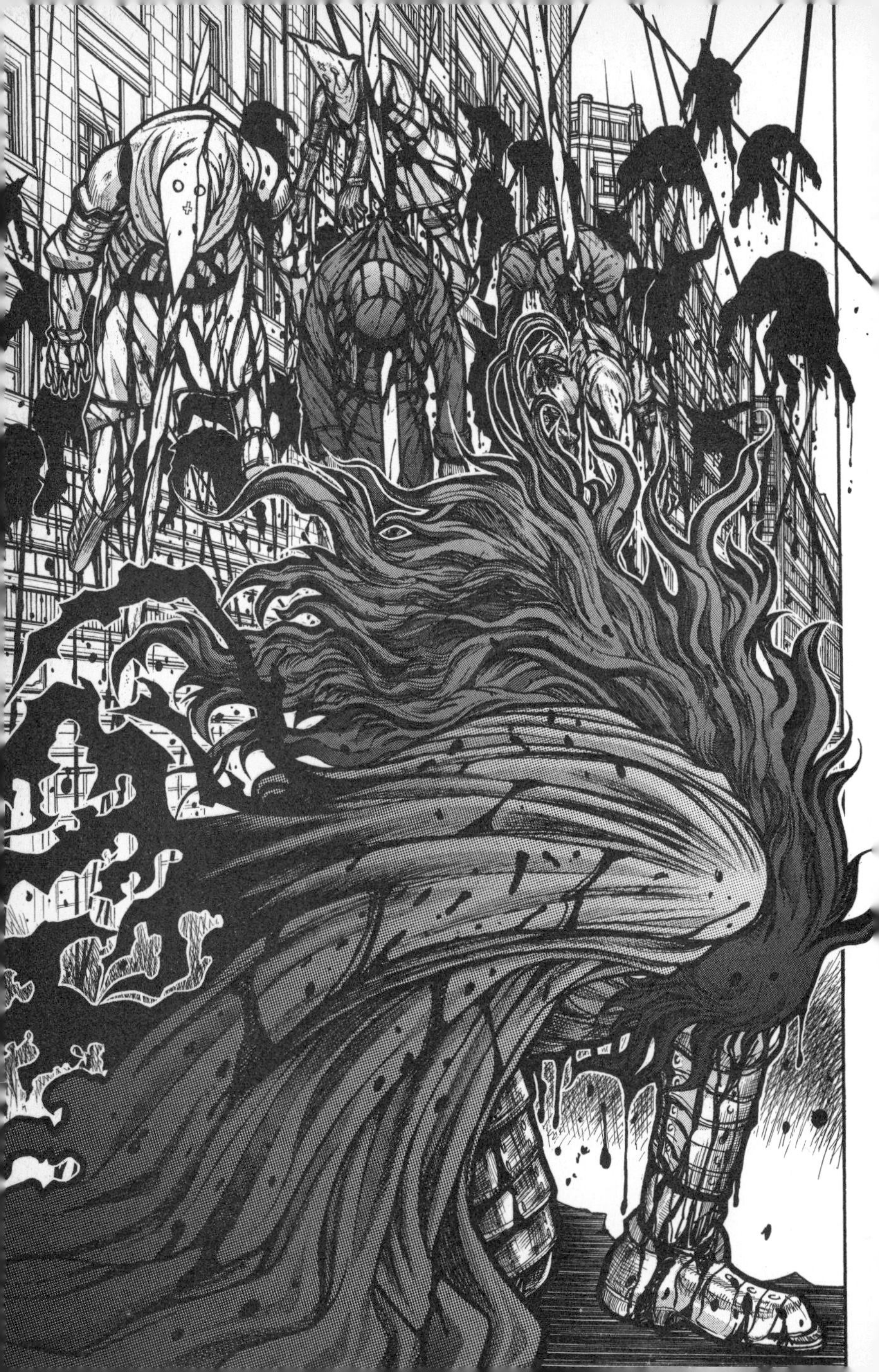

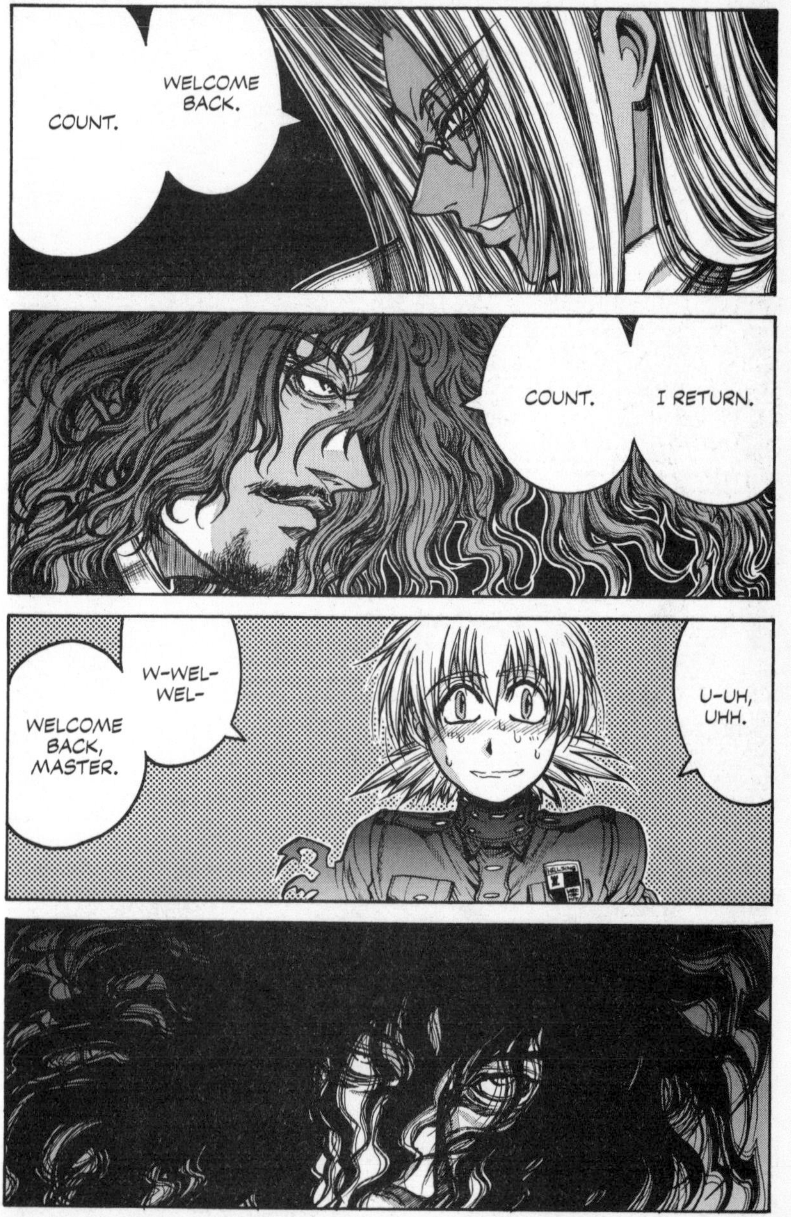
WELCOME BACK.
COUNT.
I RETURN.
COUNT.
U-UH, UHH.
W-WEL- WEL-
WELCOME BACK, MASTER.

MOUSTACHE.

YOU HAVE A MOUSTACHE, MASTER.

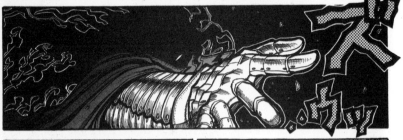

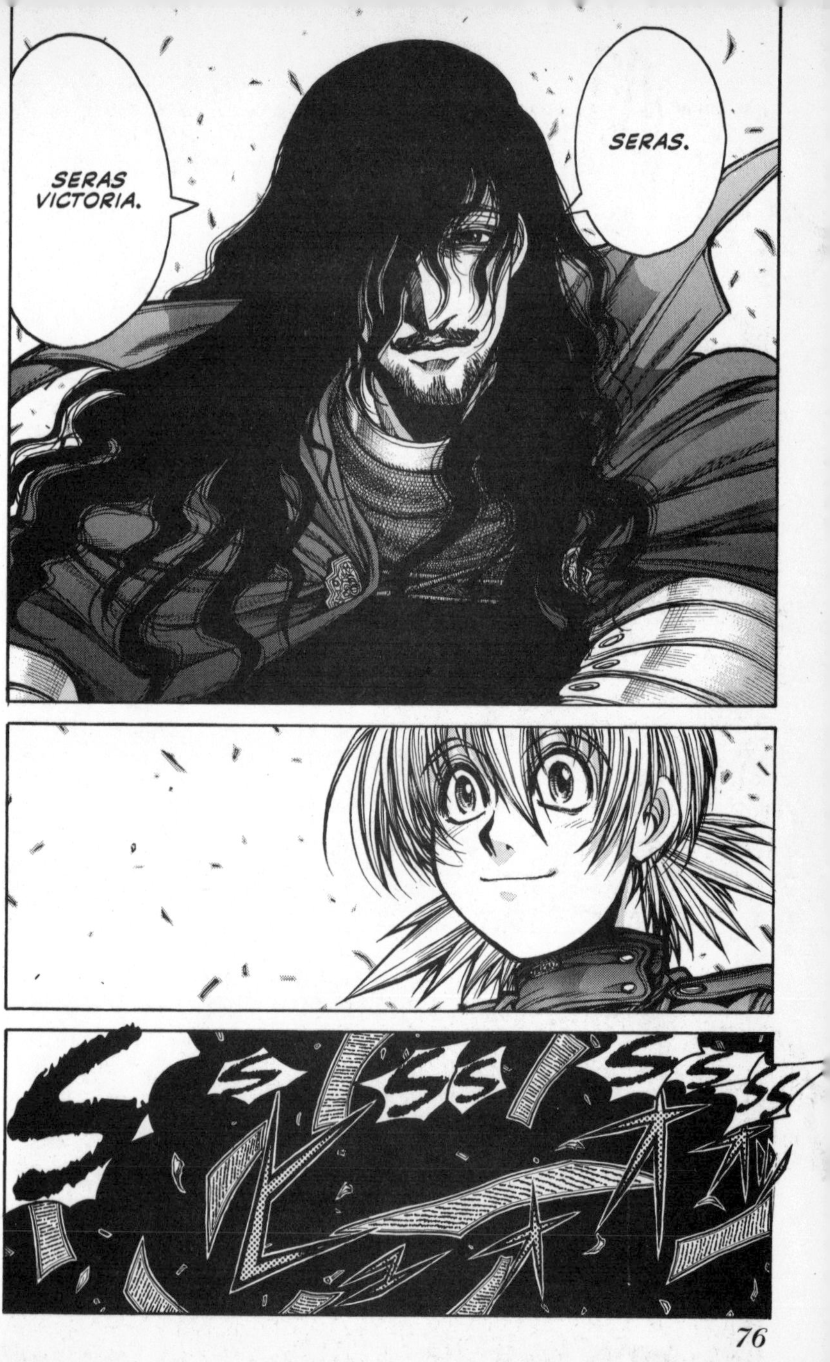
SERAS.
SERAS VICTORIA.
SSSSSSSS

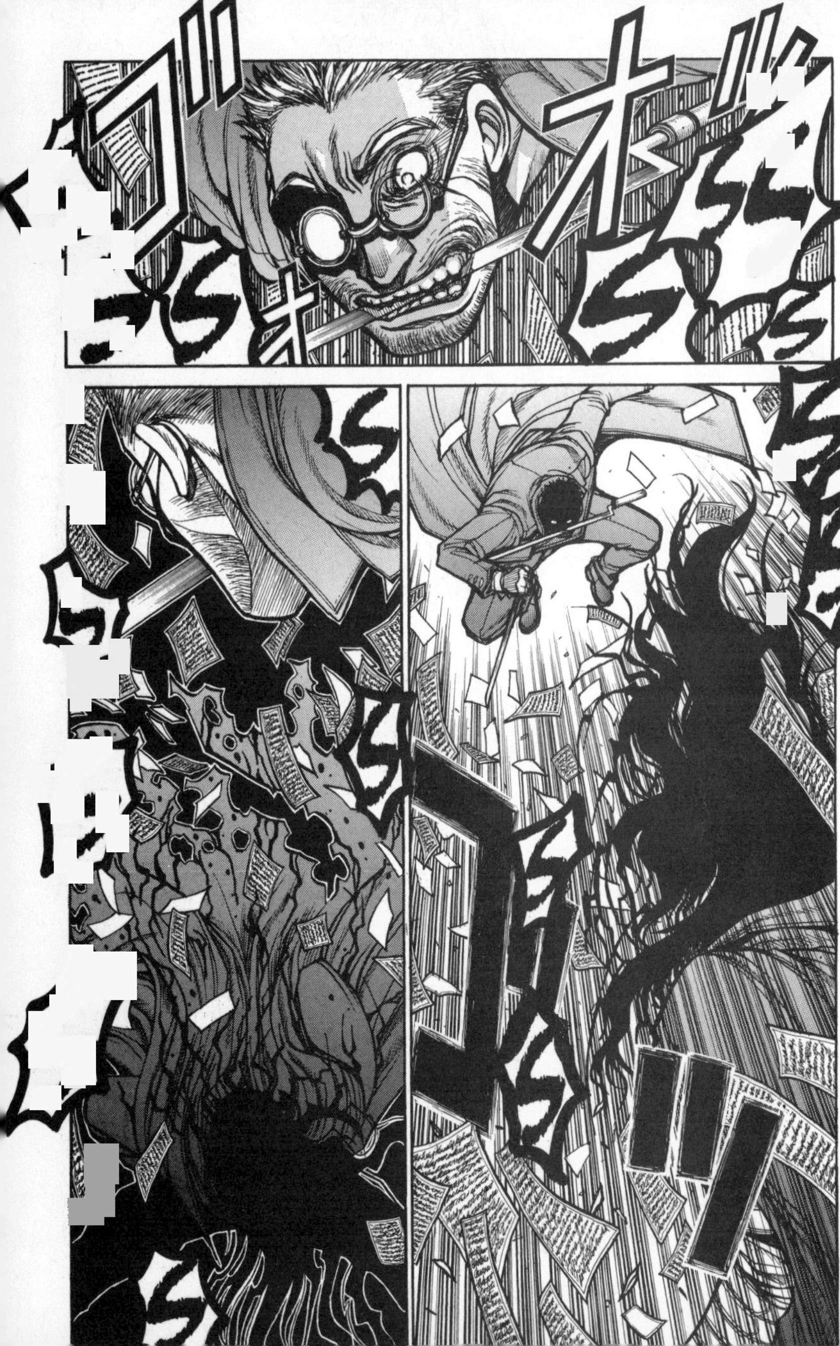
ゴオ
ゴ!!

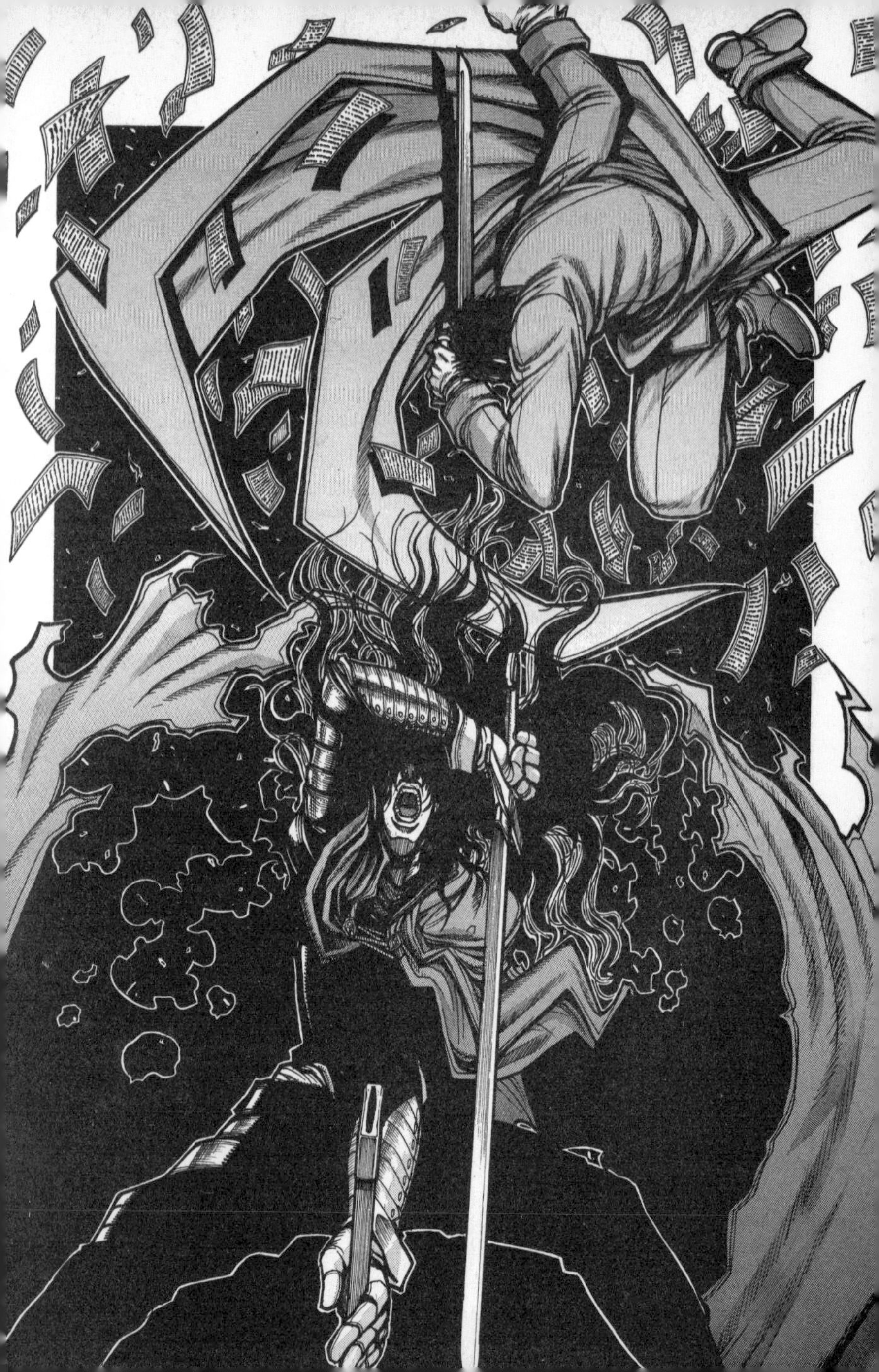

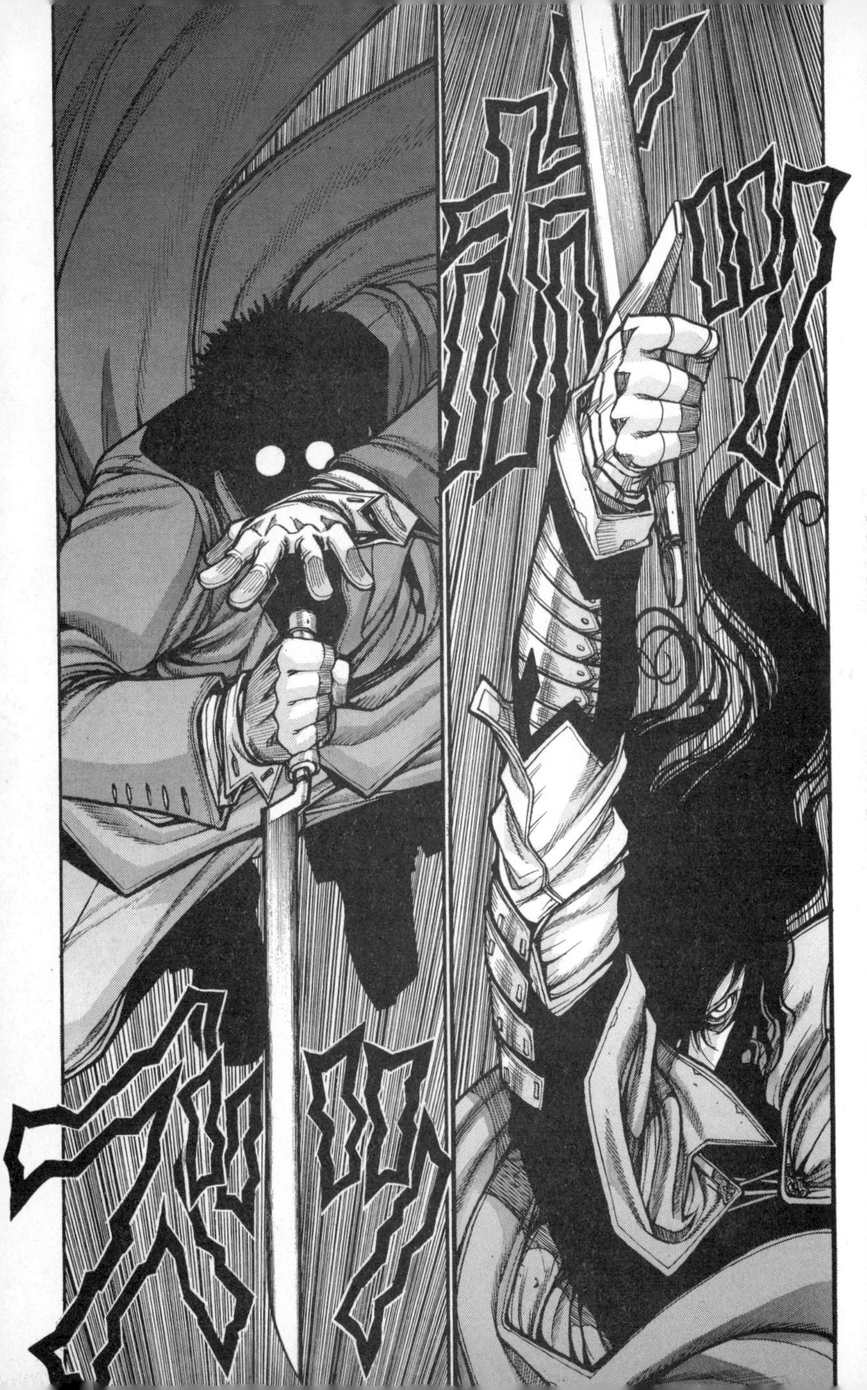

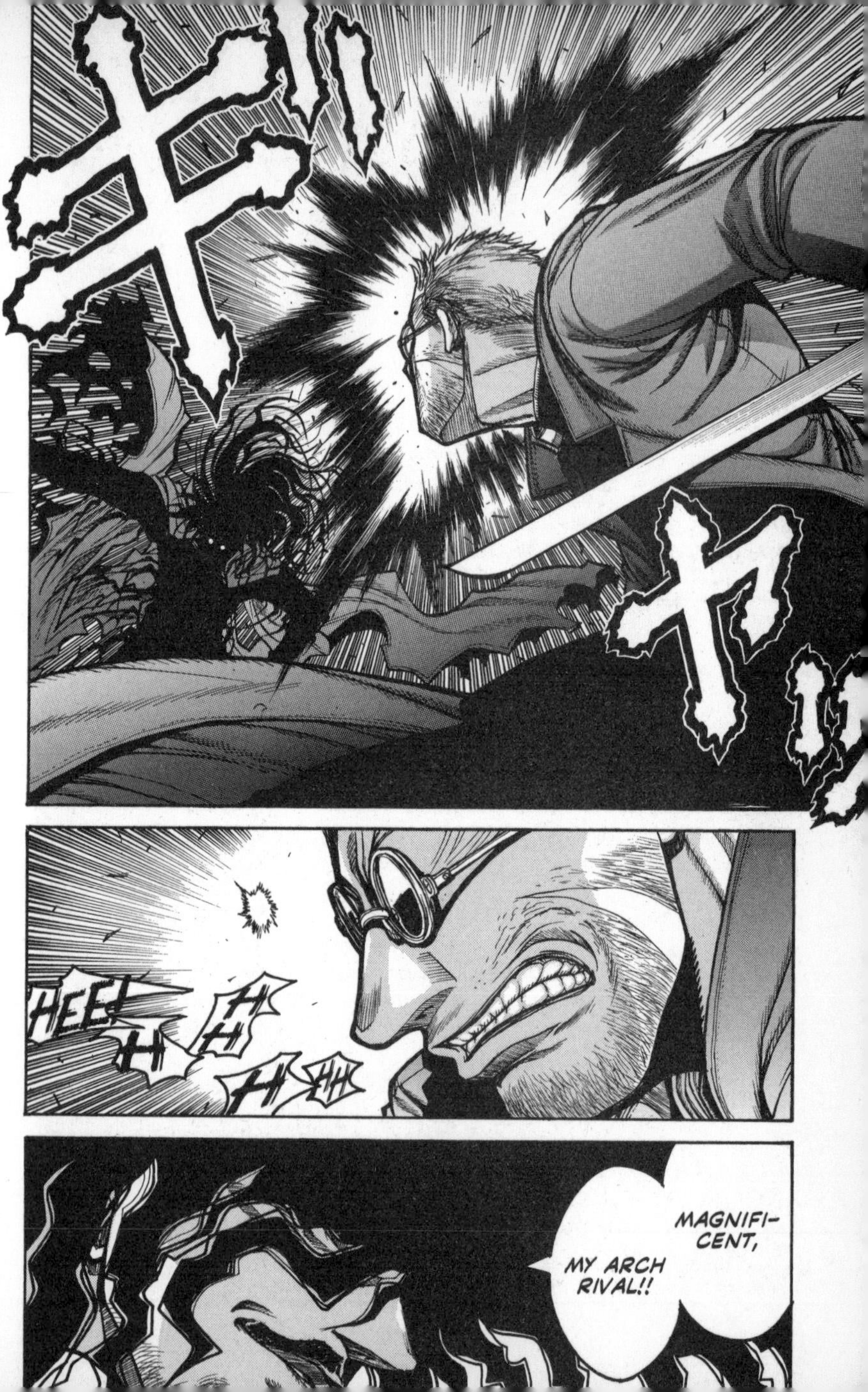
HEE!
MAGNIFI-CENT, MY ARCH RIVAL!!

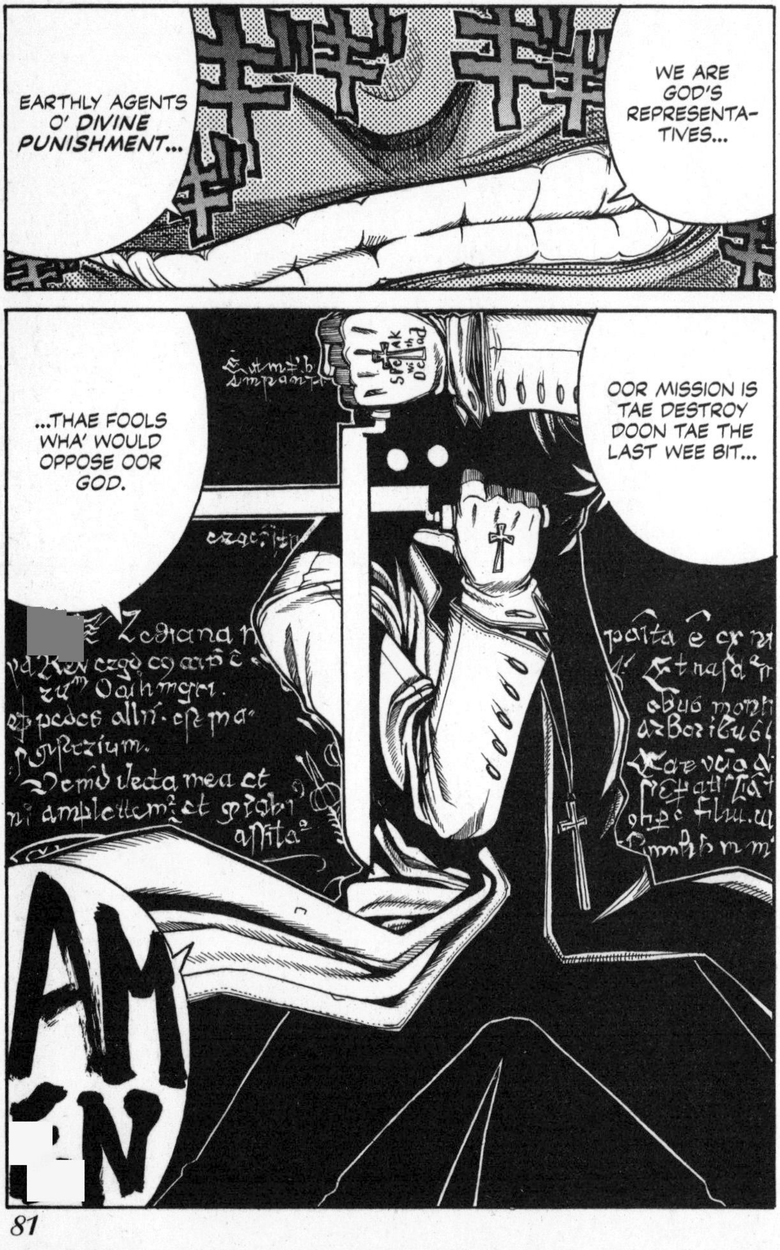
WE ARE GOD'S REPRESENTA-TIVES...
EARTHLY AGENTS O' DIVINE PUNISHMENT...
OOR MISSION IS TAE DESTROY DOON TAE THE LAST WEE BIT...
...THAE FOOLS WHA' WOULD OPPOSE OOR GOD.
AMEN

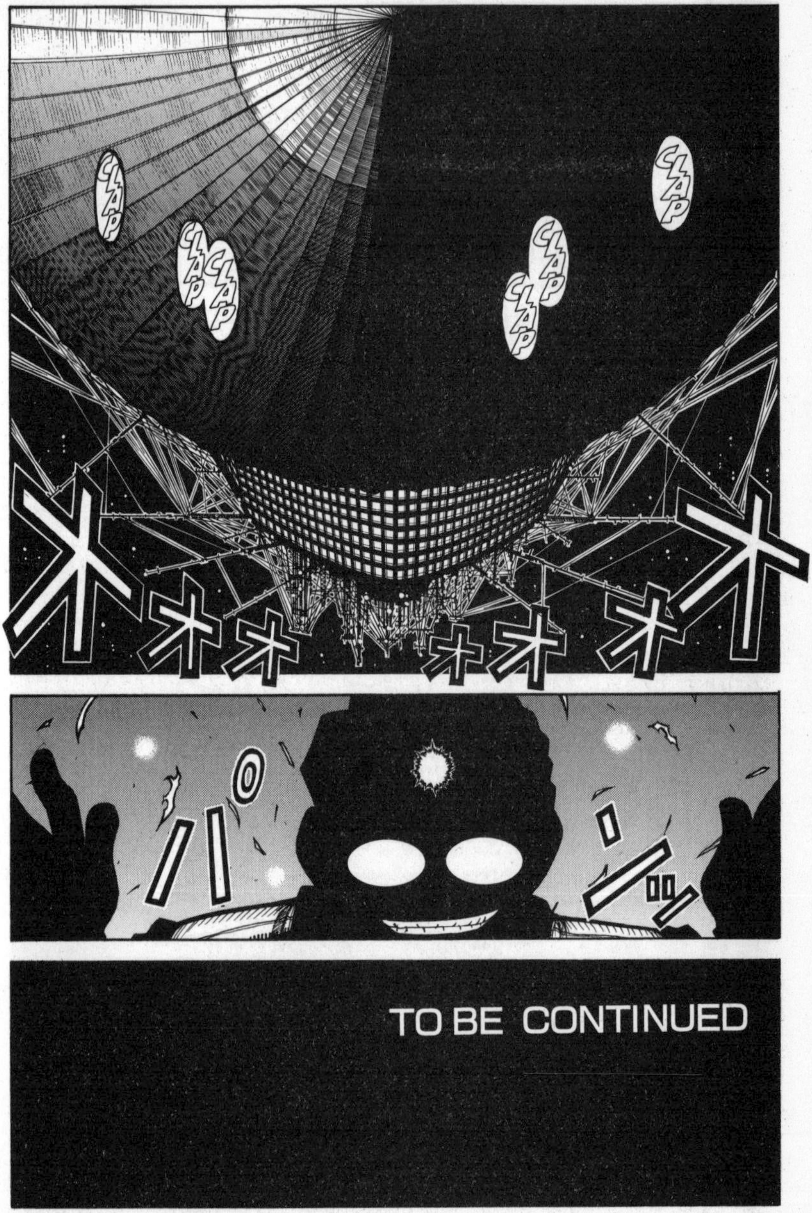
CLAP
CLAP
CLAP
CLAP
CLAP
CLAP
TO BE CONTINUED

ORDER 5

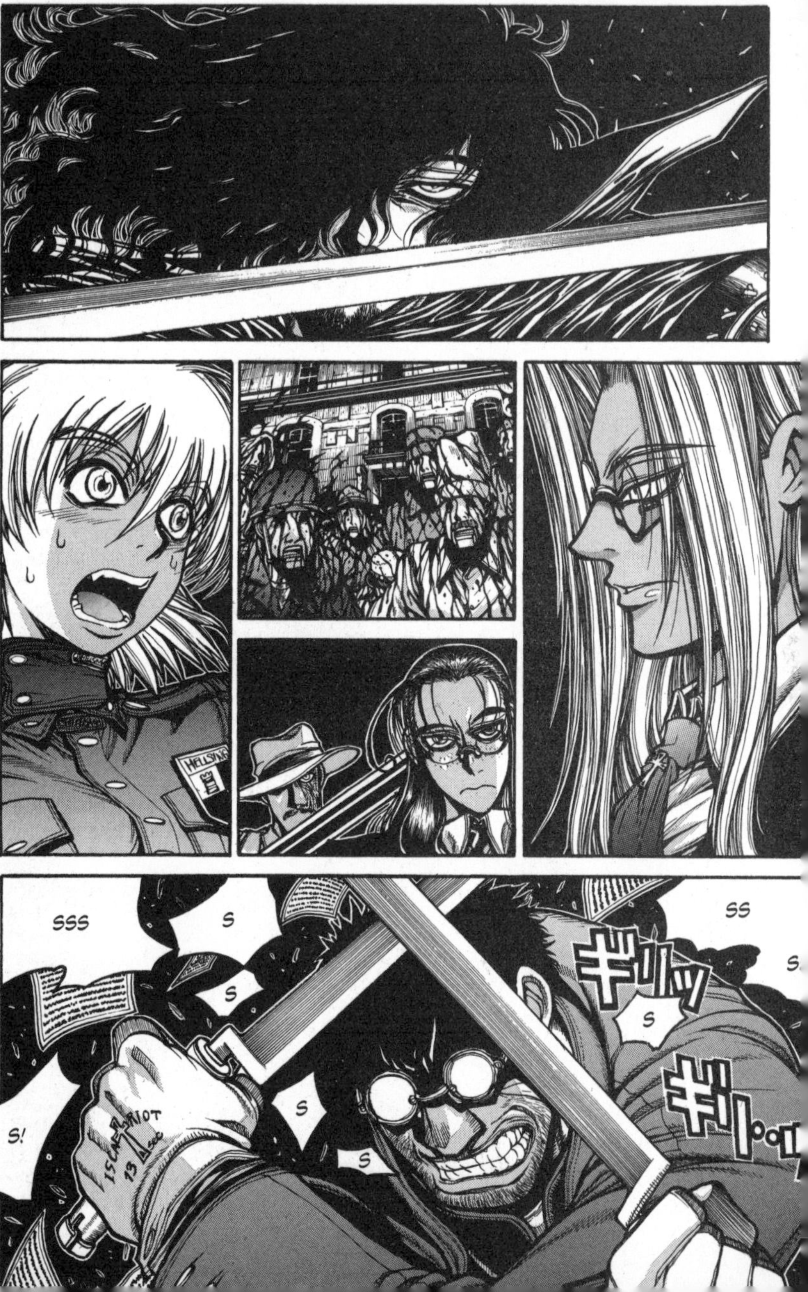

SS
ギリッ
S
S
S
S
SSS
S!
S

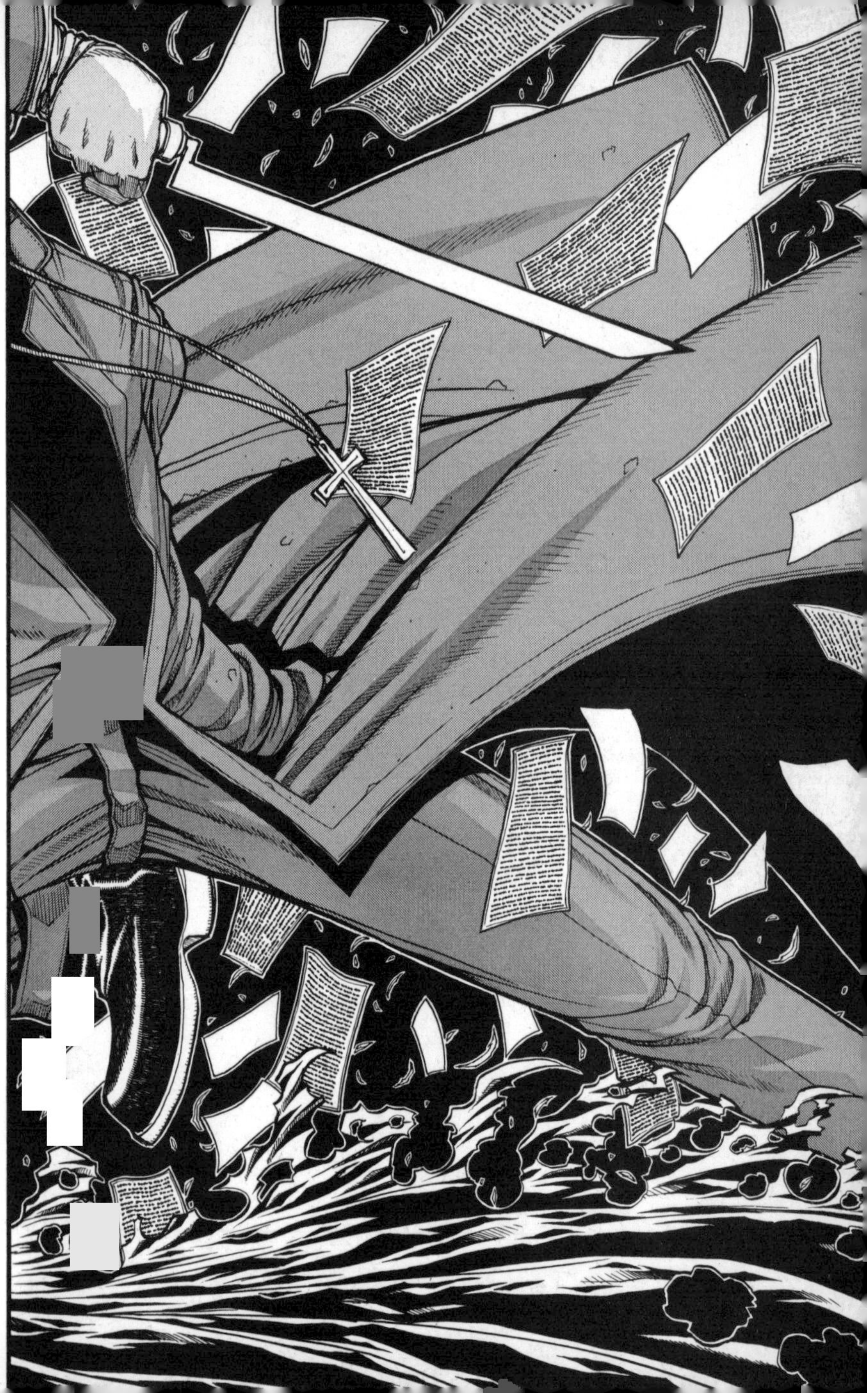

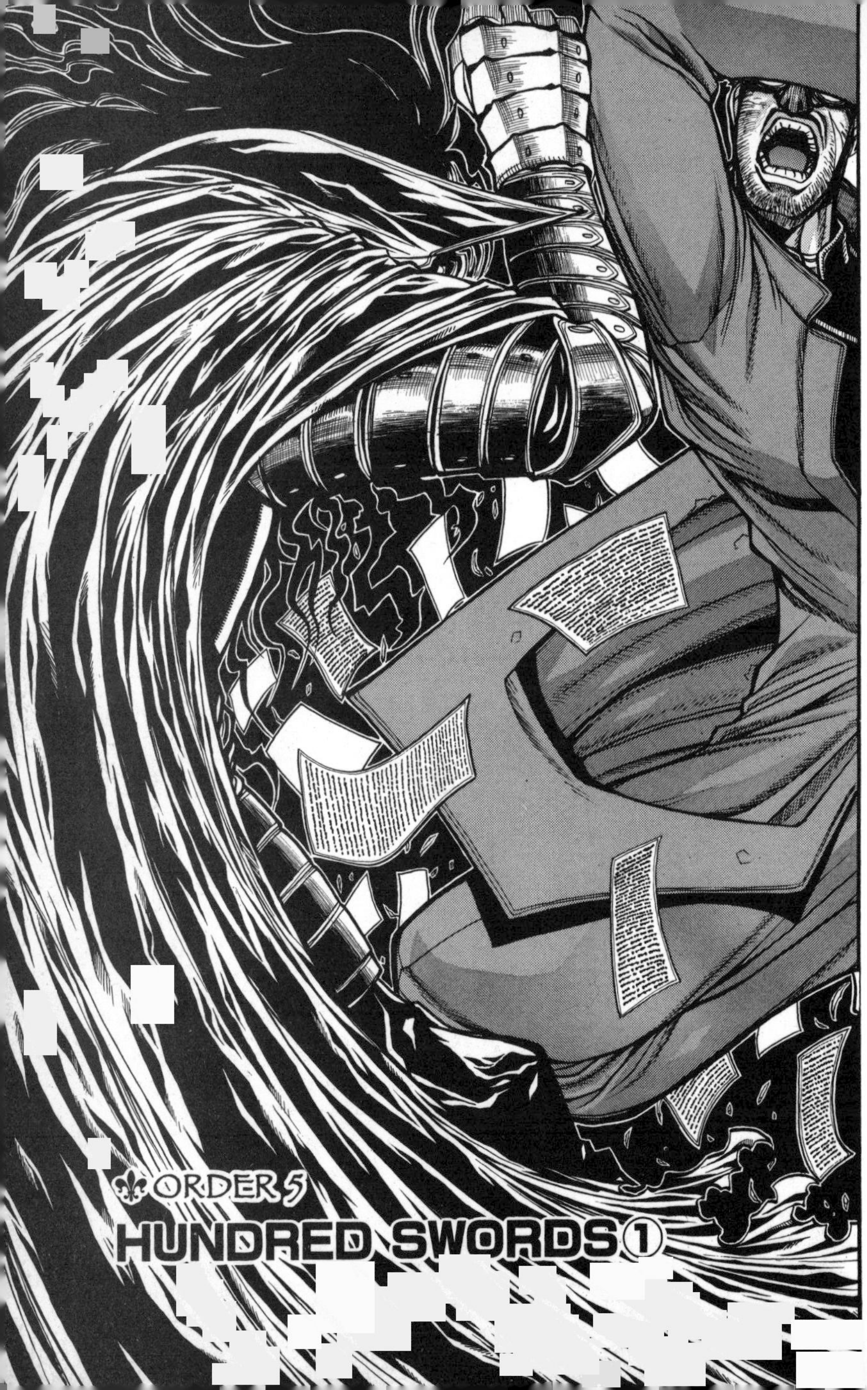
ORDER 5
HUNDRED SWORDS 1

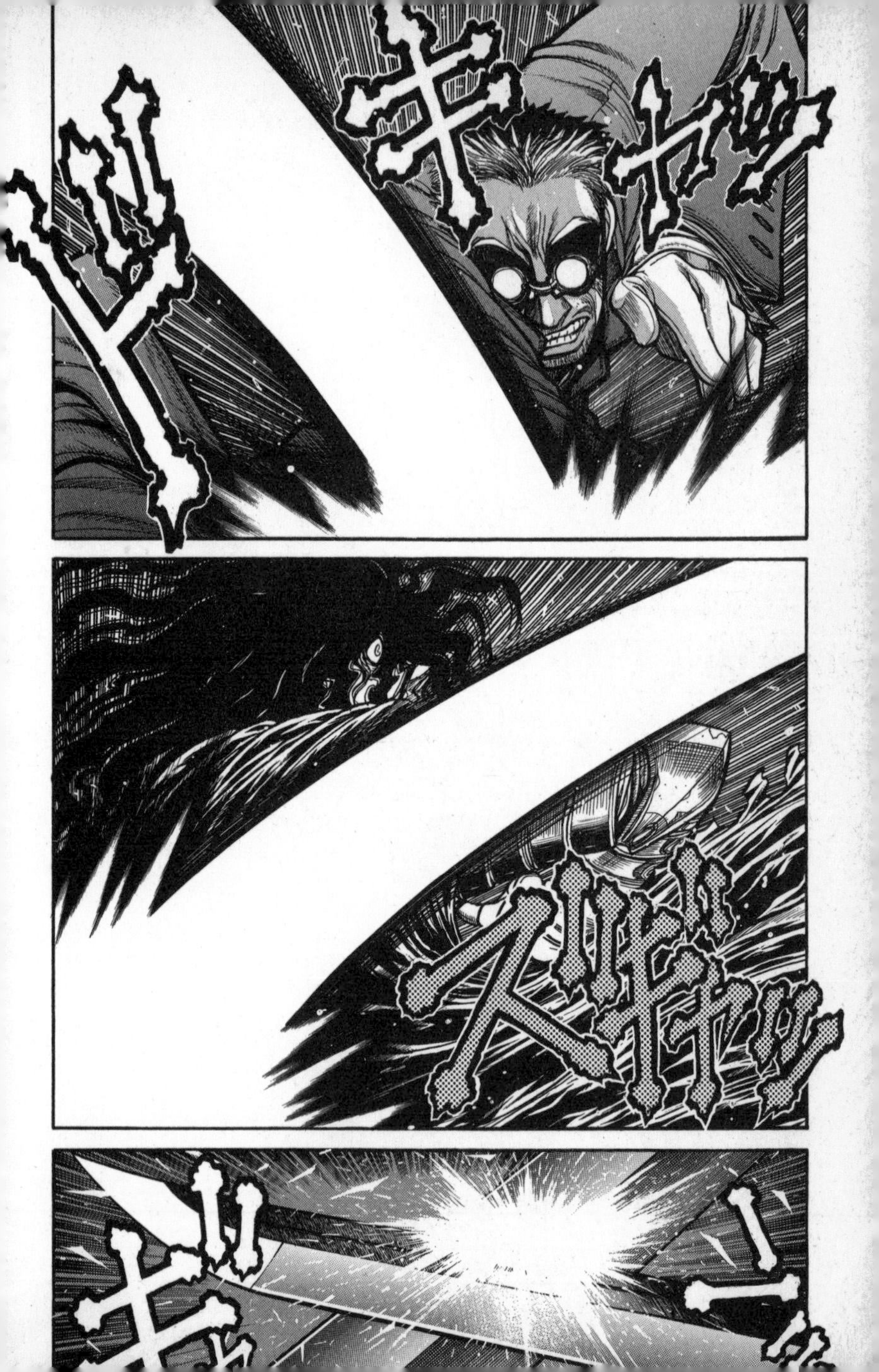

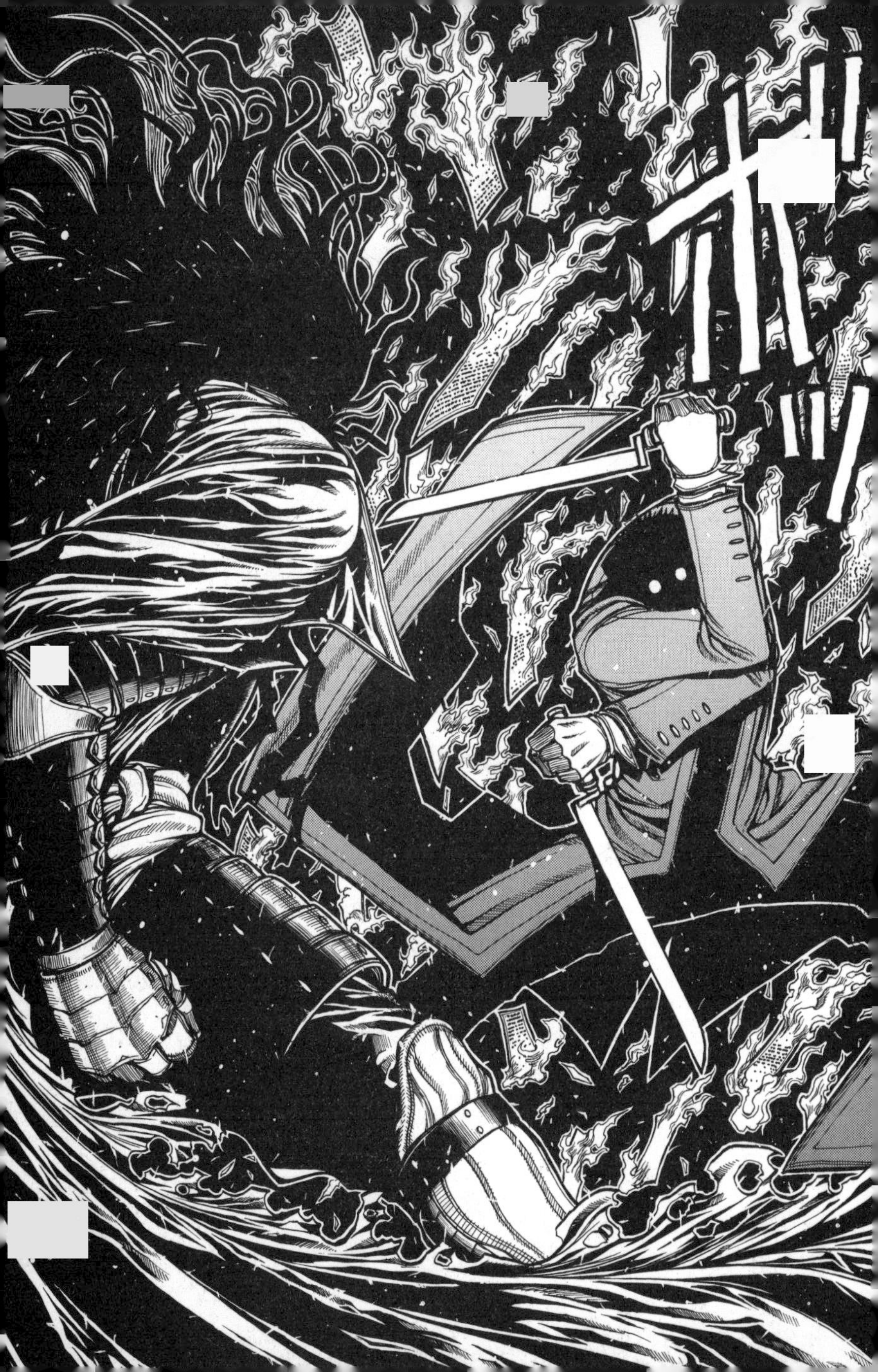

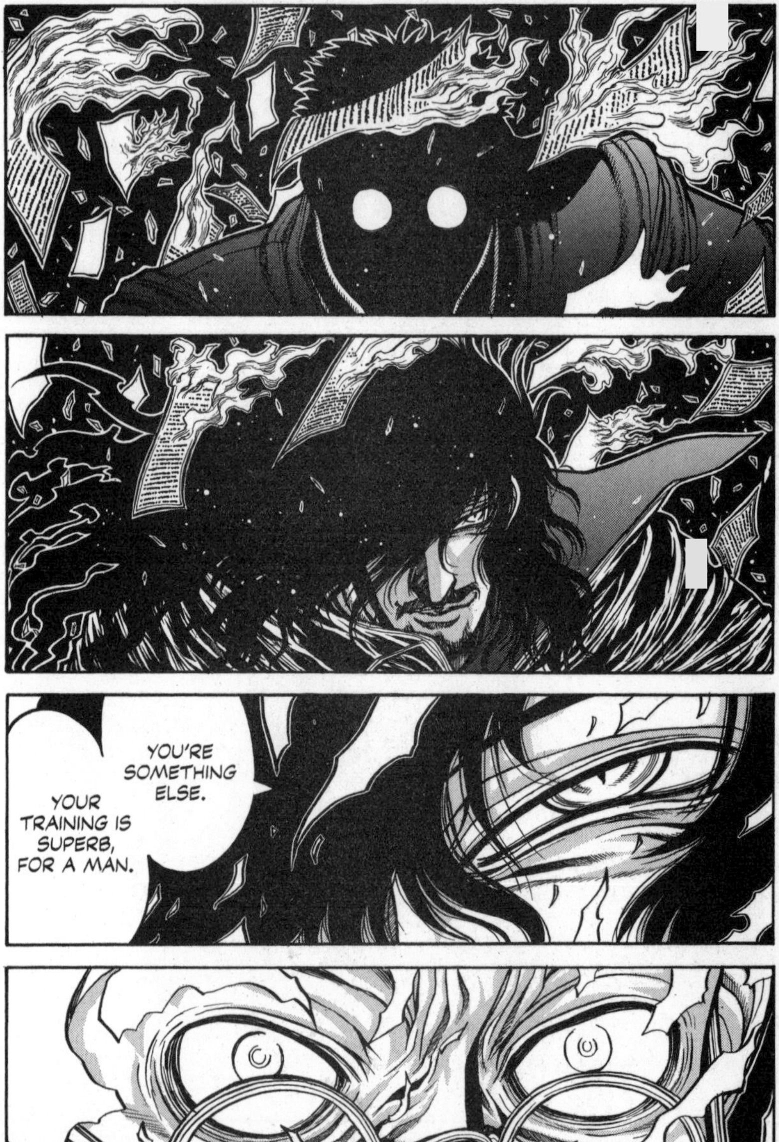
YOU'RE SOMETHING ELSE.
YOUR TRAINING IS SUPERB, FOR A MAN.

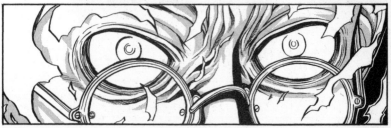

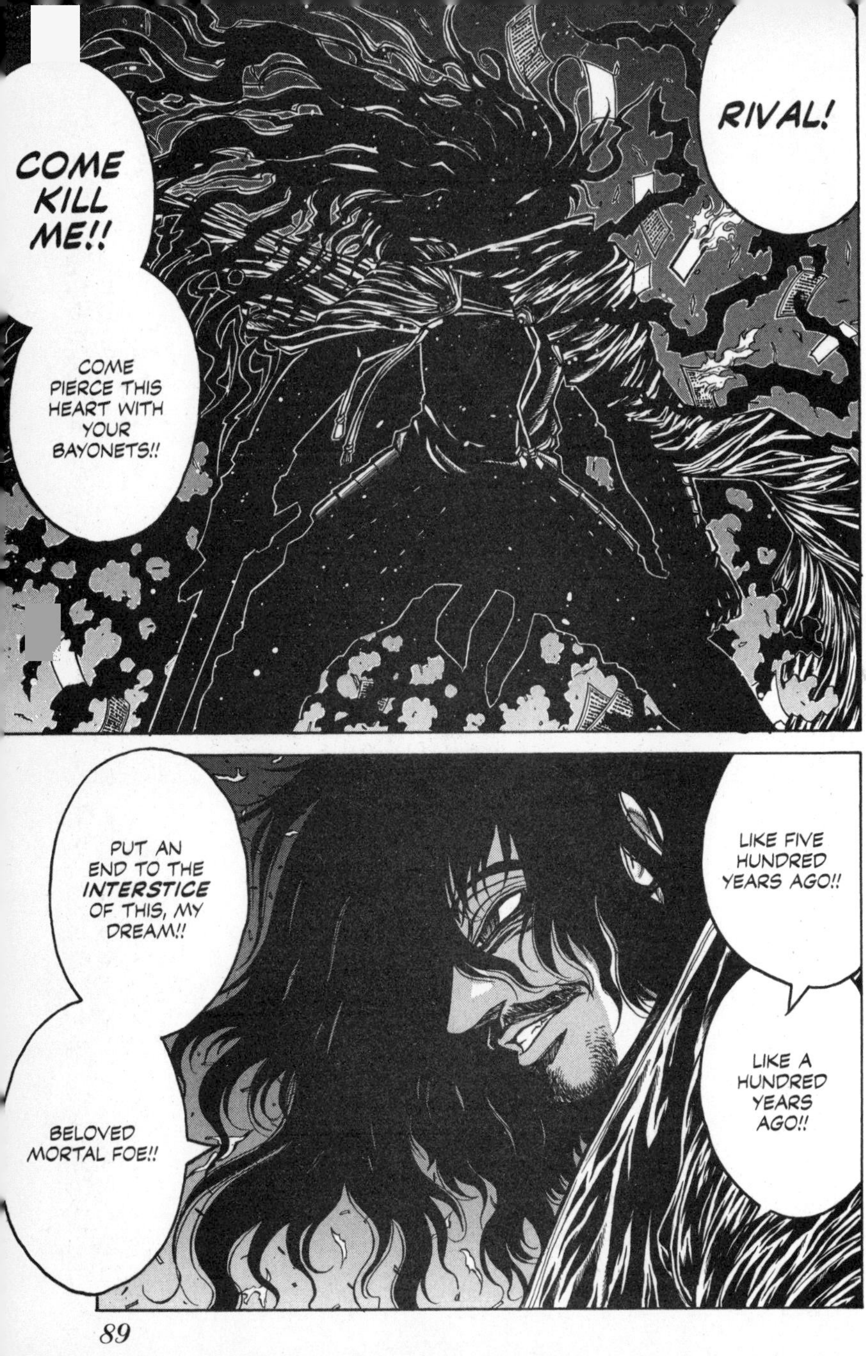
RIVAL!
COME KILL ME!!
COME PIERCE THIS HEART WITH YOUR BAYONETS!!
LIKE FIVE HUNDRED YEARS AGO!!
LIKE A HUNDRED YEARS AGO!!
PUT AN END TO THE INTERSTICE OF THIS, MY DREAM!!
BELOVED MORTAL FOE!!

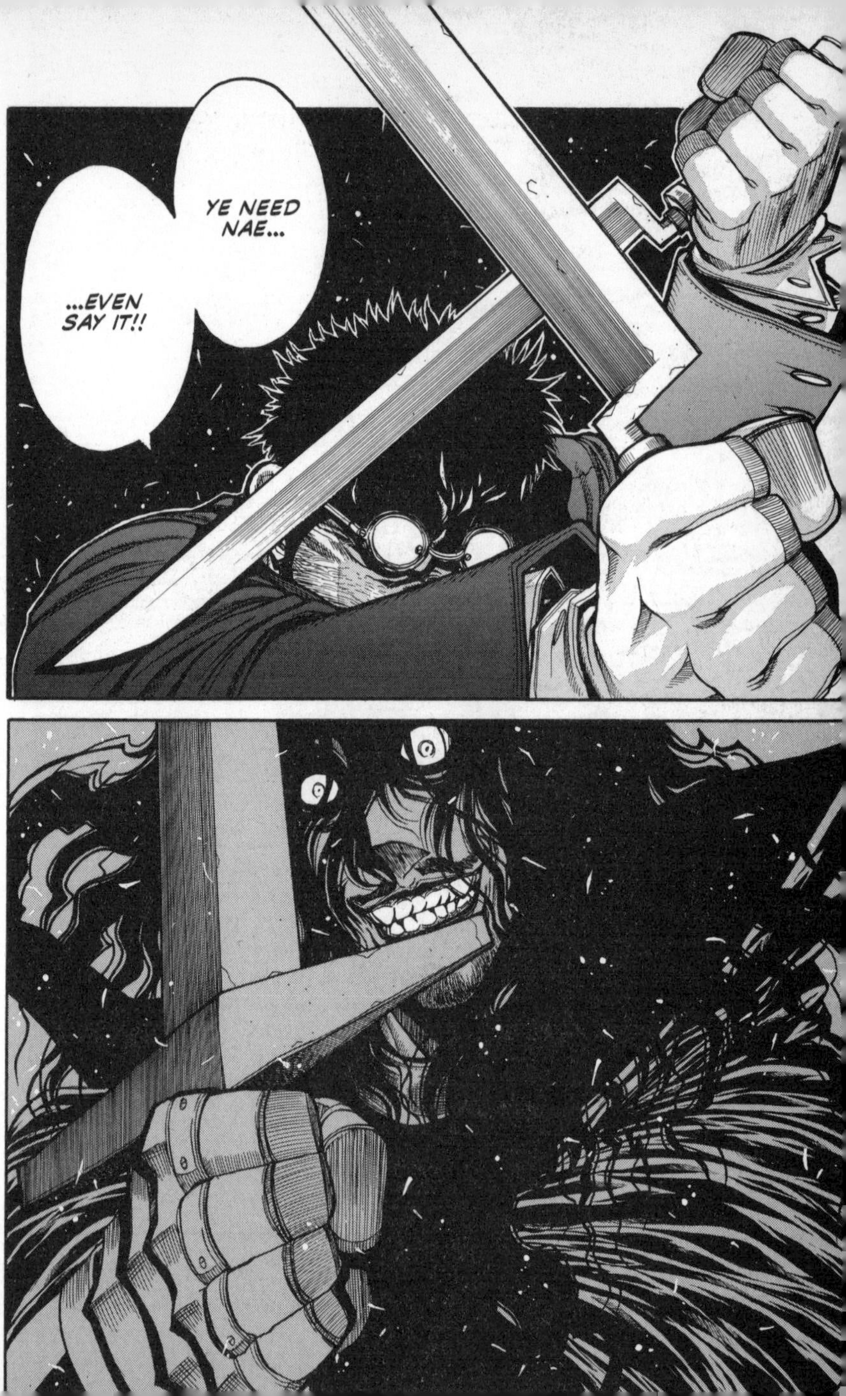
YE NEED NAE...
...EVEN SAY IT!!

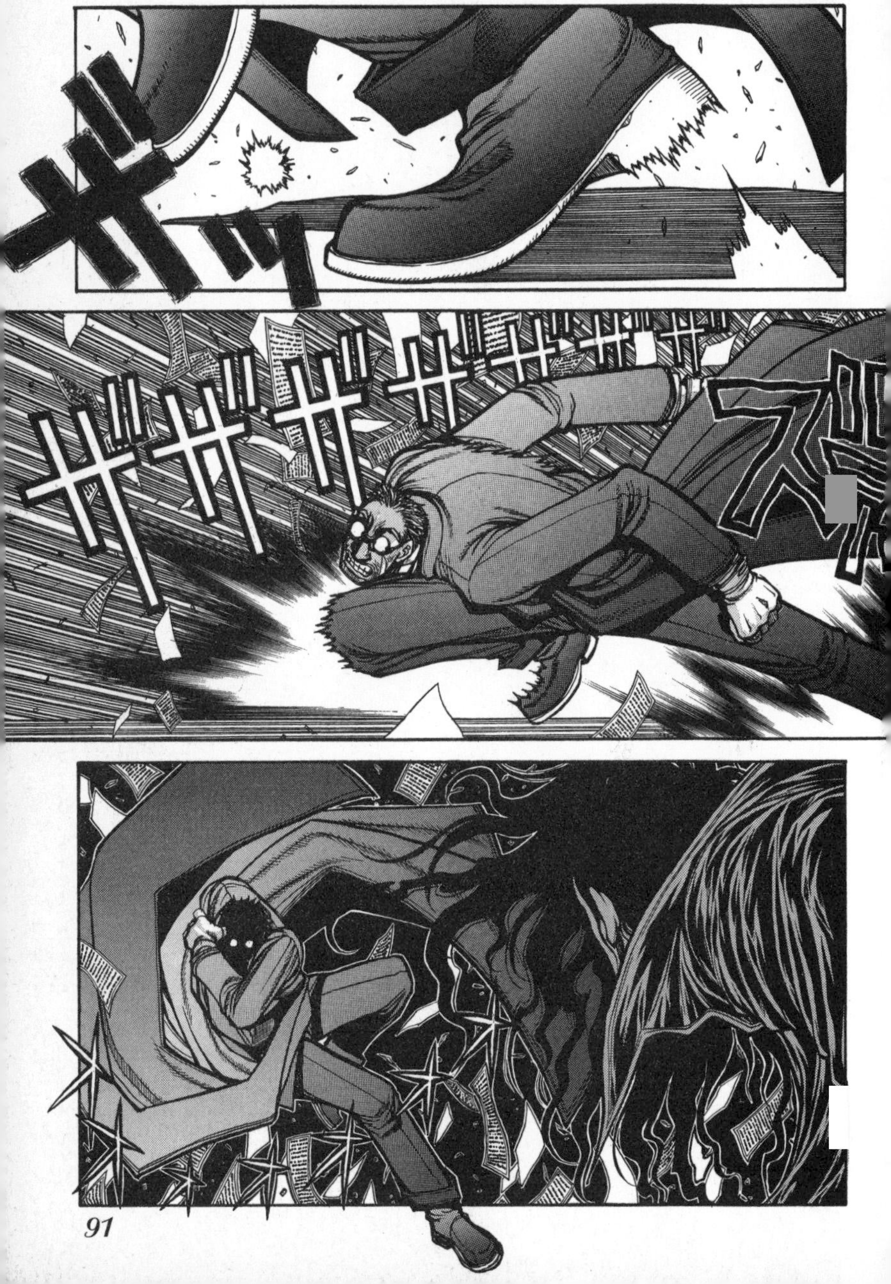
ギッ
ズ
ザザザザザザザ

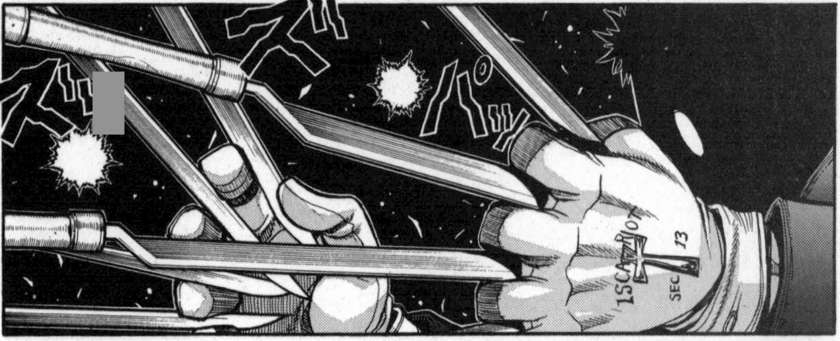
パッ
ズ
ズッ
ISCARIOT
SEC 13

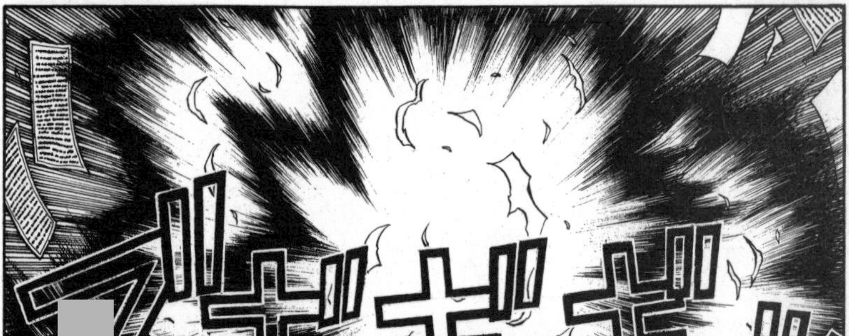
ズギャギャギャッ

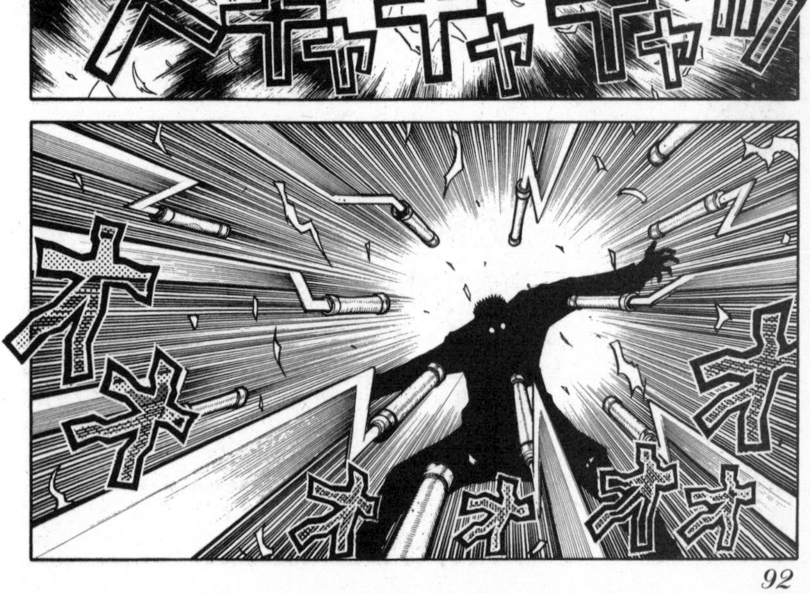
オオオオ
オオ

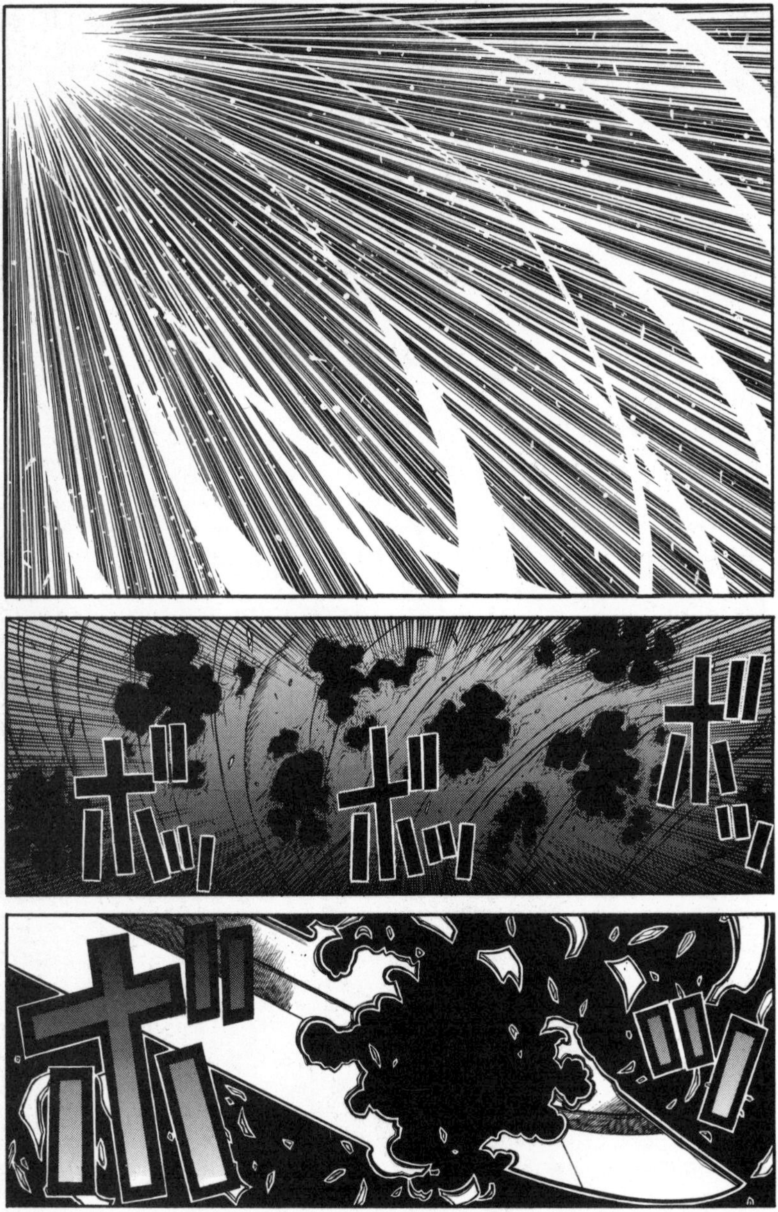
ボッ
ボッ
ボッ
ボッ

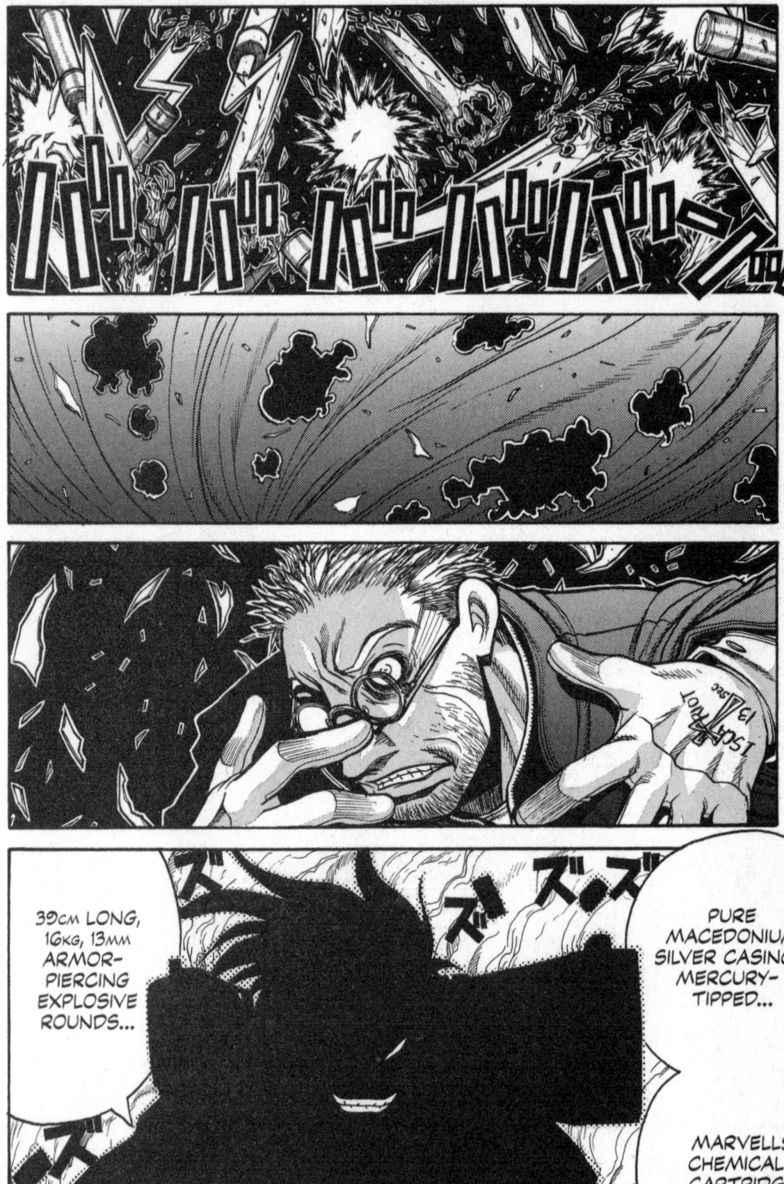
ISCARIOT
13 Sec
PURE MACEDONIUM SILVER CASINGS, MERCURY-TIPPED...
MARVELLS CHEMICALS CARTRIDGE N.N.A.9...
39cm LONG, 16kg, 13mm ARMOR-PIERCING EXPLOSIVE ROUNDS...

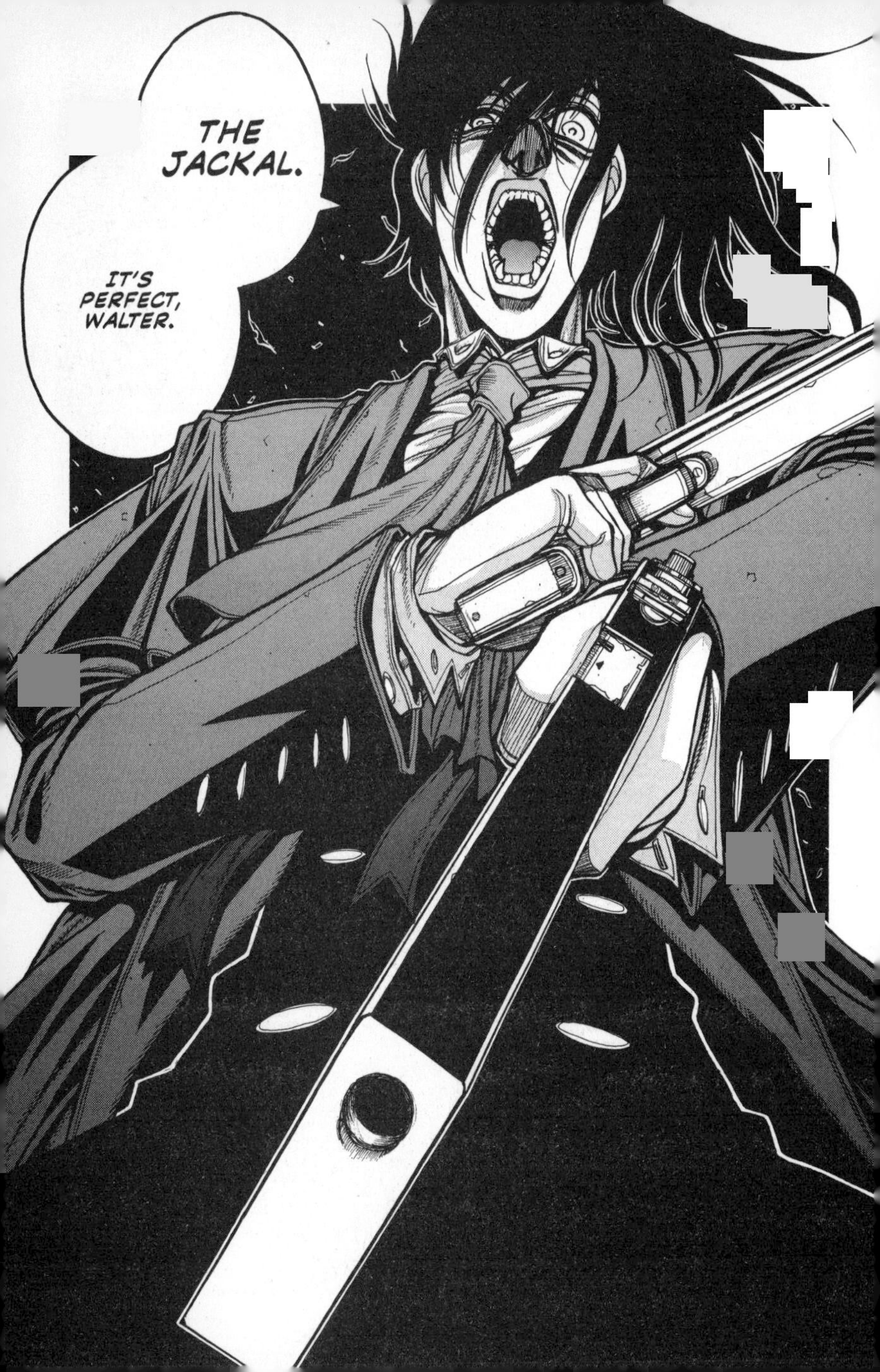
THE JACKAL.
IT'S PERFECT, WALTER.

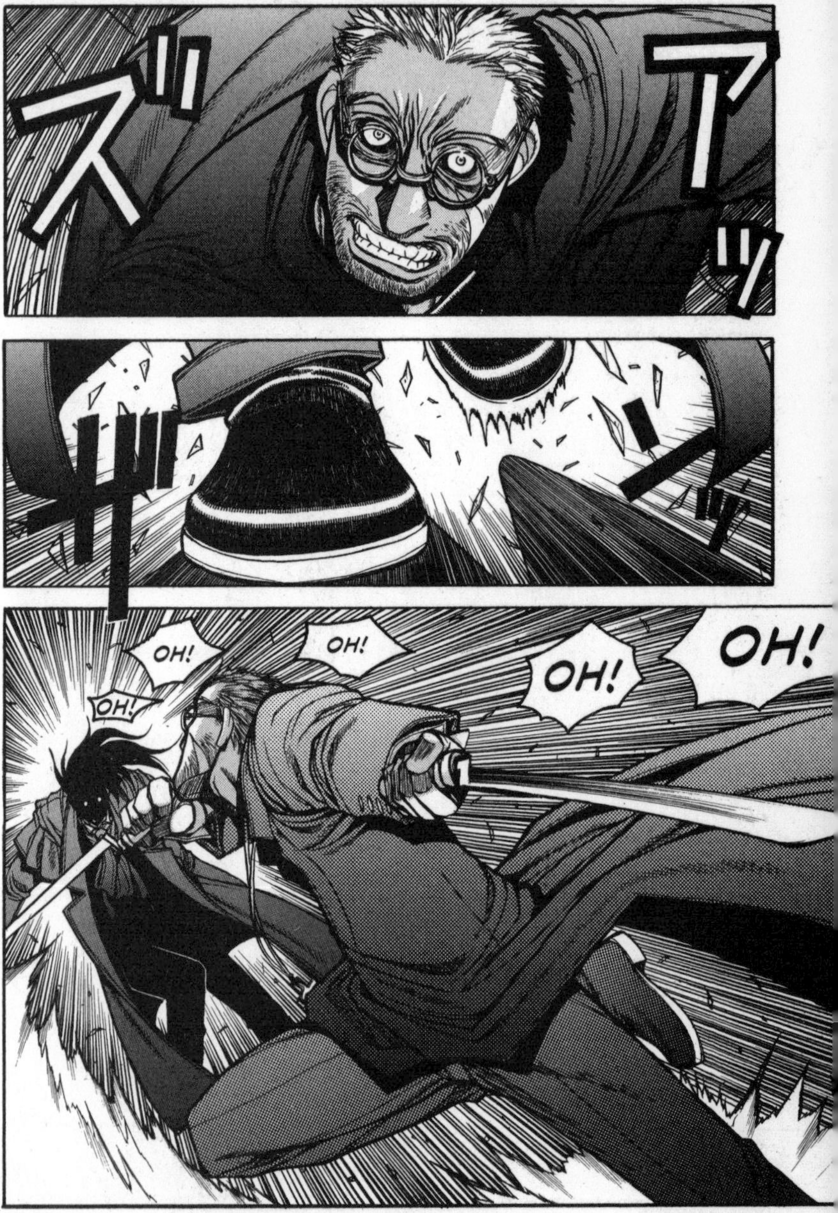
ズアッ
OH!
OH!
OH!
OH!
OH!

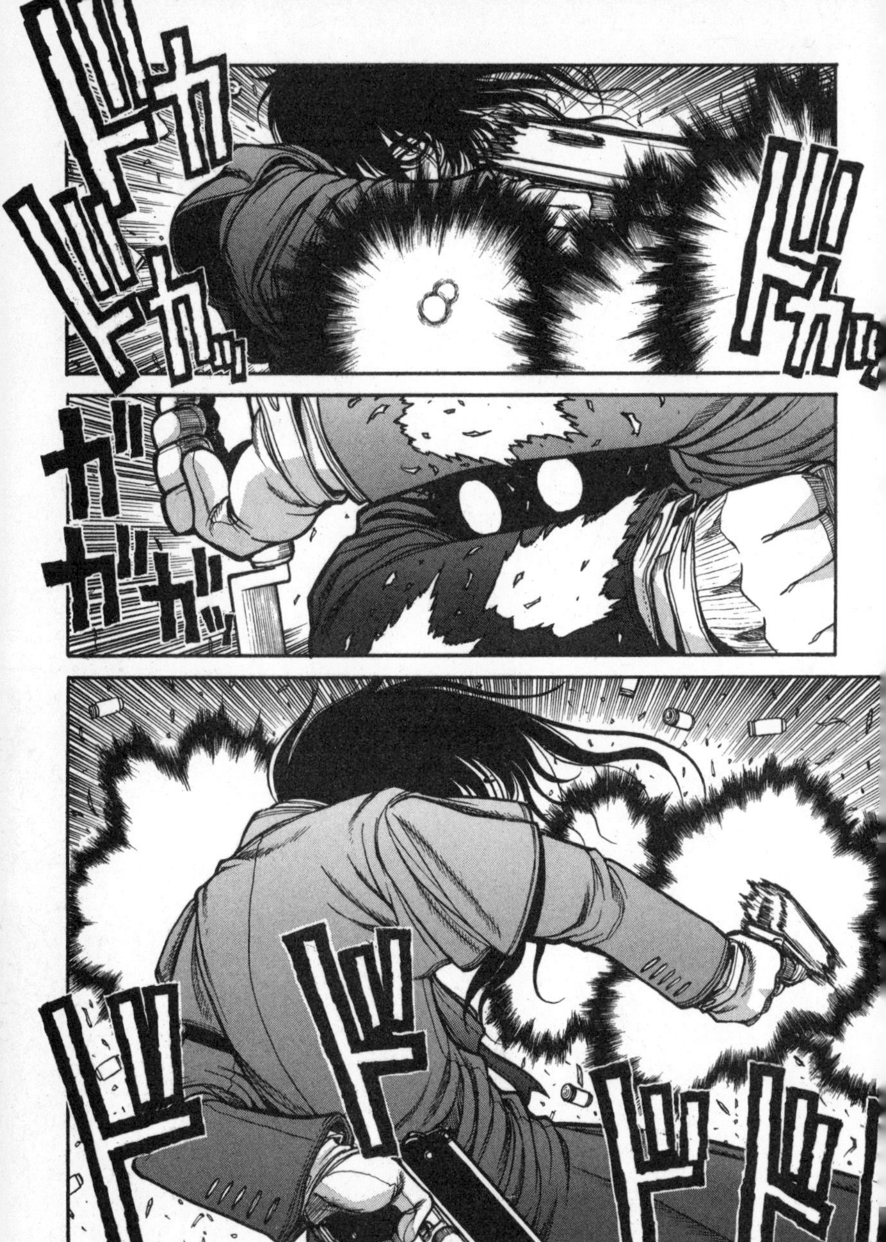
ドカッ
ドカドカッ
ガガガガッ
ドドドドド

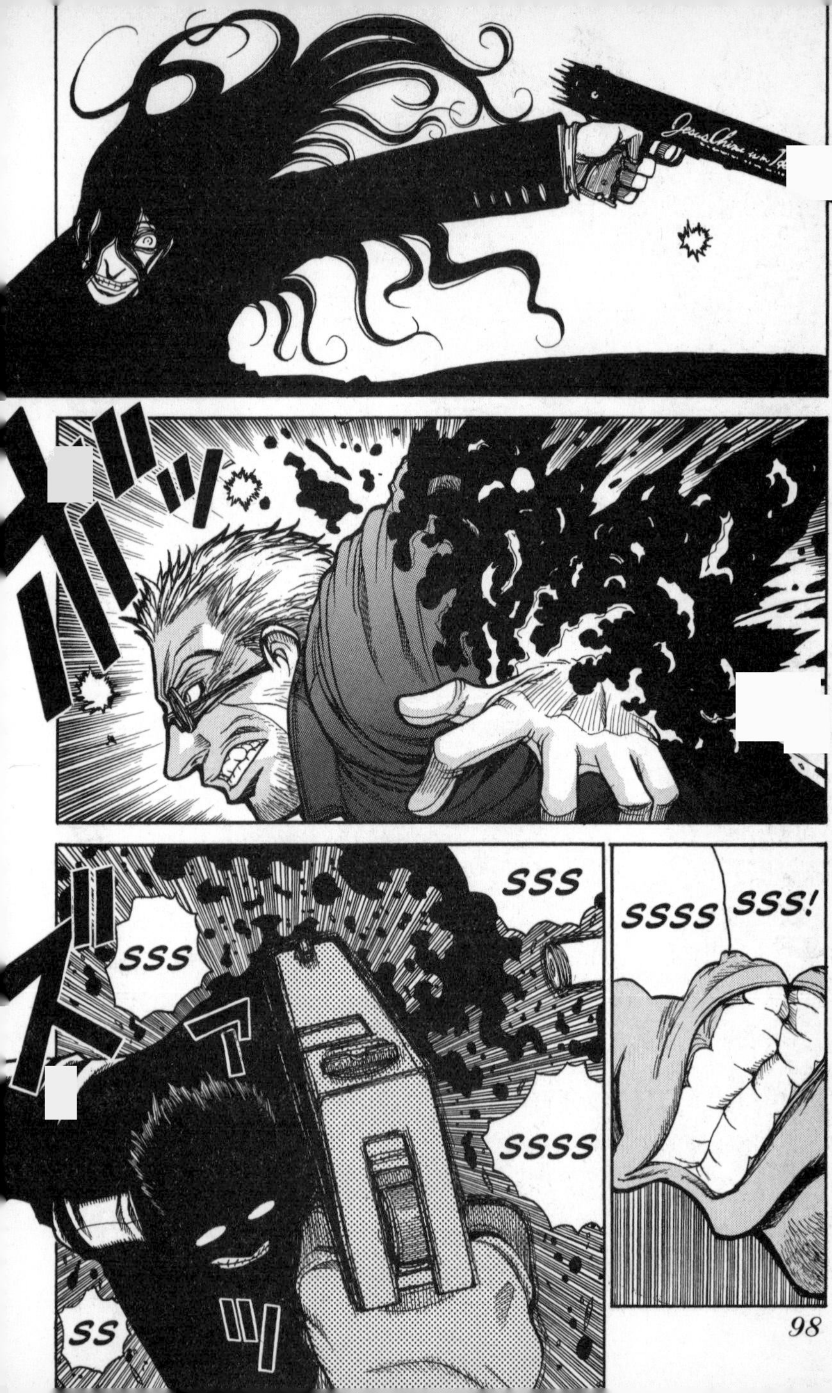
SSS!
SSSS
SSS
SSS
SSSS
SS

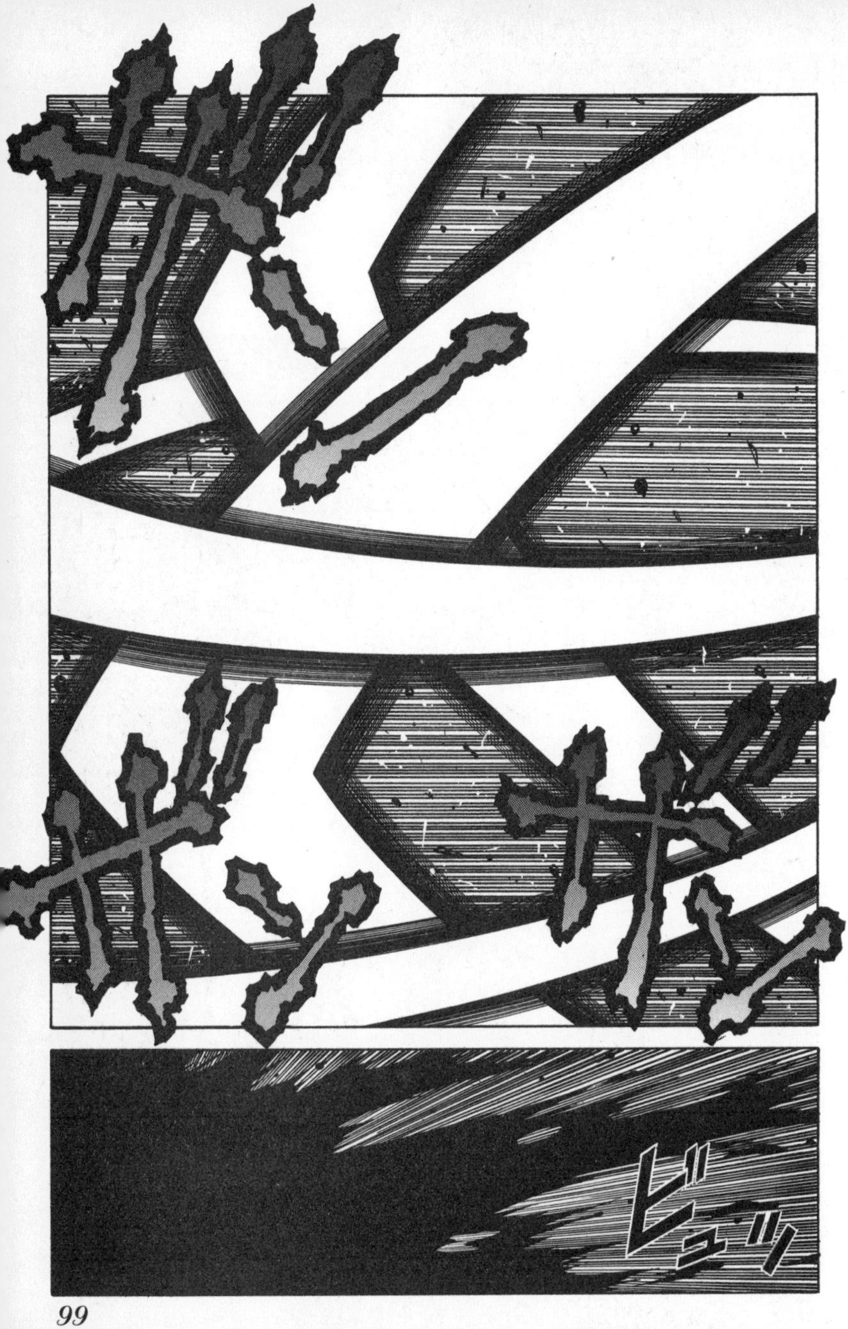
ボッ
ボッ
ボッ
ビュッ

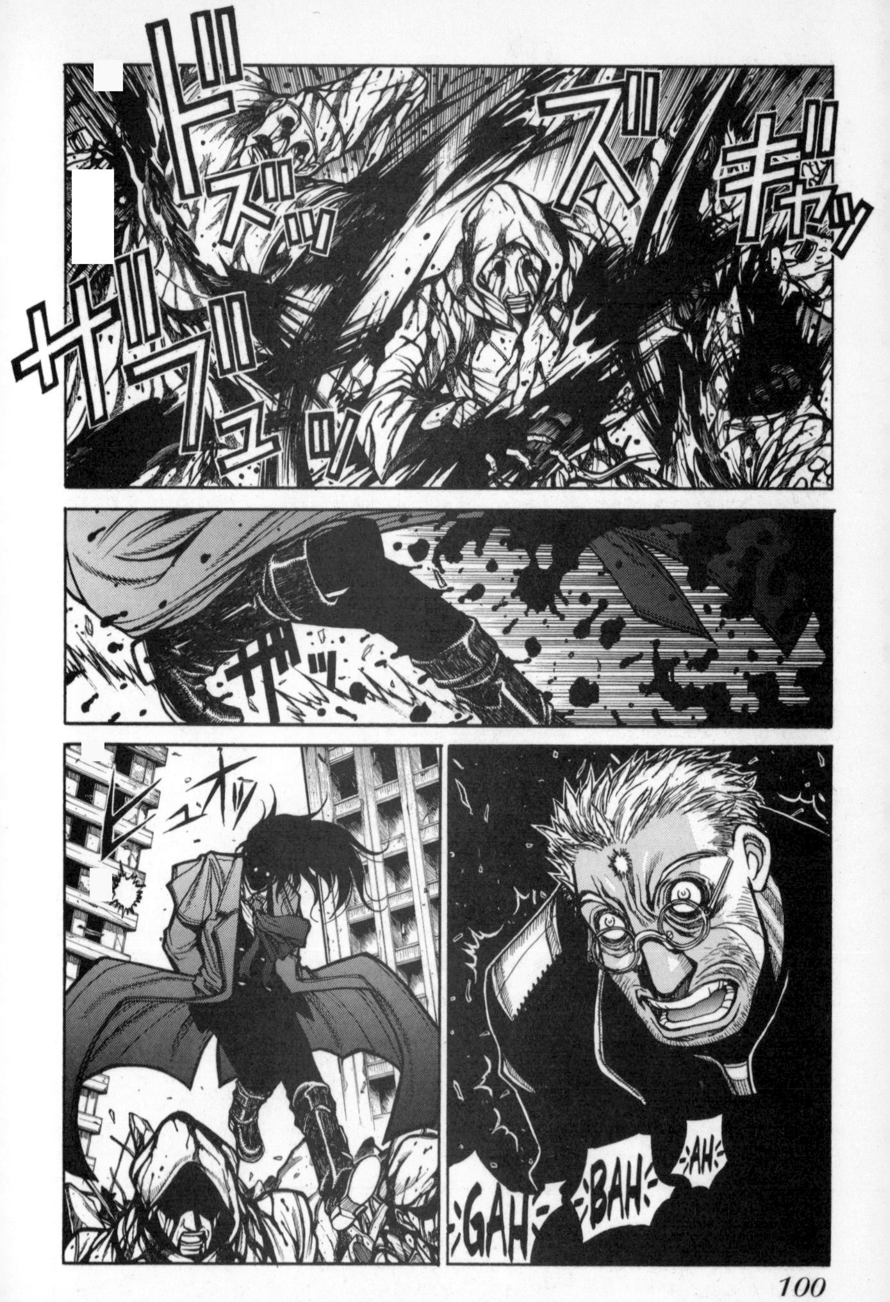
GAH
BAH
AH

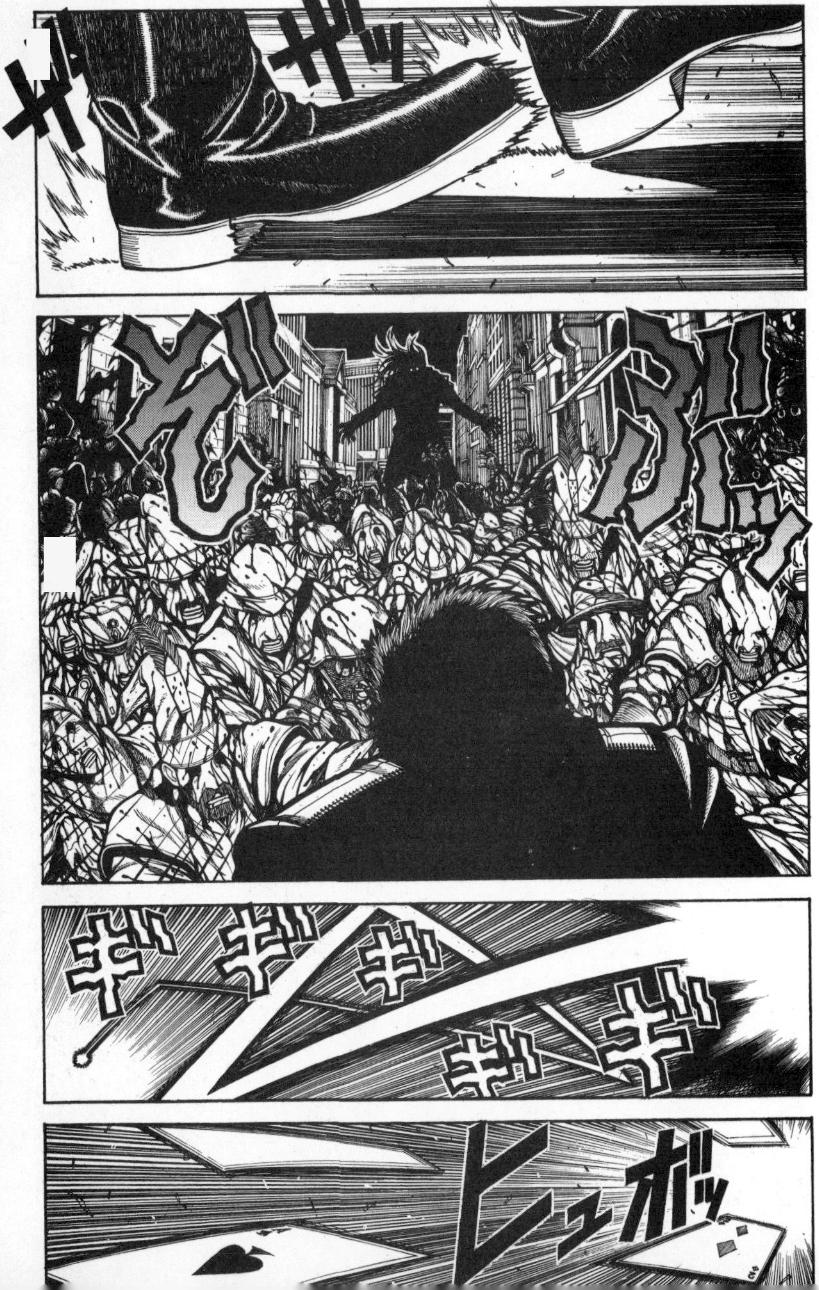
ザッ
ギ
ギ
ギ
ギ
ギ
ヒュオ゛ッ

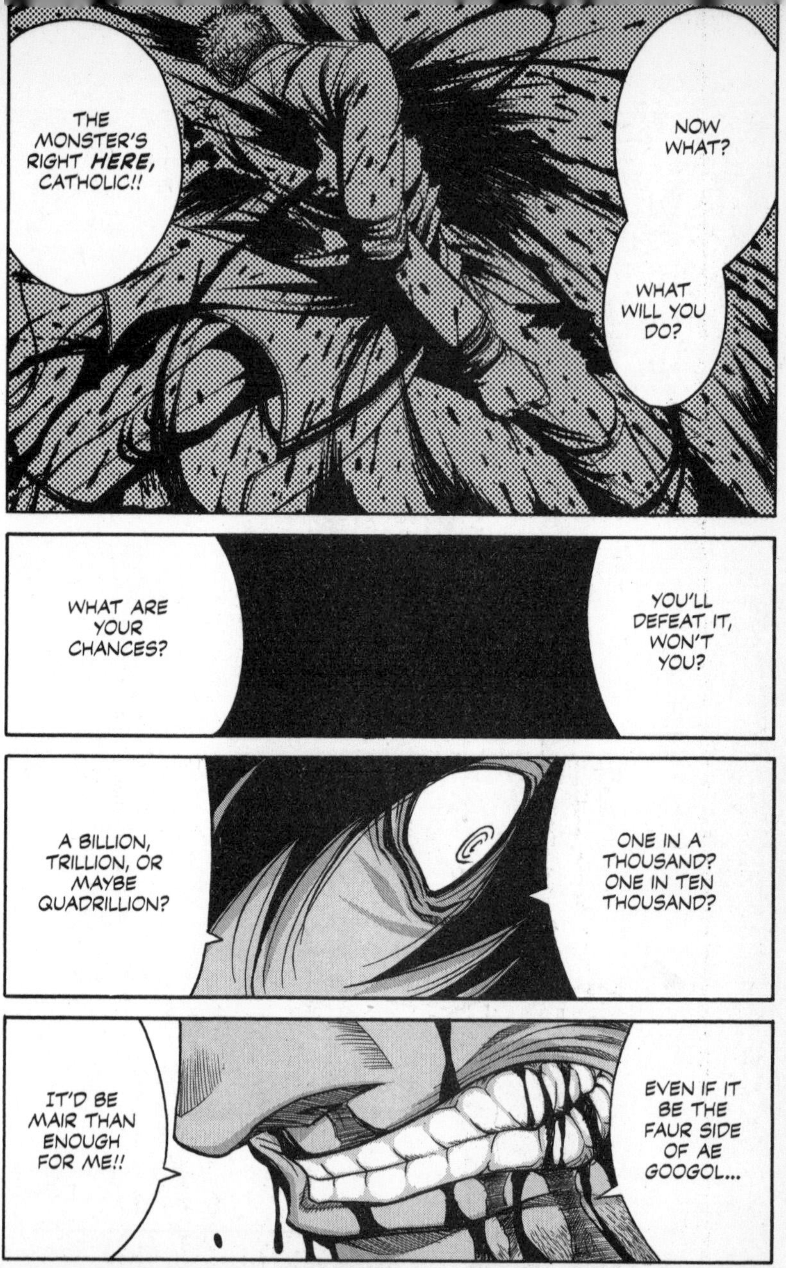
NOW WHAT?
WHAT WILL YOU DO?
THE MONSTER'S RIGHT **HERE**, CATHOLIC!!
YOU'LL DEFEAT IT, WON'T YOU?
WHAT ARE YOUR CHANCES?
ONE IN A THOUSAND? ONE IN TEN THOUSAND?
A BILLION, TRILLION, OR MAYBE QUADRILLION?
EVEN IF IT BE THE FAUR SIDE OF AE GOOGOL...
IT'D BE MAIR THAN ENOUGH FOR ME!!

TO BE CONTINUED

ORDER 5 / END

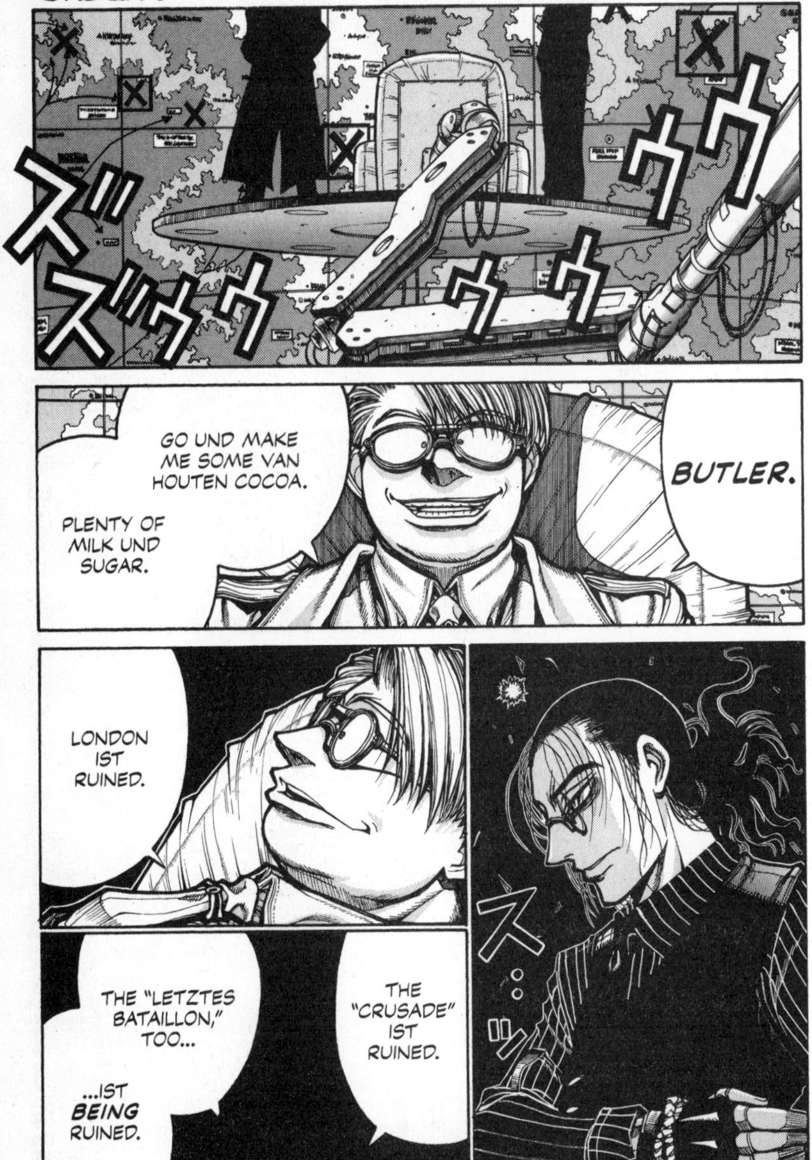
BUTLER.
GO UND MAKE ME SOME VAN HOUTEN COCOA.
PLENTY OF MILK UND SUGAR.
LONDON IST RUINED.
THE "CRUSADE" IST RUINED.
THE "LETZTES BATAILLON," TOO...
...IST *BEING* RUINED.

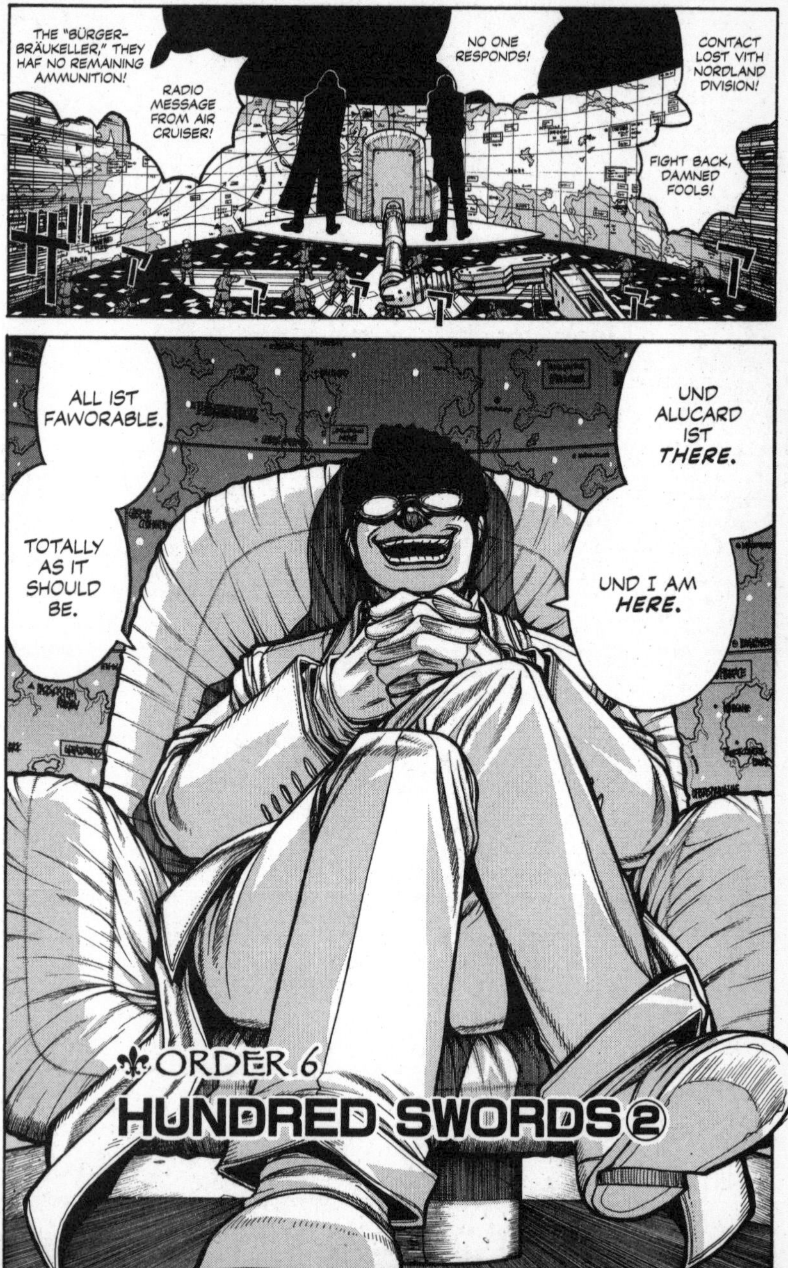
CONTACT LOST VITH NORDLAND DIVISION!
NO ONE RESPONDS!
THE "BÜRGER-BRÄUKELLER," THEY HAF NO REMAINING AMMUNITION!
FIGHT BACK, DAMNED FOOLS!
RADIO MESSAGE FROM AIR CRUISER!
UND ALUCARD IST *THERE.*
ALL IST FAWORABLE.
UND I AM *HERE.*
TOTALLY AS IT SHOULD BE.

ORDER 6

HUNDRED SWORDS 2

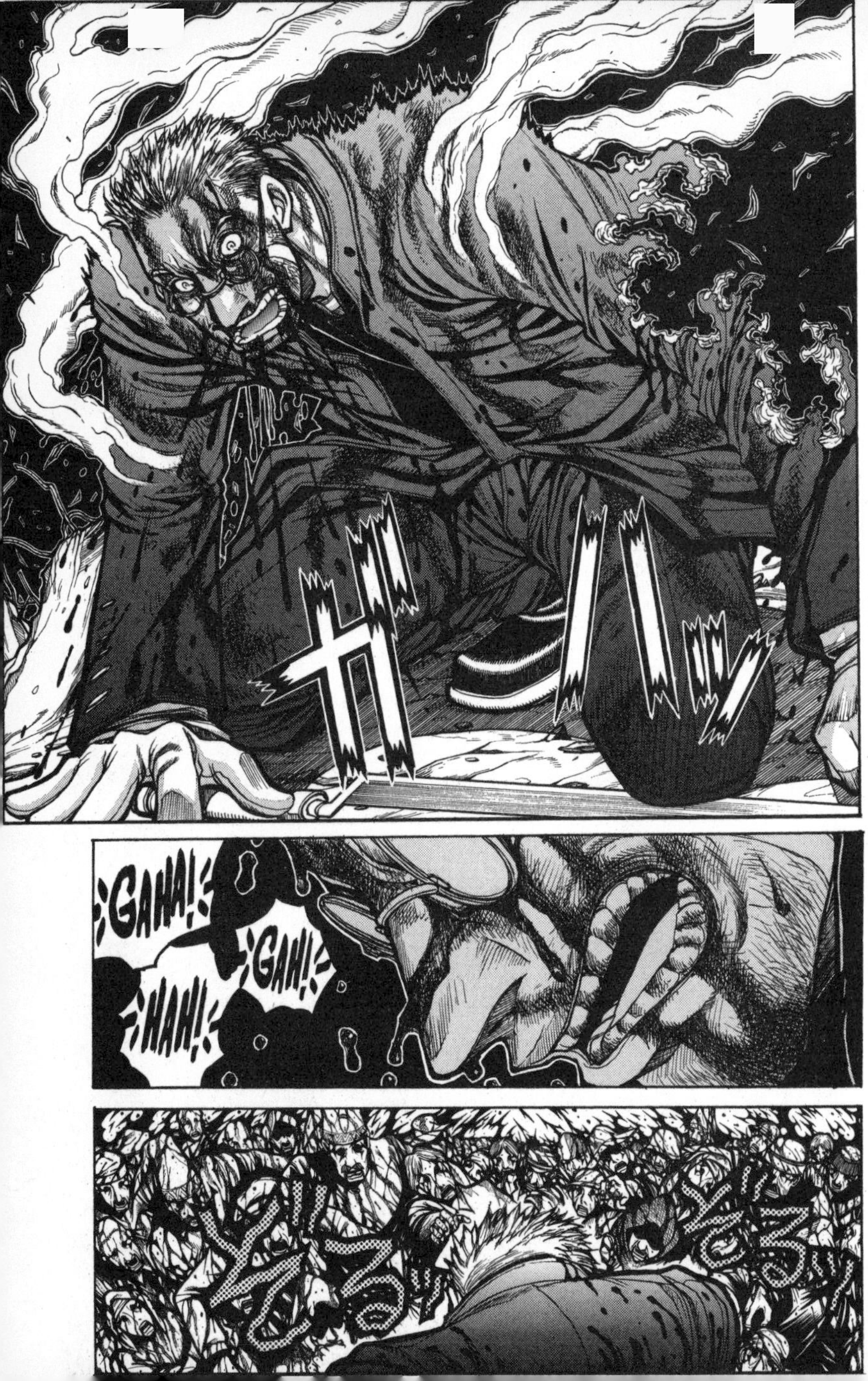
GAHA!
GAH!
HAH!

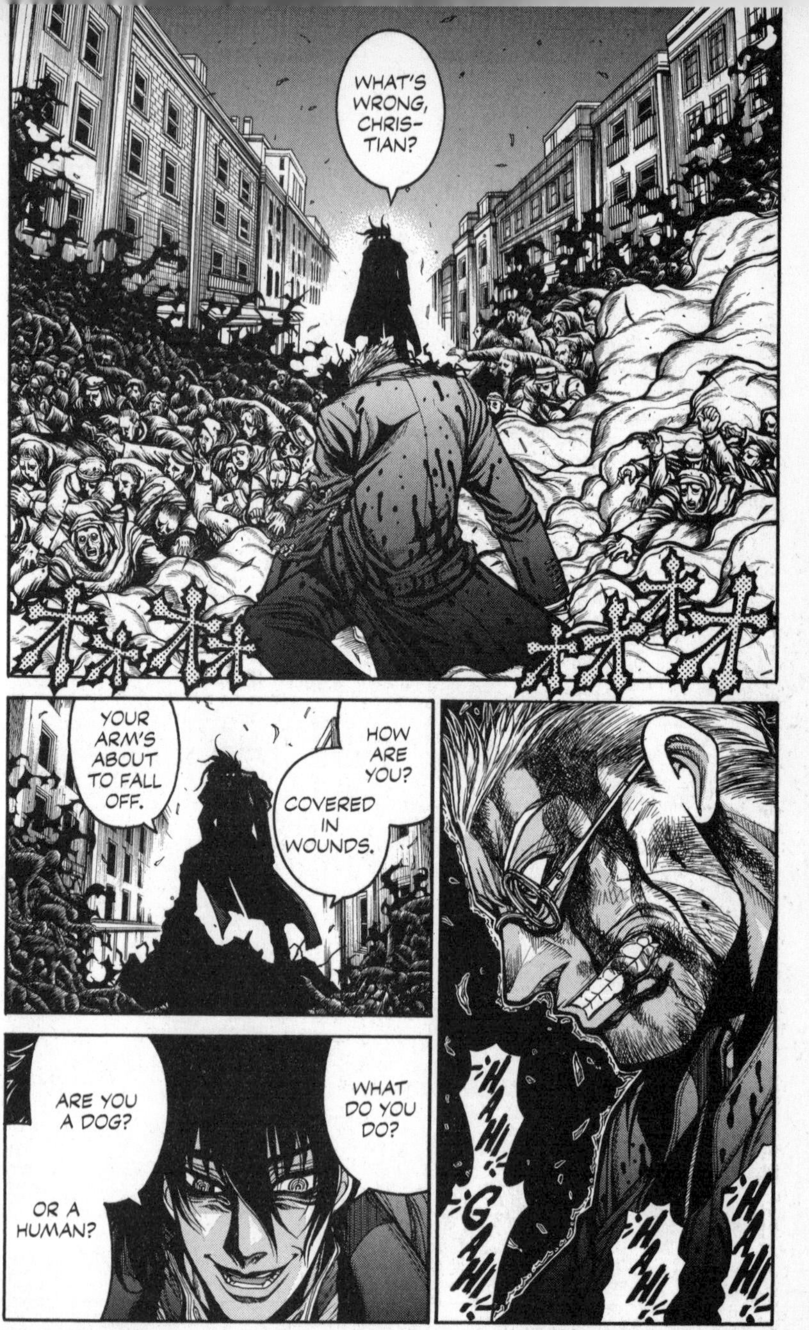
WHAT'S WRONG, CHRIS-TIAN?
オオオオ
オオオオ
HAAH!
HAAH!
HAAH!
GAAH!
HOW ARE YOU?
COVERED IN WOUNDS.
YOUR ARM'S ABOUT TO FALL OFF.
WHAT DO YOU DO?
ARE YOU A DOG?
OR A HUMAN?

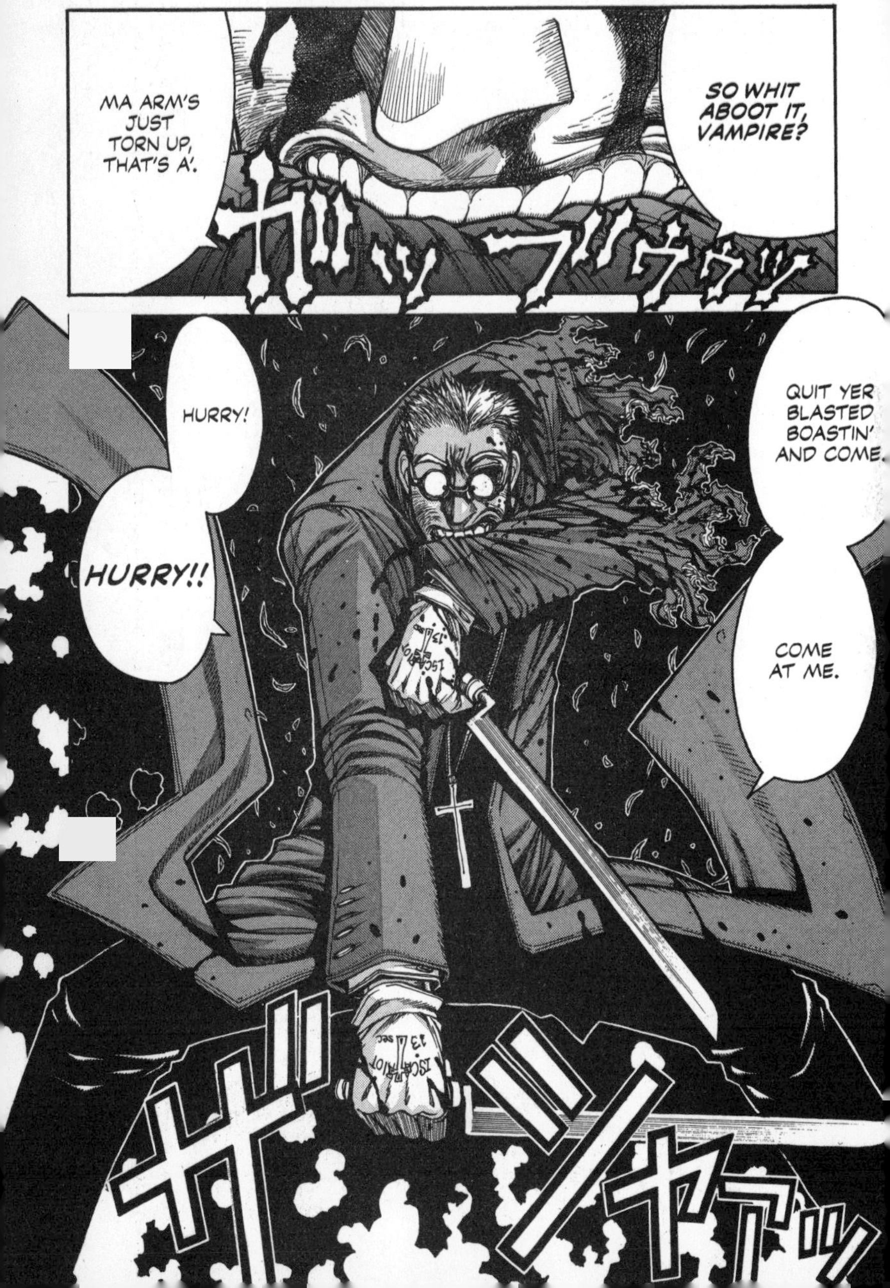
SO WHIT ABOOT IT, VAMPIRE?
MA ARM'S JUST TORN UP, THAT'S A'.
QUIT YER BLASTED BOASTIN' AND COME.
COME AT ME.
HURRY!
HURRY!!

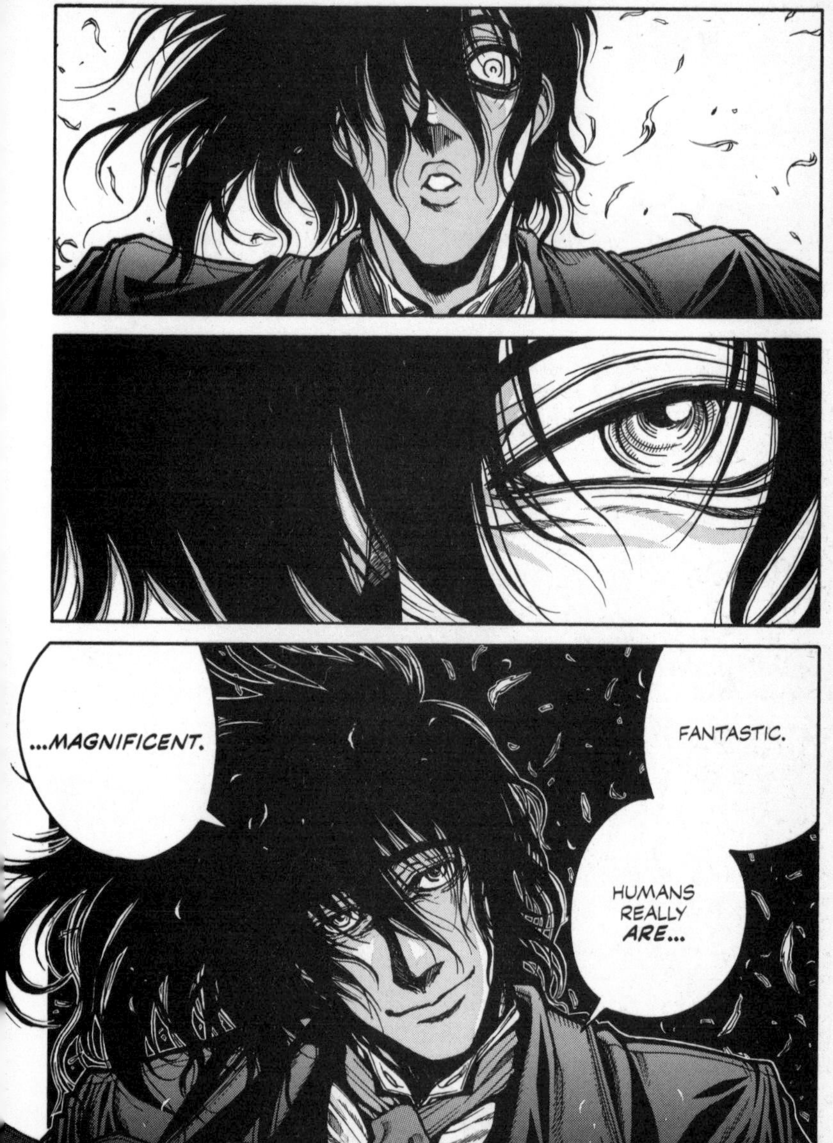
FANTASTIC.
HUMANS REALLY ARE...
...MAGNIFICENT.

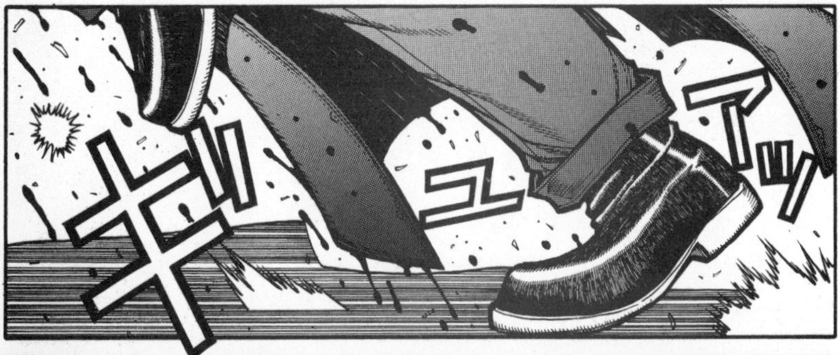
ギュアッ
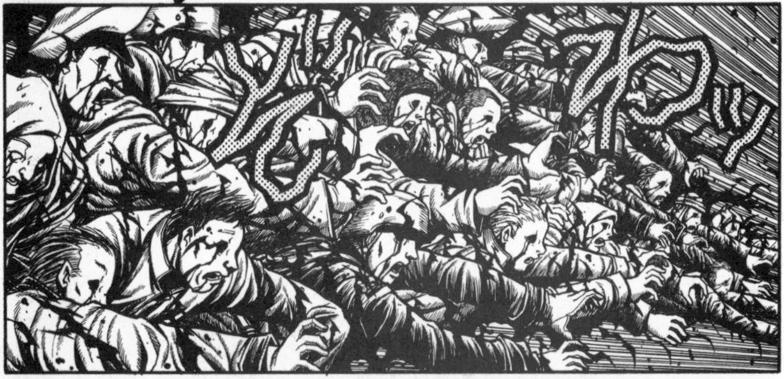
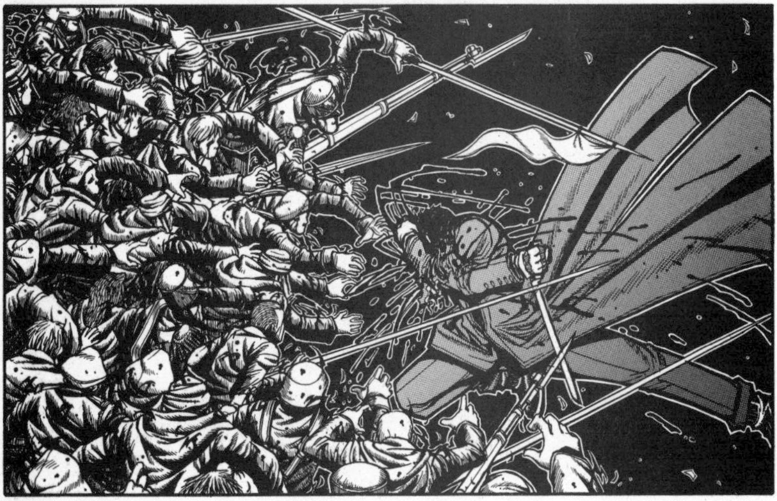

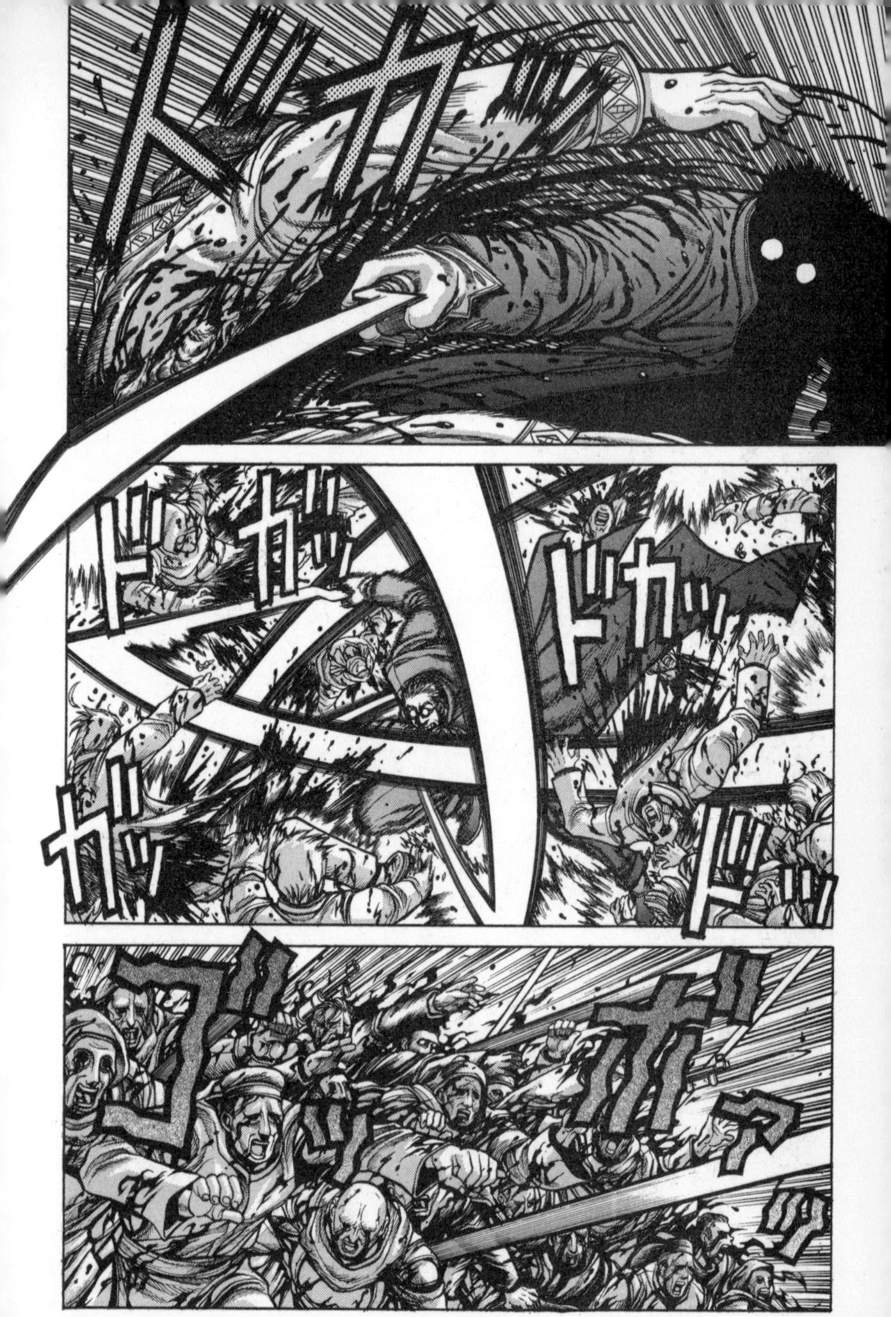
ドガッ
ドカッ
ドッ
ドガッ
ガッ
ゴッガァッ

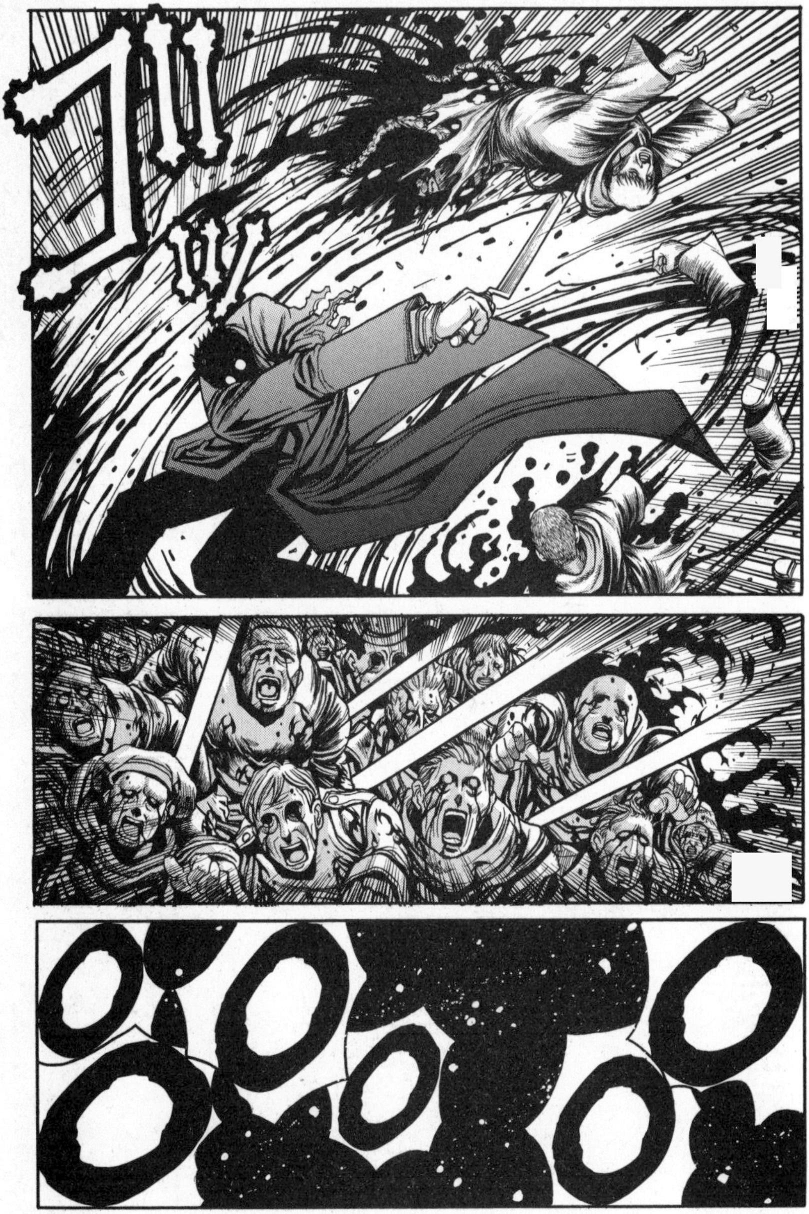

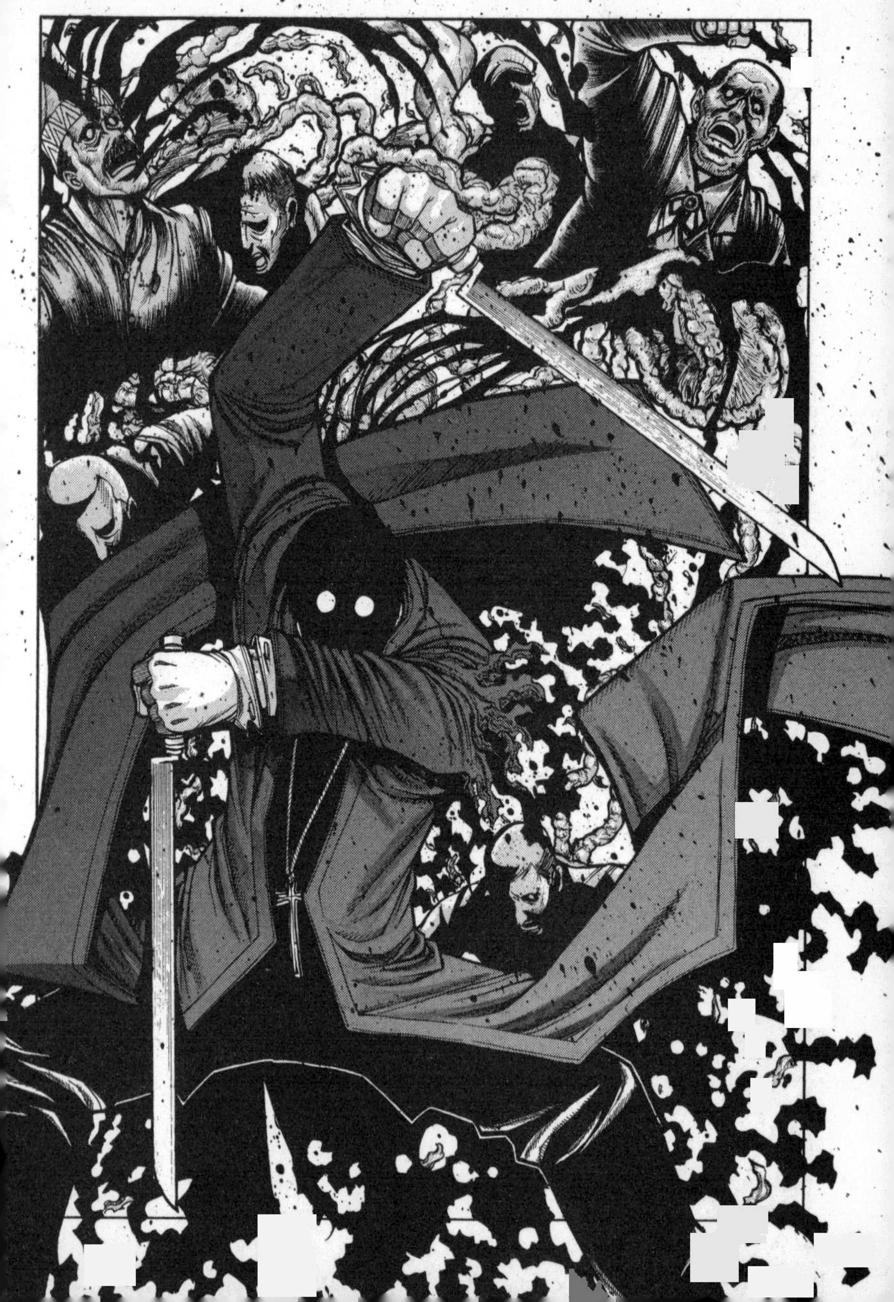

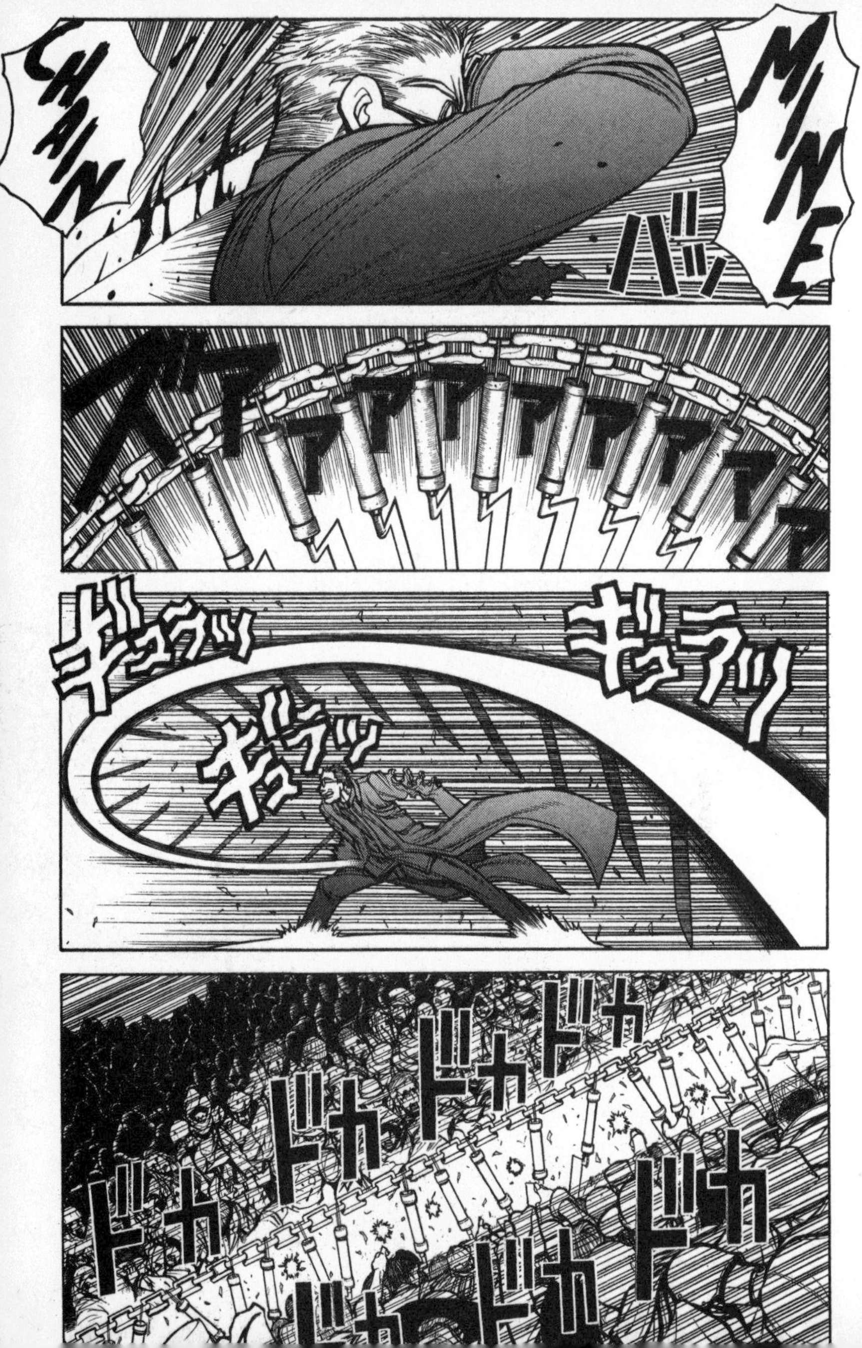
MINE
バッ
CHAIN
ズァアアアアアアアアアア
ギュラッ
ギュラッ
ギュラッ
ドカ
ドカ
ドカ
ドカ
ドカ
ドカ
ドカ
ドカ

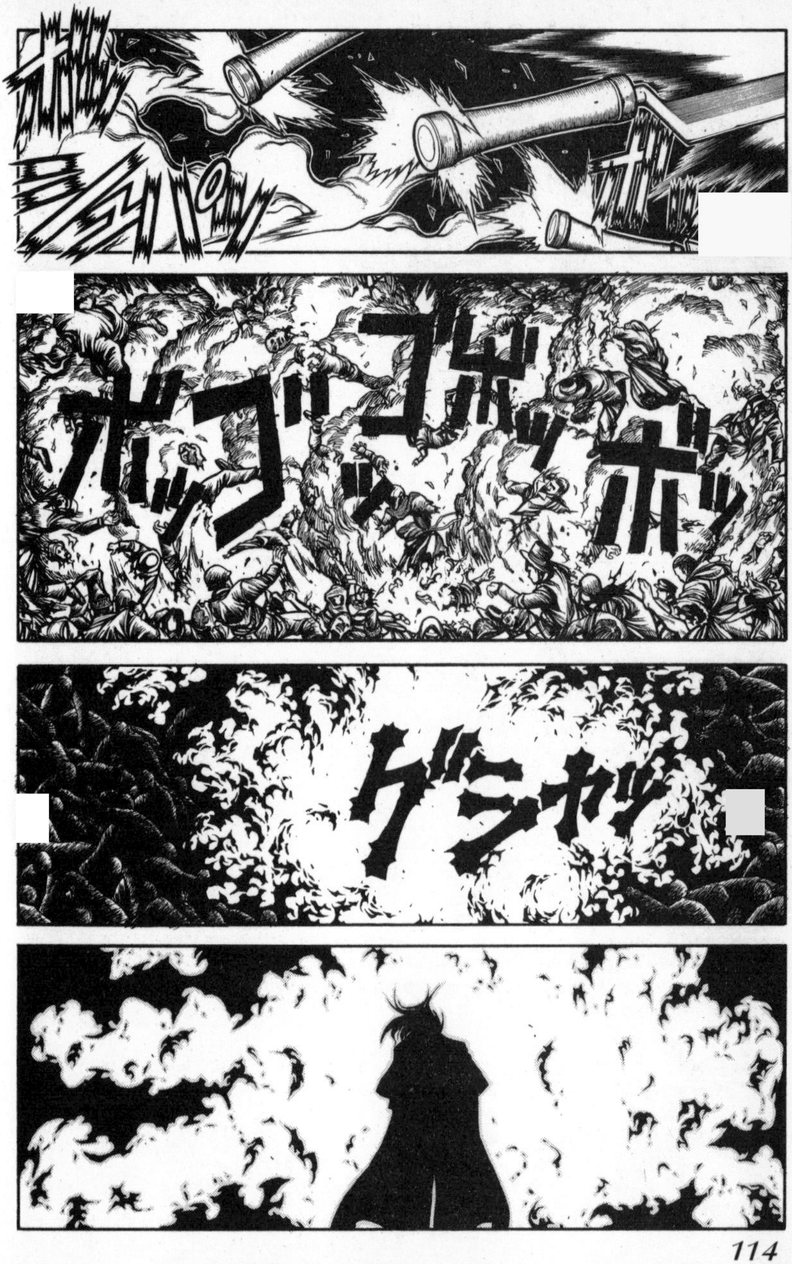
ボッ
ゴボッ
ゴッ
ボッ
グシャッ

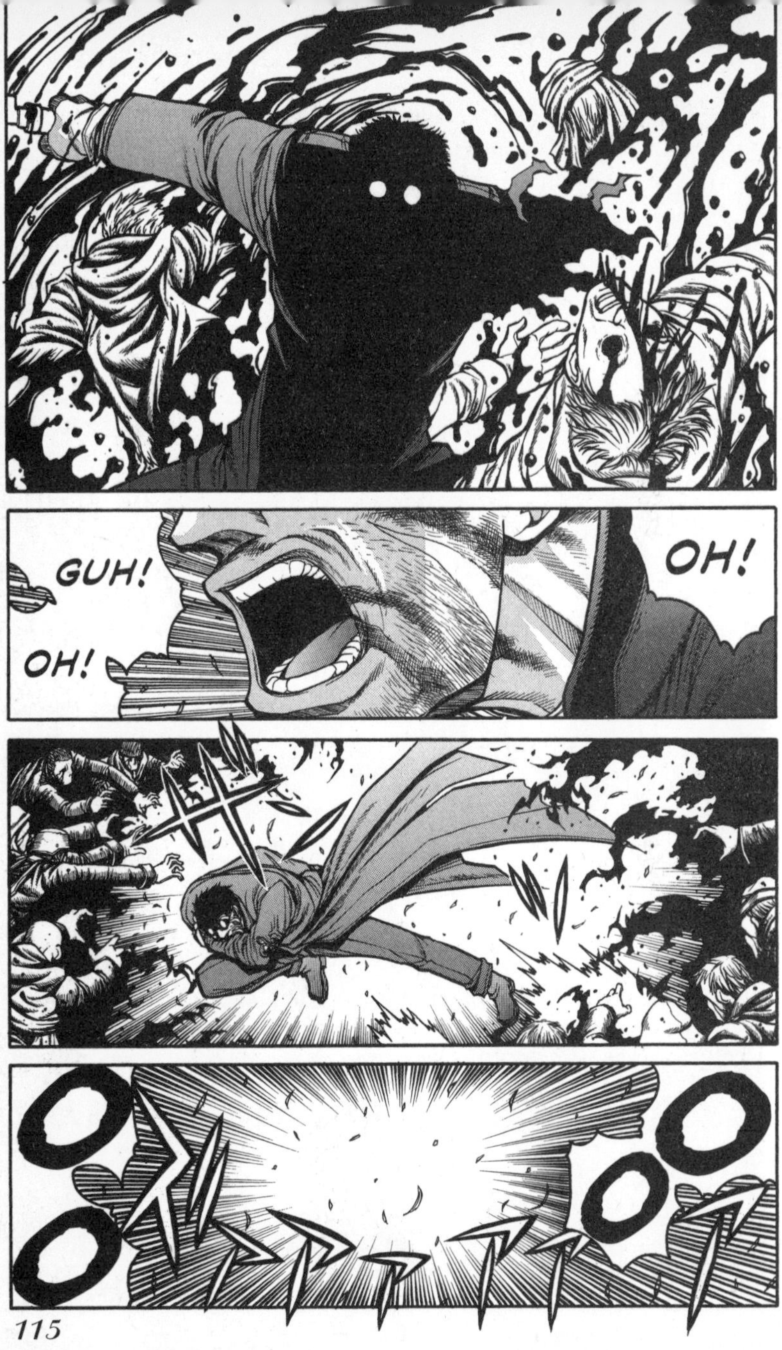
OH!
GUH!
OH!

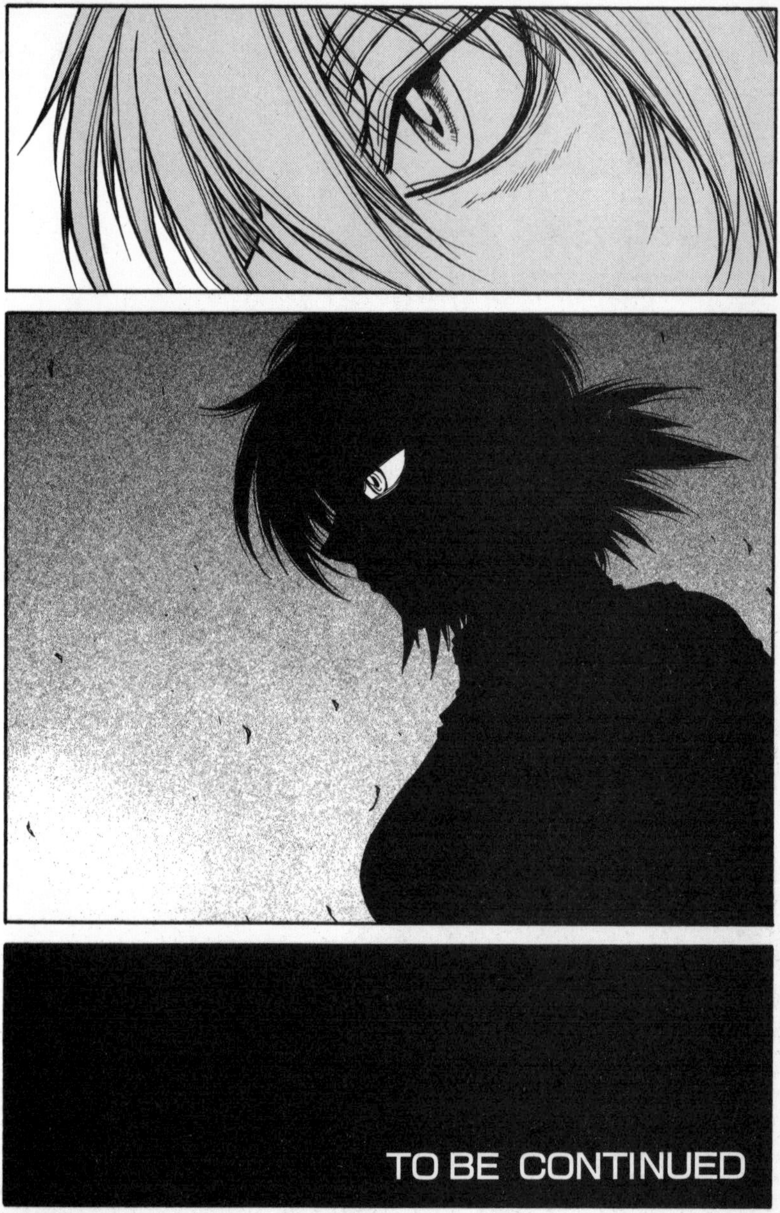
TO BE CONTINUED

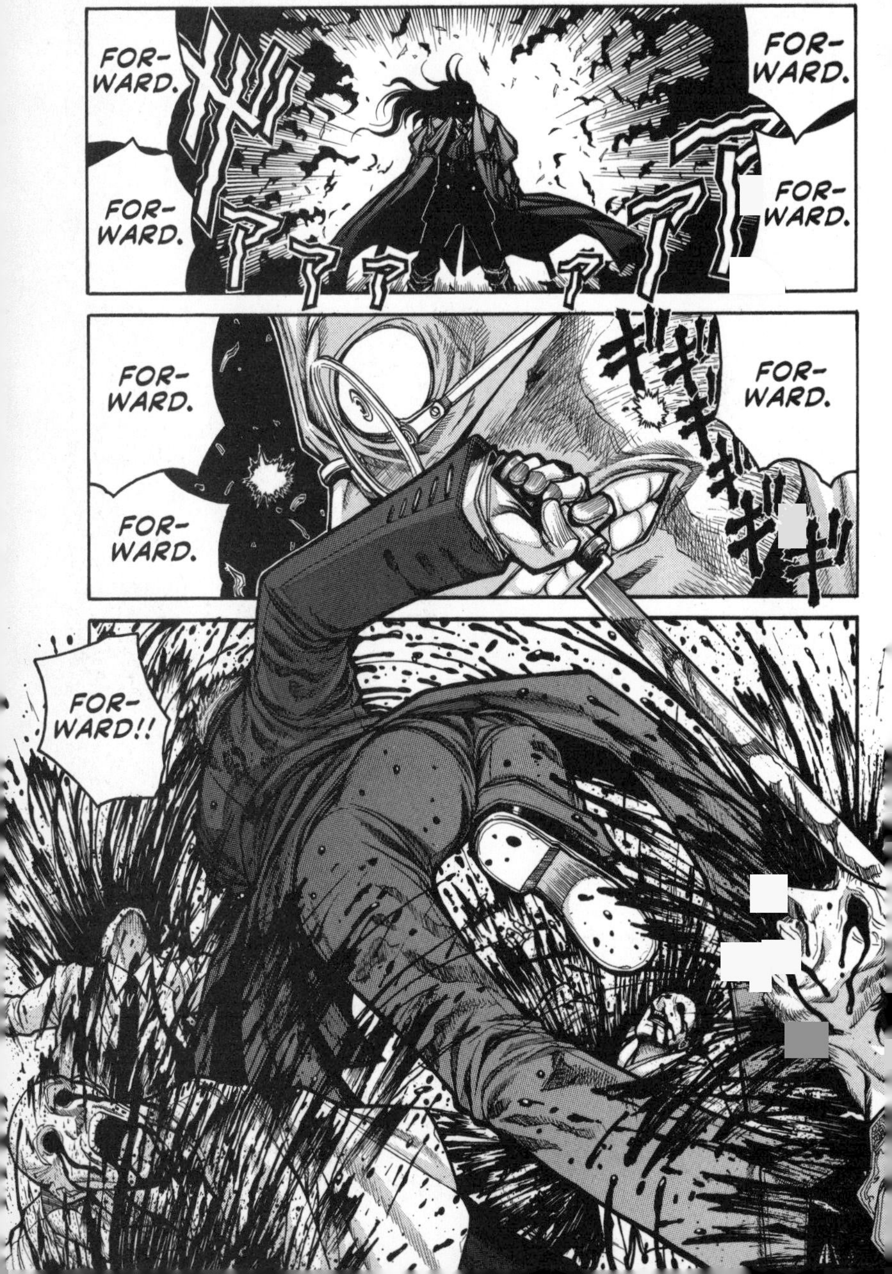
FOR-WARD.
FOR-WARD.
FOR-WARD.
FOR-WARD.
FOR-WARD.
FOR-WARD.
FOR-WARD.
FOR-WARD!!

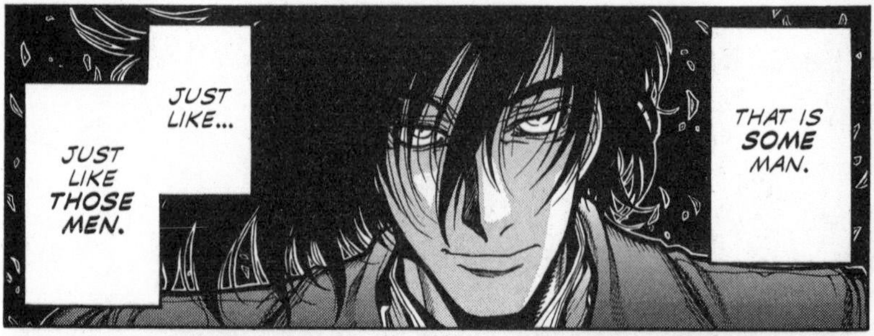
THAT IS SOME MAN.
JUST LIKE...
JUST LIKE THOSE MEN.

ORDER 7
HUNDRED SWORDS ③

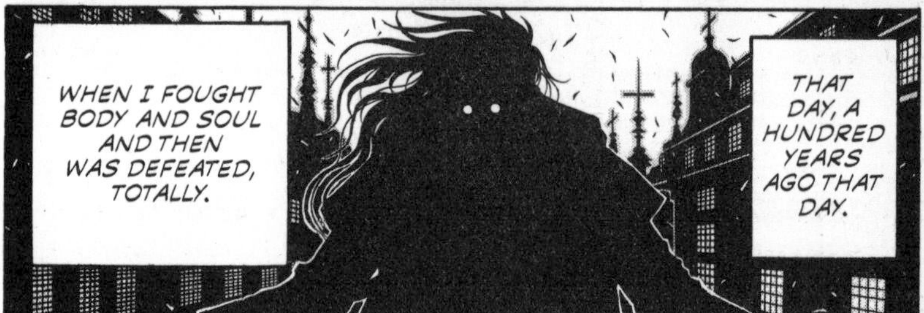
THAT DAY, A HUNDRED YEARS AGO THAT DAY.
WHEN I FOUGHT BODY AND SOUL AND THEN WAS DEFEATED, TOTALLY.

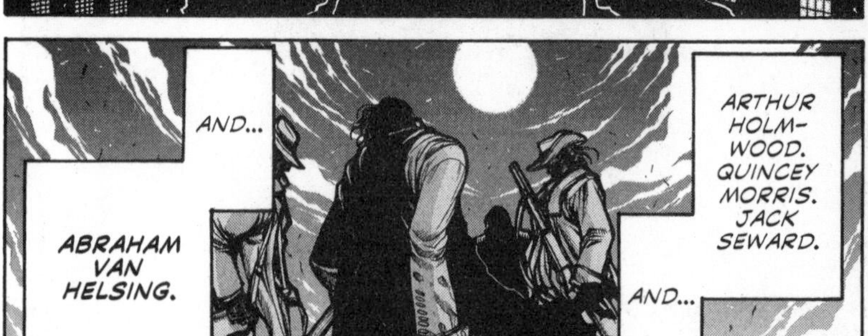
ARTHUR HOLMWOOD. QUINCEY MORRIS. JACK SEWARD.
AND...
AND...
ABRAHAM VAN HELSING.

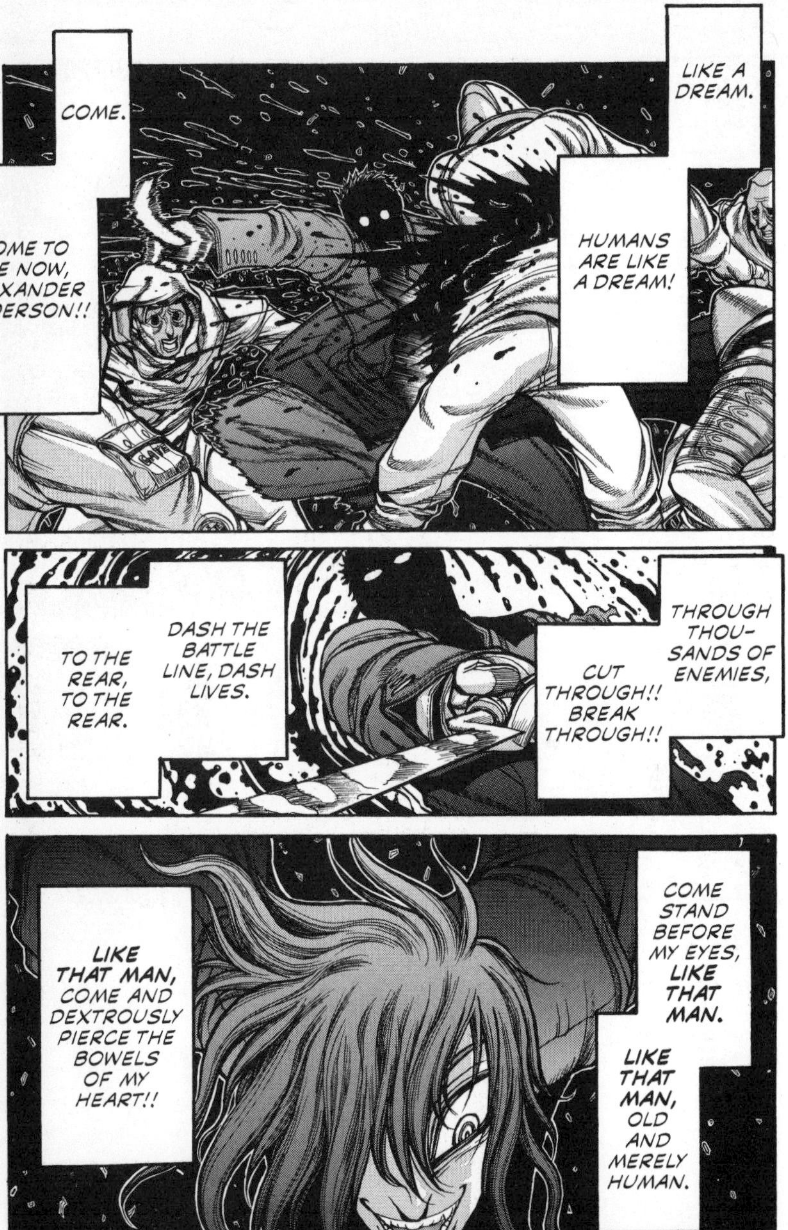
LIKE A DREAM.
HUMANS ARE LIKE A DREAM!
COME.
COME TO ME NOW, ALEXANDER ANDERSON!!
THROUGH THOUSANDS OF ENEMIES,
CUT THROUGH!! BREAK THROUGH!!
DASH THE BATTLE LINE, DASH LIVES.
TO THE REAR, TO THE REAR.
COME STAND BEFORE MY EYES, **LIKE THAT MAN.**
LIKE THAT MAN, OLD AND MERELY HUMAN.
LIKE THAT MAN, COME AND DEXTROUSLY PIERCE THE BOWELS OF MY HEART!!

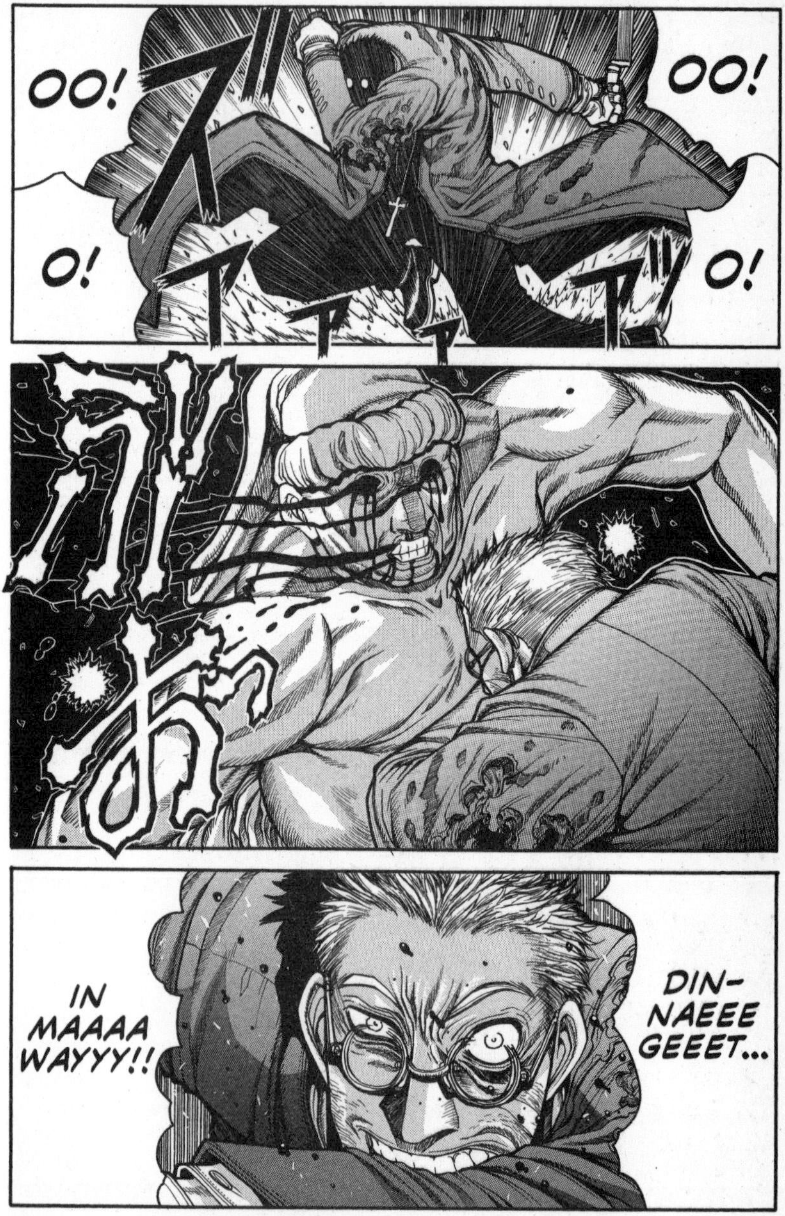
OO!
OO!
O!
O!
DIN-
NAEEE
GEEET...
IN
MAAAA
WAYYY!!

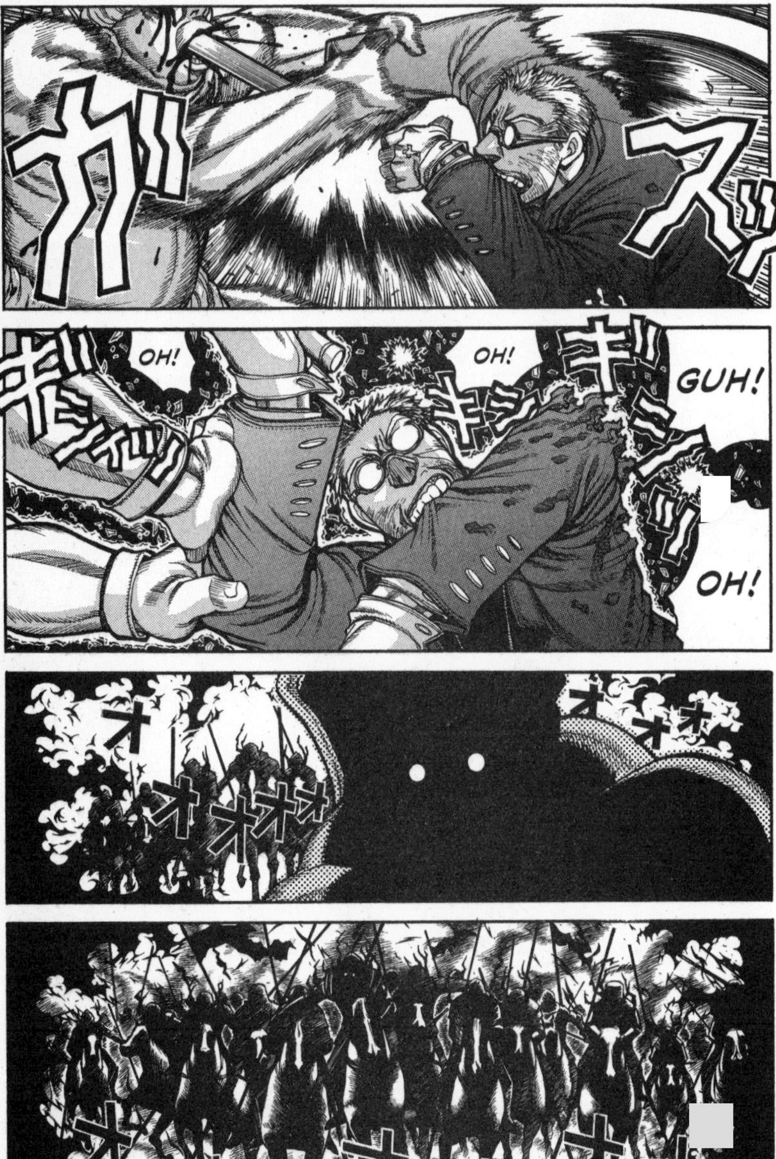
GUH!
OH!
OH!
OH!

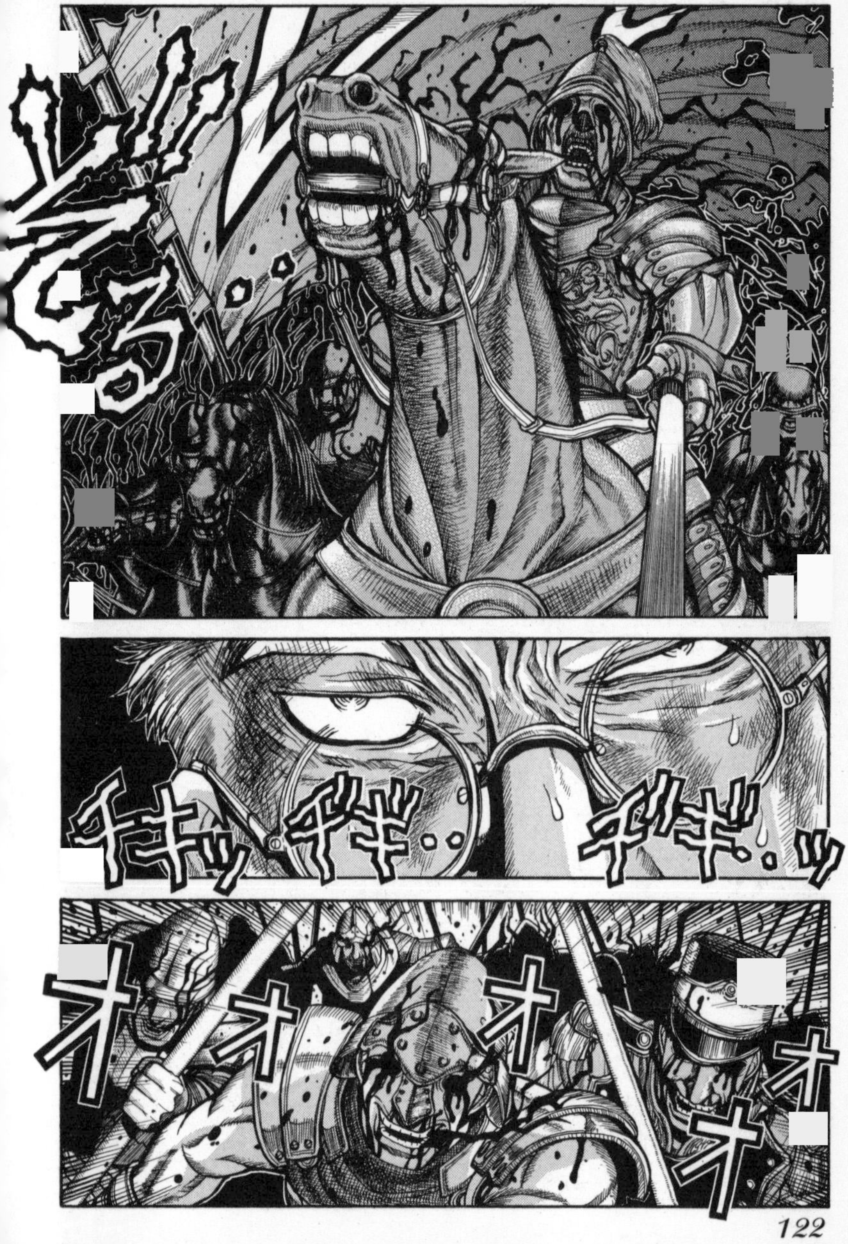
ギリギ・ッ
チキッ ギリギ・・
オオ
オオオ

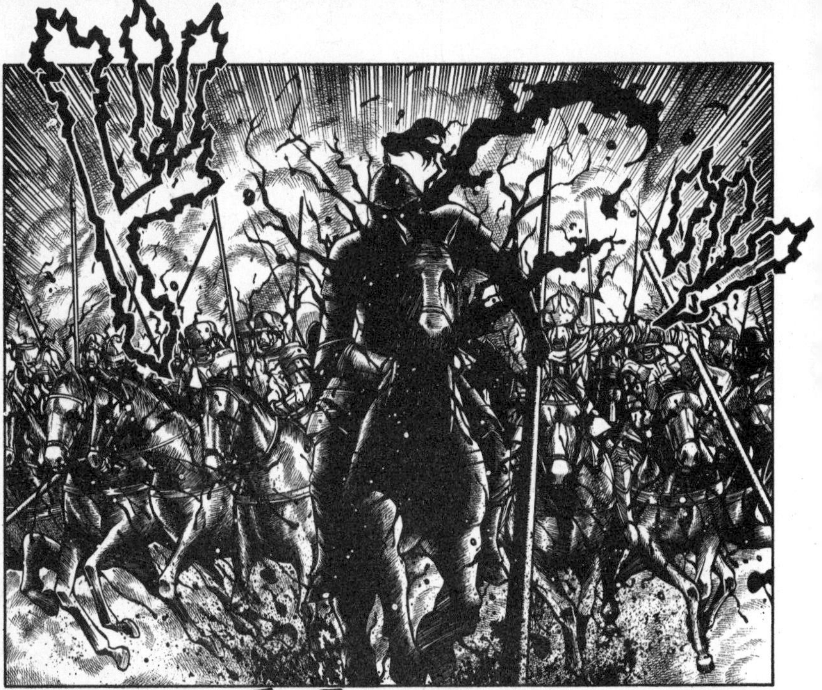
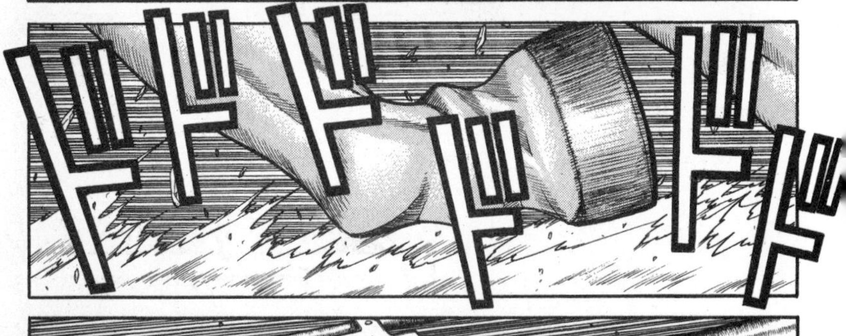
ドドドドドド
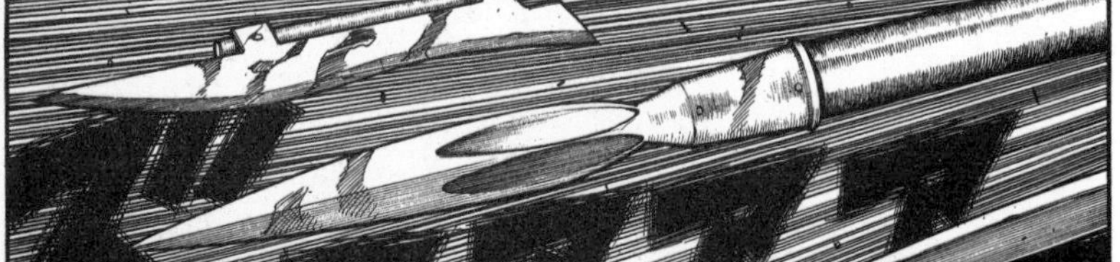

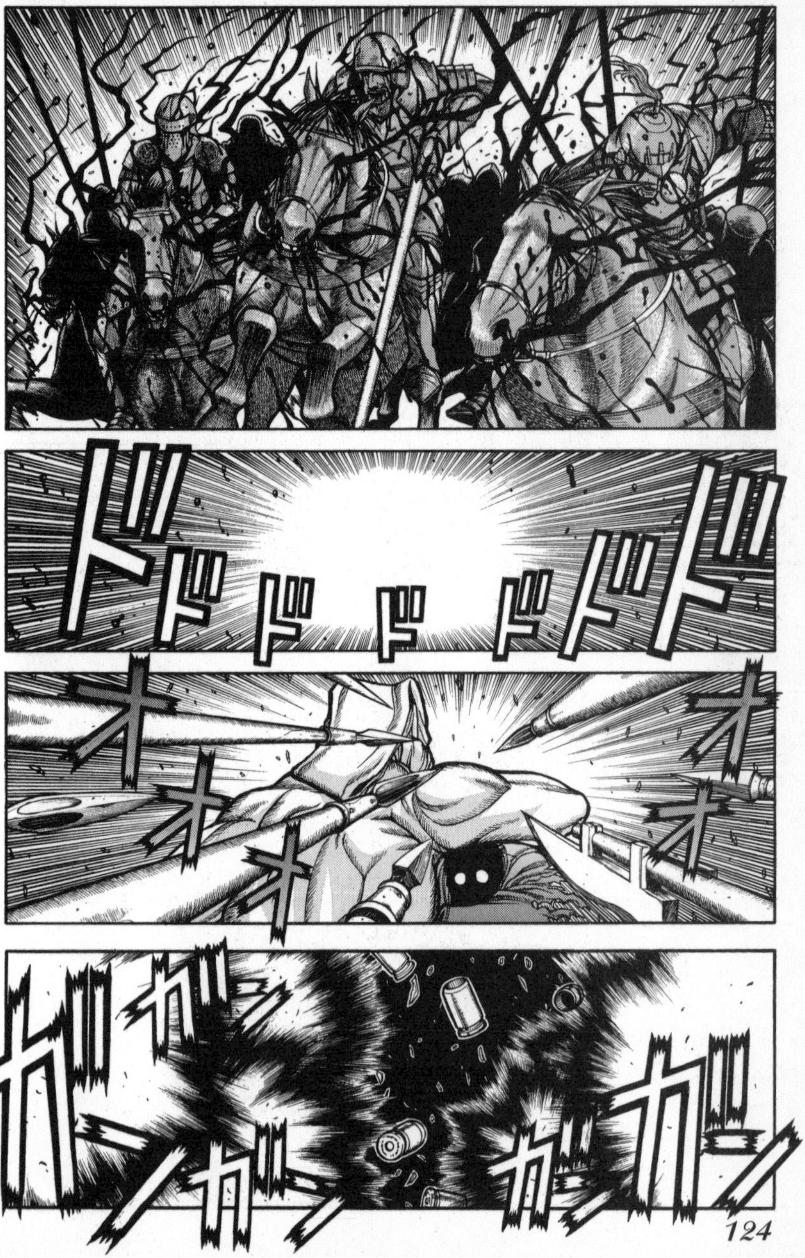
ドドドドドドド
オオ
オオオ
ガーンガーン
ガガガン
ガーンガーン

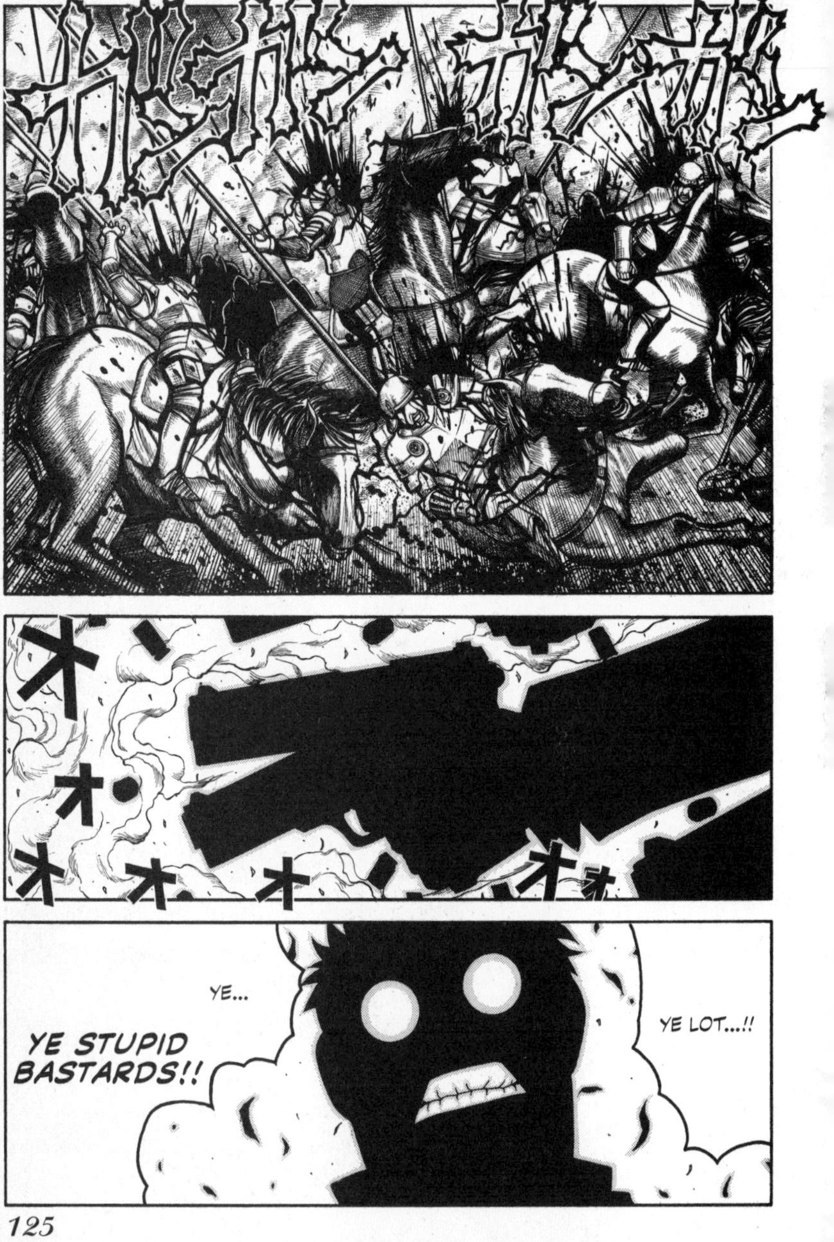
YE...
YE LOT...!!
YE STUPID BASTARDS!!

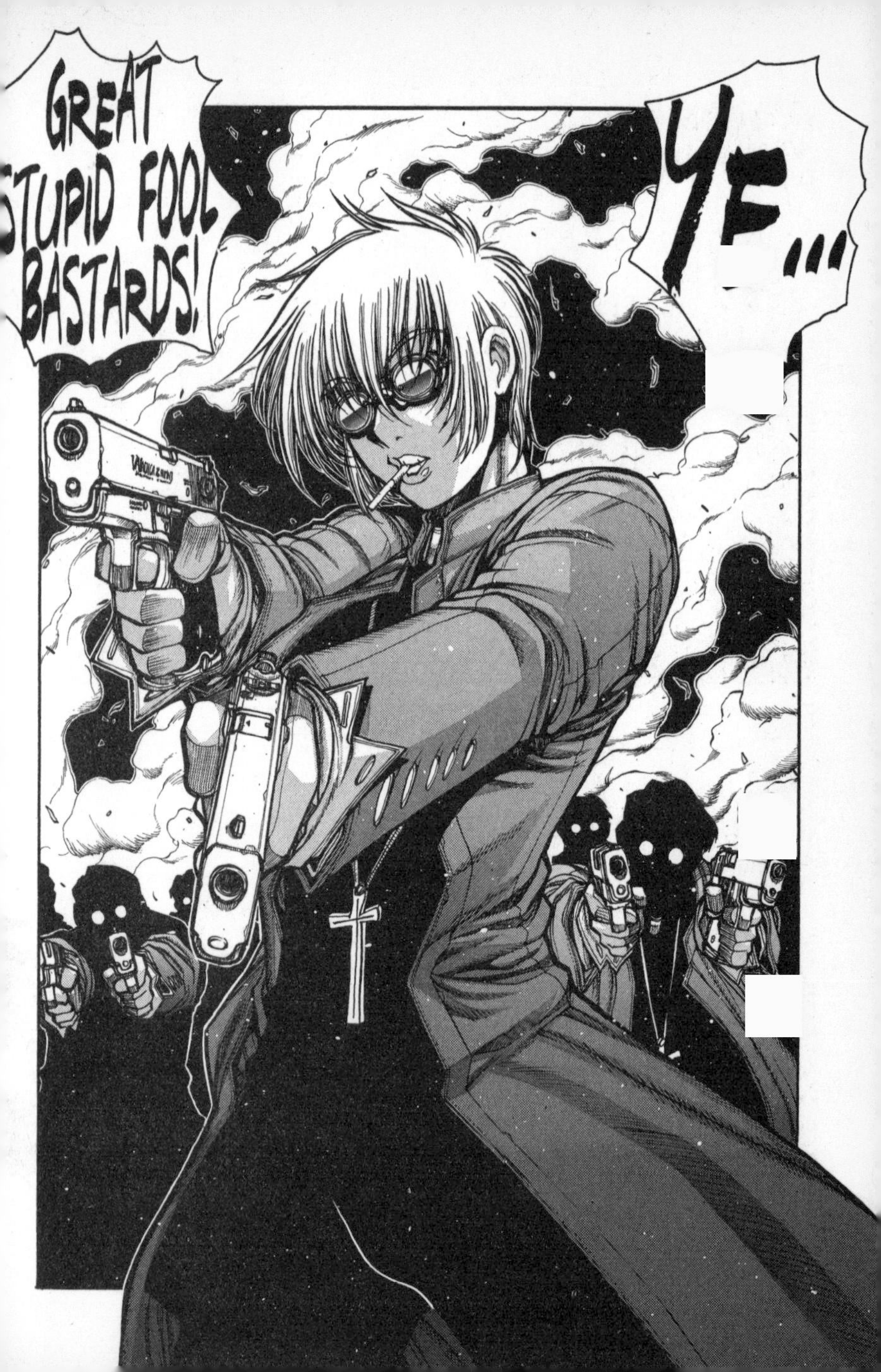
YE...
GREAT STUPID FOOL BASTARDS!

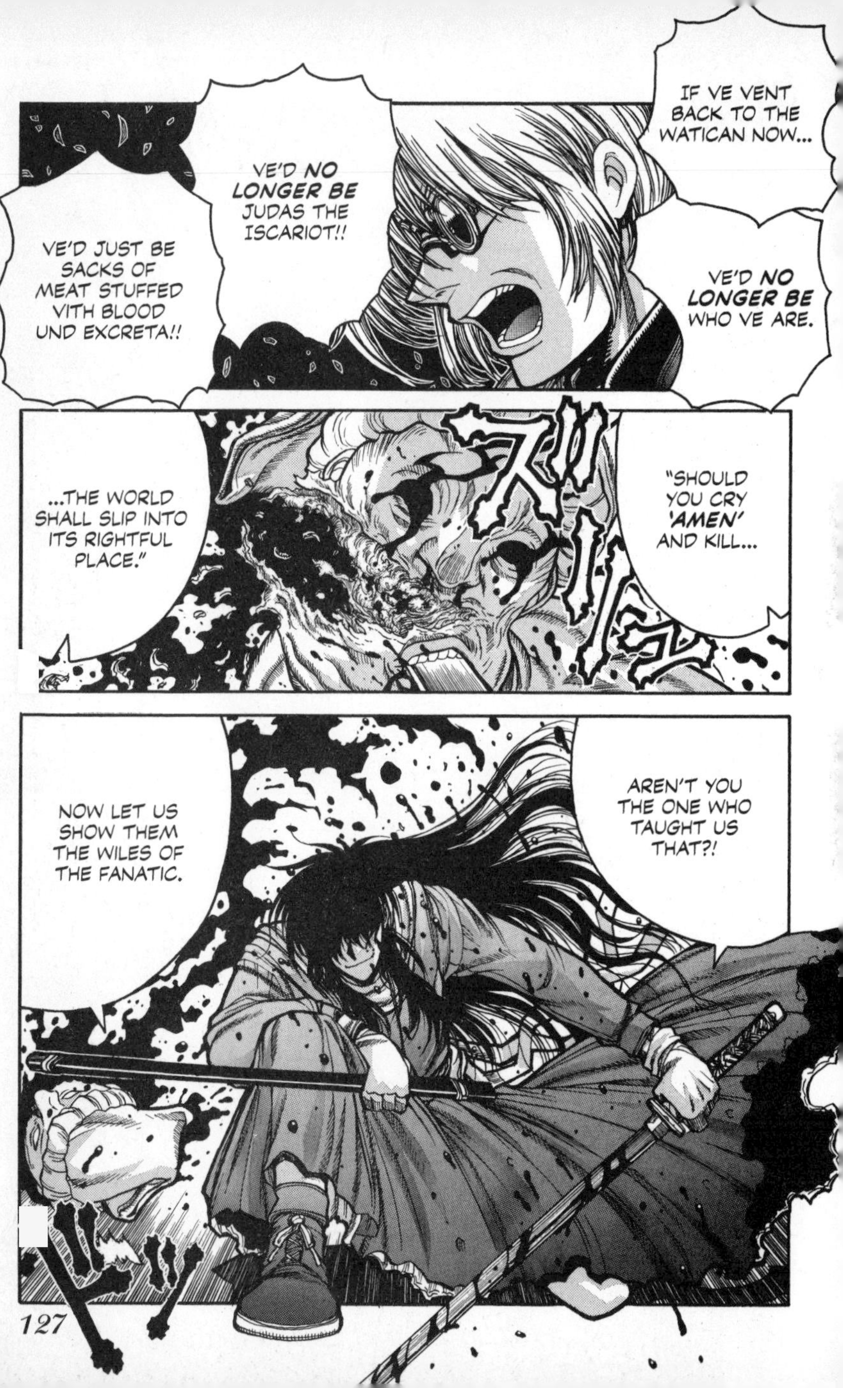
IF VE VENT BACK TO THE WATICAN NOW...
VE'D **NO LONGER BE** WHO VE ARE.
VE'D **NO LONGER BE** JUDAS THE ISCARIOT!!
VE'D JUST BE SACKS OF MEAT STUFFED VITH BLOOD UND EXCRETA!!
"SHOULD YOU CRY ***'AMEN'*** AND KILL...
...THE WORLD SHALL SLIP INTO ITS RIGHTFUL PLACE."
AREN'T YOU THE ONE WHO TAUGHT US THAT?!
NOW LET US SHOW THEM THE WILES OF THE FANATIC.

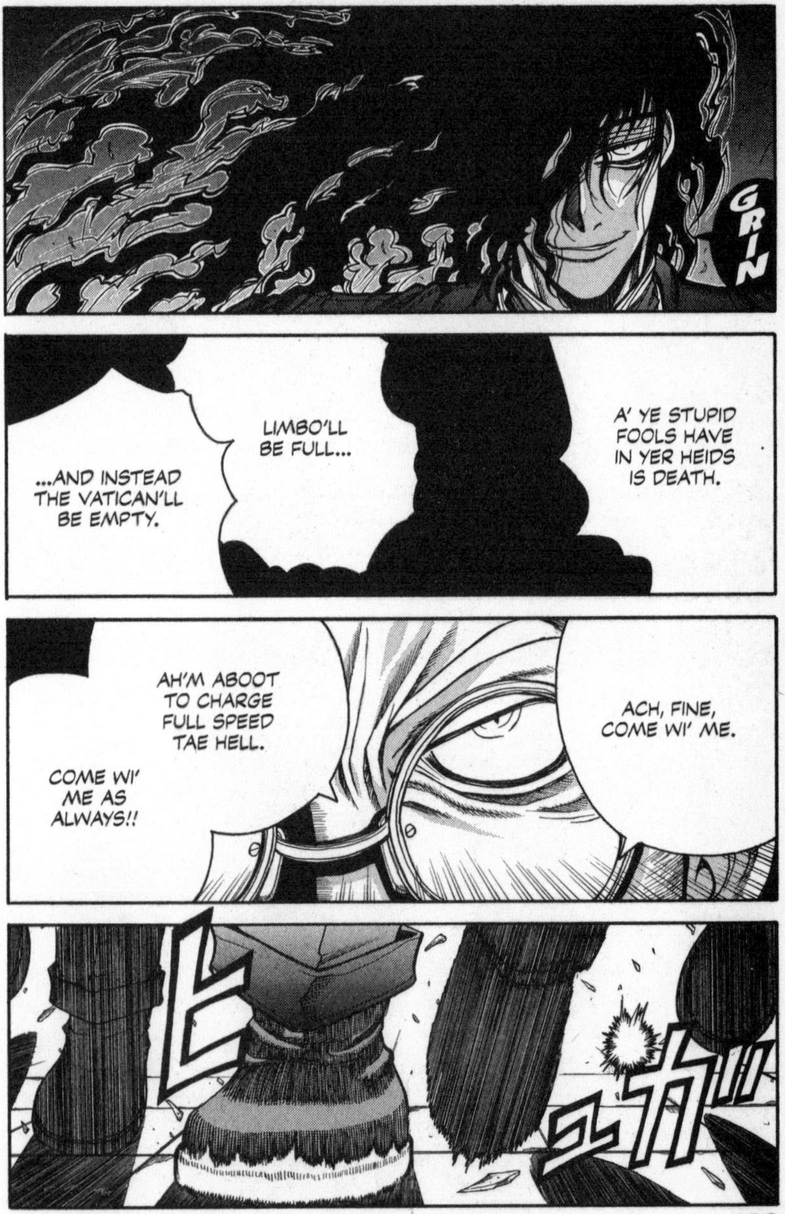
GRIN
A' YE STUPID FOOLS HAVE IN YER HEIDS IS DEATH.
LIMBO'LL BE FULL...
...AND INSTEAD THE VATICAN'LL BE EMPTY.
ACH, FINE, COME WI' ME.
AH'M ABOOT TO CHARGE FULL SPEED TAE HELL.
COME WI' ME AS ALWAYS!!

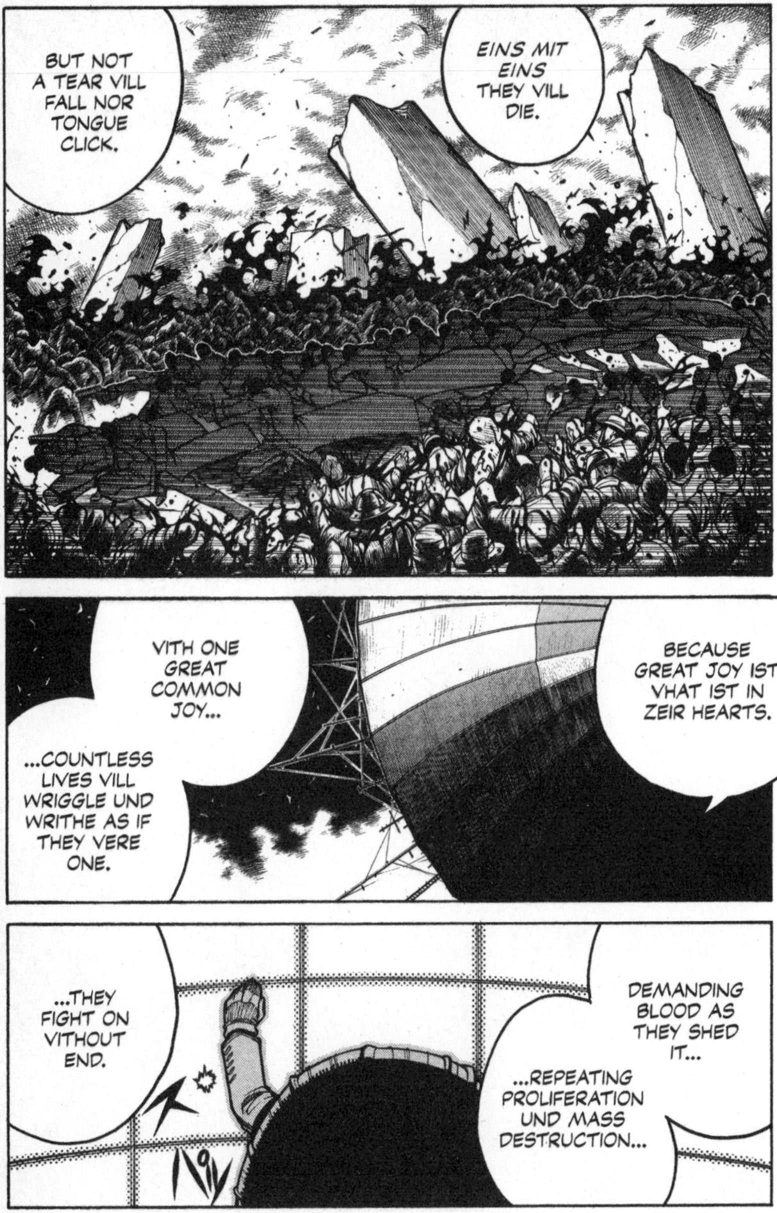
EINS MIT EINS THEY VILL DIE.
BUT NOT A TEAR VILL FALL NOR TONGUE CLICK.
BECAUSE GREAT JOY IST VHAT IST IN ZEIR HEARTS.
VITH ONE GREAT COMMON JOY...
...COUNTLESS LIVES VILL WRIGGLE UND WRITHE AS IF THEY VERE ONE.
DEMANDING BLOOD AS THEY SHED IT...
...REPEATING PROLIFERATION UND MASS DESTRUCTION...
...THEY FIGHT ON VITHOUT END.

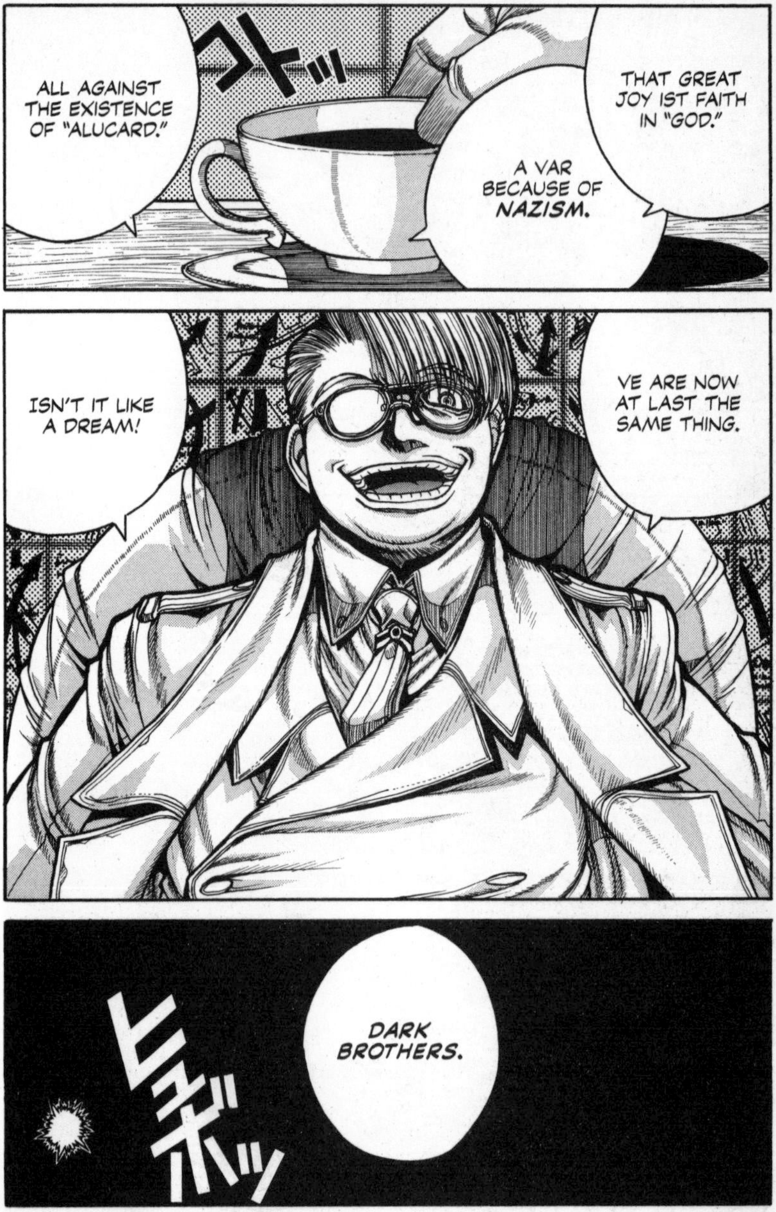
THAT GREAT JOY IST FAITH IN "GOD."
A VAR BECAUSE OF **NAZISM.**
コトッ
ALL AGAINST THE EXISTENCE OF "ALUCARD."
VE ARE NOW AT LAST THE SAME THING.
ISN'T IT LIKE A DREAM!
DARK BROTHERS.
ヒュボッ

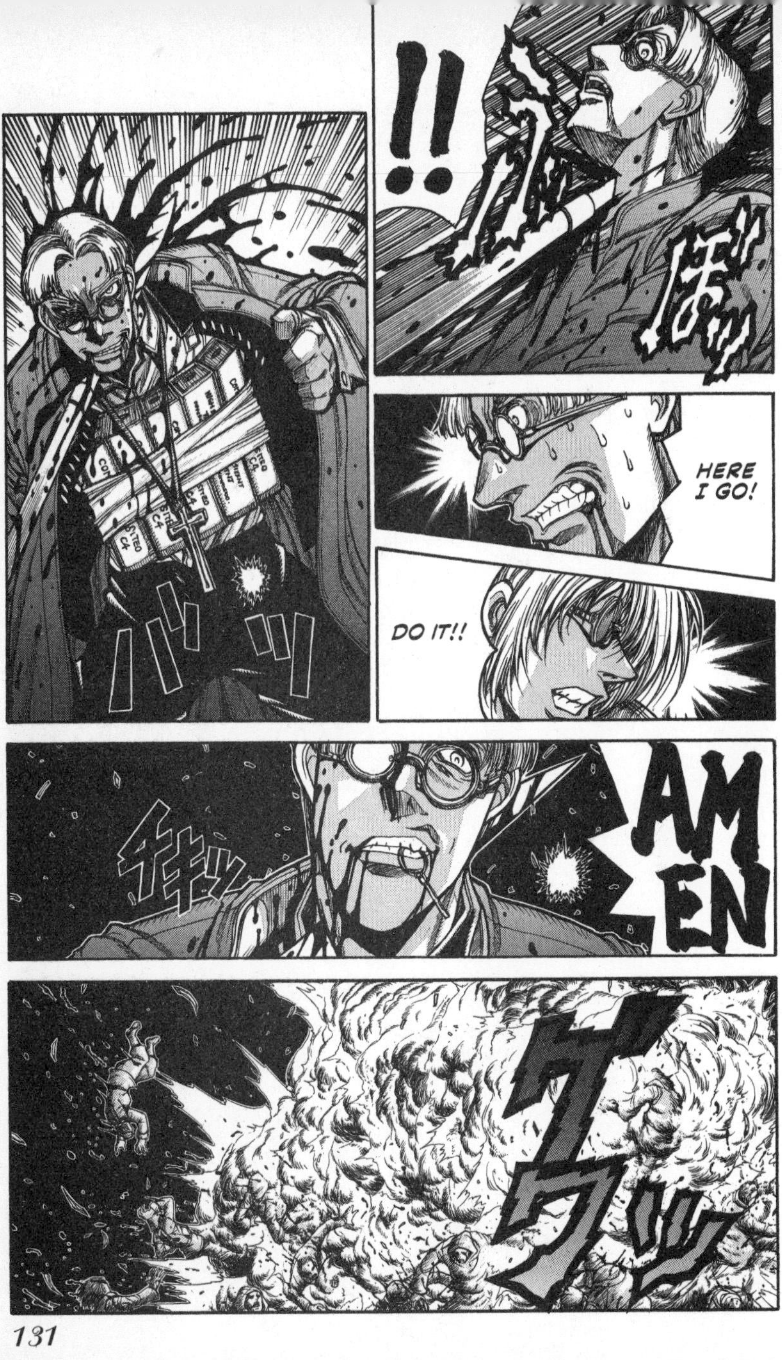
!!
HERE I GO!
DO IT!!
AMEN
チキッ

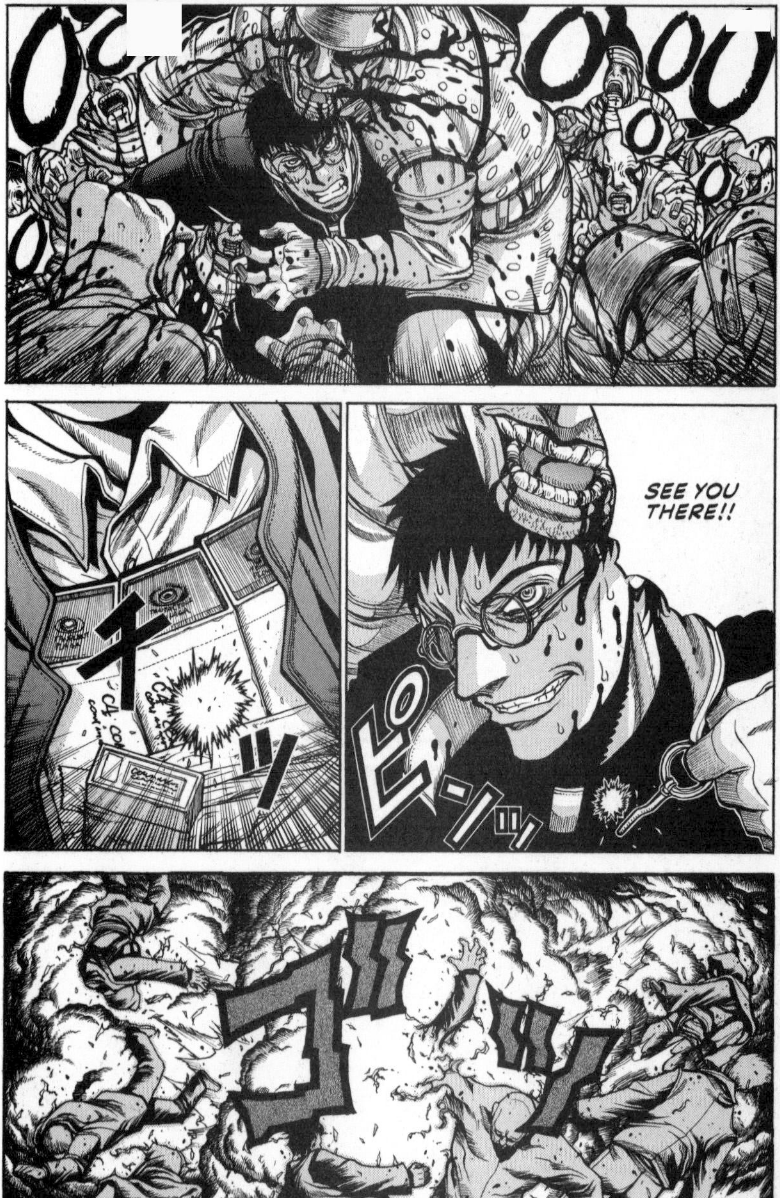
SEE YOU THERE!!

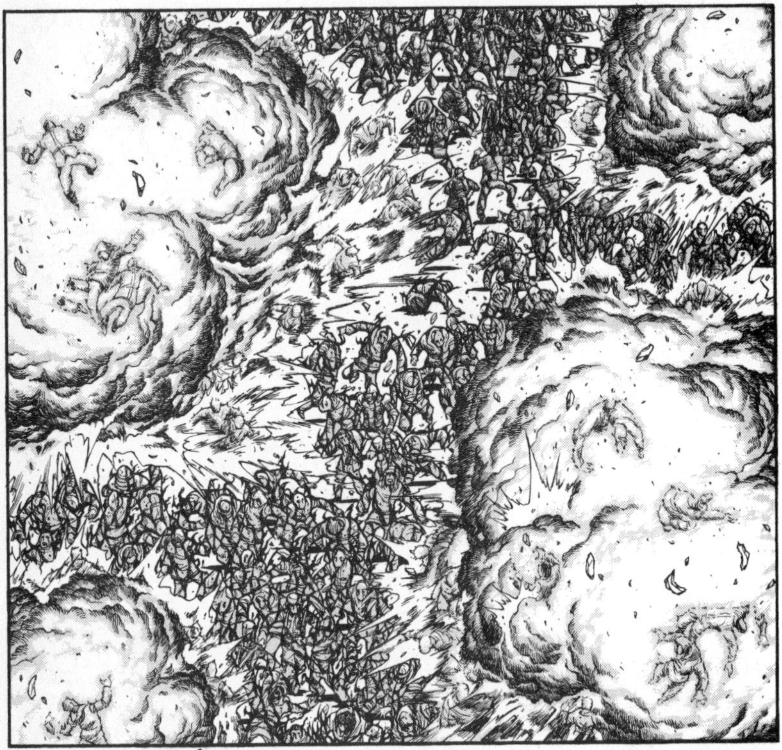

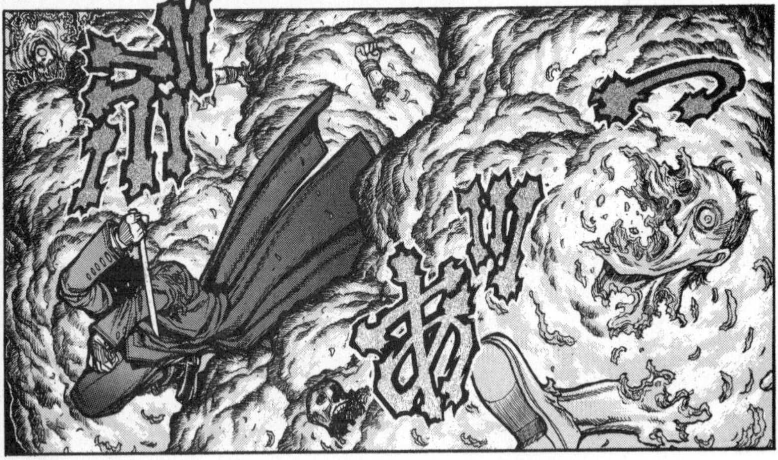

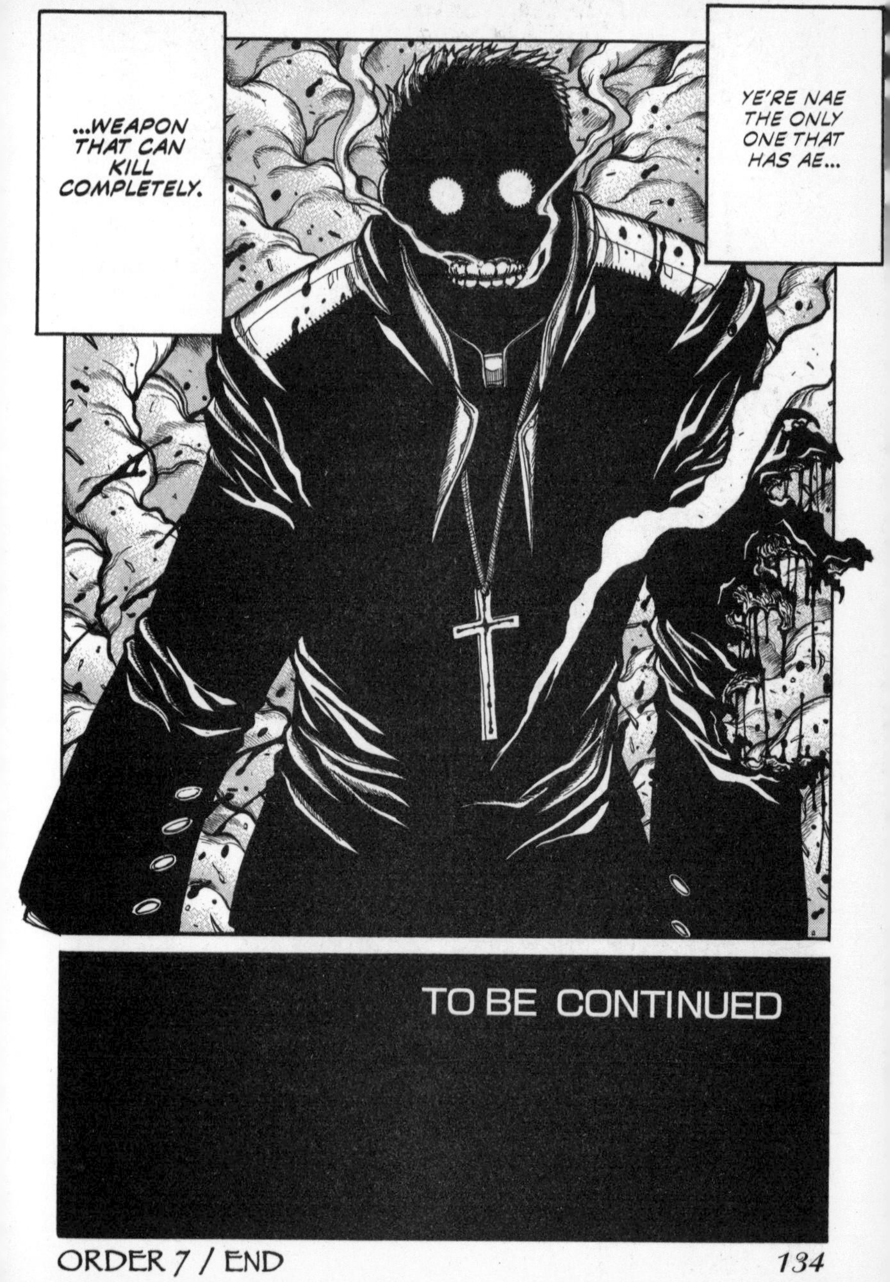
YE'RE NAE THE ONLY ONE THAT HAS AE...
...WEAPON THAT CAN KILL COMPLETELY.

TO BE CONTINUED

KKkK
KkKK

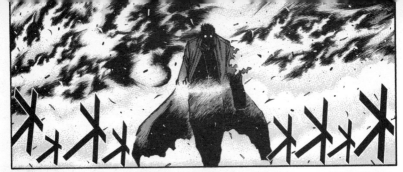

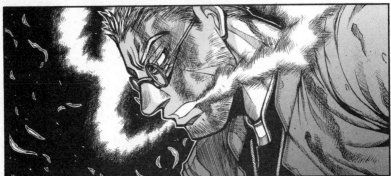

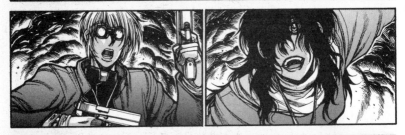

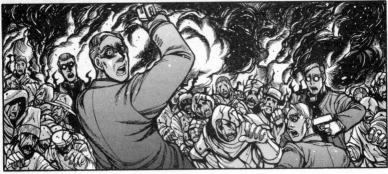

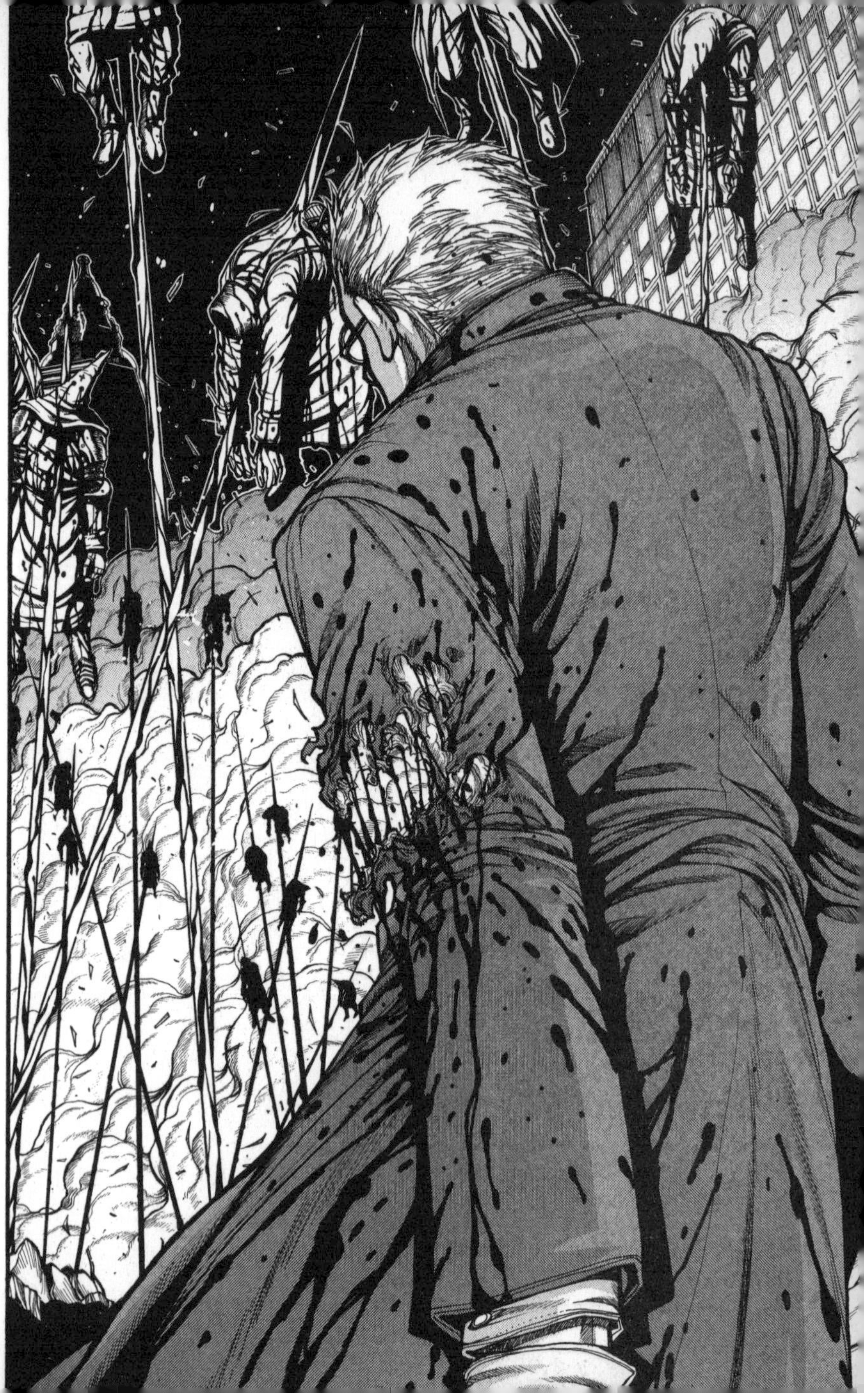

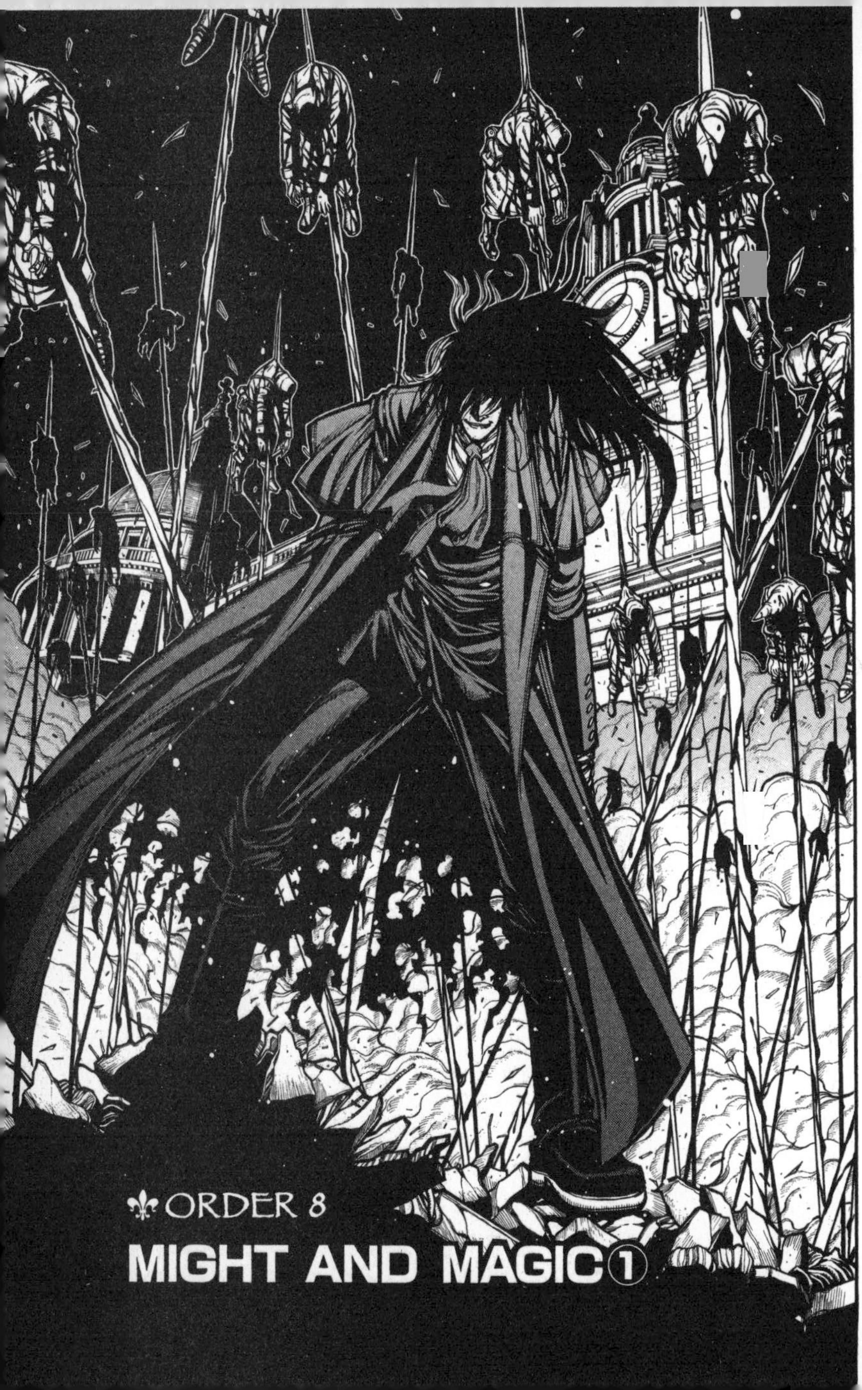
ORDER 8
MIGHT AND MAGIC ①

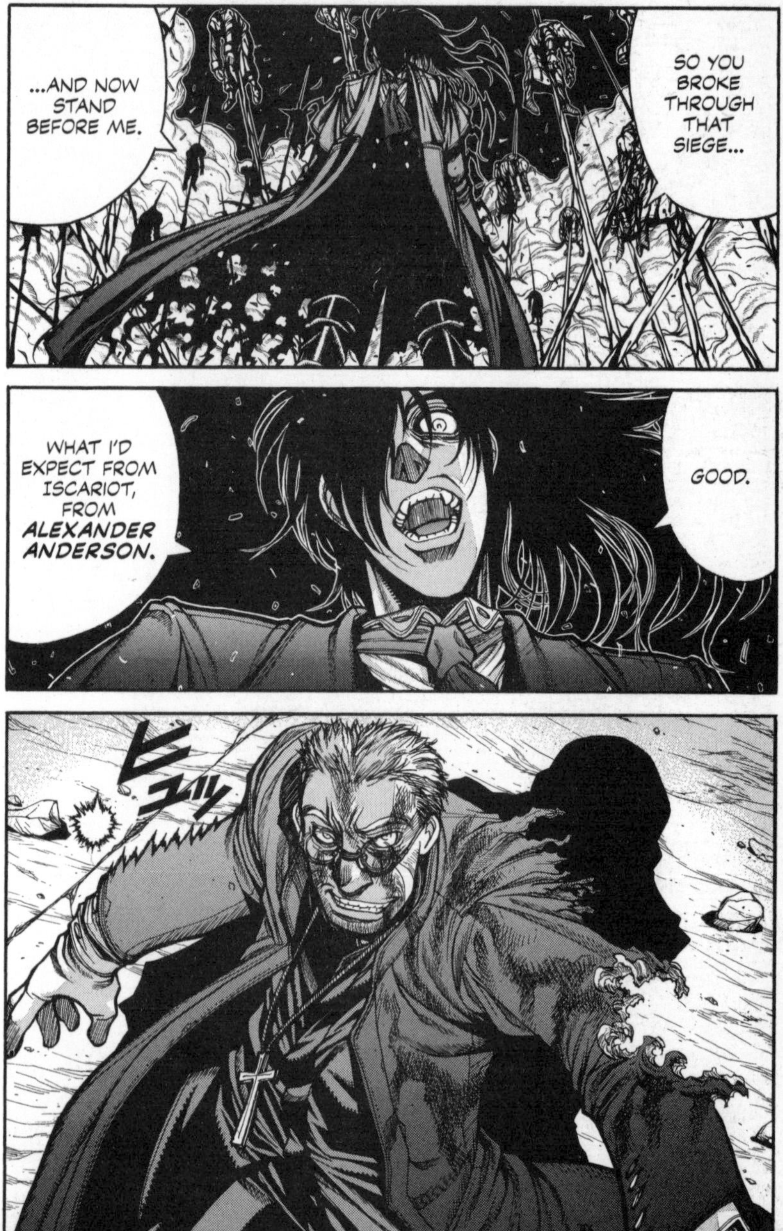
SO YOU BROKE THROUGH THAT SIEGE...
...AND NOW STAND BEFORE ME.
GOOD.
WHAT I'D EXPECT FROM ISCARIOT, FROM ALEXANDER ANDERSON.

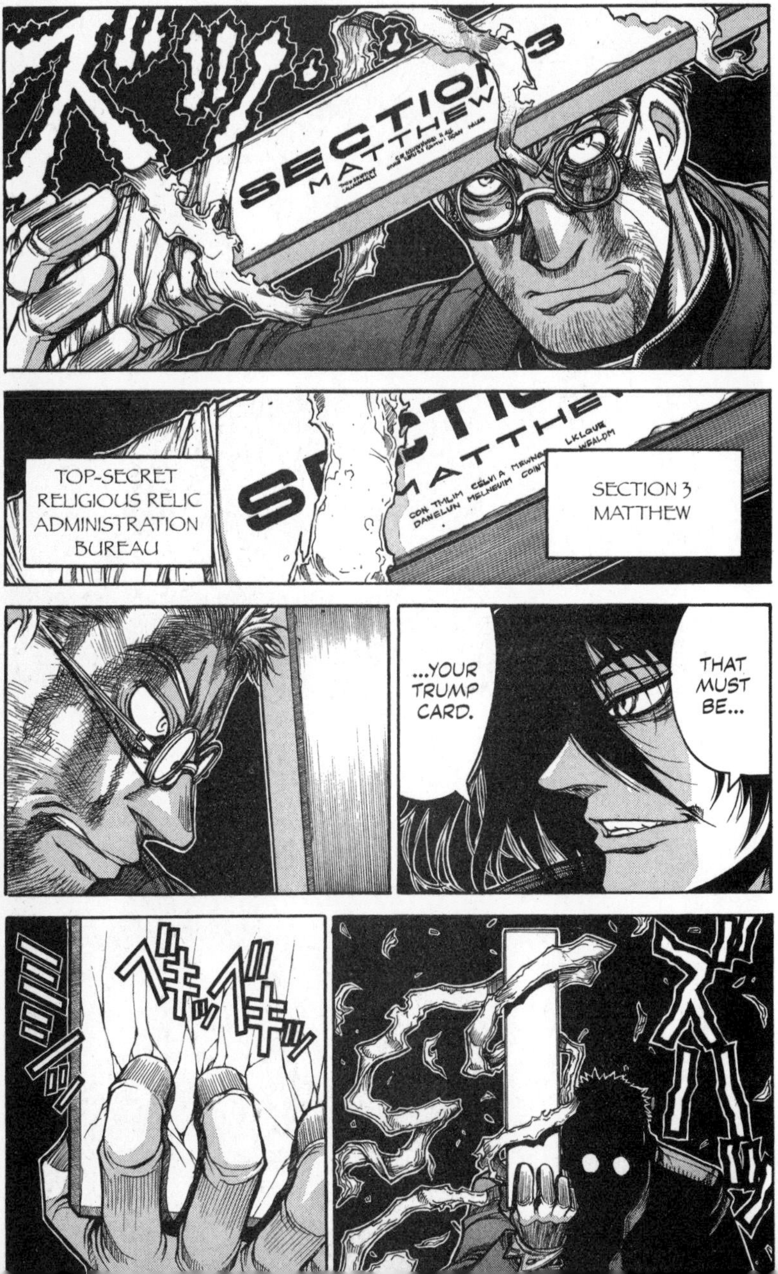
SECTION 3
MATTHEW
SECTION 3 MATTHEW
TOP-SECRET RELIGIOUS RELIC ADMINISTRATION BUREAU
THAT MUST BE...
...YOUR TRUMP CARD.
ベキッベキッ
ミシッ

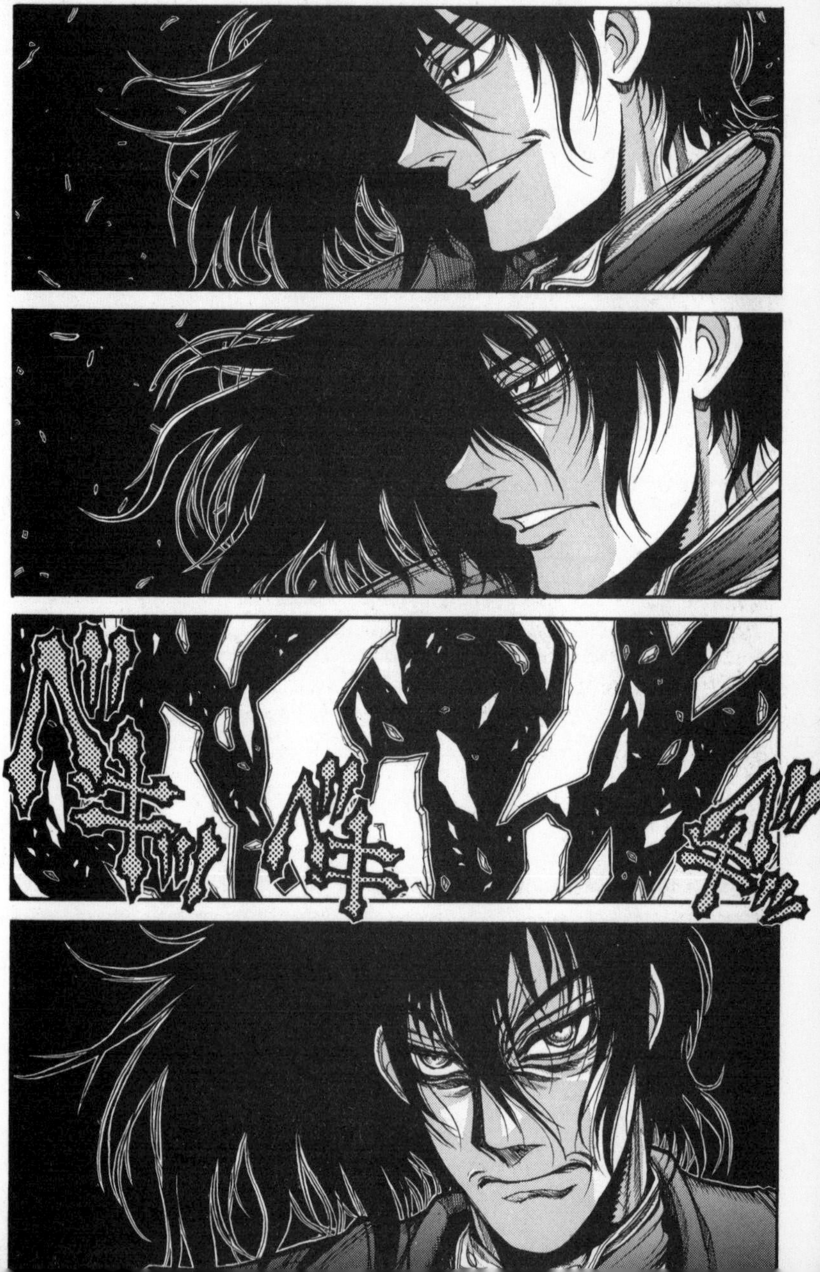

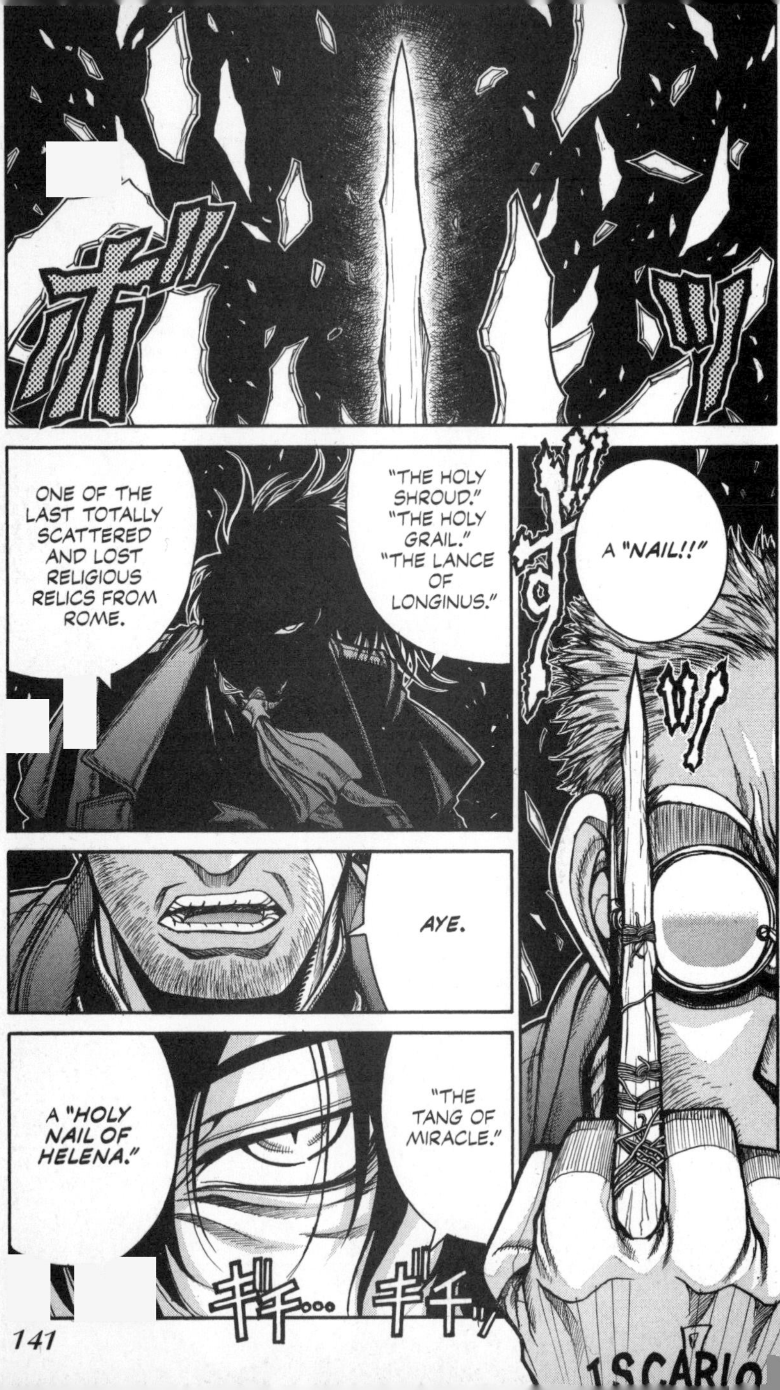
A "NAIL!!"
ISCARIO
"THE HOLY SHROUD." "THE HOLY GRAIL." "THE LANCE OF LONGINUS."
ONE OF THE LAST TOTALLY SCATTERED AND LOST RELIGIOUS RELICS FROM ROME.
AYE.
"THE TANG OF MIRACLE."
A "HOLY NAIL OF HELENA."
ギチ... ギチッ

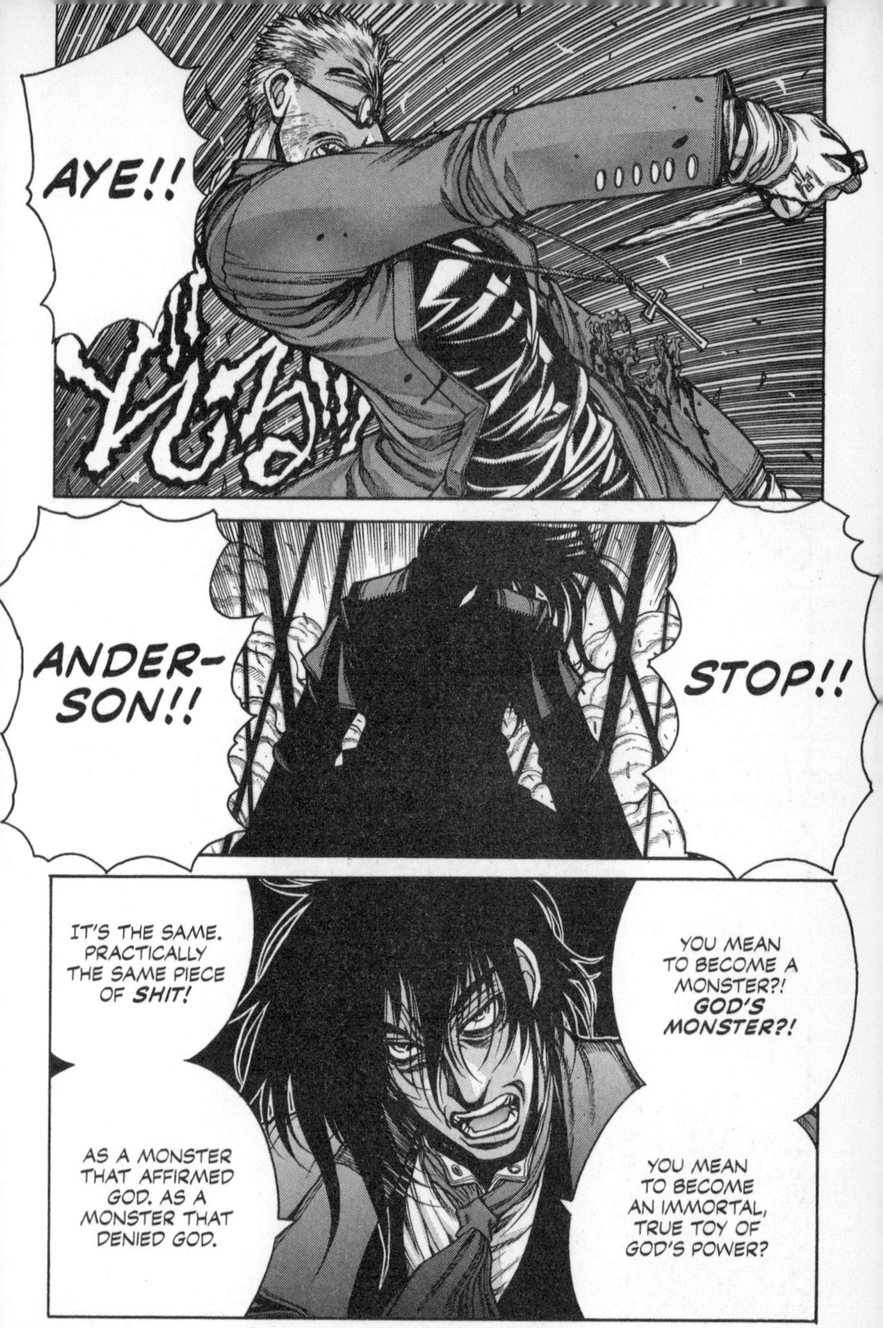
AYE!!
STOP!!
ANDER-SON!!
YOU MEAN TO BECOME A MONSTER?! **GOD'S MONSTER?!**
IT'S THE SAME. PRACTICALLY THE SAME PIECE OF ***SHIT!***
YOU MEAN TO BECOME AN IMMORTAL, TRUE TOY OF GOD'S POWER?
AS A MONSTER THAT AFFIRMED GOD. AS A MONSTER THAT DENIED GOD.

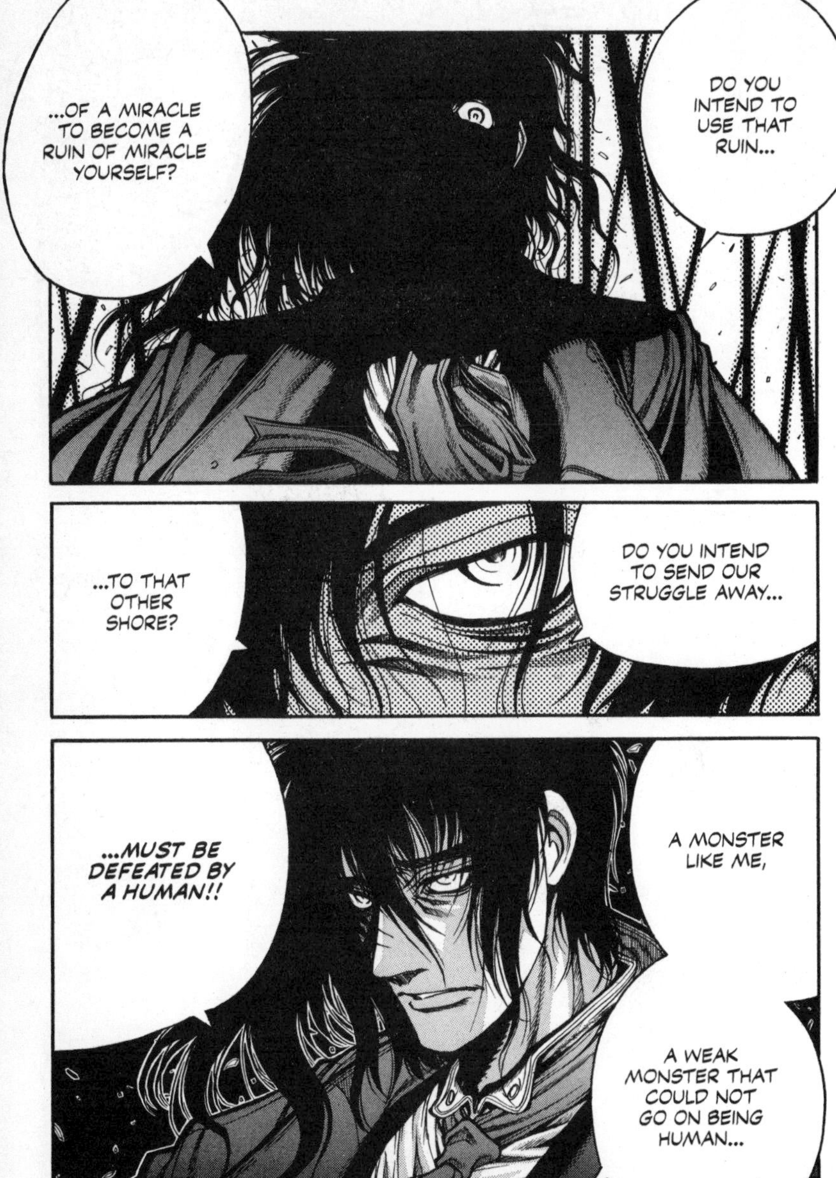
DO YOU INTEND TO USE THAT RUIN...
...OF A MIRACLE TO BECOME A RUIN OF MIRACLE YOURSELF?
DO YOU INTEND TO SEND OUR STRUGGLE AWAY...
...TO THAT OTHER SHORE?
A MONSTER LIKE ME,
A WEAK MONSTER THAT COULD NOT GO ON BEING HUMAN...
...MUST BE DEFEATED BY A HUMAN!!

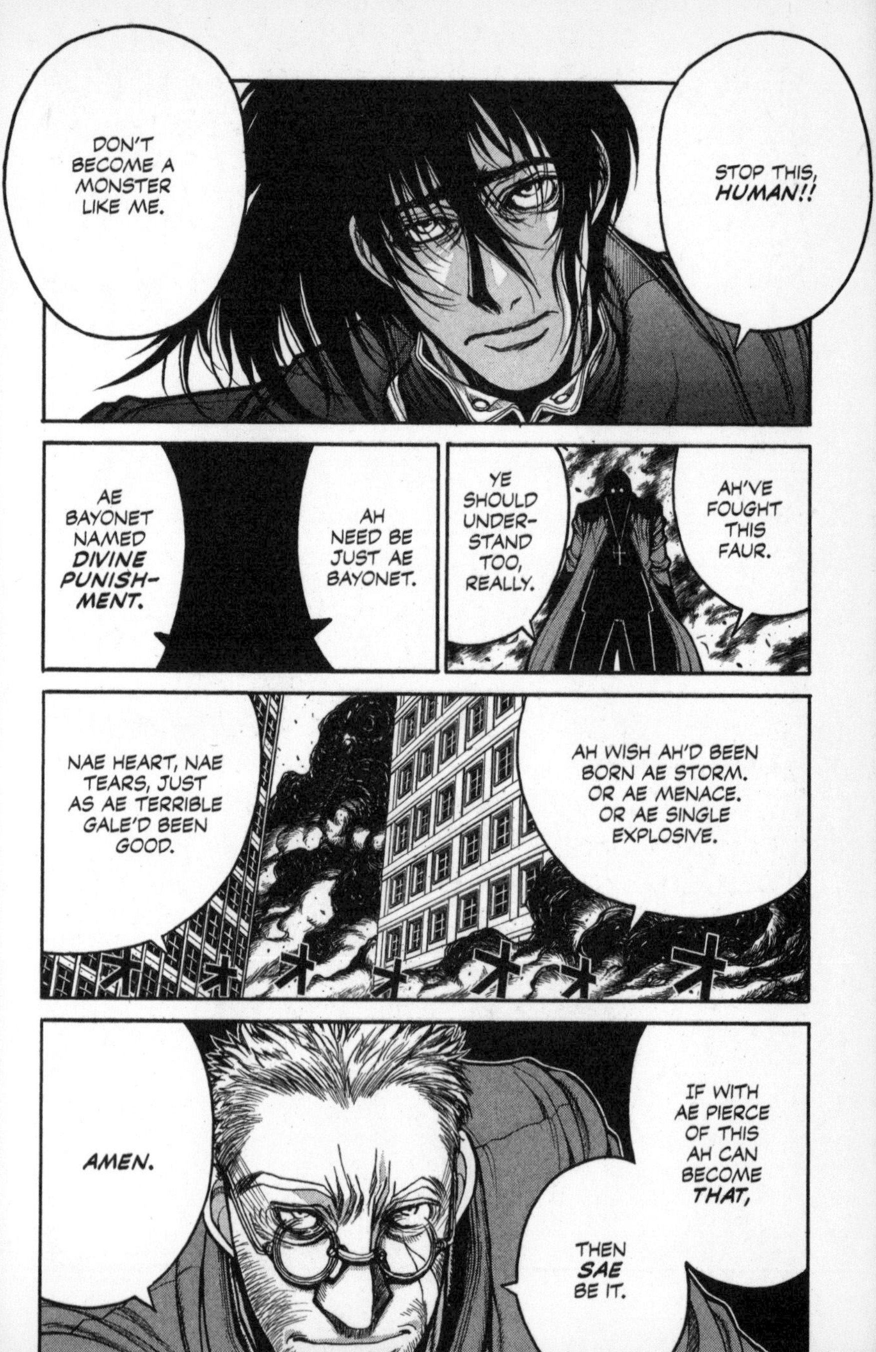
STOP THIS, HUMAN!!
DON'T BECOME A MONSTER LIKE ME.
AH'VE FOUGHT THIS FAUR.
YE SHOULD UNDER-STAND TOO, REALLY.
AH NEED BE JUST AE BAYONET.
AE BAYONET NAMED DIVINE PUNISH-MENT.
AH WISH AH'D BEEN BORN AE STORM. OR AE MENACE. OR AE SINGLE EXPLOSIVE.
NAE HEART, NAE TEARS, JUST AS AE TERRIBLE GALE'D BEEN GOOD.
IF WITH AE PIERCE OF THIS AH CAN BECOME THAT,
THEN SAE BE IT.
AMEN.

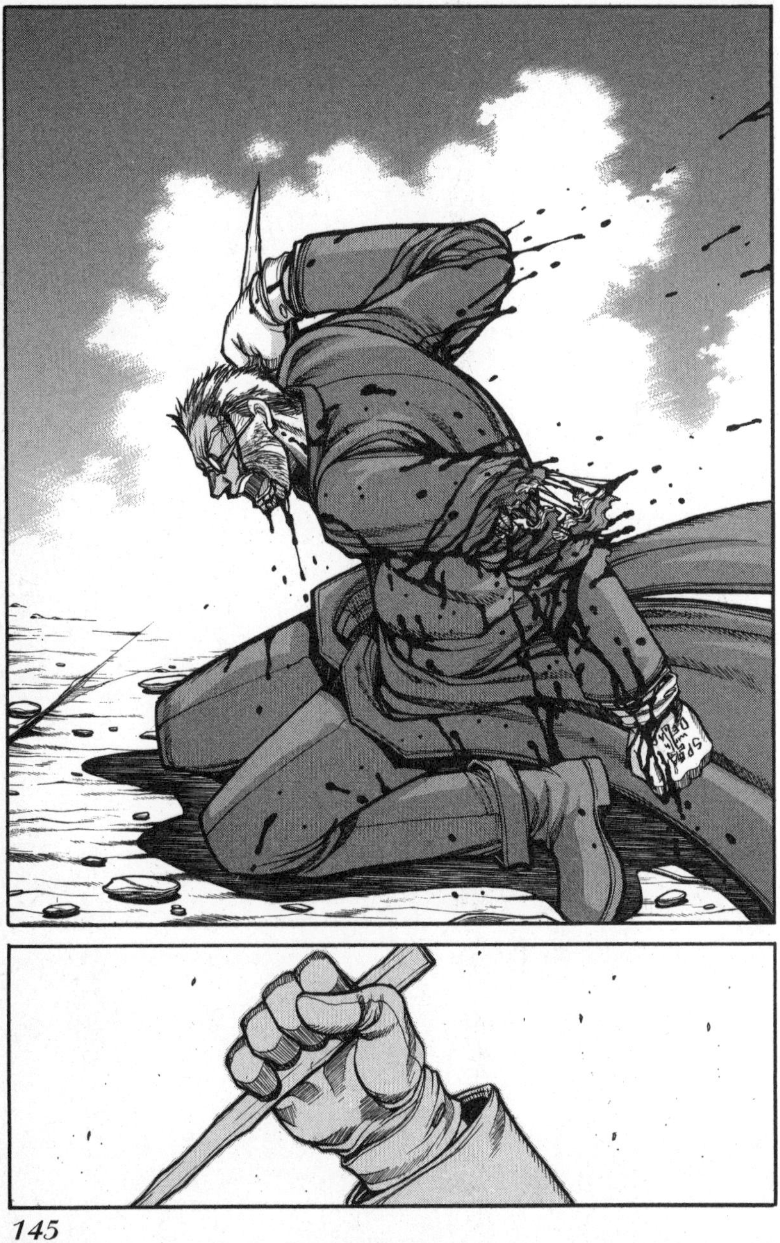

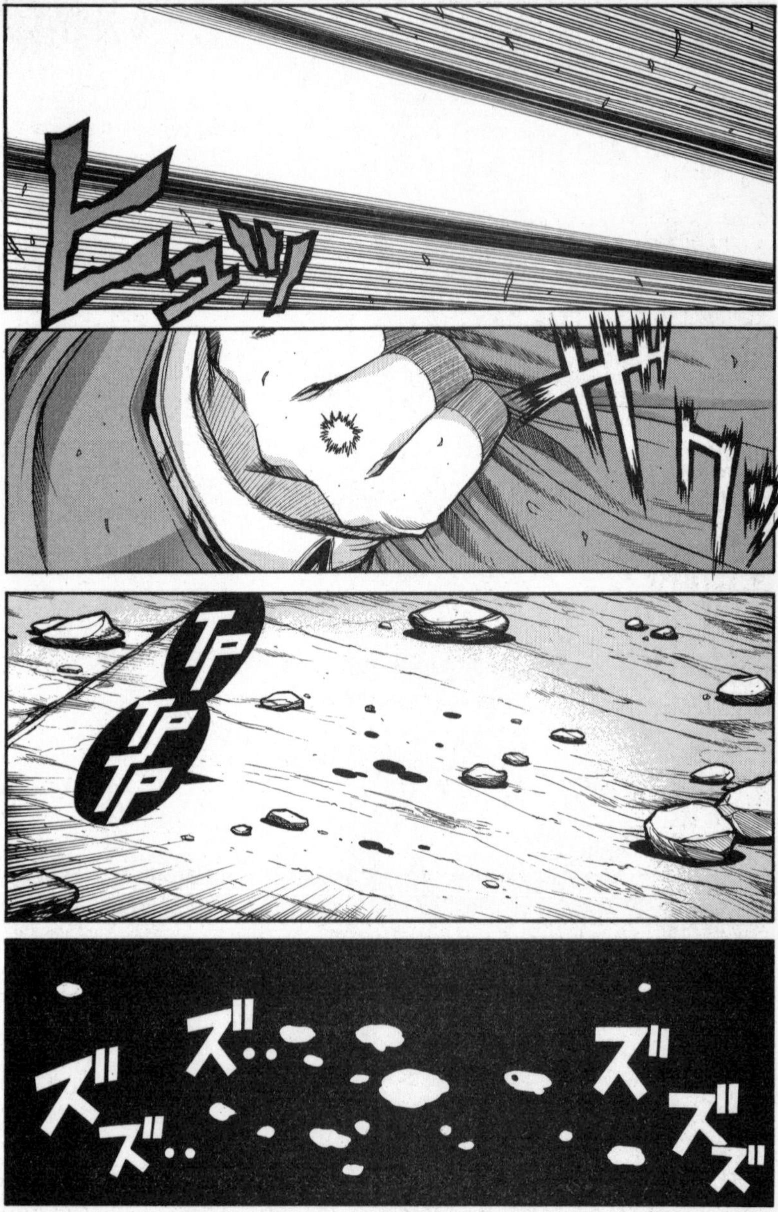
ヒュッ
ザクッ
TP TP TP
ズズズ
ズ‥ ズ‥
ズズ‥

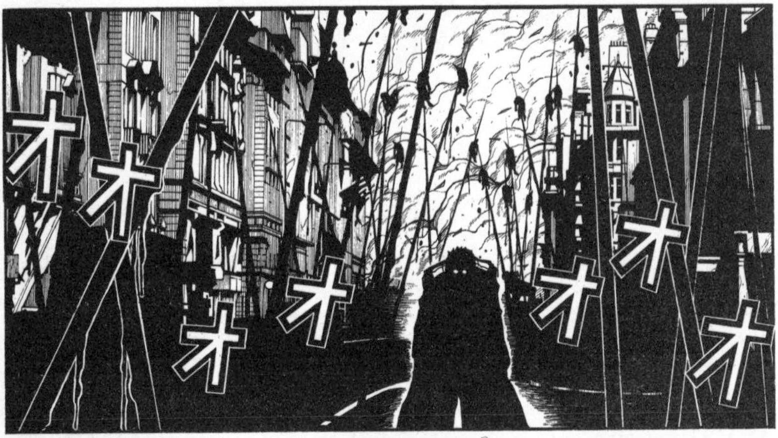
オオオ
オオオオ
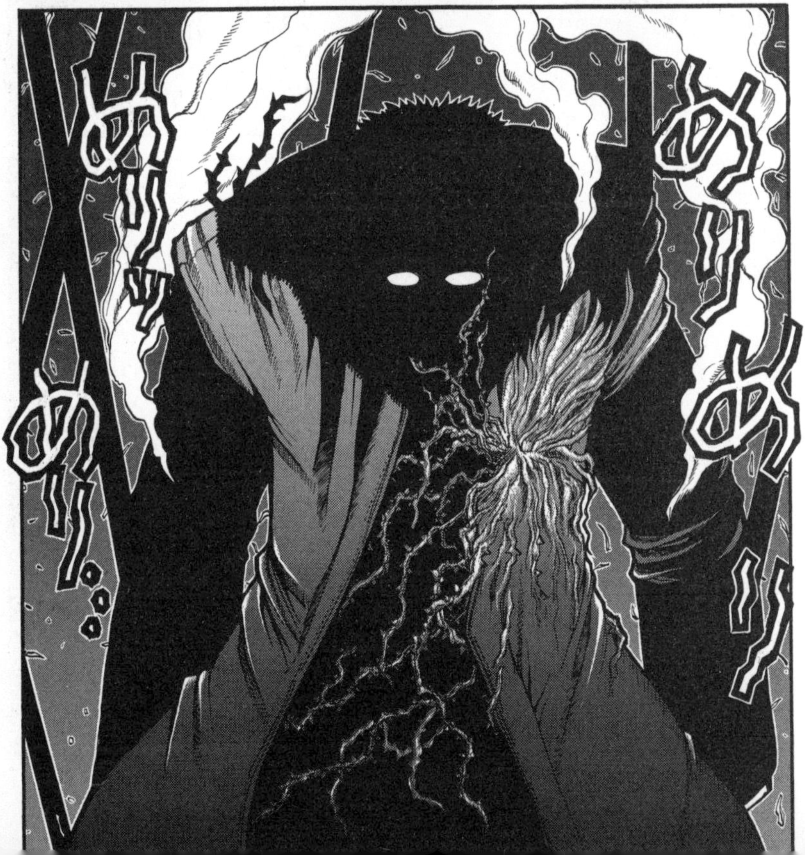
めりめりッ
めりッ
めりー…

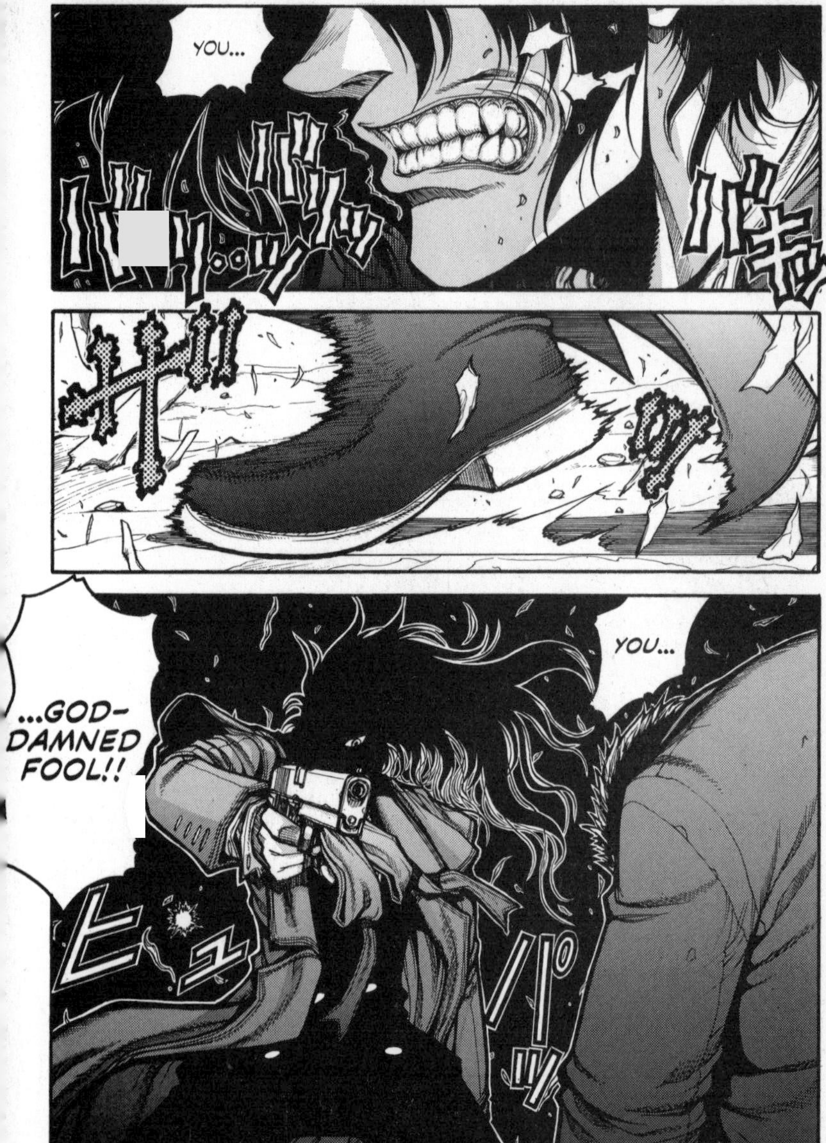
YOU...
YOU...
...GOD-DAMNED FOOL!!

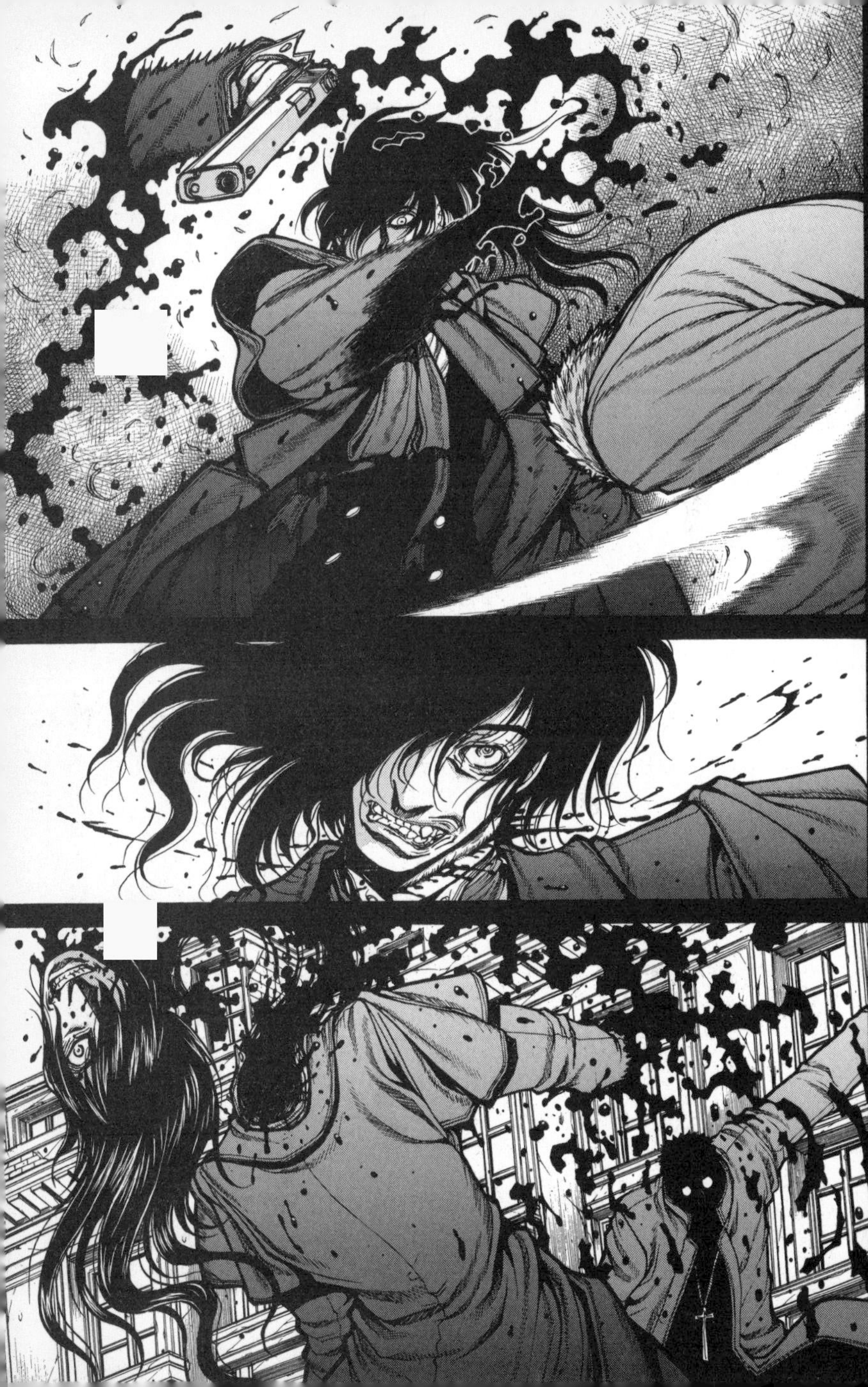

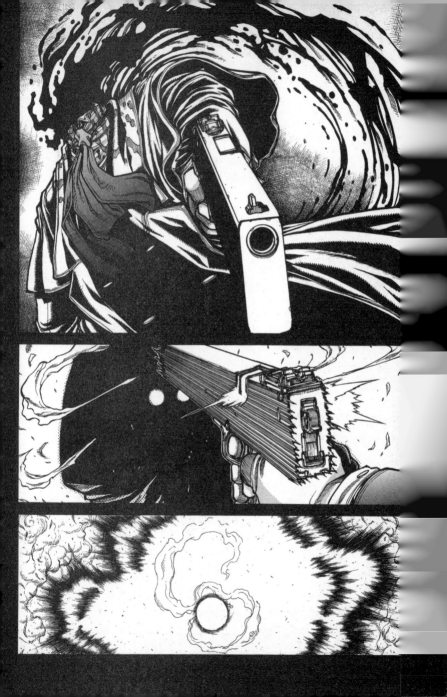

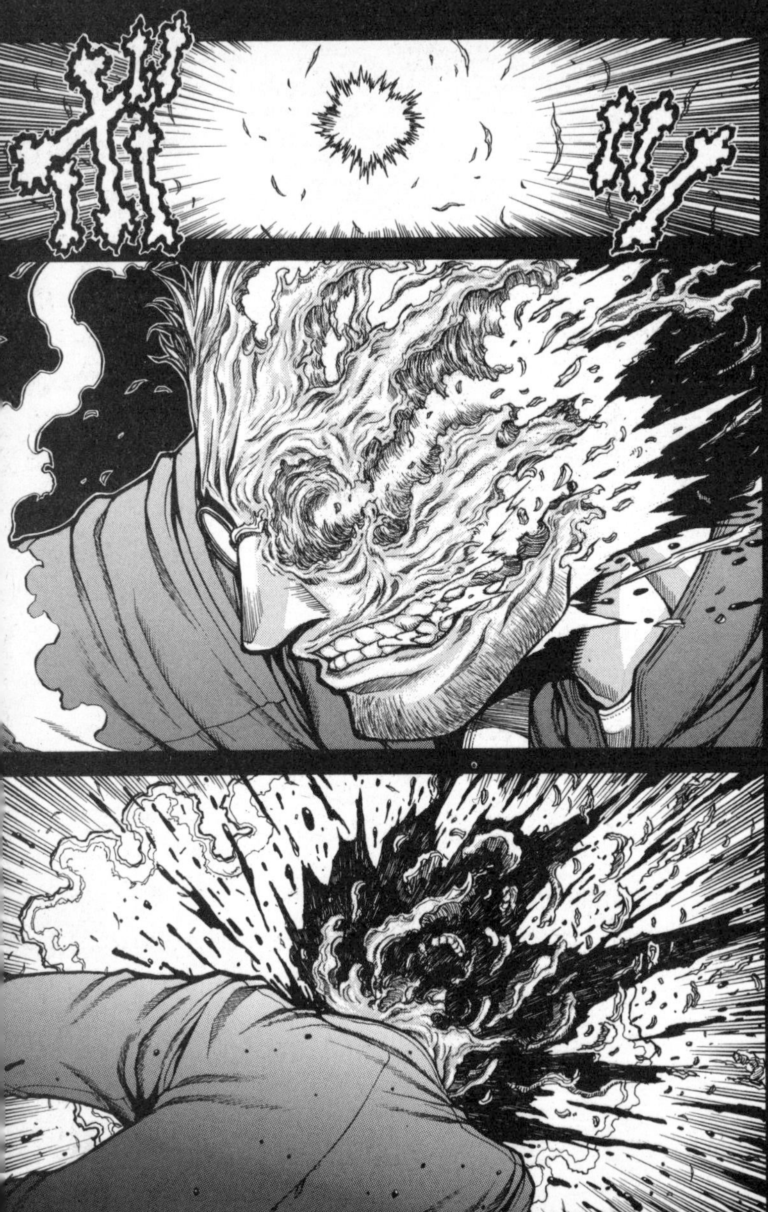

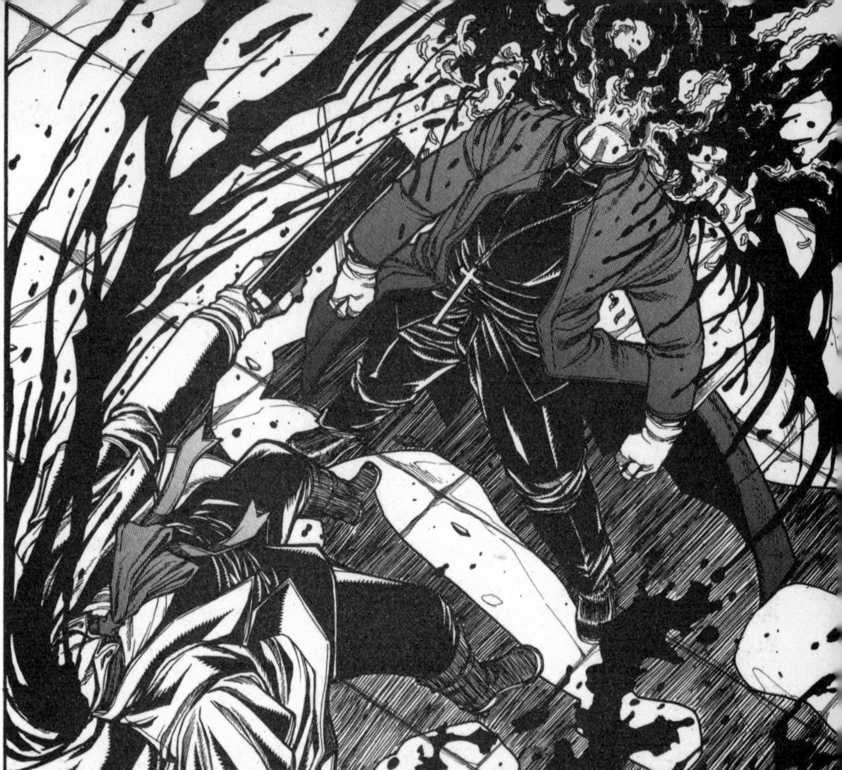
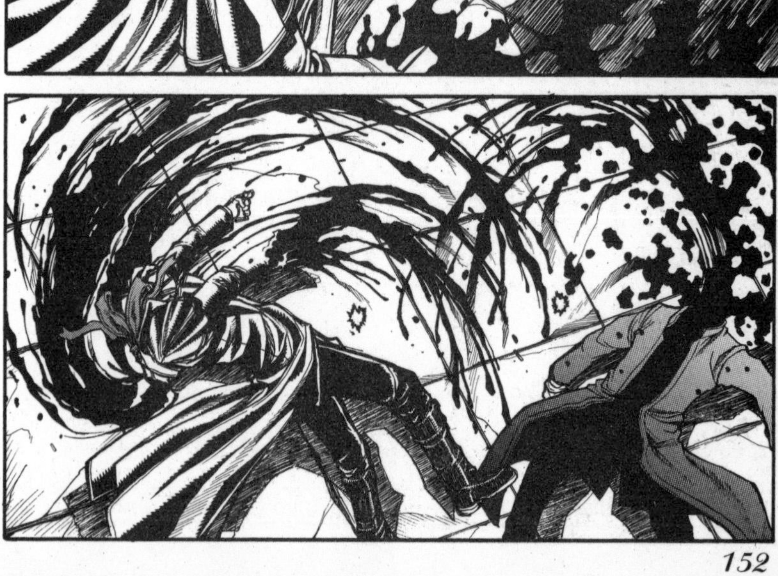

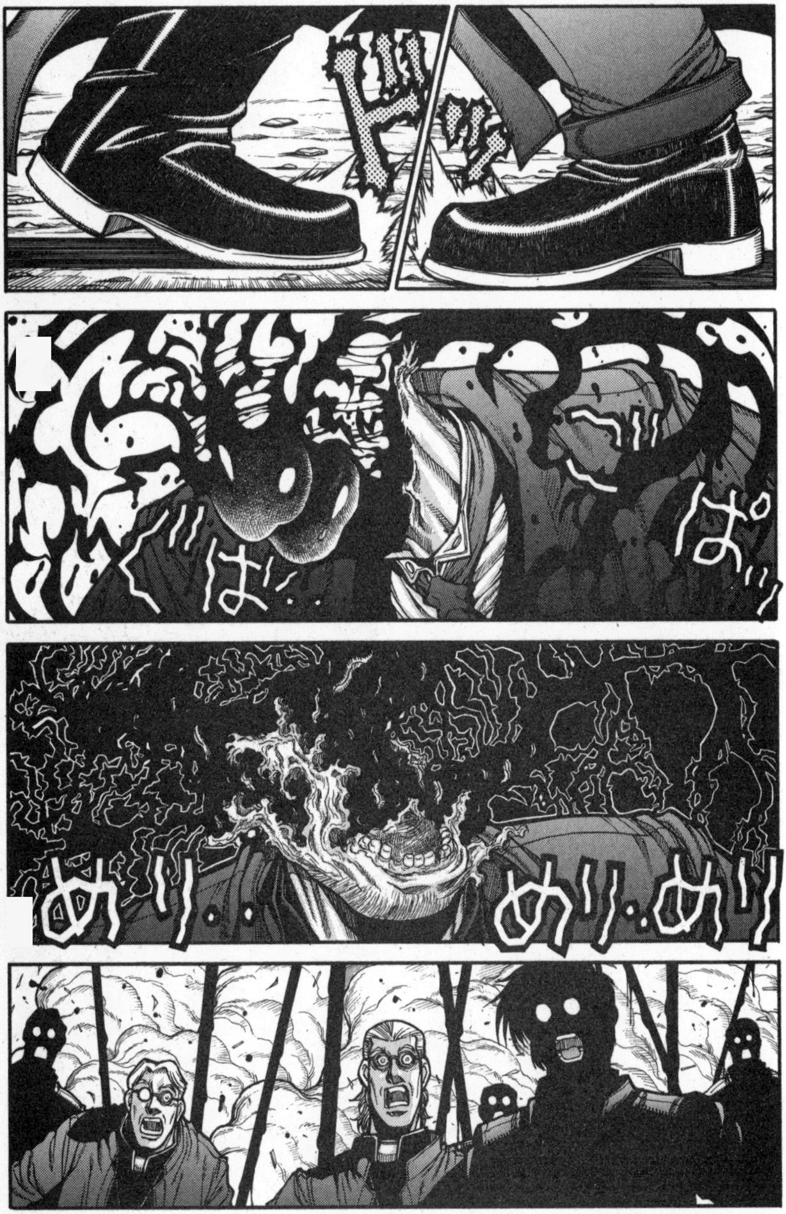
ぱッ
めり・めり
めり・・

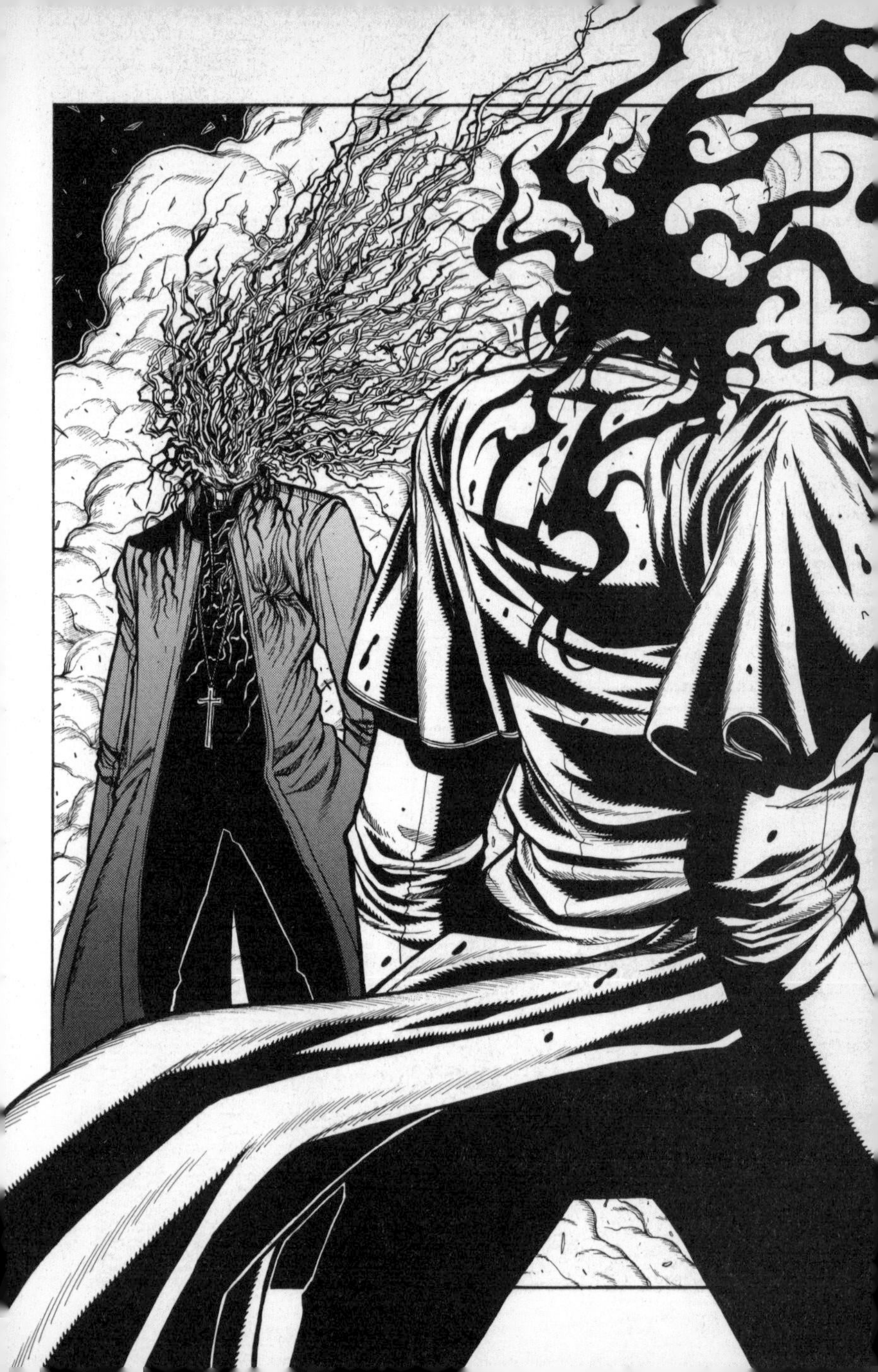

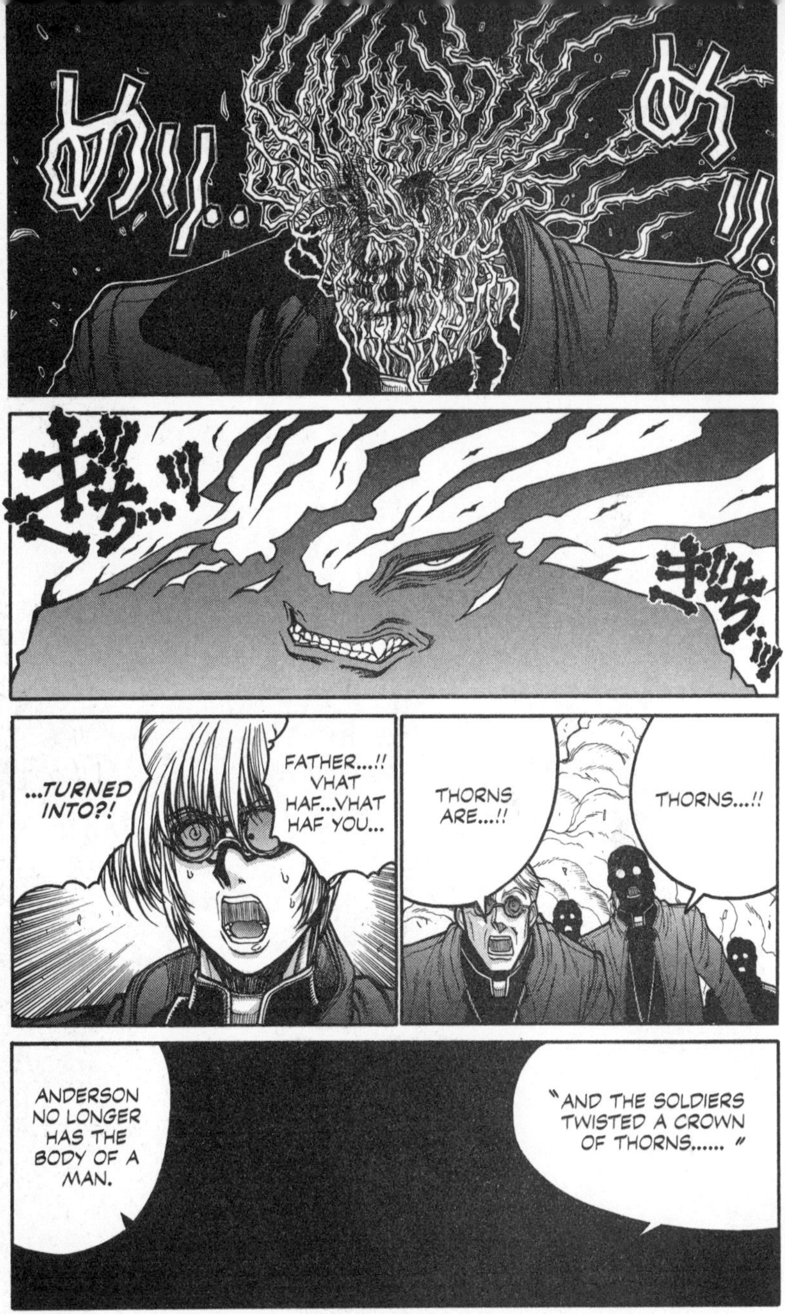

めり..
めり!!.
ぎち...!!
ぎち...!!
THORNS...!!
THORNS ARE...!!
FATHER...!! VHAT HAF...VHAT HAF YOU...
...TURNED INTO?!
"AND THE SOLDIERS TWISTED A CROWN OF THORNS......"
ANDERSON NO LONGER HAS THE BODY OF A MAN.

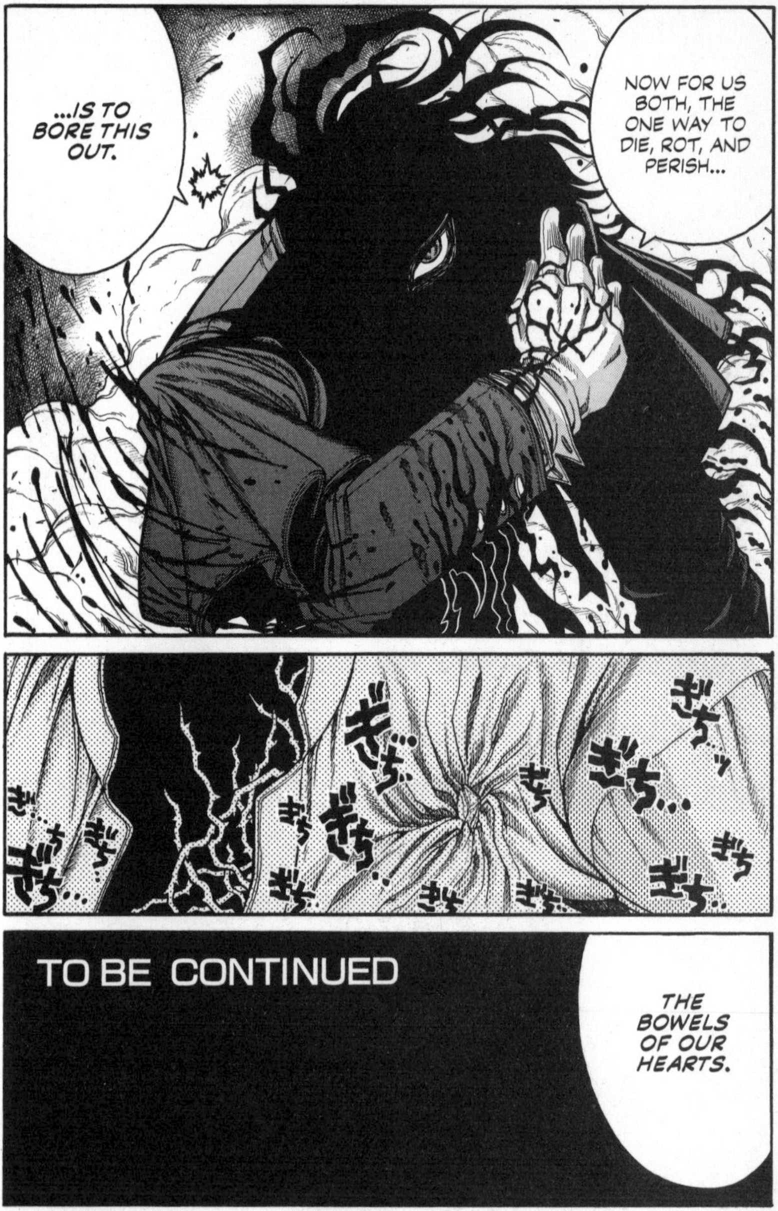
NOW FOR US BOTH, THE ONE WAY TO DIE, ROT, AND PERISH...
...IS TO BORE THIS OUT.
ぎち…ッ
ぎち…
ぎち
ぎち…
ぎぢ
ぎち
ぎち…
THE BOWELS OF OUR HEARTS.
TO BE CONTINUED

ORDER 9

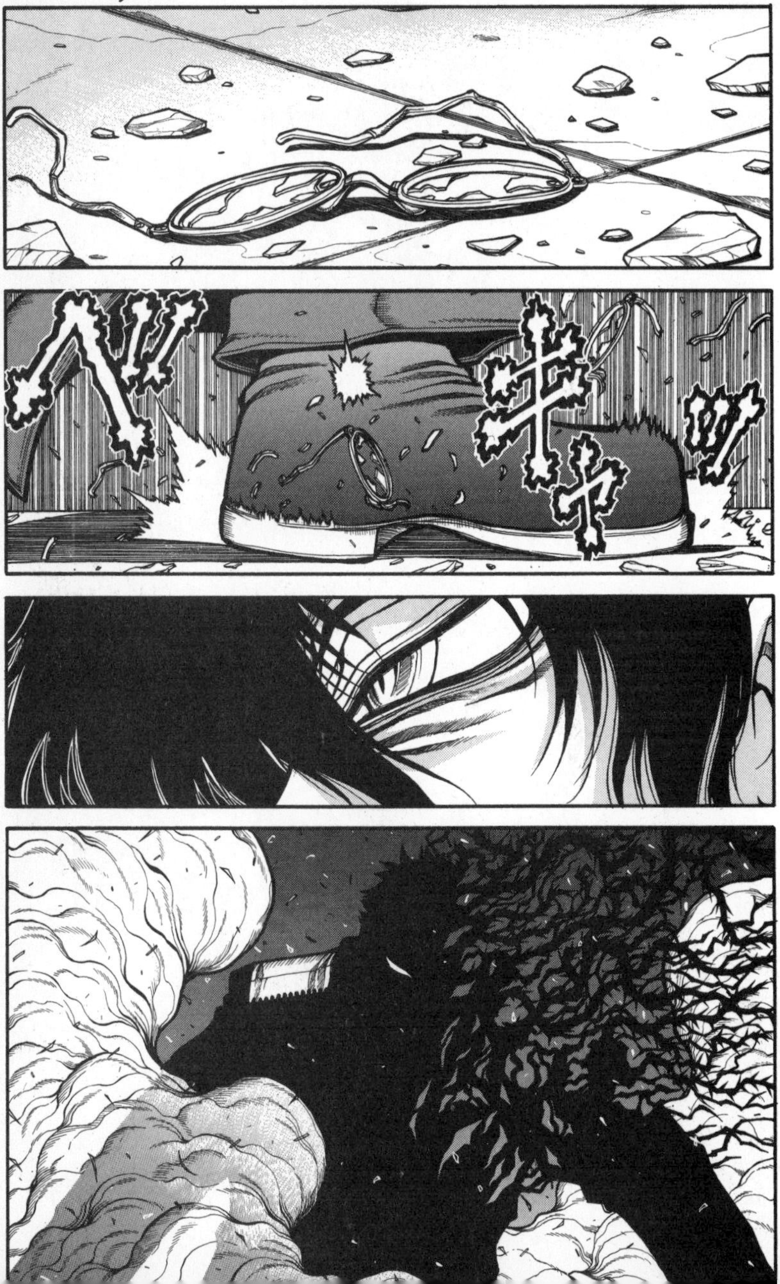

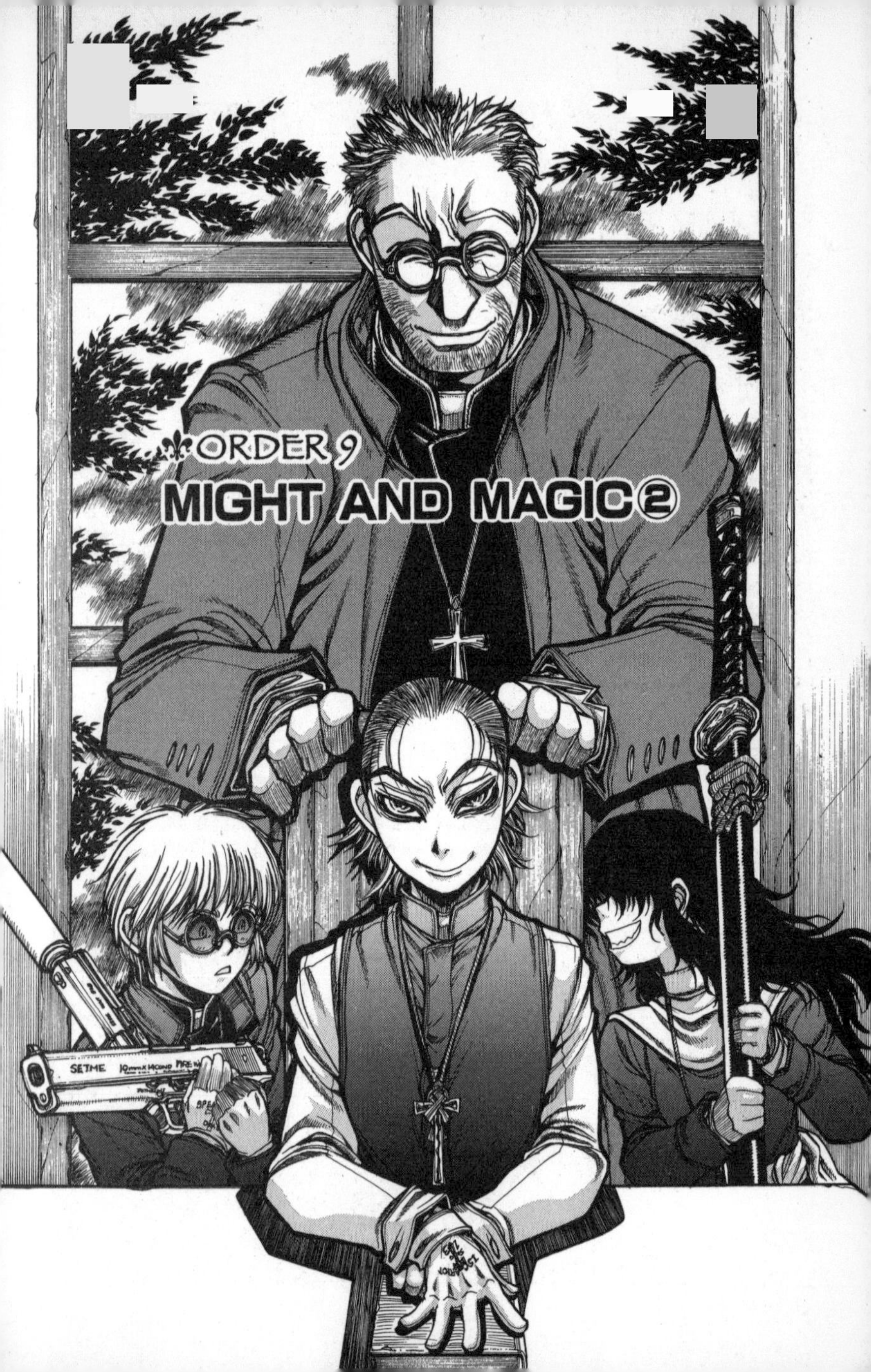
ORDER 9
MIGHT AND MAGIC ②

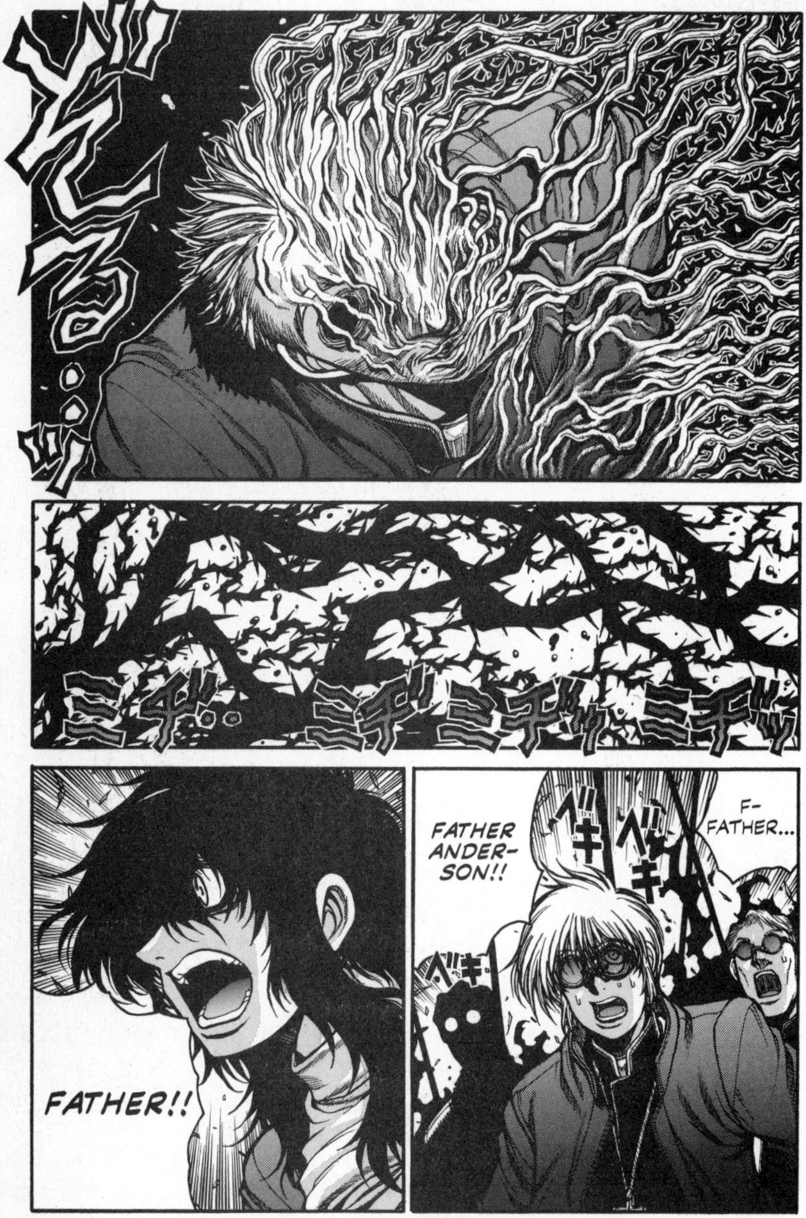
F-
FATHER...
FATHER
ANDER-
SON!!
FATHER!!

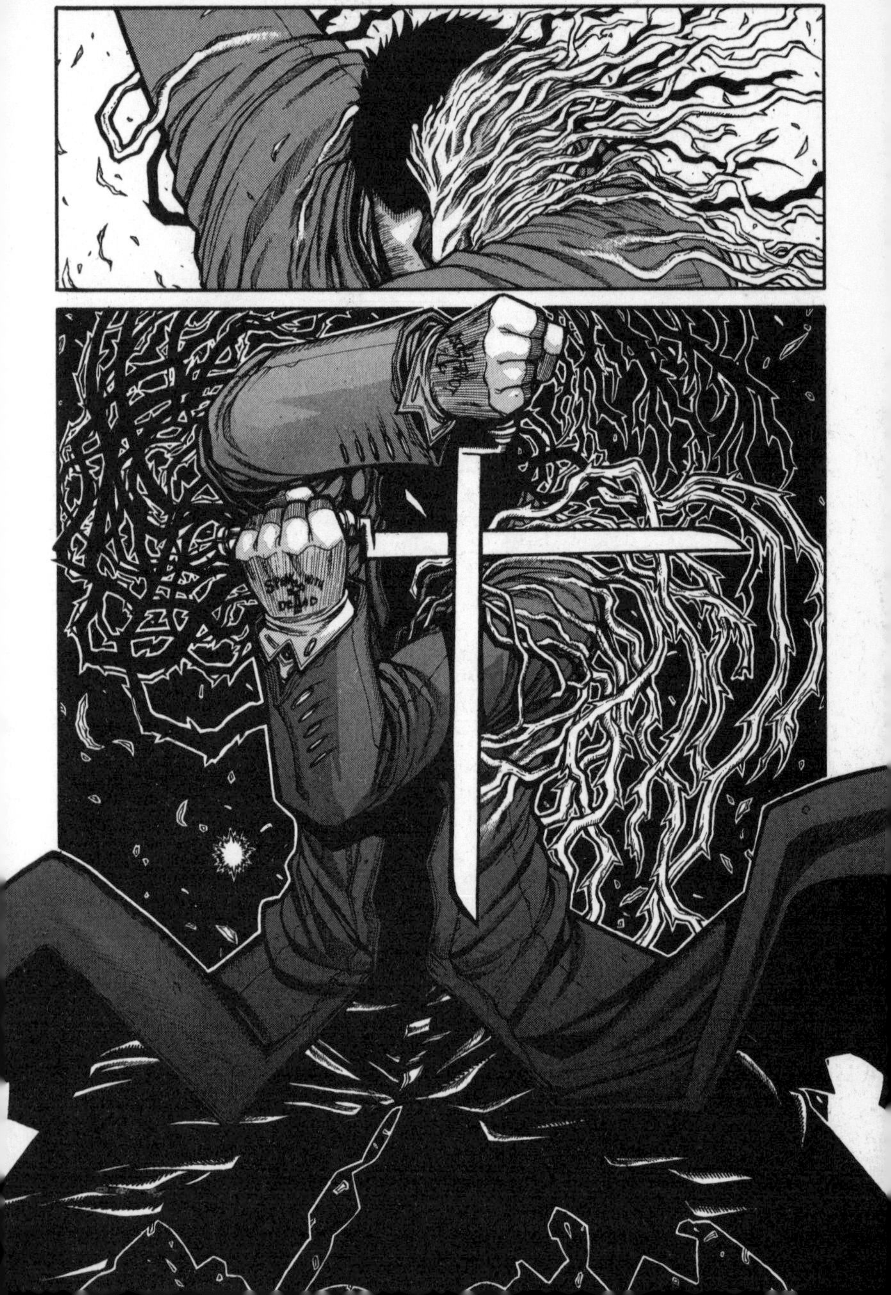

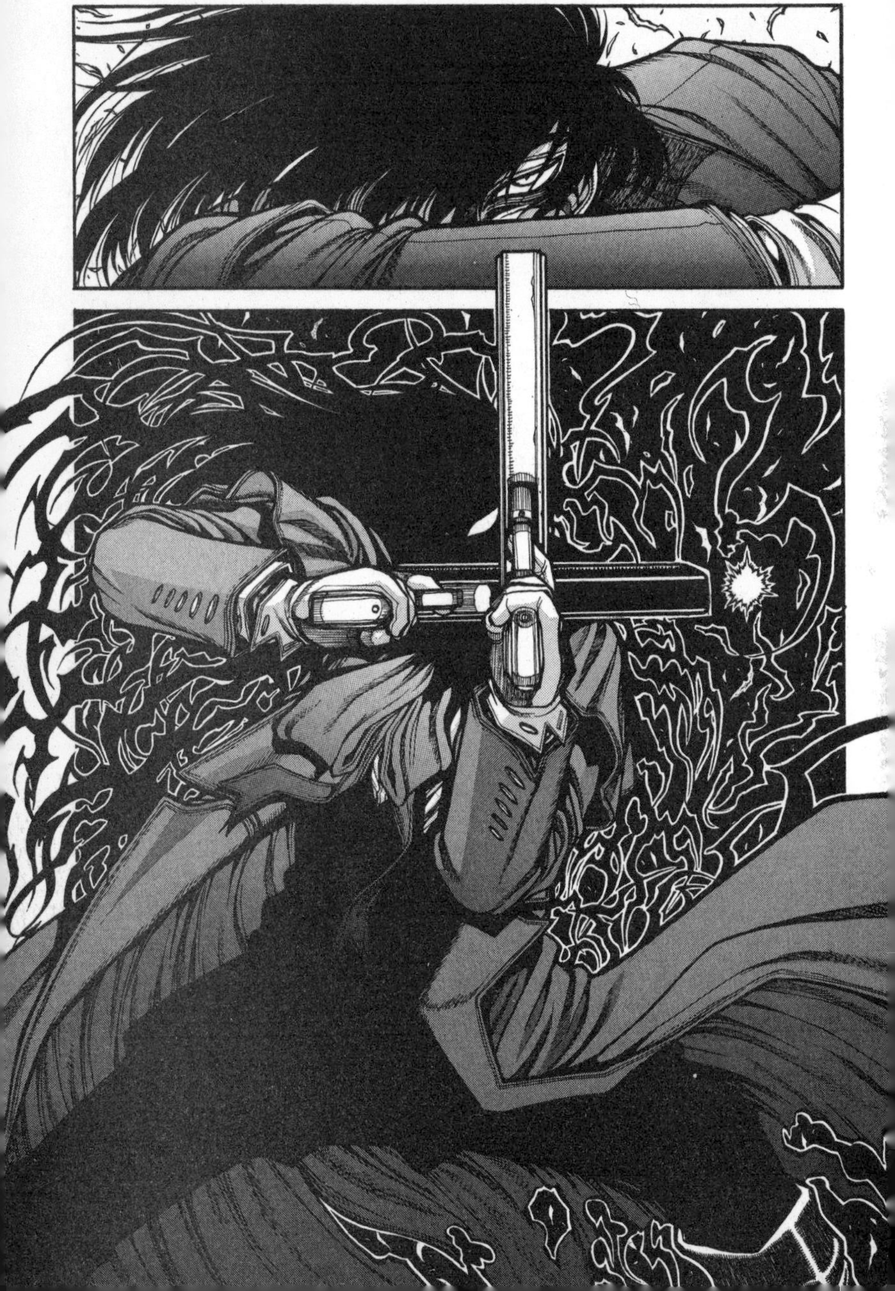

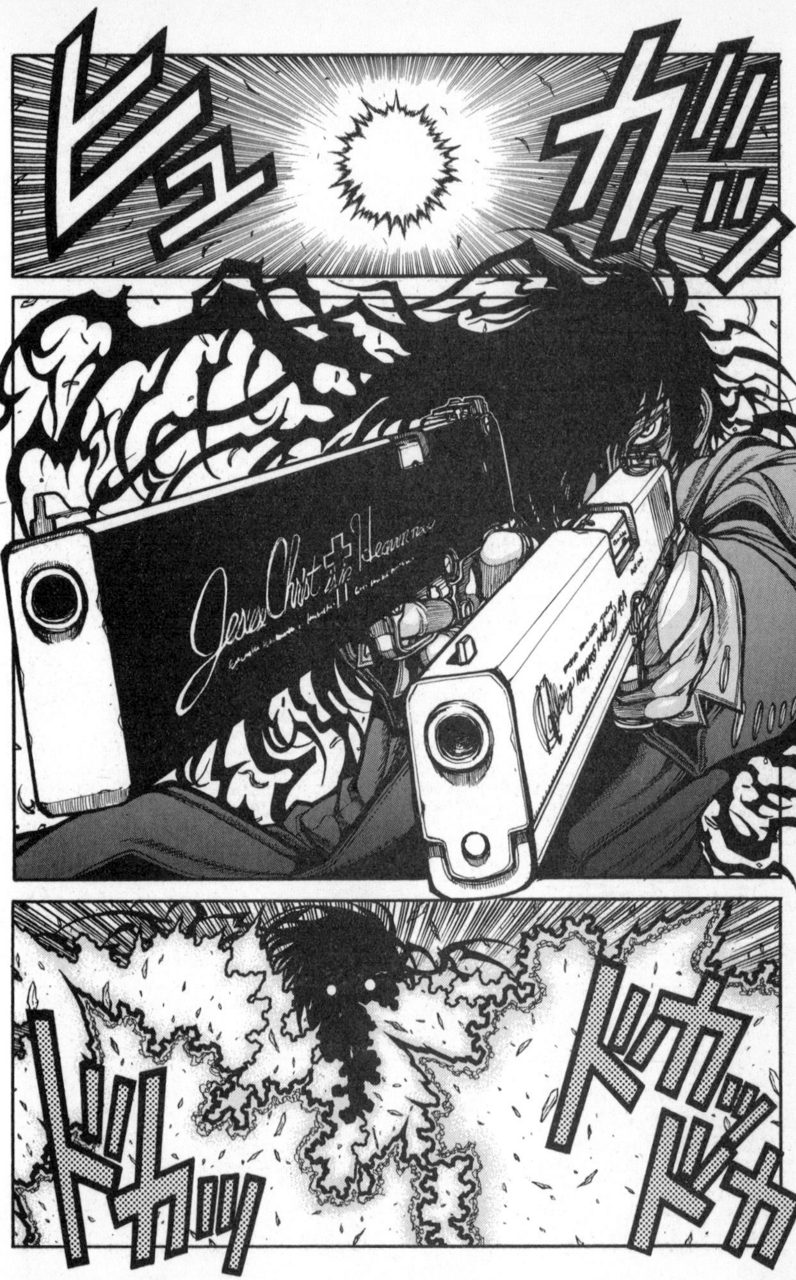
ガッ
ヒュ
Jesus Christ is in Heaven now
ドカッ ドカ
ドカッ

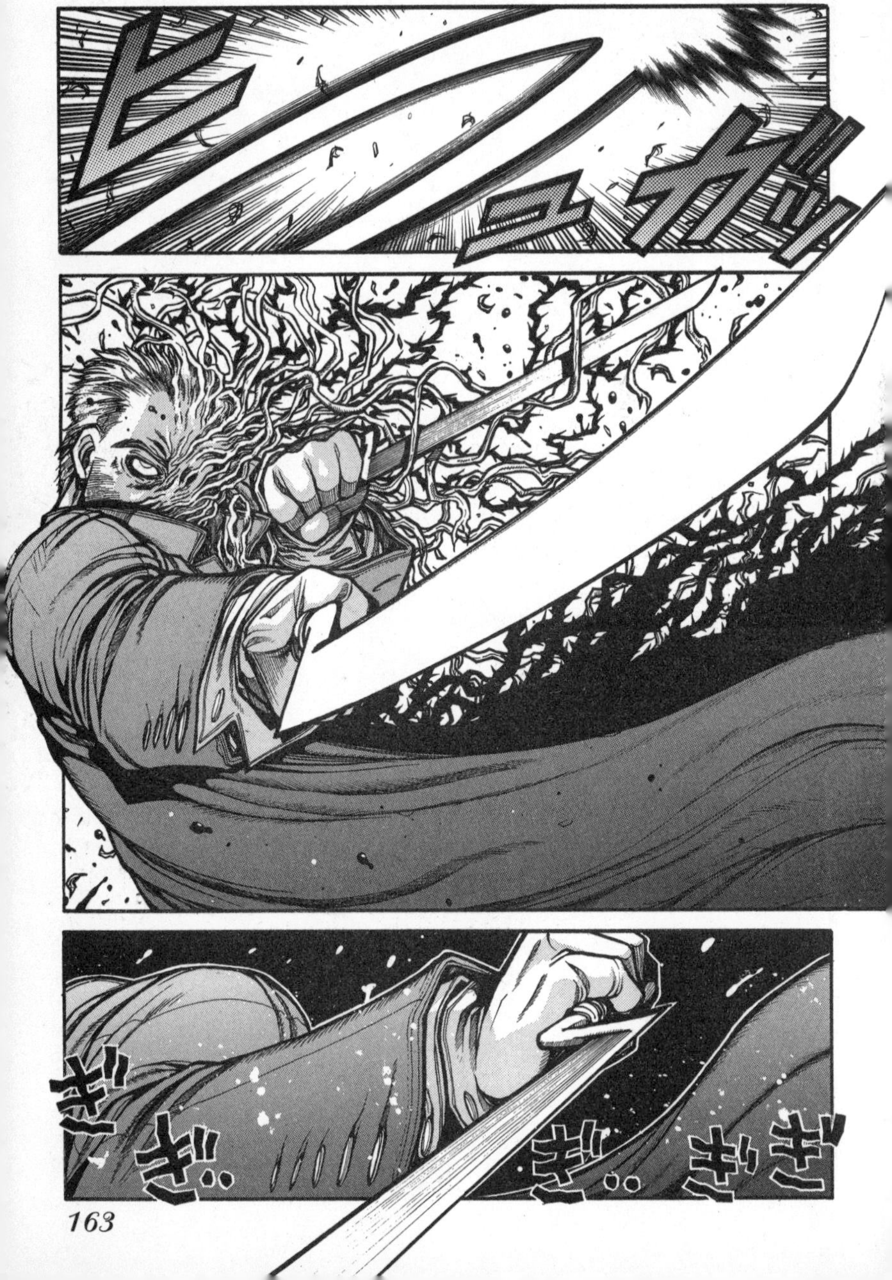
ヒュ
ガッ
ぎぎ..
ぎ..ぎぎ

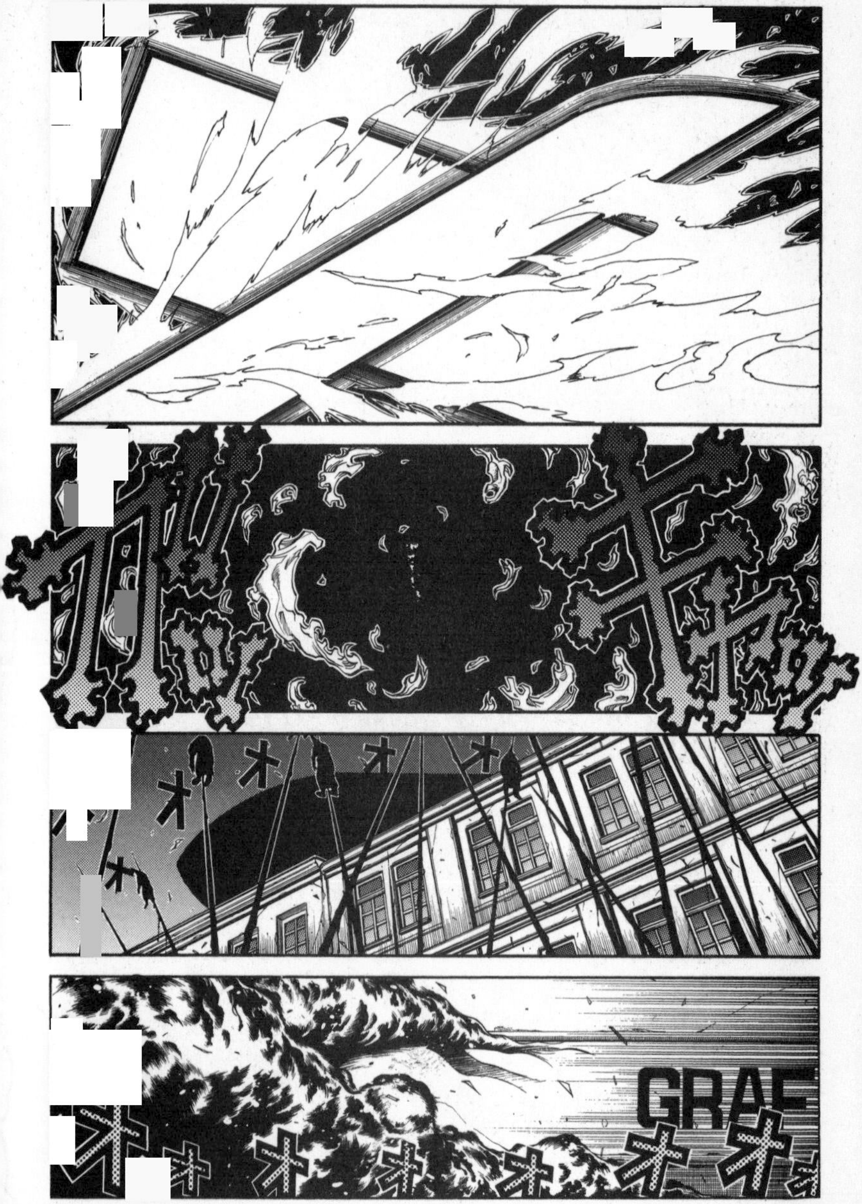
オ
オ
オ
オ
GRAF
オ
オ
オ
オ
オ

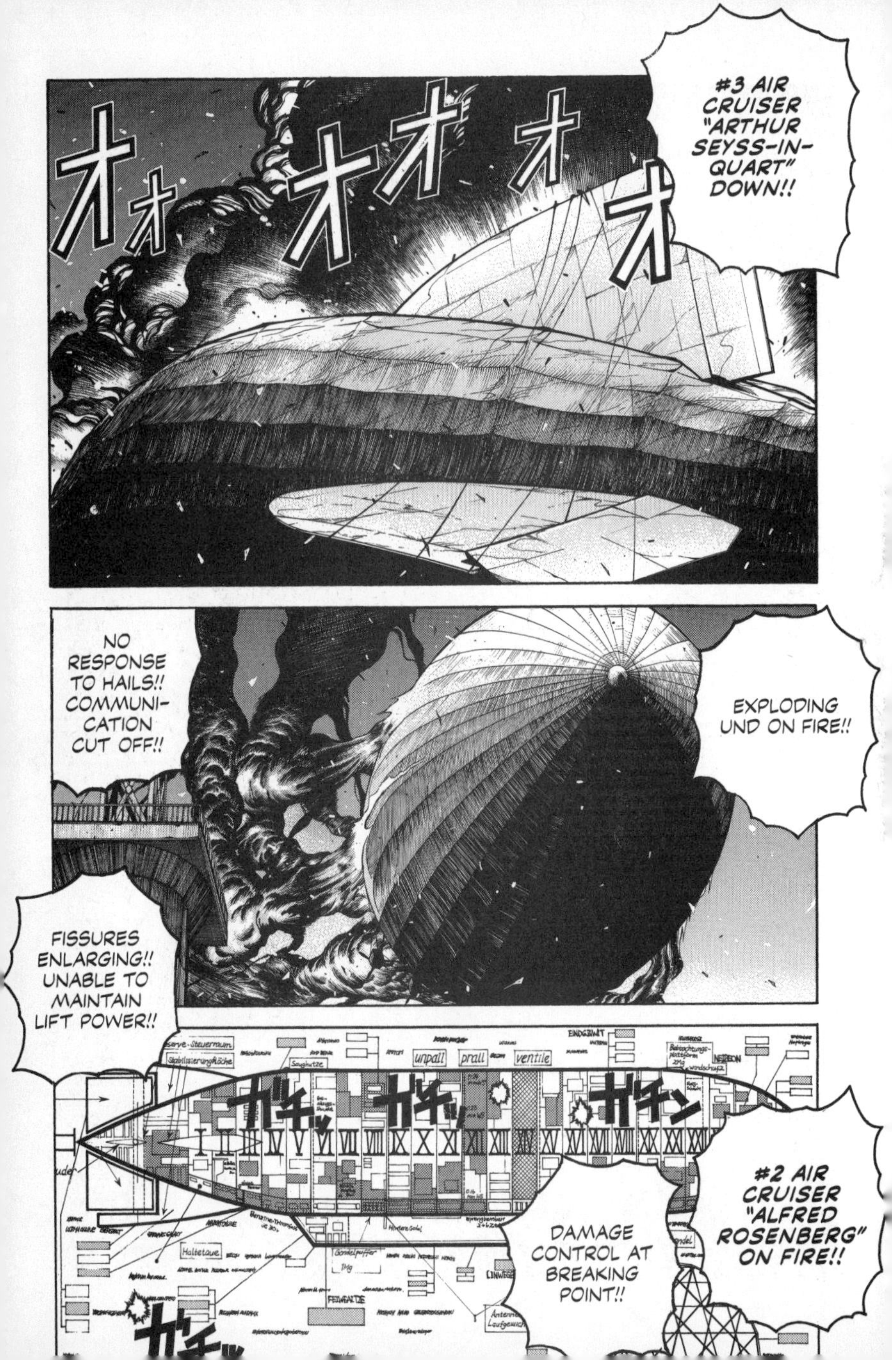
#3 AIR CRUISER "ARTHUR SEYSS-INQUART" DOWN!!
オォオオオオ
EXPLODING UND ON FIRE!!
NO RESPONSE TO HAILS!! COMMUNICATION CUT OFF!!
FISSURES ENLARGING!! UNABLE TO MAINTAIN LIFT POWER!!
#2 AIR CRUISER "ALFRED ROSENBERG" ON FIRE!!
DAMAGE CONTROL AT BREAKING POINT!!
ガチッ
ガチッ
ガチン
ガチッ

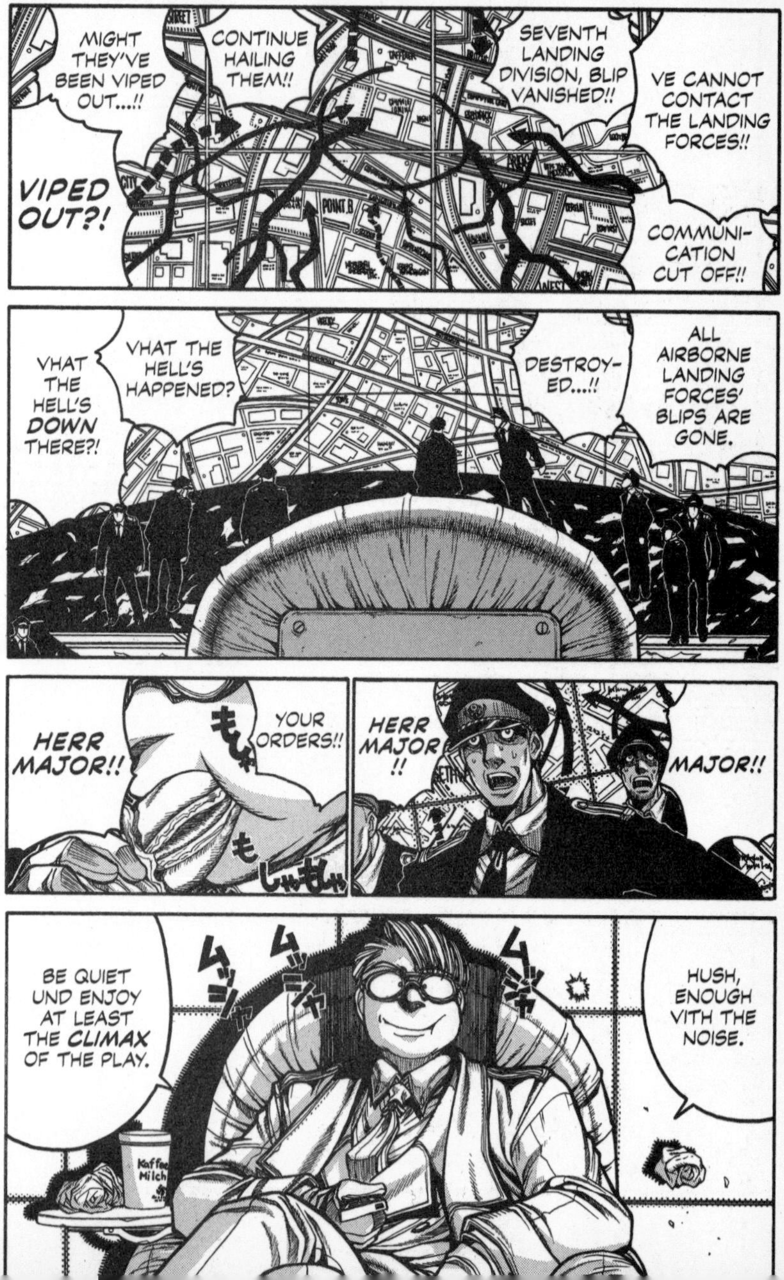
VE CANNOT CONTACT THE LANDING FORCES!!
COMMUNICATION CUT OFF!!
SEVENTH LANDING DIVISION, BLIP VANISHED!!
CONTINUE HAILING THEM!!
MIGHT THEY'VE BEEN VIPED OUT...!!
VIPED OUT?!
ALL AIRBORNE LANDING FORCES' BLIPS ARE GONE.
DESTROYED...!!
VHAT THE HELL'S HAPPENED?
VHAT THE HELL'S DOWN THERE?!
MAJOR!!
HERR MAJOR!!
YOUR ORDERS!!
もしゃ
もしゃもしゃ
HERR MAJOR!!
HUSH, ENOUGH VITH THE NOISE.
BE QUIET UND ENJOY AT LEAST THE CLIMAX OF THE PLAY.
Kaffee Milch

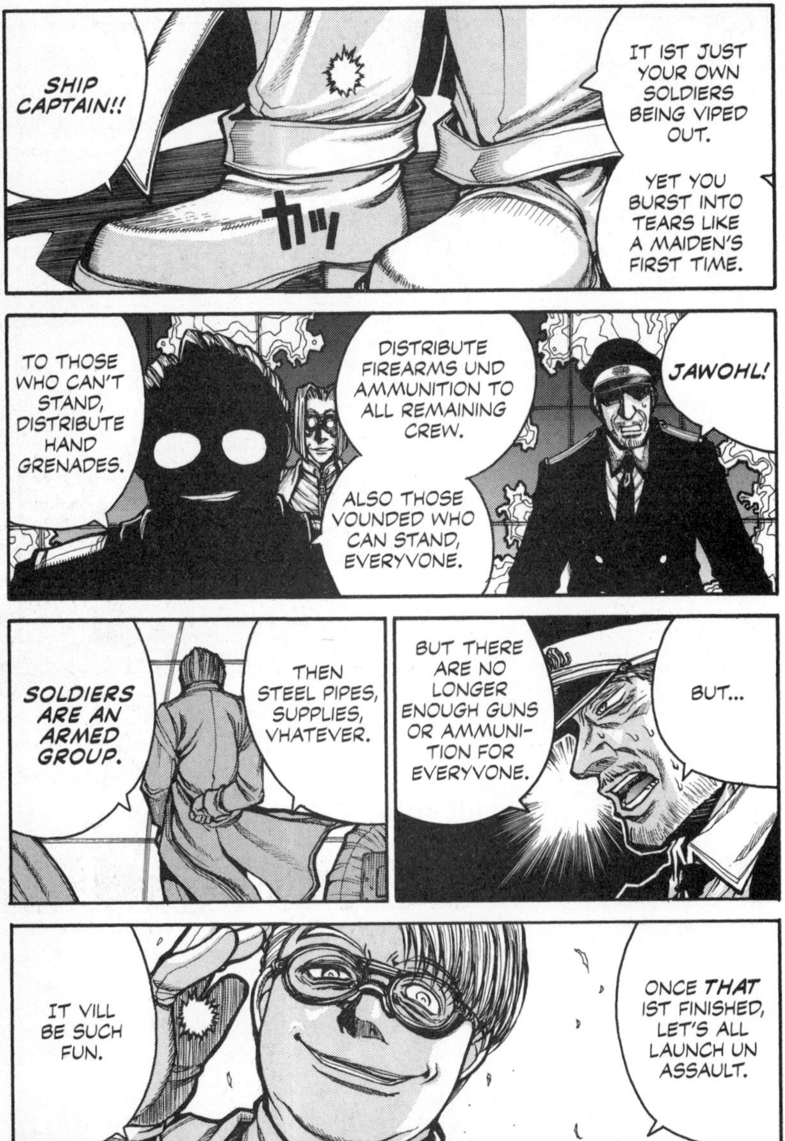
IT IST JUST YOUR OWN SOLDIERS BEING VIPED OUT.
YET YOU BURST INTO TEARS LIKE A MAIDEN'S FIRST TIME.
カッ
SHIP CAPTAIN!!
JAWOHL!
DISTRIBUTE FIREARMS UND AMMUNITION TO ALL REMAINING CREW.
ALSO THOSE VOUNDED WHO CAN STAND, EVERYVONE.
TO THOSE WHO CAN'T STAND, DISTRIBUTE HAND GRENADES.
BUT...
BUT THERE ARE NO LONGER ENOUGH GUNS OR AMMUNITION FOR EVERYVONE.
THEN STEEL PIPES, SUPPLIES, VHATEVER.
SOLDIERS ARE AN ARMED GROUP.
ONCE THAT IST FINISHED, LET'S ALL LAUNCH UN ASSAULT.
IT VILL BE SUCH FUN.

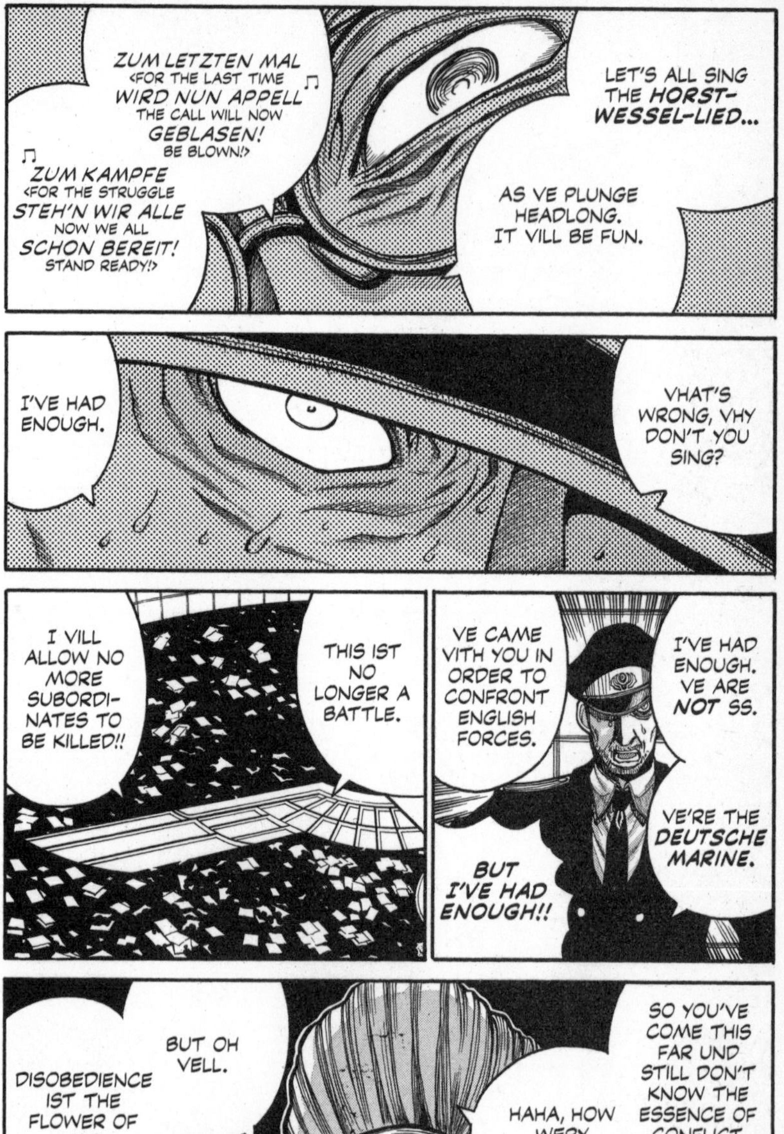
LET'S ALL SING THE HORST-WESSEL-LIED...
AS VE PLUNGE HEADLONG. IT VILL BE FUN.
♫ ZUM LETZTEN MAL <FOR THE LAST TIME WIRD NUN APPELL THE CALL WILL NOW GEBLASEN! BE BLOWN!>
♫ ZUM KAMPFE <FOR THE STRUGGLE STEH'N WIR ALLE NOW WE ALL SCHON BEREIT! STAND READY!>
VHAT'S WRONG, VHY DON'T YOU SING?
I'VE HAD ENOUGH.
I'VE HAD ENOUGH. VE ARE NOT SS.
VE CAME VITH YOU IN ORDER TO CONFRONT ENGLISH FORCES.
VE'RE THE DEUTSCHE MARINE.
BUT I'VE HAD ENOUGH!!
THIS IST NO LONGER A BATTLE.
I VILL ALLOW NO MORE SUBORDINATES TO BE KILLED!!
SO YOU'VE COME THIS FAR UND STILL DON'T KNOW THE ESSENCE OF CONFLICT.
HAHA, HOW WERY UNPERCEPTIVE.
BUT OH VELL.
DISOBEDIENCE IST THE FLOWER OF VAR.

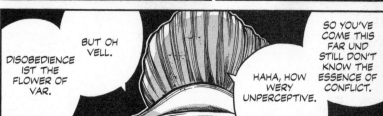

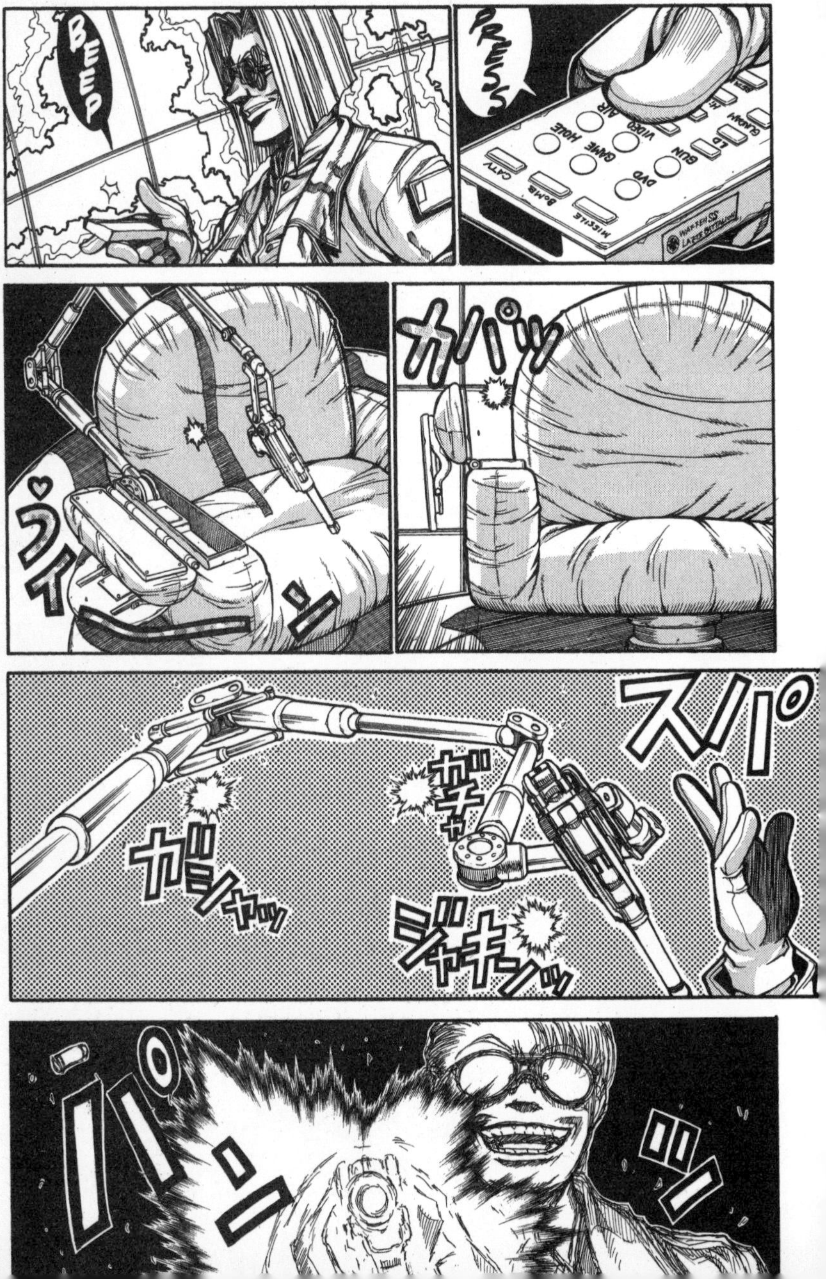
PRESS
BEEP
カパッ
♥ウィイーン
スパ
ガチャ
ガシャッ
ジャキーン
ドパーン

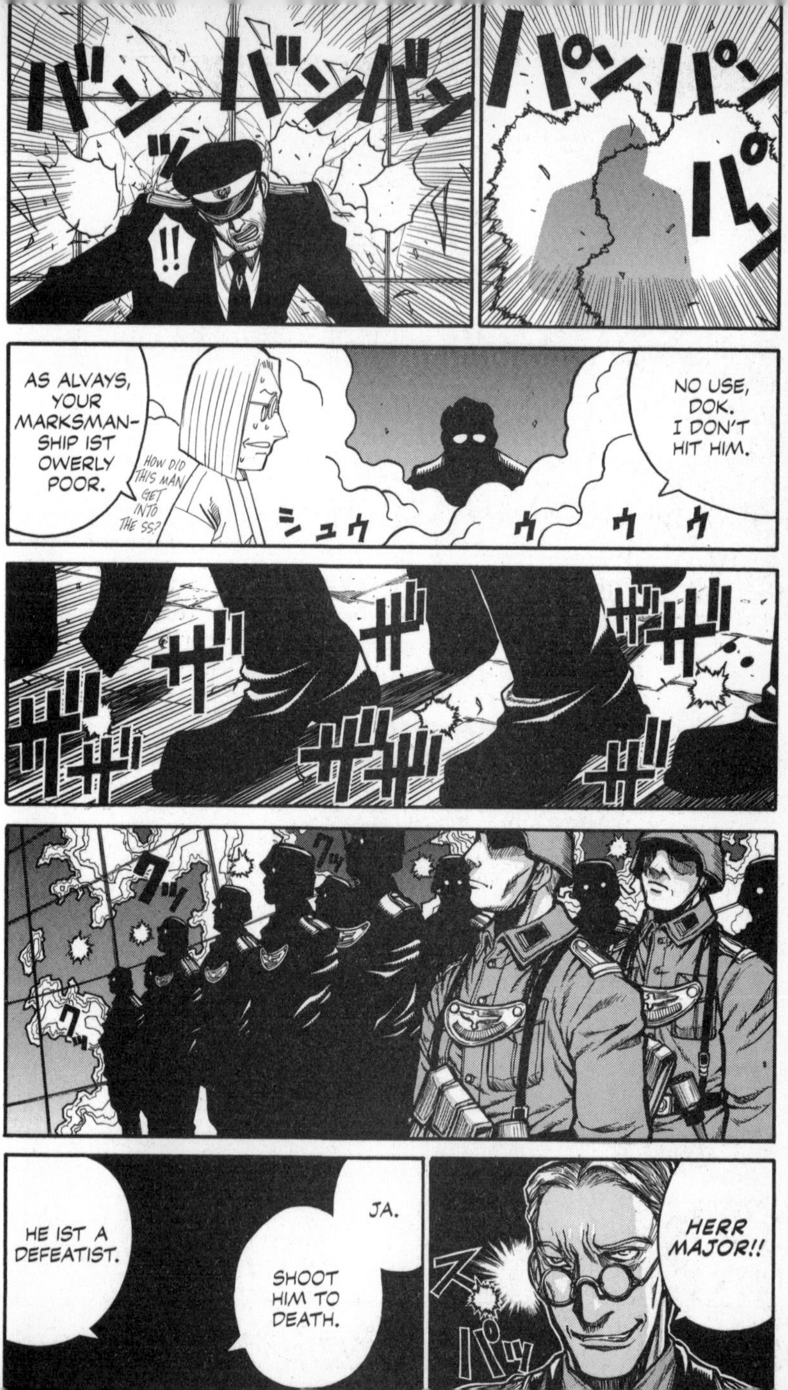
!!
NO USE, DOK. I DON'T HIT HIM.
AS ALVAYS, YOUR MARKSMAN-SHIP IST OWERLY POOR.
HOW DID THIS MAN GET INTO THE SS?
HERR MAJOR!!
JA.
HE IST A DEFEATIST.
SHOOT HIM TO DEATH.

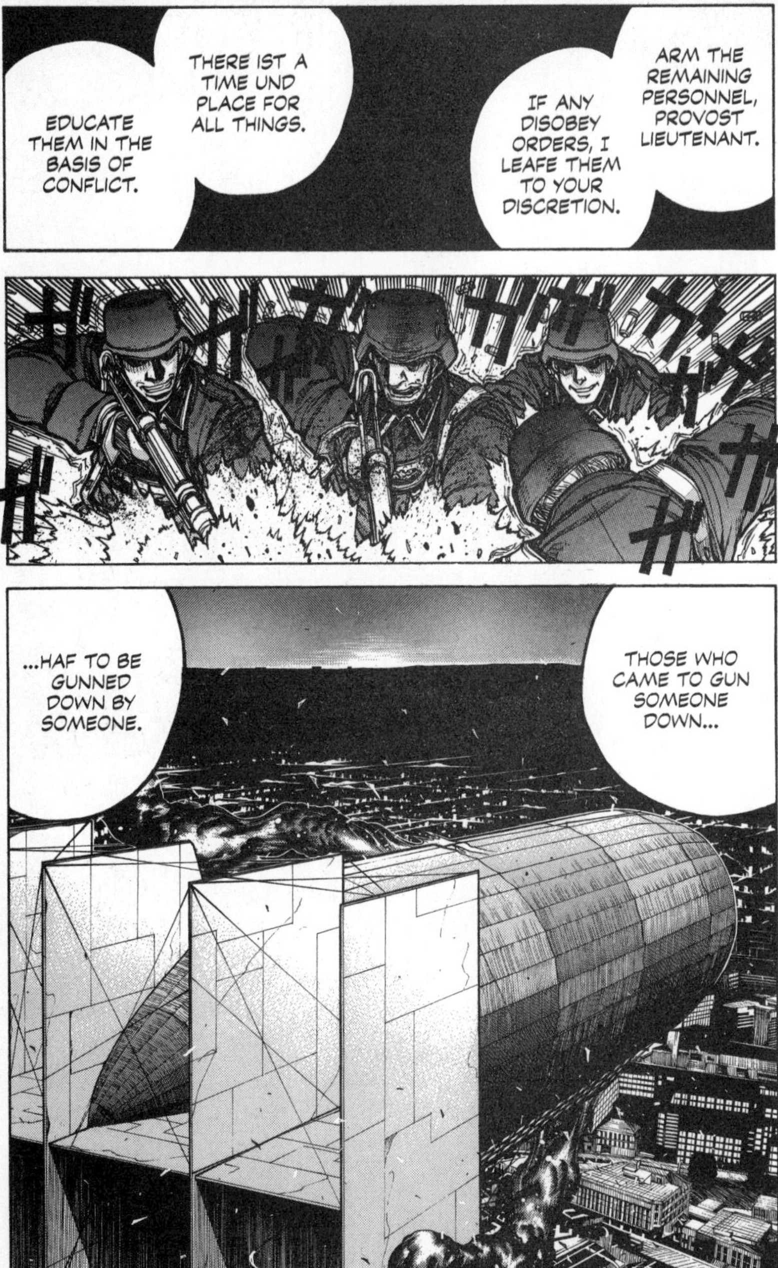
ARM THE REMAINING PERSONNEL, PROVOST LIEUTENANT.
IF ANY DISOBEY ORDERS, I LEAFE THEM TO YOUR DISCRETION.
THERE IST A TIME UND PLACE FOR ALL THINGS.
EDUCATE THEM IN THE BASIS OF CONFLICT.
THOSE WHO CAME TO GUN SOMEONE DOWN...
...HAF TO BE GUNNED DOWN BY SOMEONE.

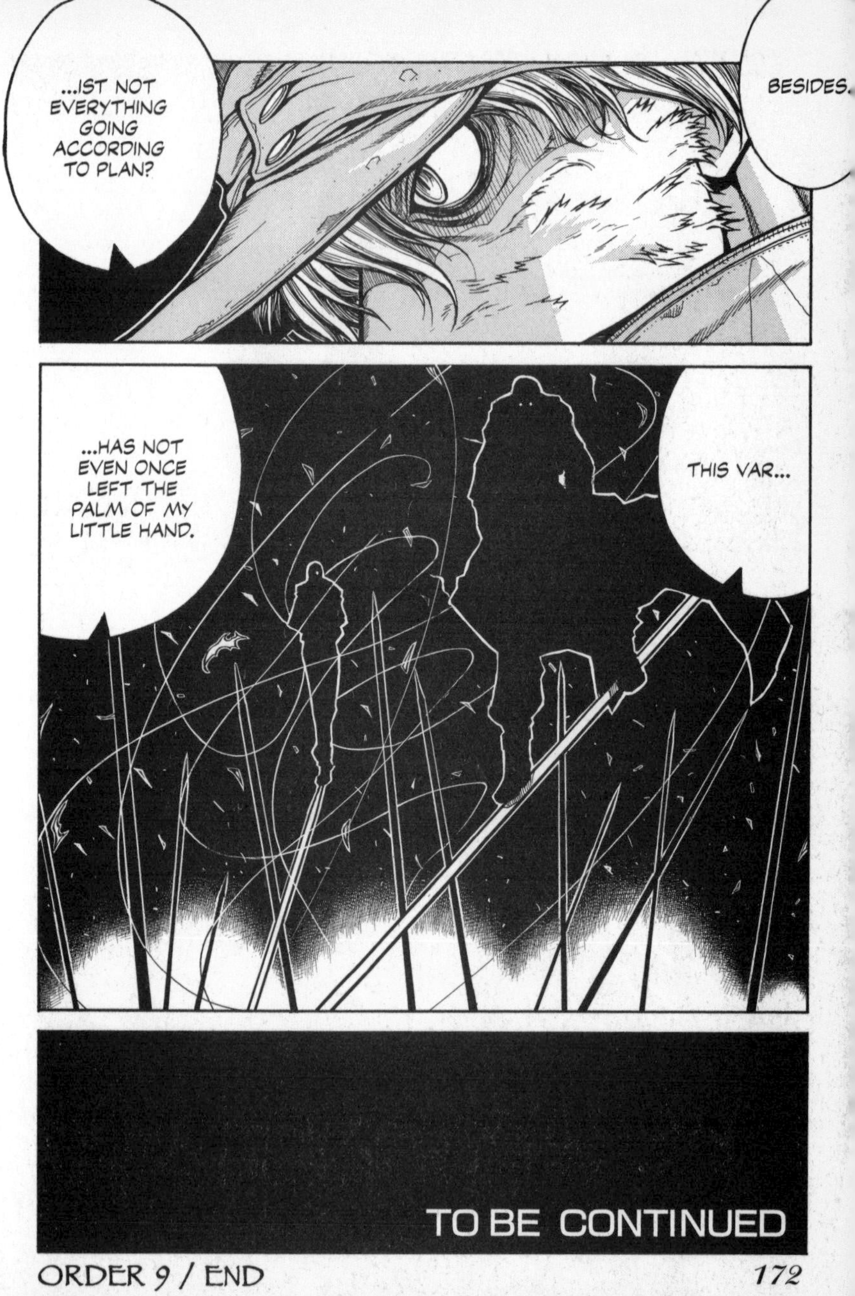
BESIDES.
...IST NOT EVERYTHING GOING ACCORDING TO PLAN?
THIS VAR...
...HAS NOT EVEN ONCE LEFT THE PALM OF MY LITTLE HAND.
TO BE CONTINUED

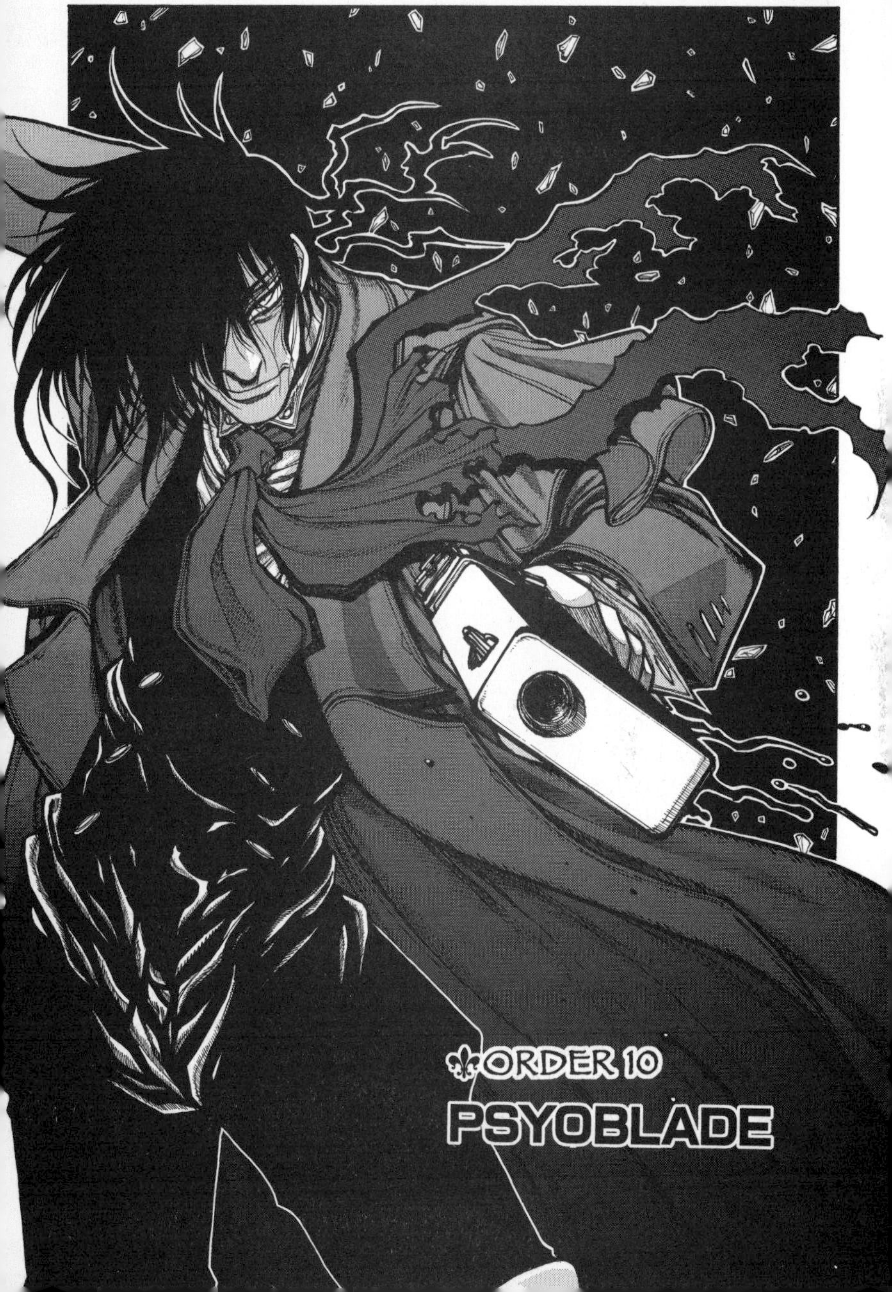
ORDER 10
PSYOBLADE

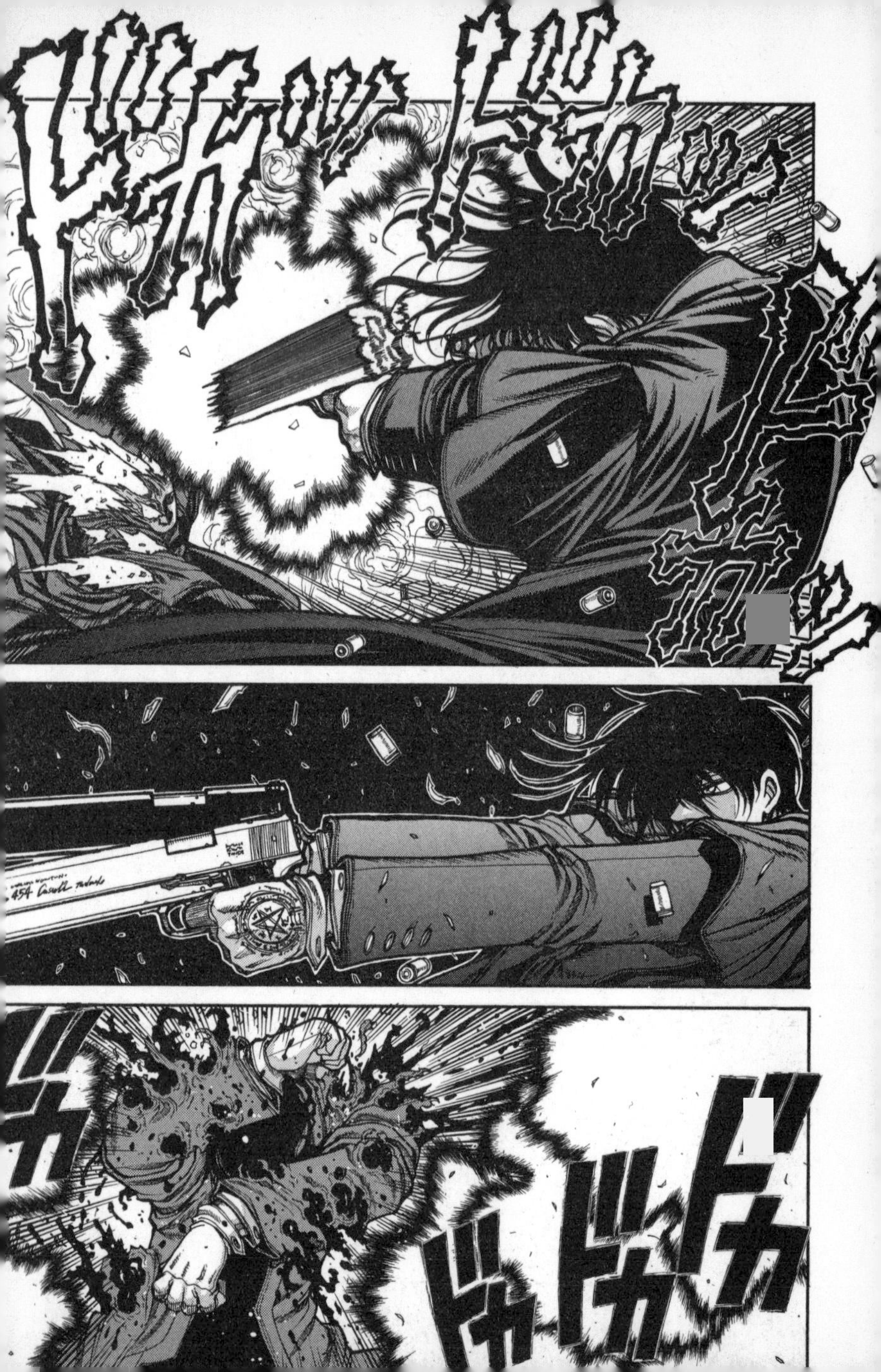
454 Casull

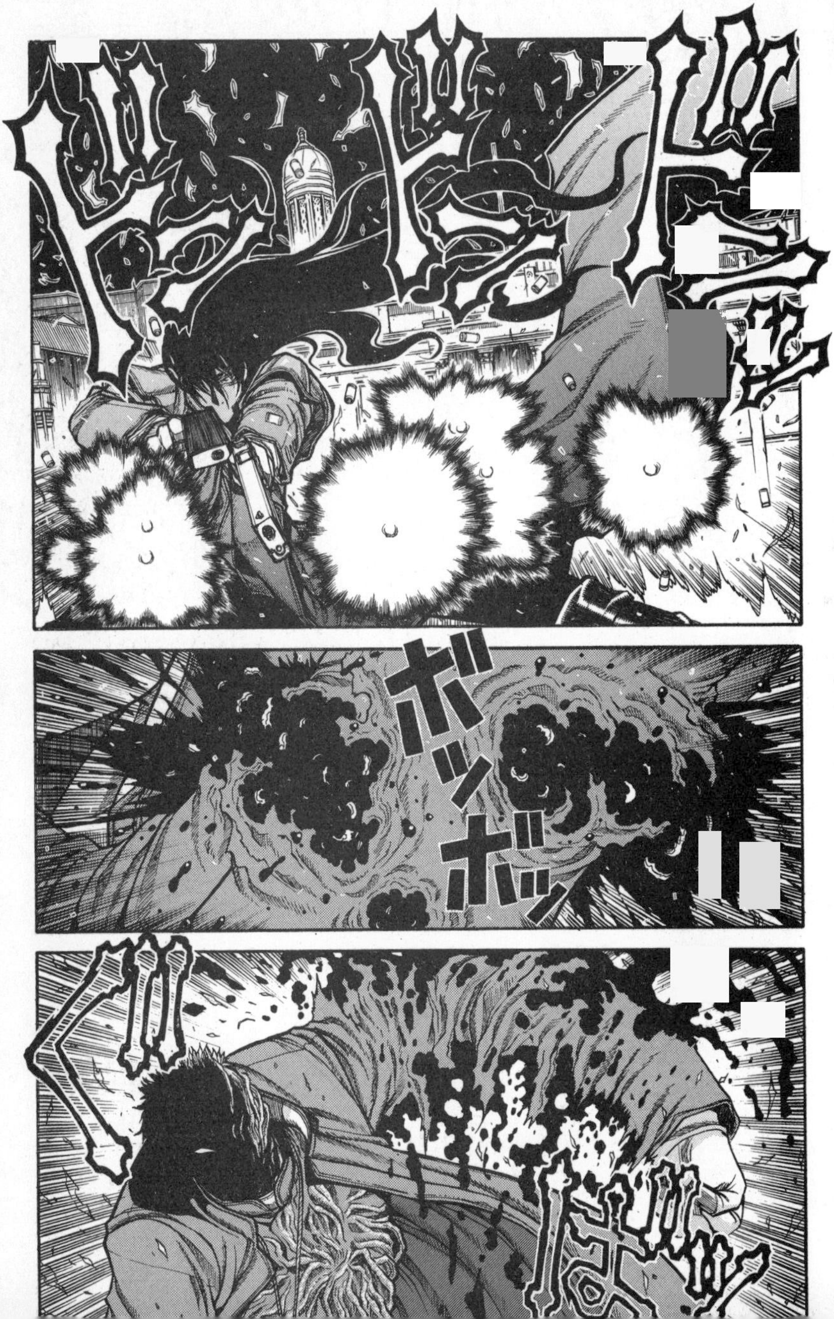
ボッ
ボッ

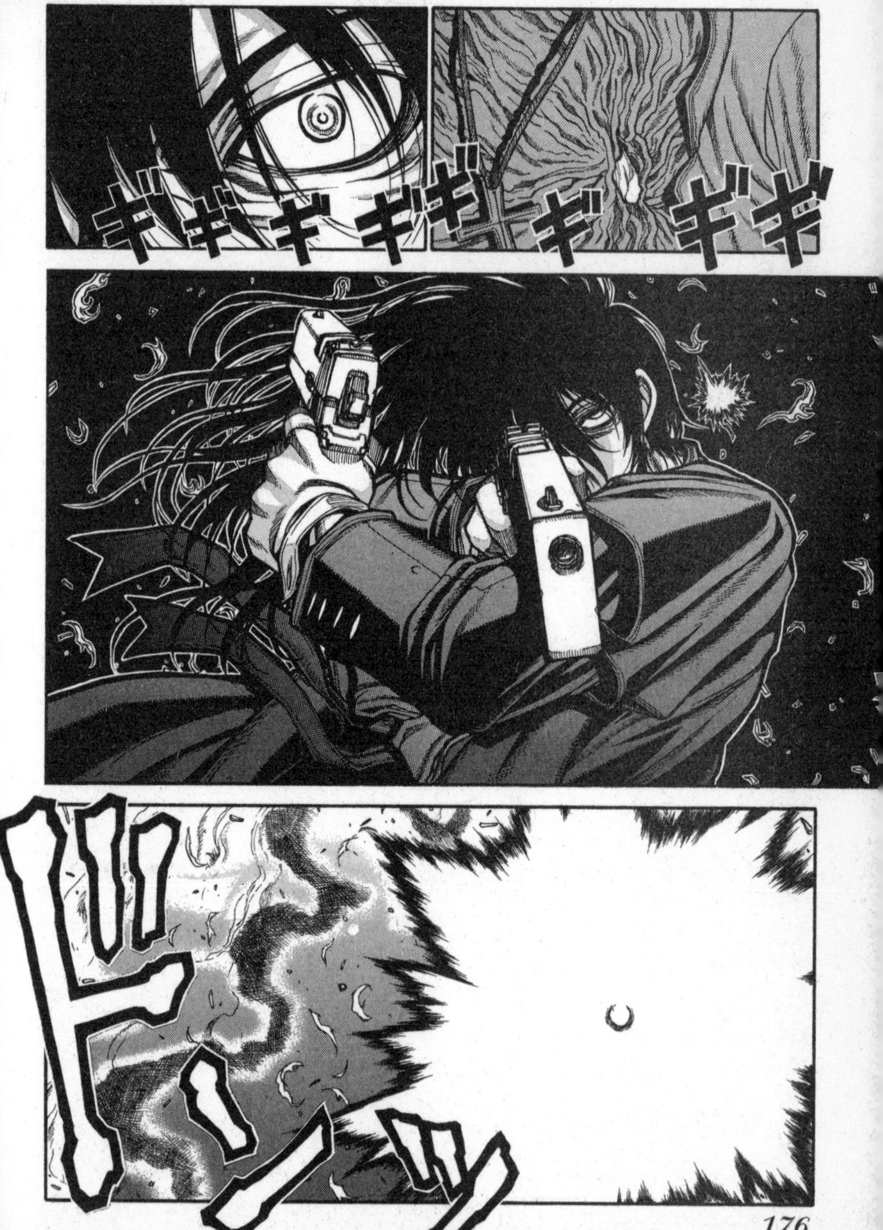
ギギギギギギギギ
ドンッ

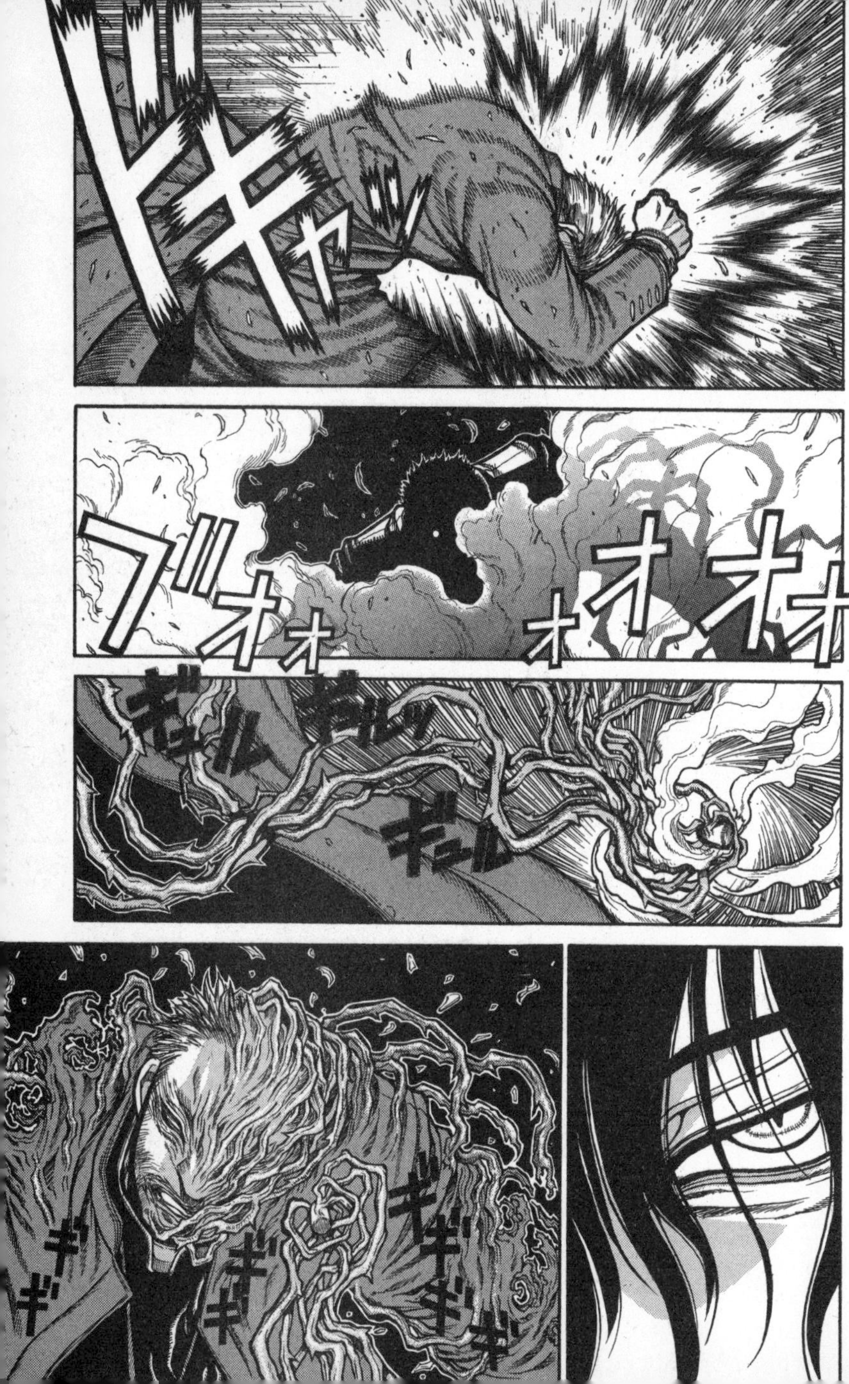
ドギャッ
ブオオォオオオ
ギュル
ギュルッ
ギュル
ギギ
ギギ
ギギ

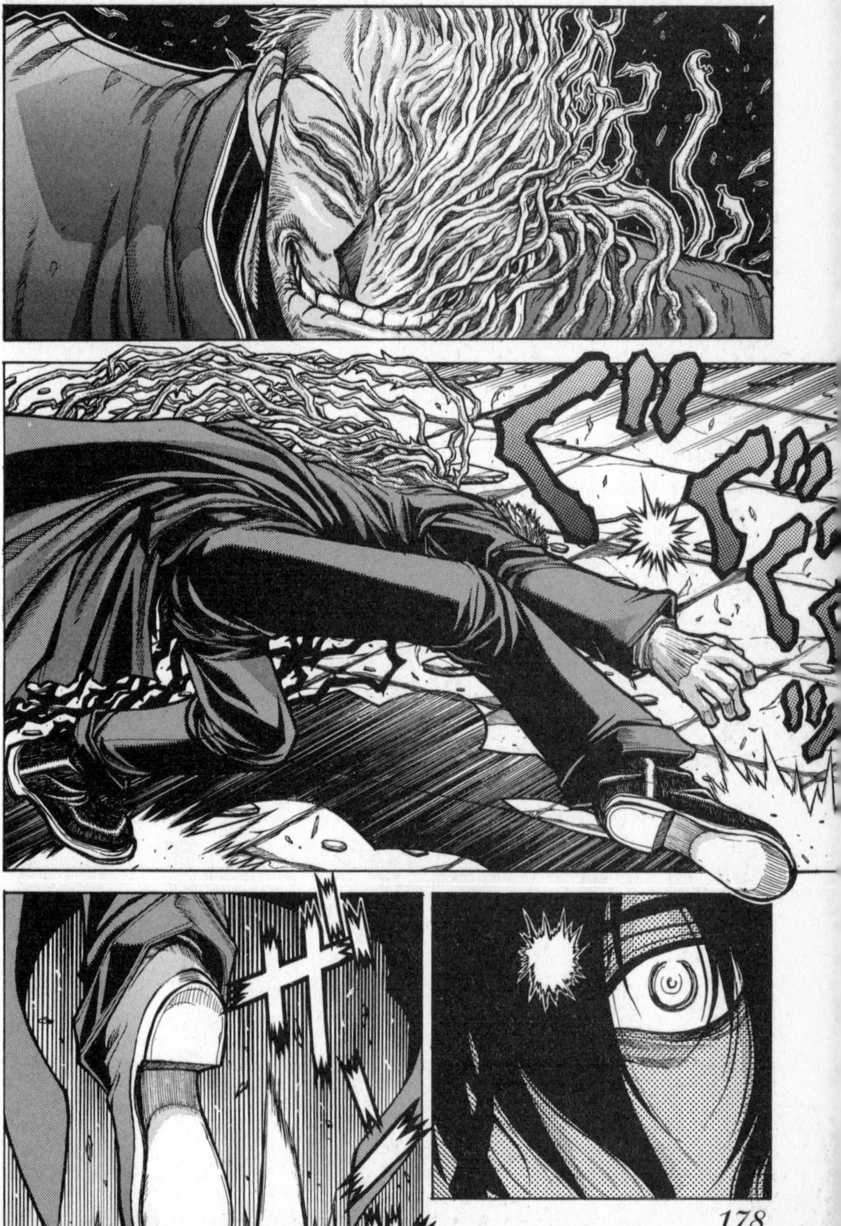

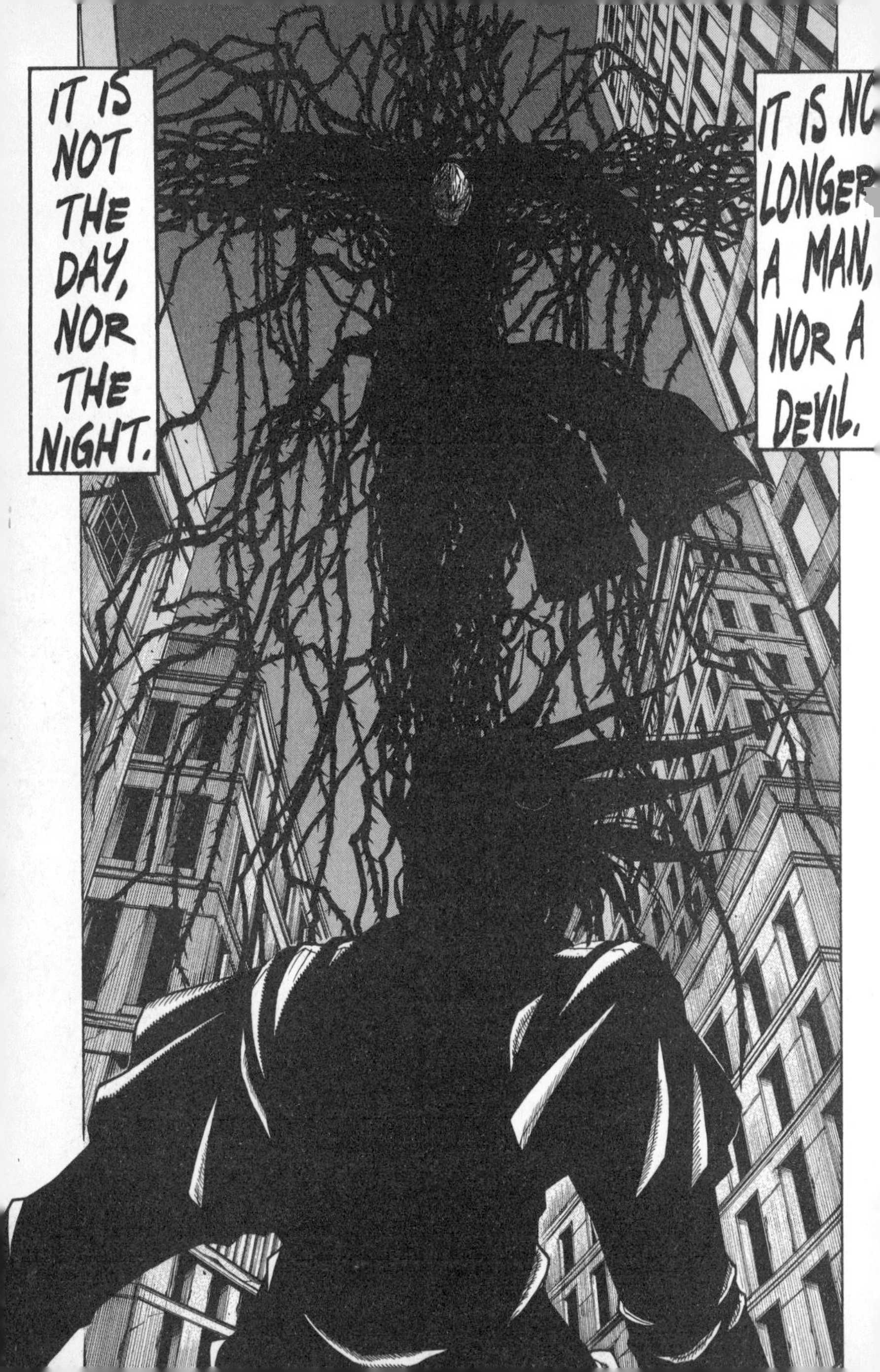
IT IS NO LONGER A MAN, NOR A DEVIL.
IT IS NOT THE DAY, NOR THE NIGHT.

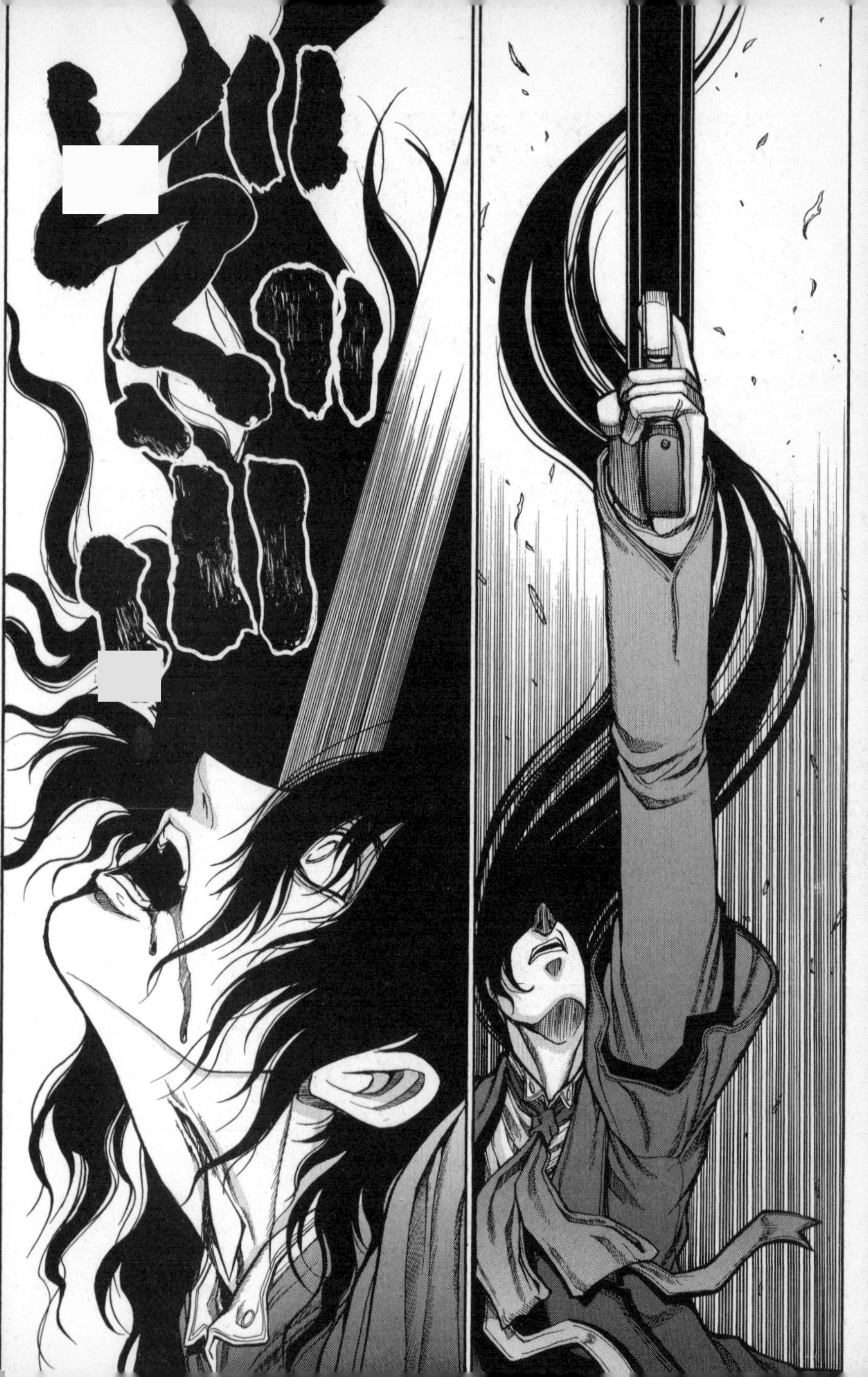

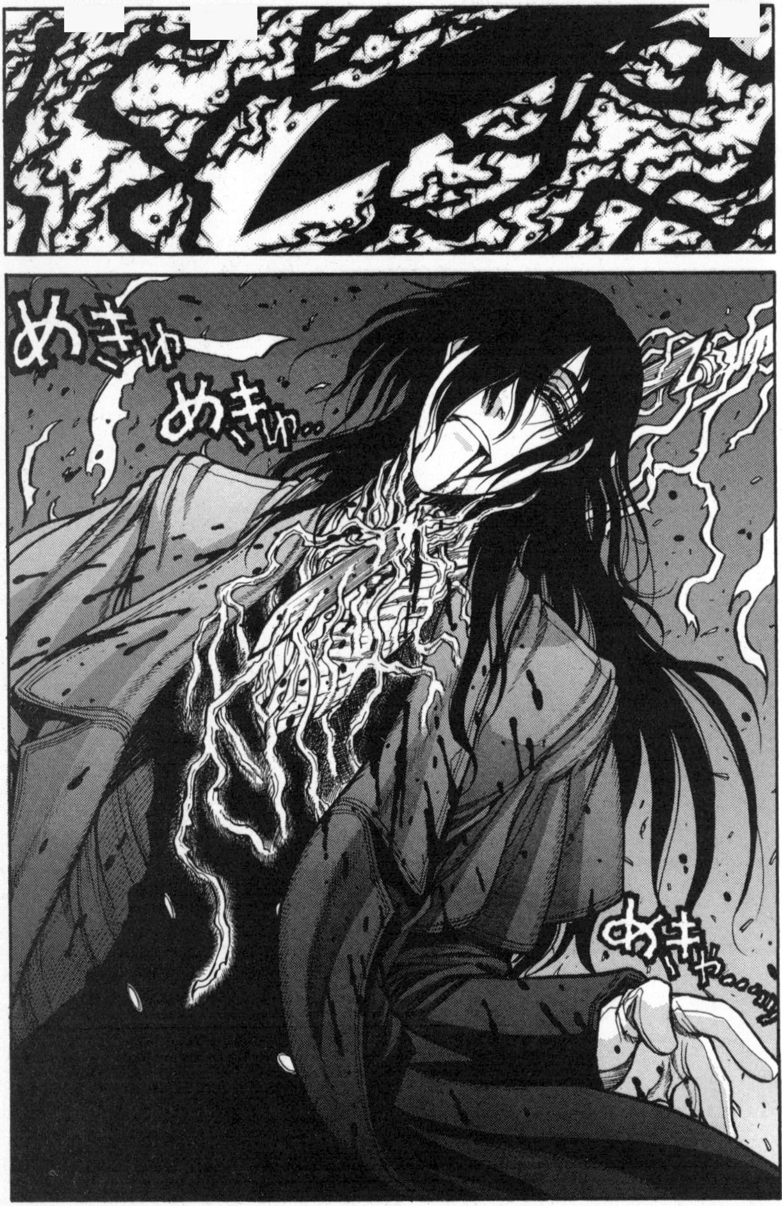
めきゅ
めきゅ..
めきゃ……

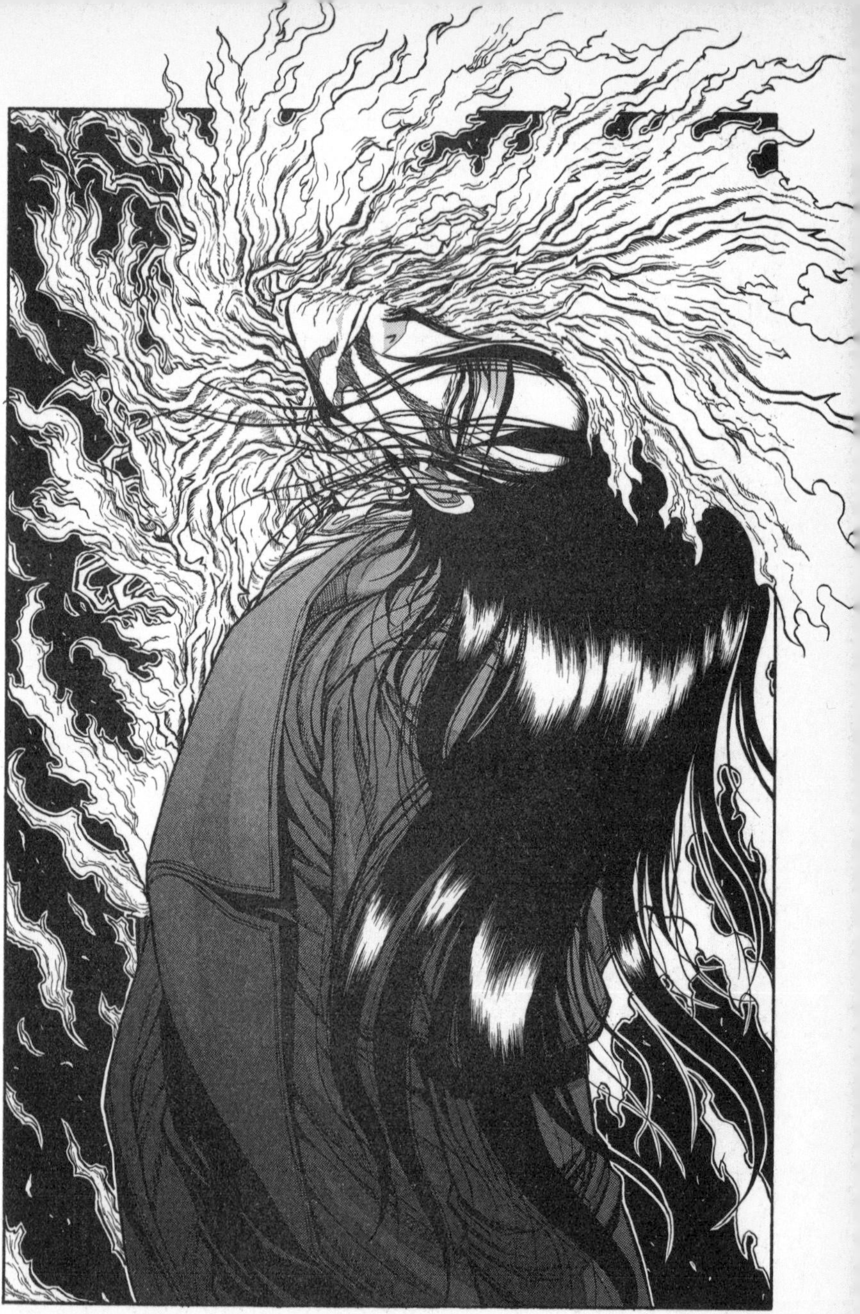

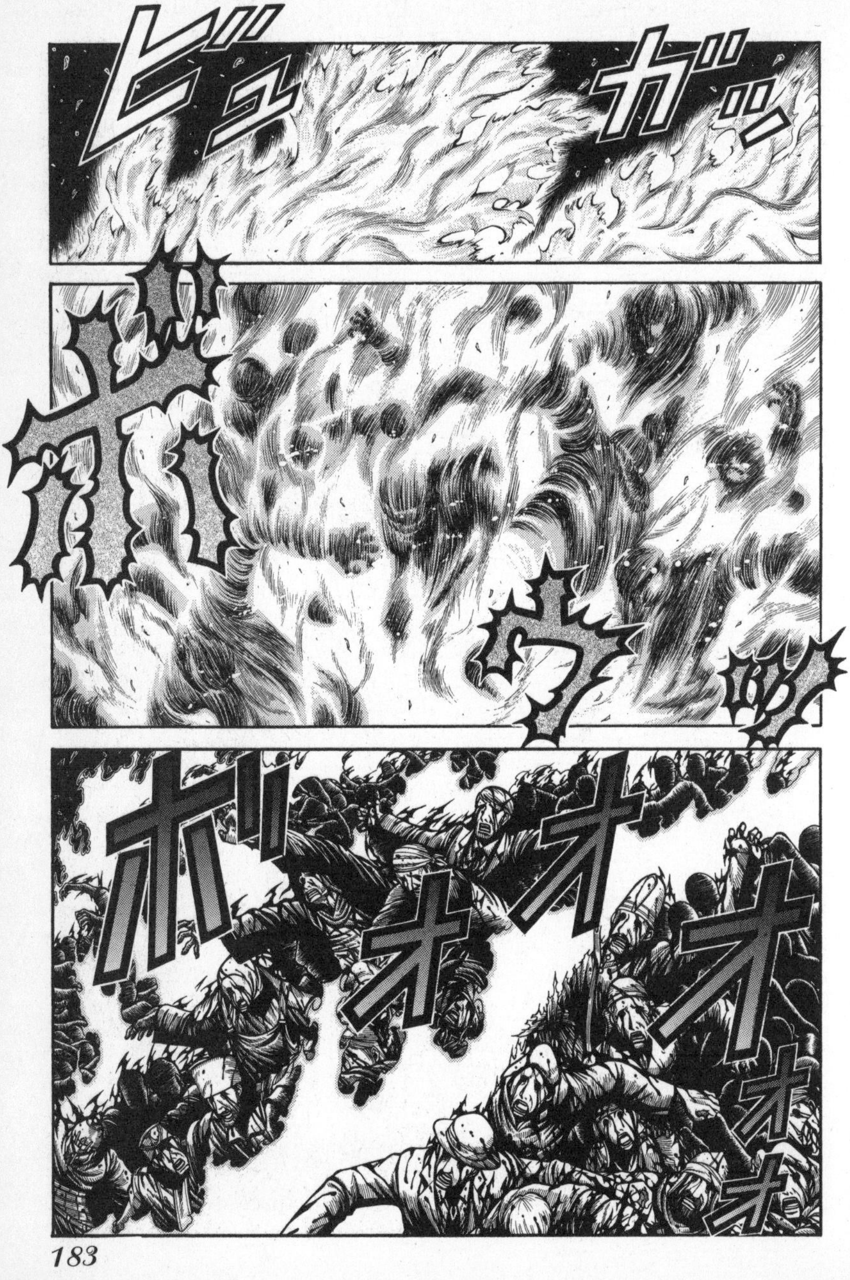
ビュ
ガッ
ボウッ
ボオオオオオ

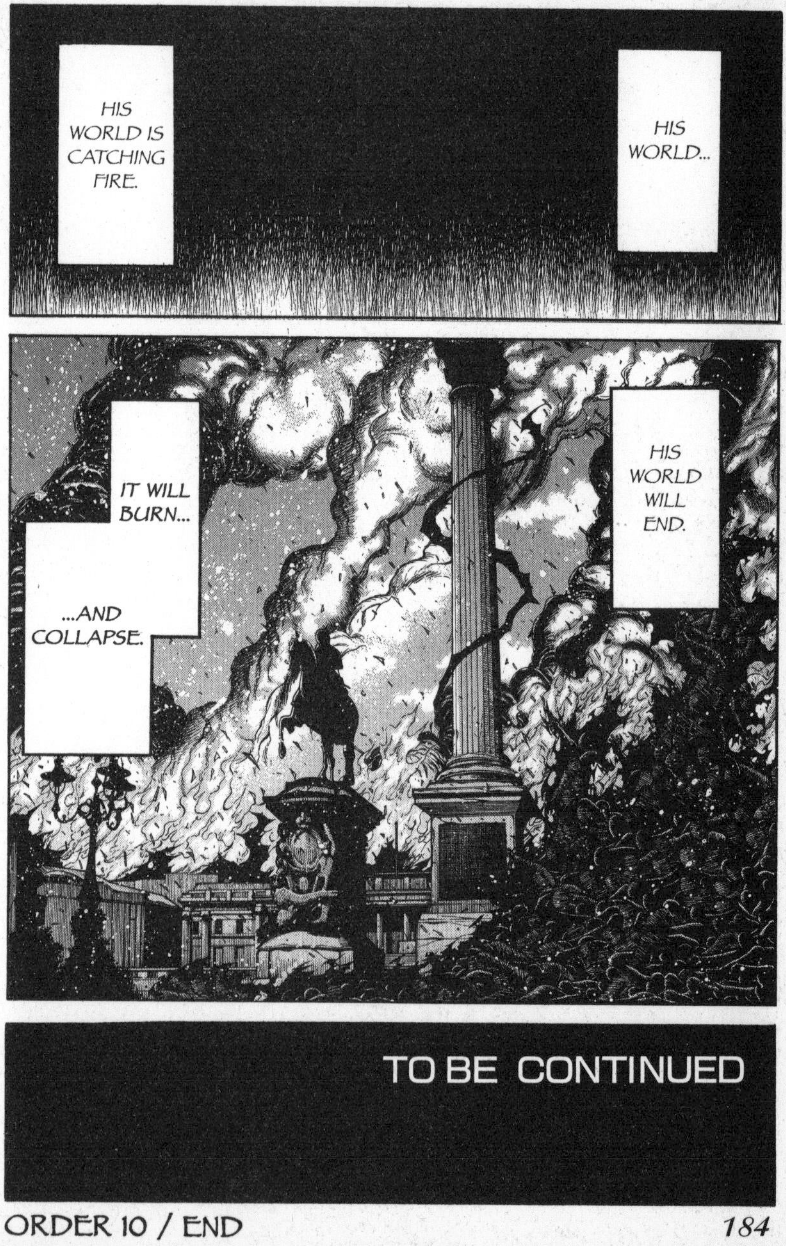
HIS WORLD...
HIS WORLD IS CATCHING FIRE.
HIS WORLD WILL END.
IT WILL BURN...
...AND COLLAPSE.
TO BE CONTINUED

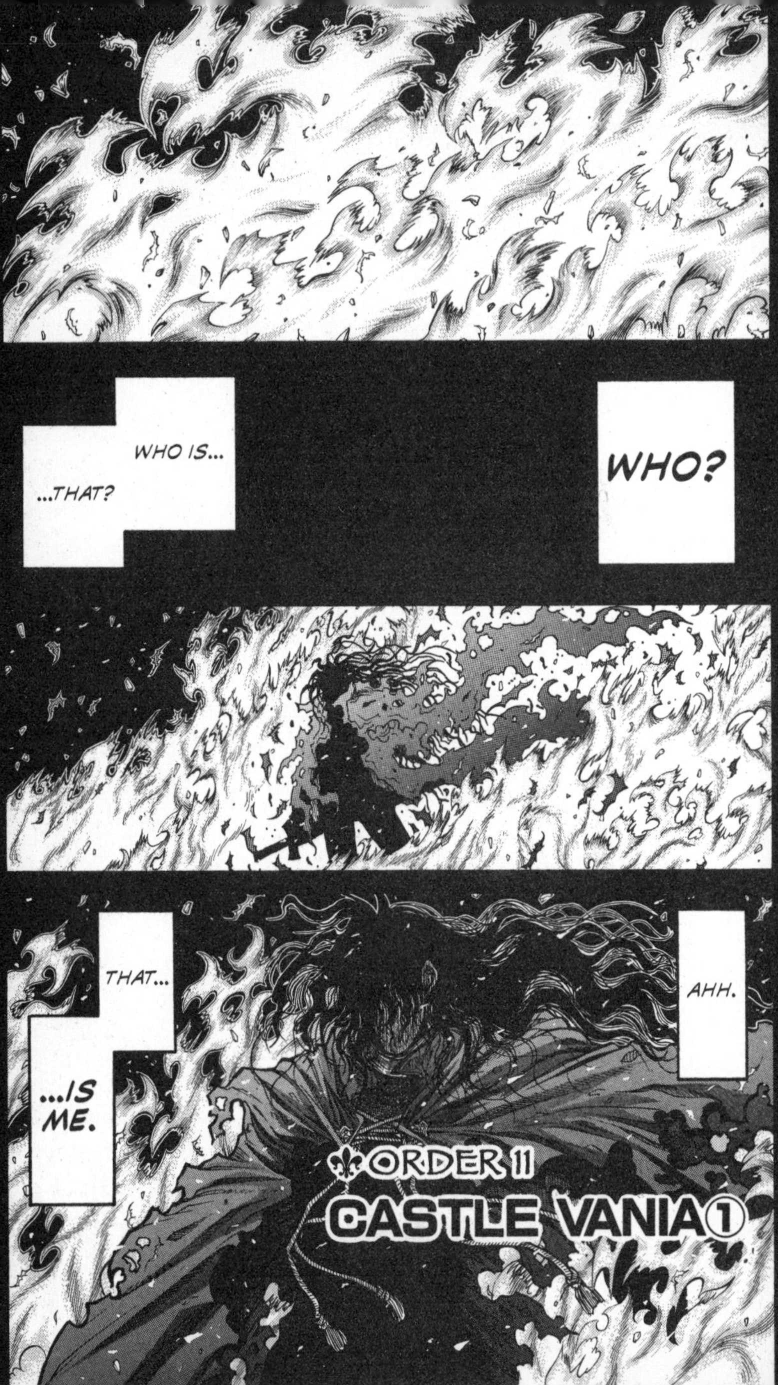
WHO?
WHO IS...
...THAT?
AHH.
THAT...
...IS ME.
ORDER 11
CASTLE VANIA①

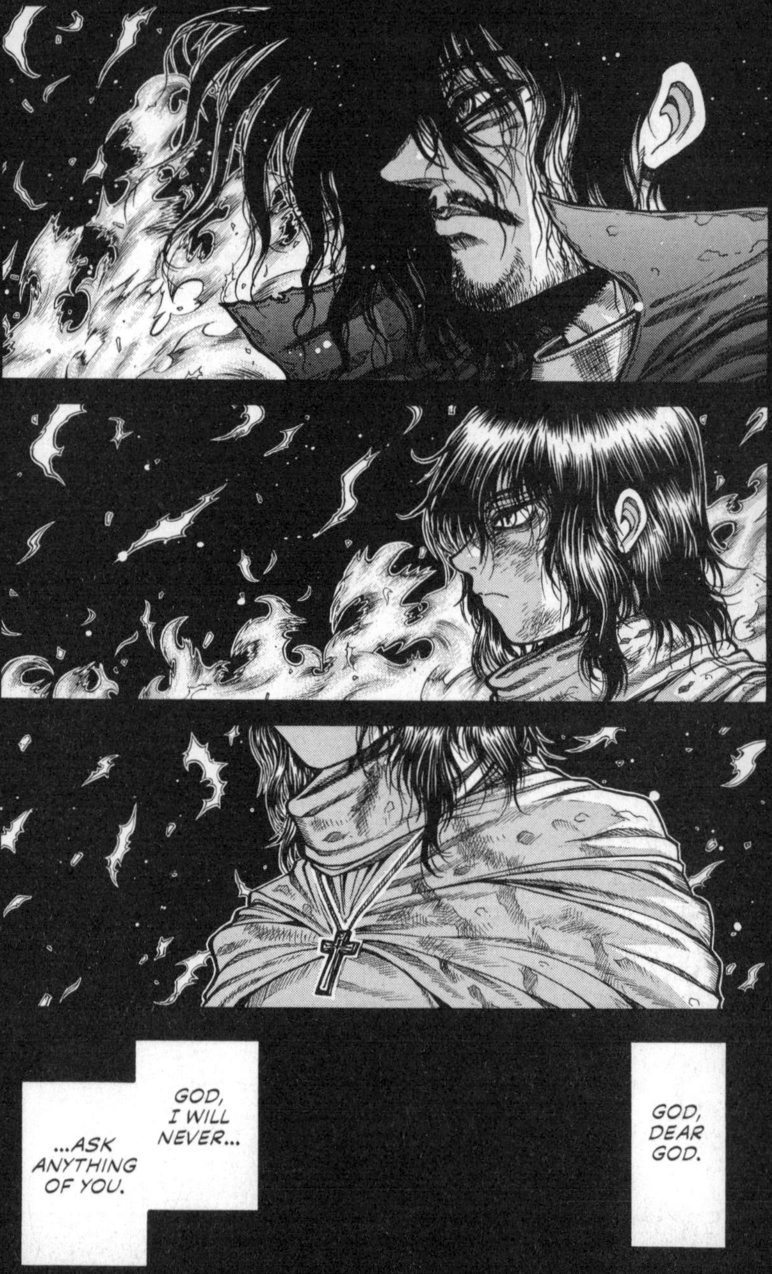
GOD, DEAR GOD.
GOD, I WILL NEVER...
...ASK ANYTHING OF YOU.

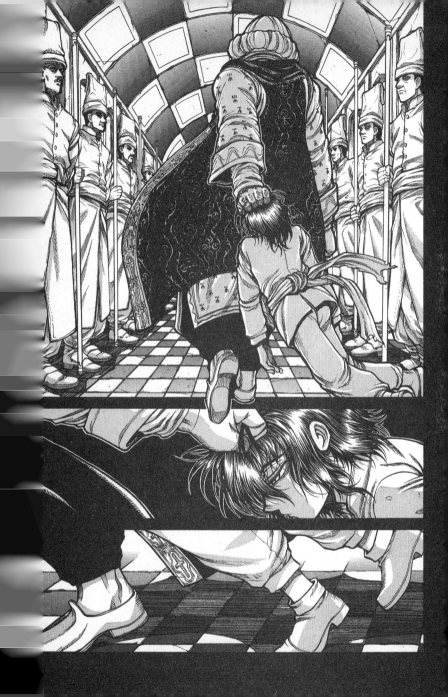

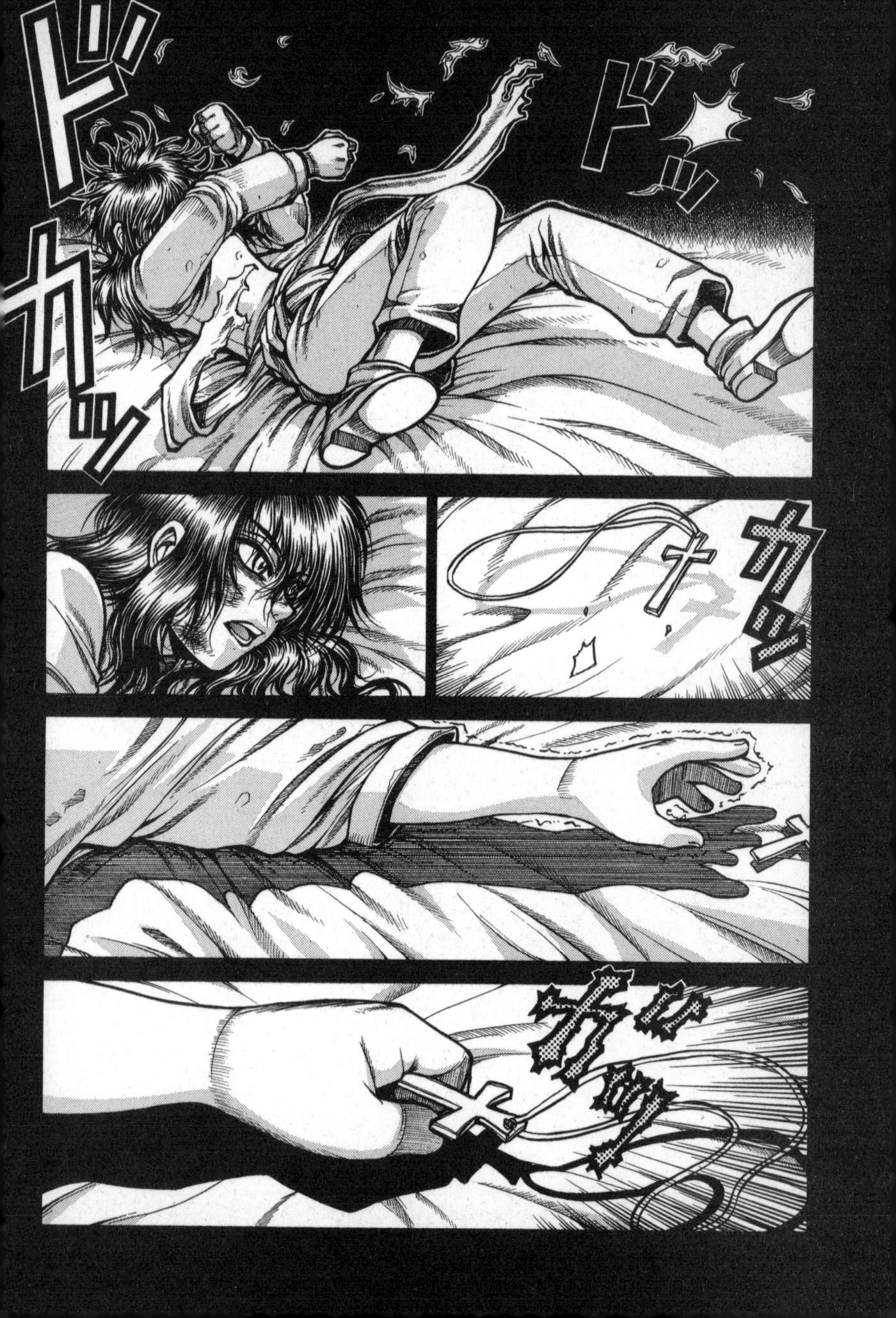
ドッ
ドカッ
カッ
ガッ

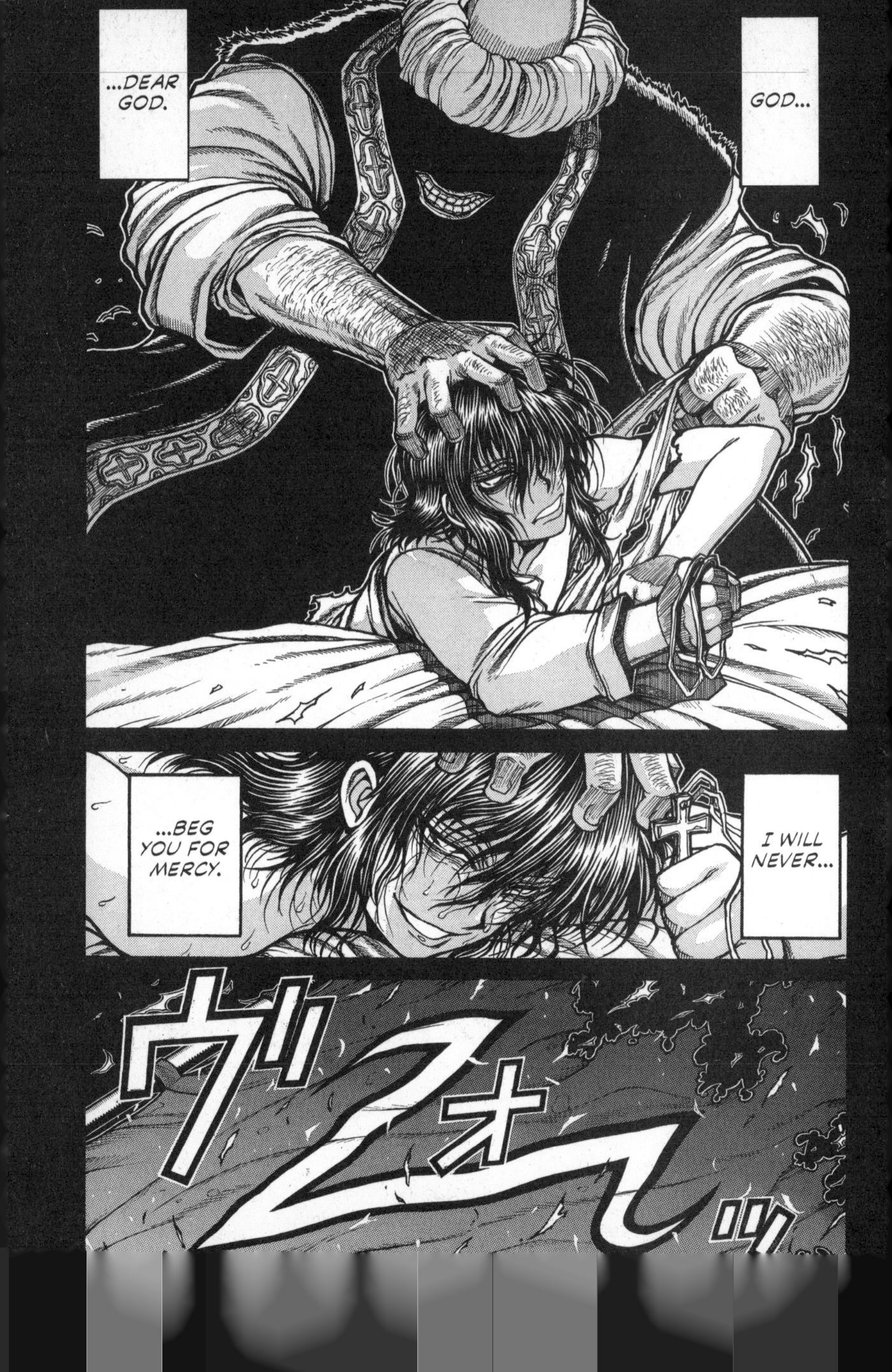
GOD...
...DEAR GOD.
I WILL NEVER...
...BEG YOU FOR MERCY.
ヴフォンッ

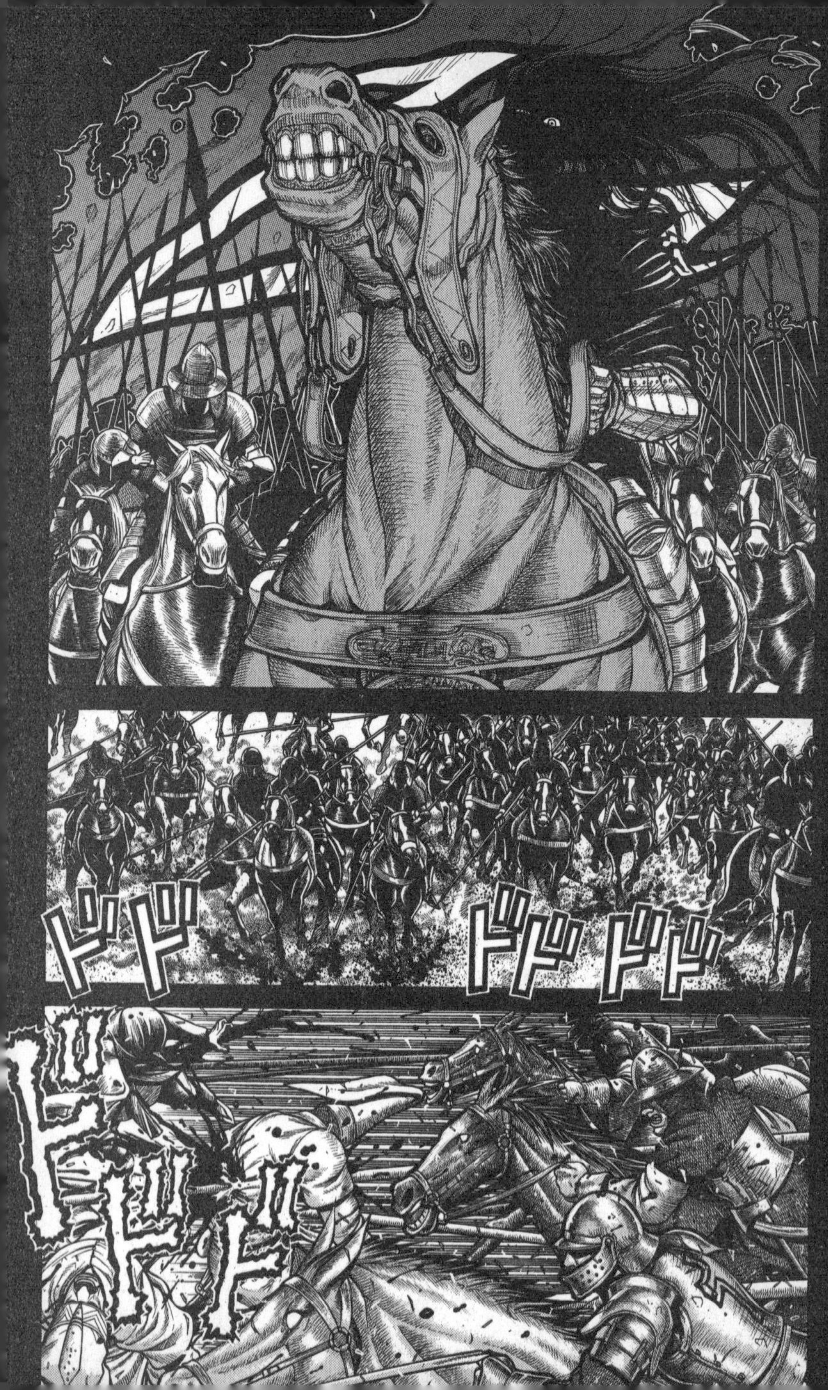
ドドドド
ドド

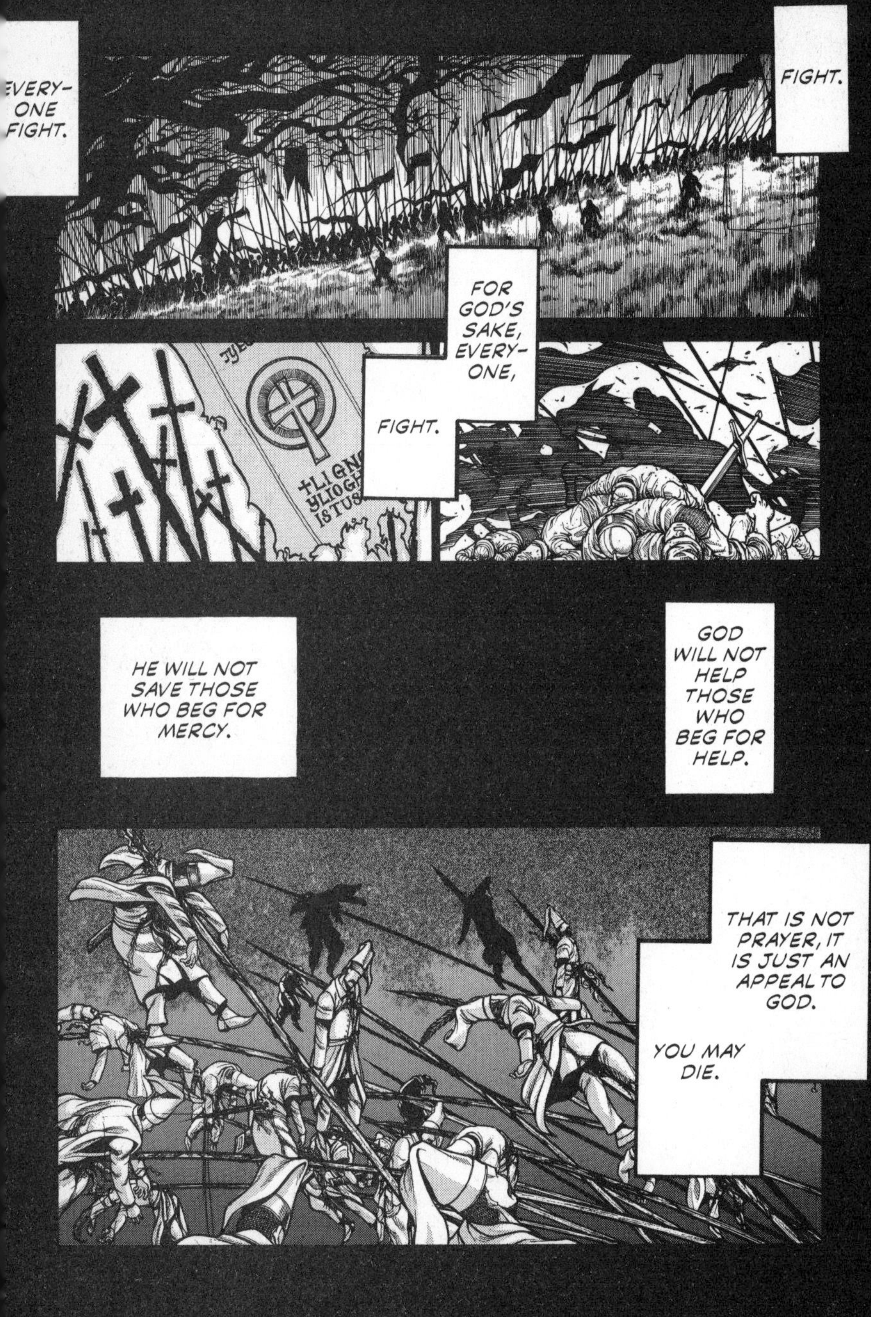
FIGHT.
EVERY-ONE FIGHT.
FOR GOD'S SAKE, EVERY-ONE,
FIGHT.
GOD WILL NOT HELP THOSE WHO BEG FOR HELP.
HE WILL NOT SAVE THOSE WHO BEG FOR MERCY.
THAT IS NOT PRAYER, IT IS JUST AN APPEAL TO GOD.
YOU MAY DIE.

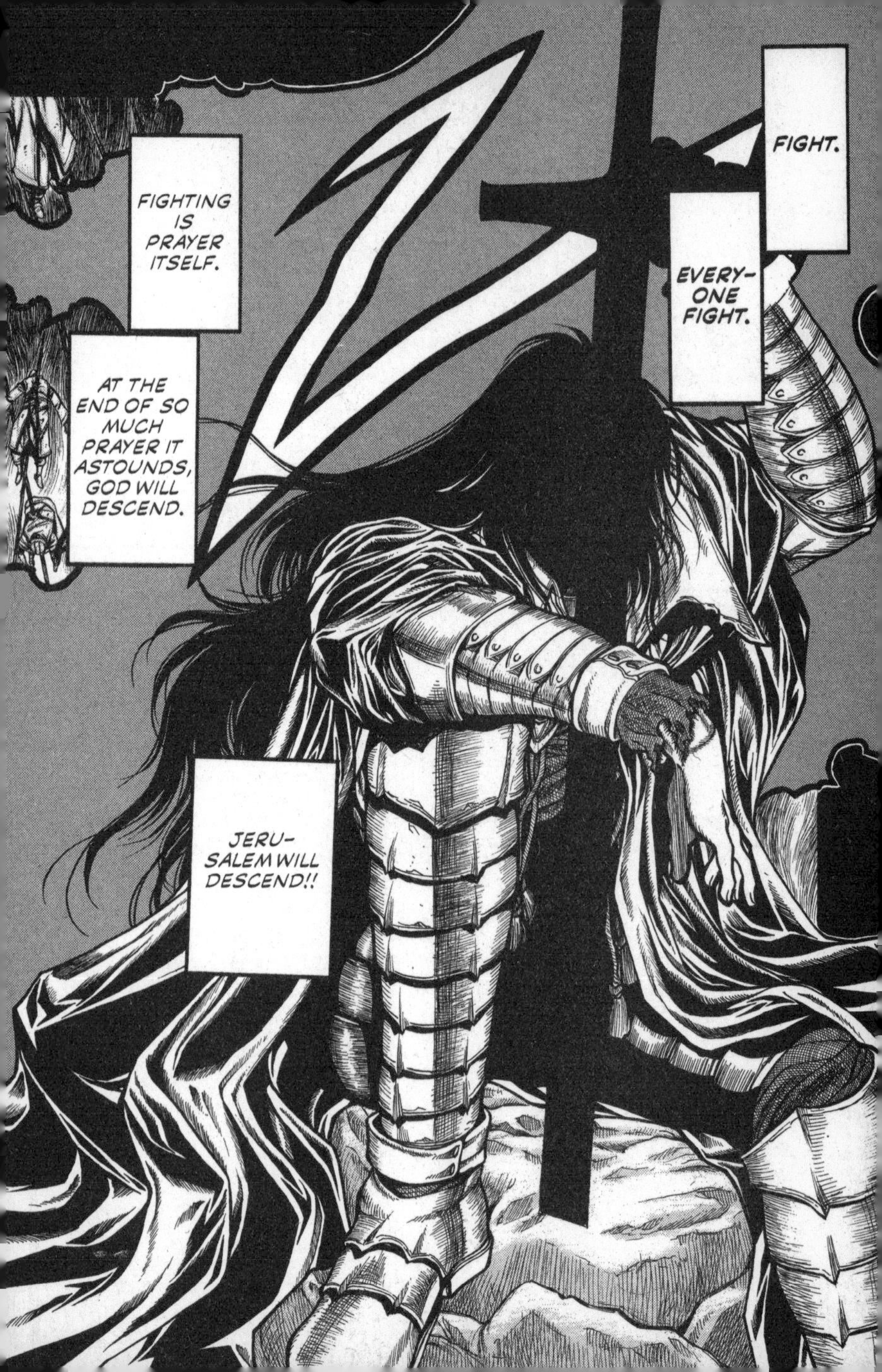
FIGHT.
EVERY-ONE FIGHT.
FIGHTING IS PRAYER ITSELF.
AT THE END OF SO MUCH PRAYER IT ASTOUNDS, GOD WILL DESCEND.
JERU-SALEM WILL DESCEND!!

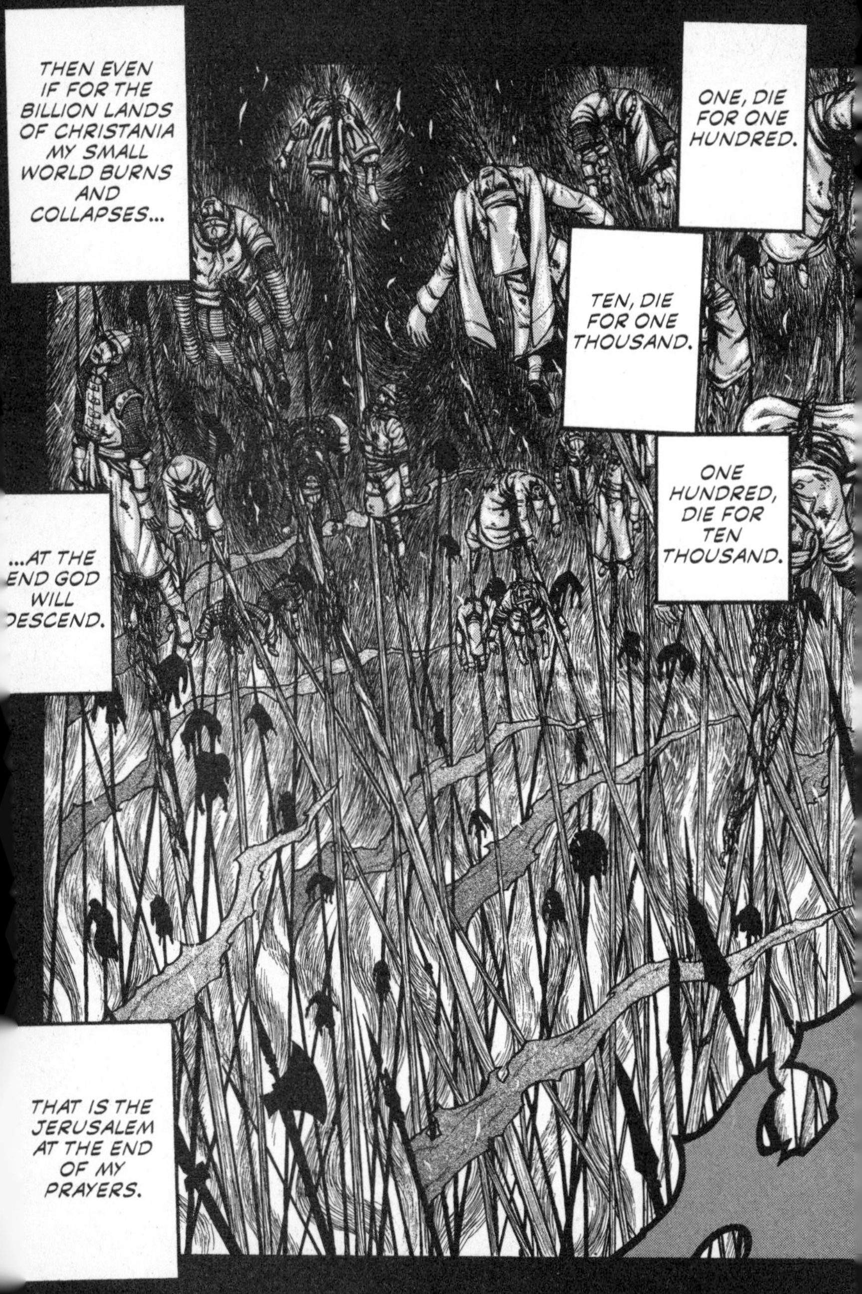
ONE, DIE FOR ONE HUNDRED.
TEN, DIE FOR ONE THOUSAND.
ONE HUNDRED, DIE FOR TEN THOUSAND.
THEN EVEN IF FOR THE BILLION LANDS OF CHRISTANIA MY SMALL WORLD BURNS AND COLLAPSES...
...AT THE END GOD WILL DESCEND.
THAT IS THE JERUSALEM AT THE END OF MY PRAYERS.

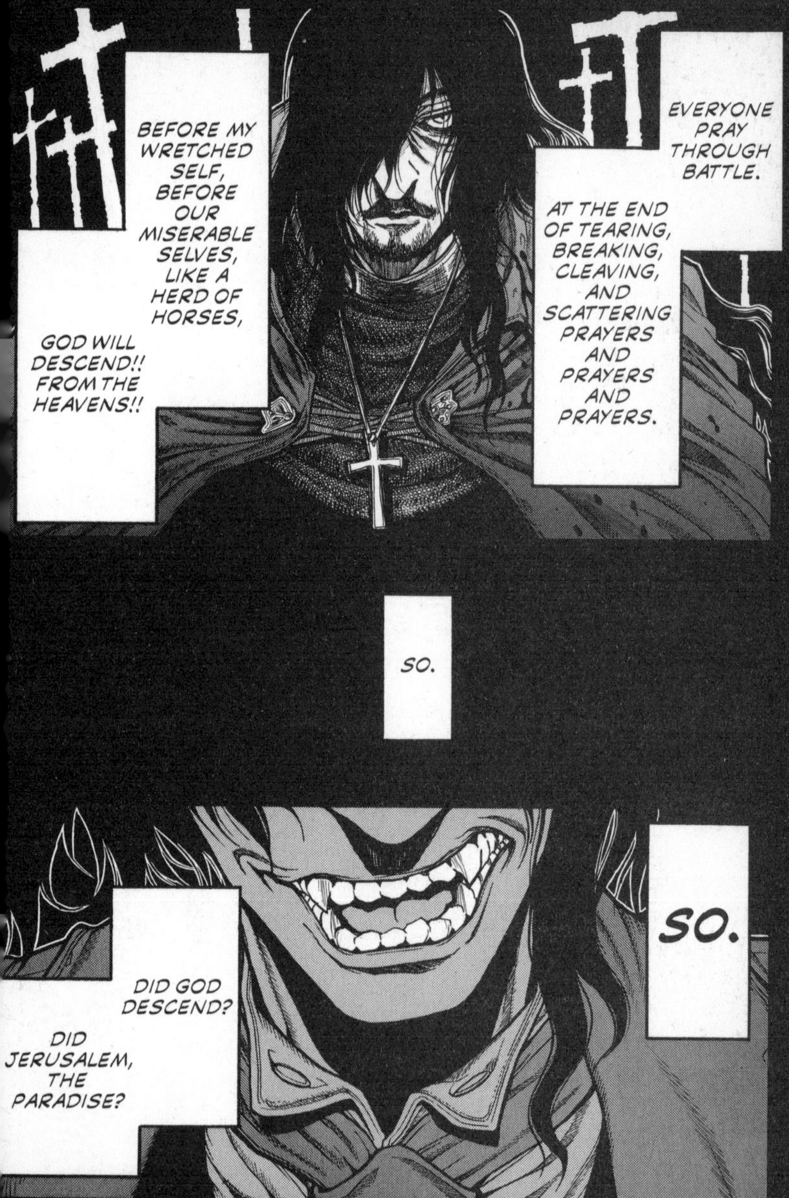
EVERYONE PRAY THROUGH BATTLE.
AT THE END OF TEARING, BREAKING, CLEAVING, AND SCATTERING PRAYERS AND PRAYERS AND PRAYERS.
BEFORE MY WRETCHED SELF, BEFORE OUR MISERABLE SELVES, LIKE A HERD OF HORSES,
GOD WILL DESCEND!! FROM THE HEAVENS!!
SO.
SO.
DID GOD DESCEND?
DID JERUSALEM, THE PARADISE?

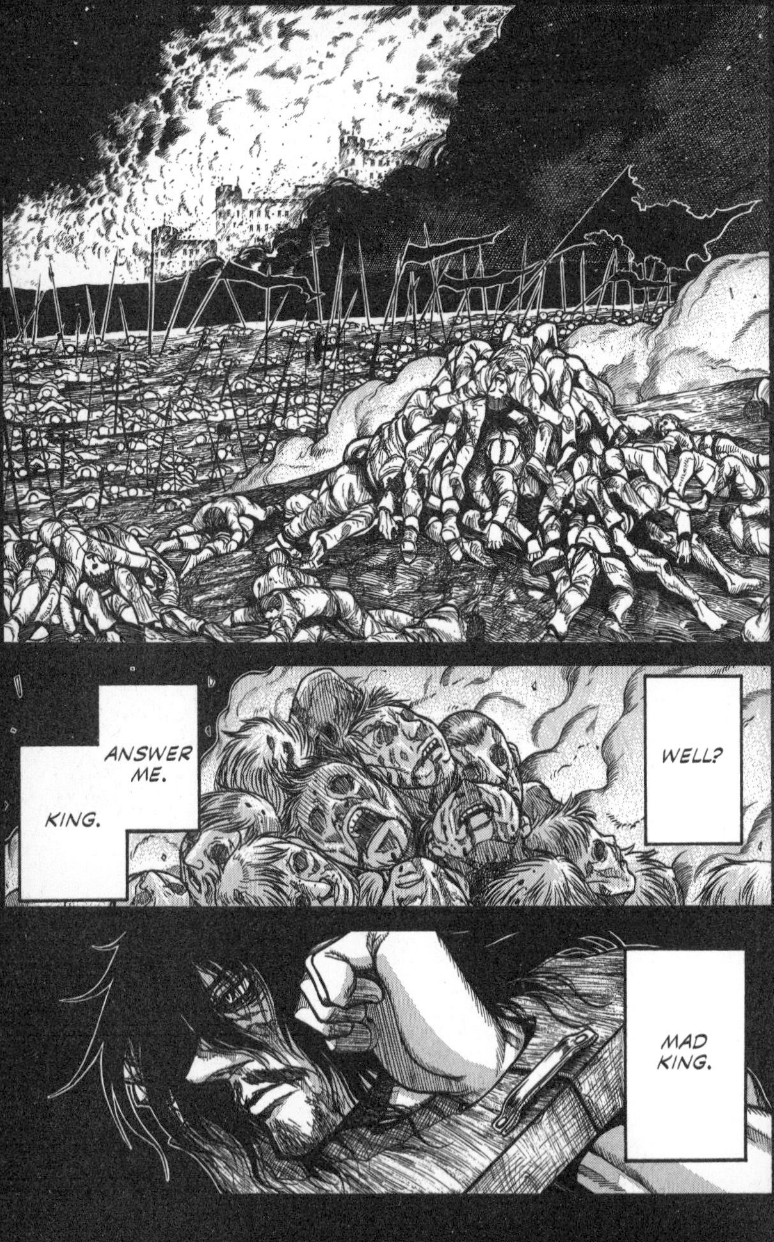
WELL?
ANSWER ME.
KING.
MAD KING.

EVERYONE
DIED.

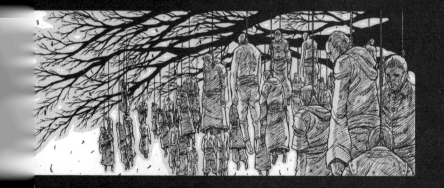

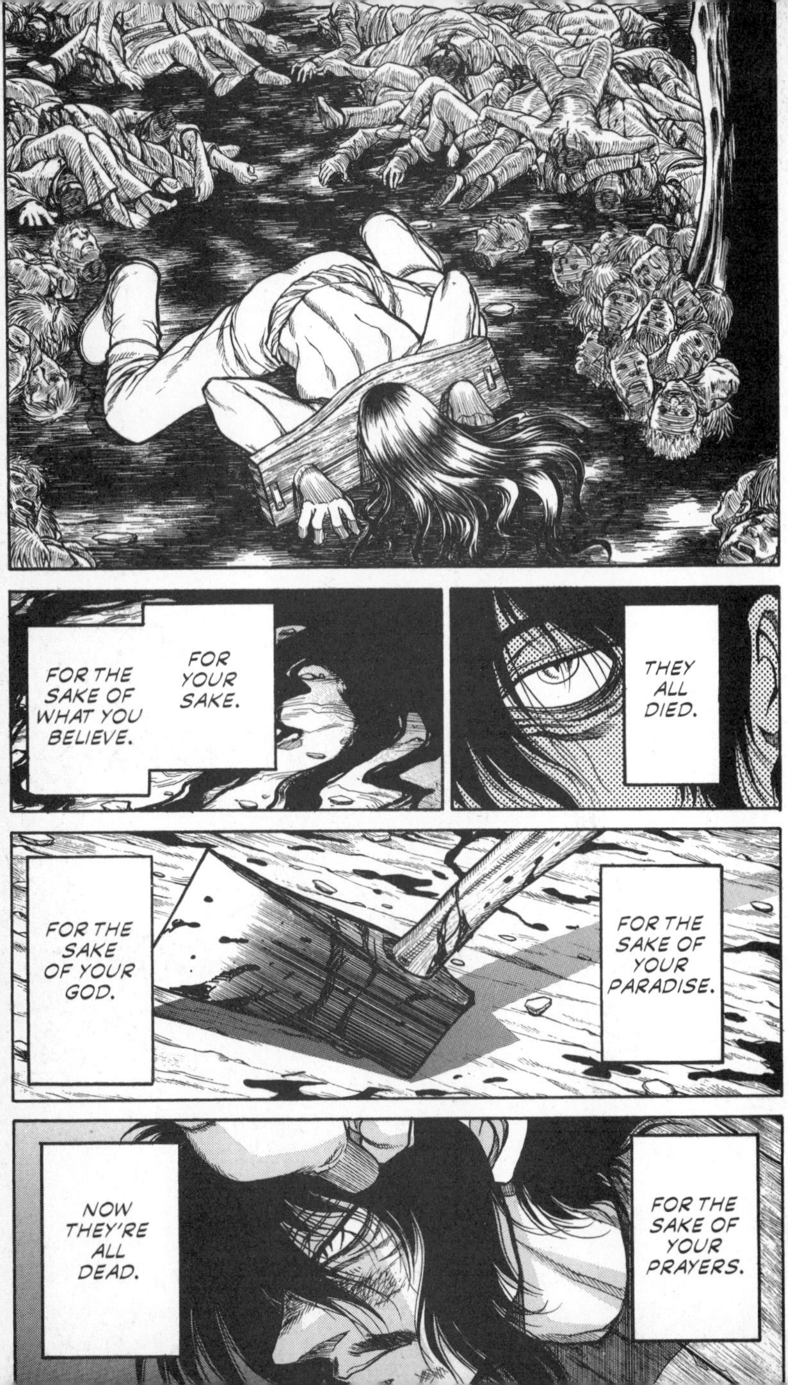
THEY ALL DIED.
FOR YOUR SAKE.
FOR THE SAKE OF WHAT YOU BELIEVE.
FOR THE SAKE OF YOUR PARADISE.
FOR THE SAKE OF YOUR GOD.
FOR THE SAKE OF YOUR PRAYERS.
NOW THEY'RE ALL DEAD.

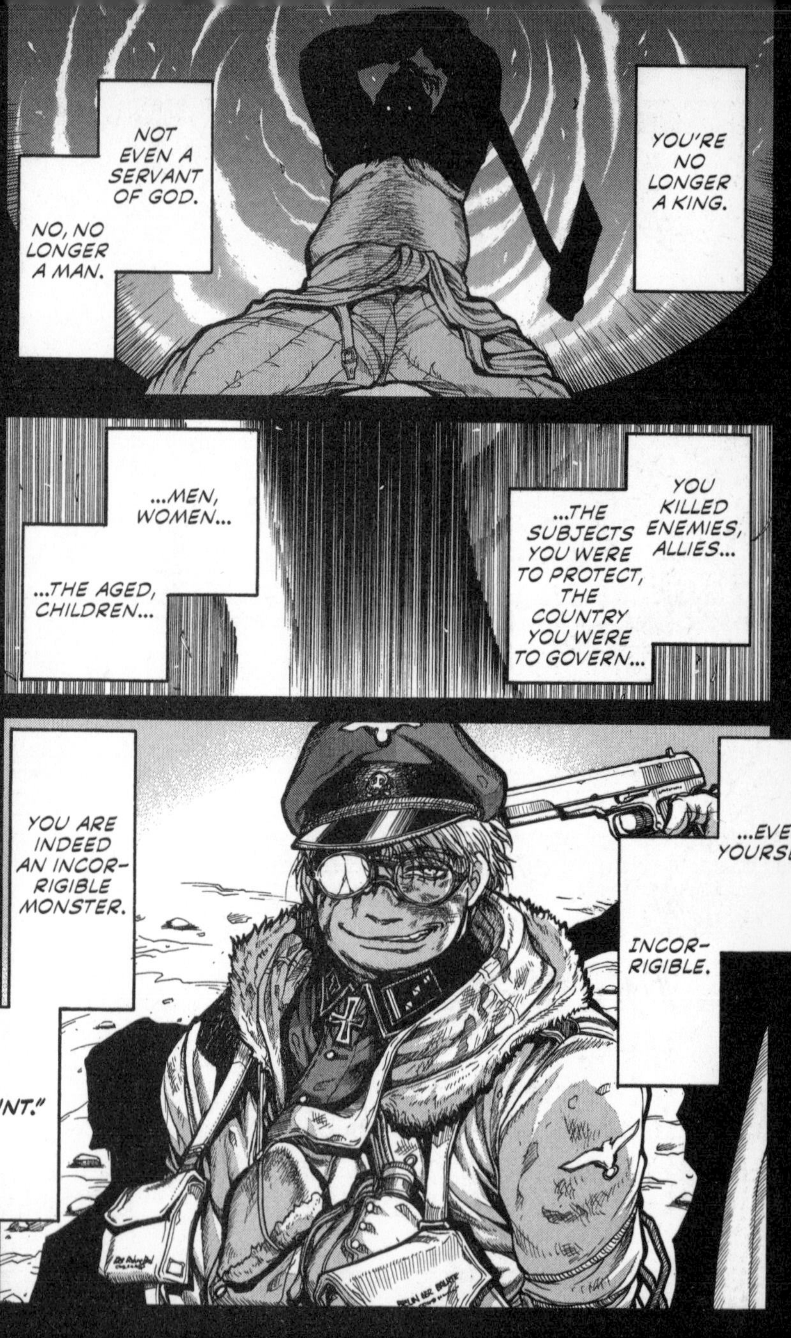
YOU'RE NO LONGER A KING.
NOT EVEN A SERVANT OF GOD.
NO, NO LONGER A MAN.
YOU KILLED ENEMIES, ALLIES...
...THE SUBJECTS YOU WERE TO PROTECT, THE COUNTRY YOU WERE TO GOVERN...
...MEN, WOMEN...
...THE AGED, CHILDREN...
...EVEN YOURSE
INCOR-RIGIBLE.
YOU ARE INDEED AN INCOR-RIGIBLE MONSTER.
"COUNT."

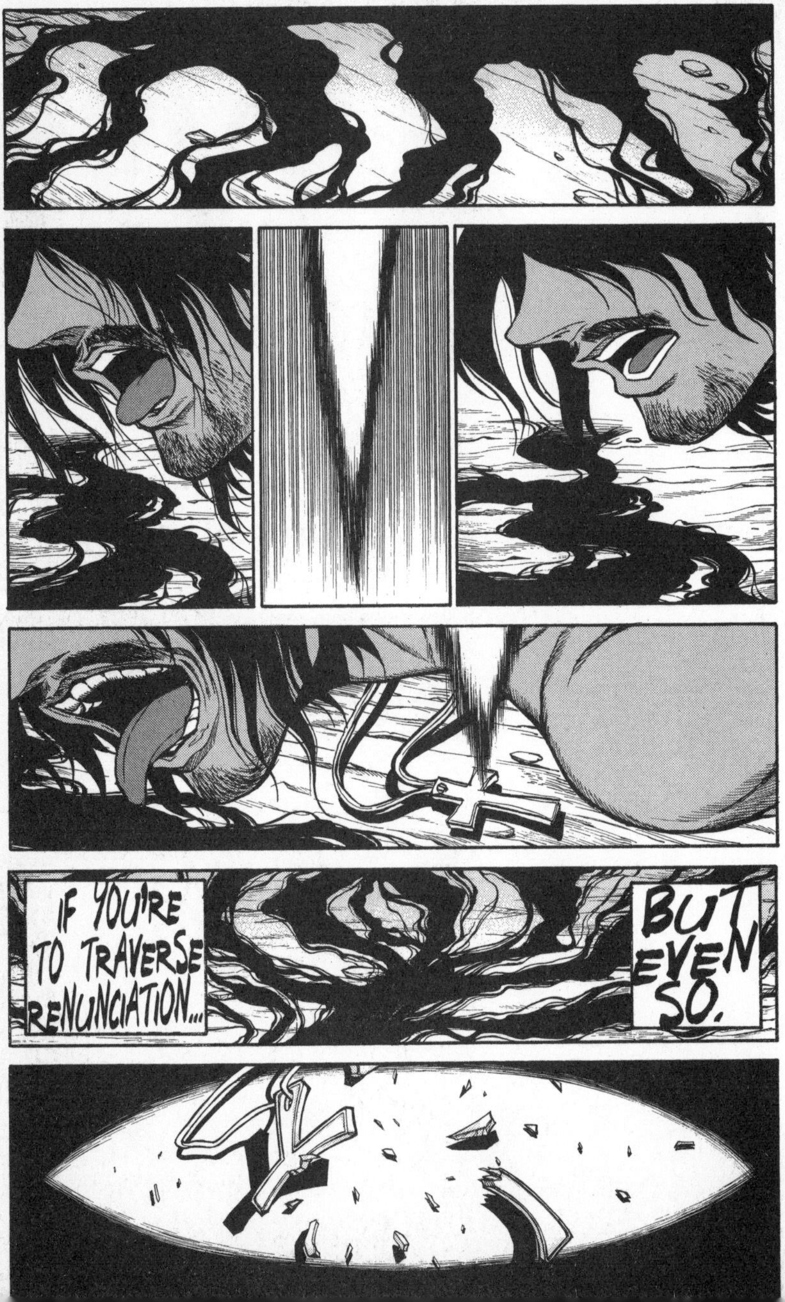
BUT EVEN SO.
IF YOU'RE TO TRAVERSE RENUNCIATION...

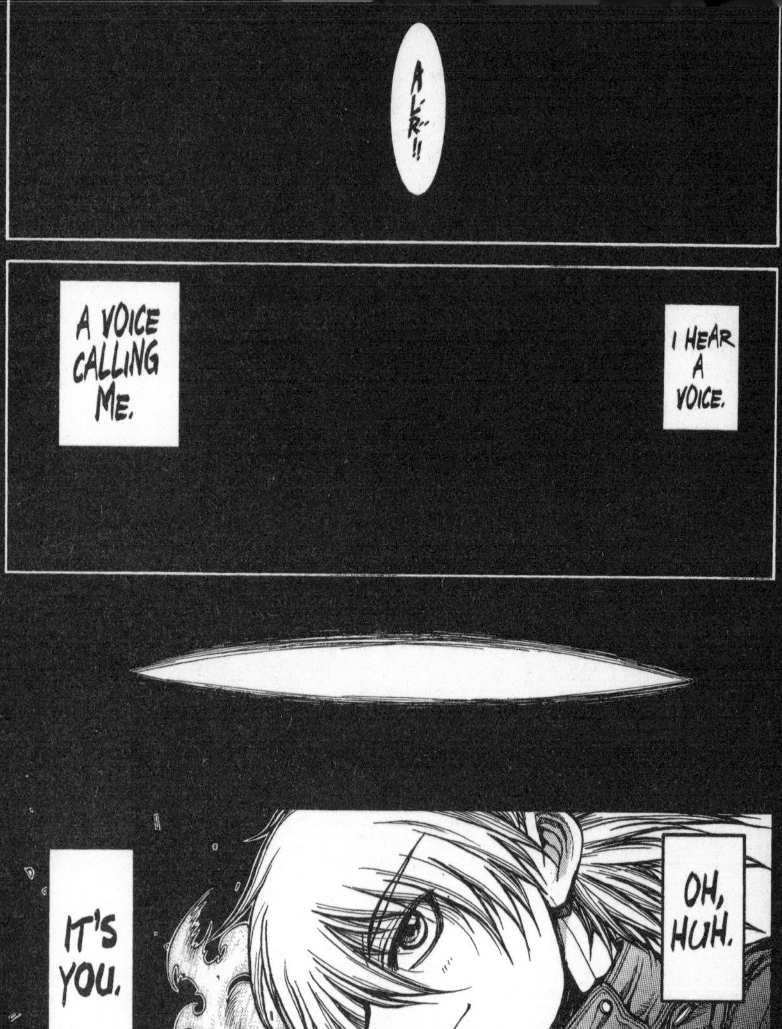
A-L-R!!
I HEAR A VOICE.
A VOICE CALLING ME.
OH, HUH.
IT'S YOU.

TO BE CONTINUED

ORDER 11 / END

KOHTA HIRANO

AHEM
AHEM

Kohta Hirano, so happy about this
volume going on sale that he dresses up
as much like an art student as he can
manage, tries to slip in between Honey
and Clover*, is mistaken for Nankai
Candies, and dies in a fit of despair.

*Note: Honey and Clover is a manga/anime set at an art school.
"Nankai Candies" is a Manzai comedy group.

Hailing from Adachi Ward, Tokyo

Hobbies
+
Being obnoxious, beating off

A bad swordsman to be chased by all night
+
Shira (from the manga Blade of the Immortal)
A bad swordsman even not all night
+
Master Kogan

Between Nina Purpleton and Katejina Loos, which would you choose to date?
+
I'd choose death

*Note: Nina is a character from Mobile Suit Gundam 0083: Stardust Memory,
and Katejina is from Mobile Suit Victory Gundam.

Long time no write!! Get's!! Kohta Hirano here!! Get's!!
I am very happy for this first book in a year
and a half! Get's!!
A lot happened over this past year and a half.
Nico Robin yelled "I wanna live!"
Ahh, thank goodness she made it back to her
companions.
You know, big breasts are great no matter how
many women there are.
Big breasts are.
Big breasts are.
Big breasts are.
To think that Death Note would come to an end...
To think that Light was the culprit...
Did all of you guess correctly who it was?

Now then, about the manga. I overdid a lot of things.
Well, hey, overdone is just about right for it.
I said it's right. What do you mean "who said?"

Ahh, I don't particularly have anything
else to talk about.

Extra space is a waste so I will sing a song.

-The Black Magician Song- Yu-Gi-Oh! Marching Song GX
When will the Black Magician Girl show up, (don)?
A Yu-Gi-Oh! marching song, todon gadon (dadon)
The President comes up, namely exit (donnn)
When will the Black Magician Girl show up, (don)?
Pegasus comes up, namely exit (donnn)
When you abbreviate "Black Magician Girl,"
you can get "brassiere," can't you?
Ah...! I'm sorry, but would you mind leaving
the room for just three minutes?

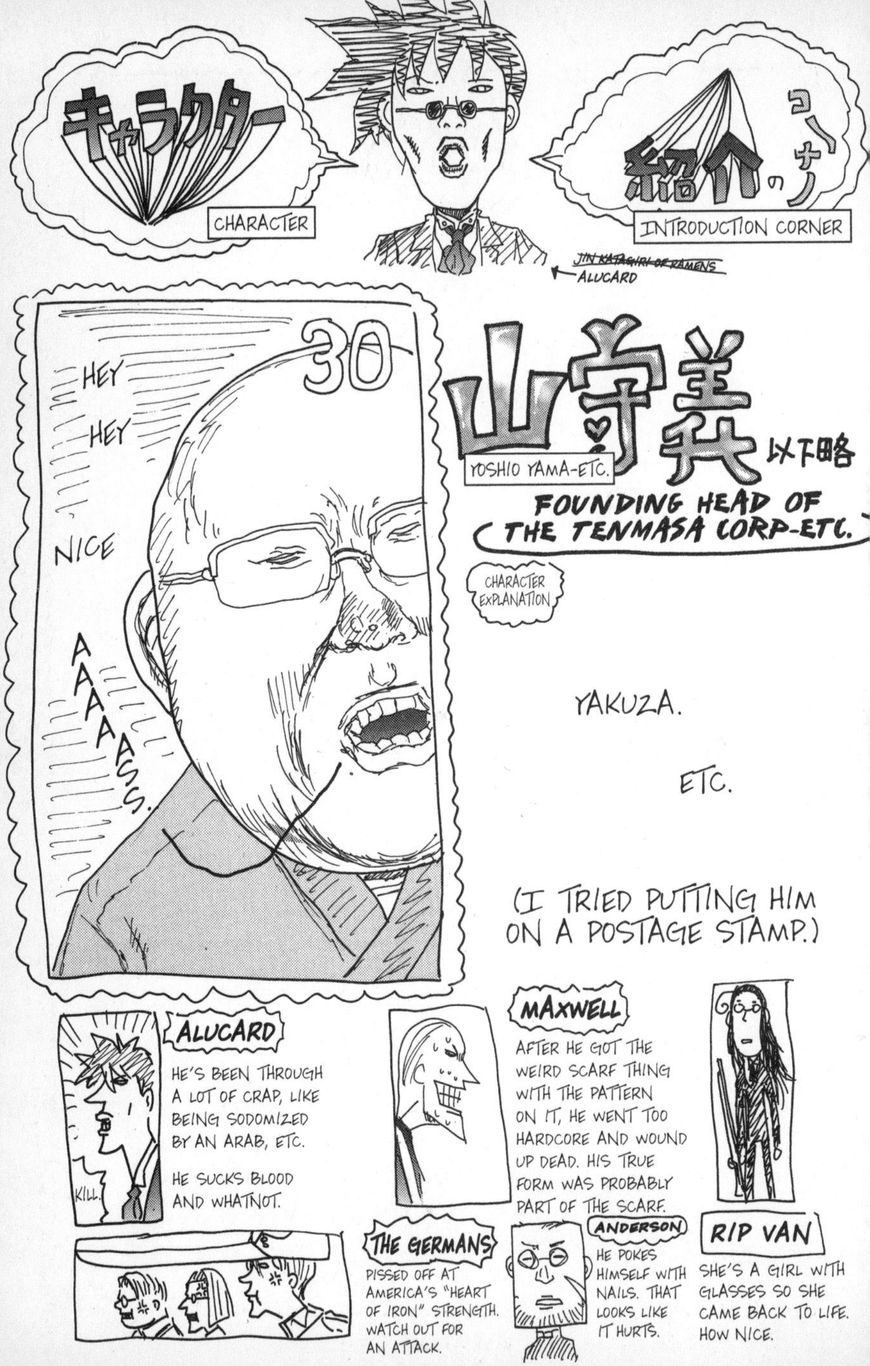
キャラクター
CHARACTER
紹介のコーナー
INTRODUCTION CORNER
JIN KATAGIRI OF RAMENS
ALUCARD
30
HEY
HEY
NICE
AAAAAASS.
山守義 以下略
YOSHIO YAMA-ETC.
FOUNDING HEAD OF THE TENMASA CORP-ETC.
CHARACTER EXPLANATION
YAKUZA.
ETC.
(I TRIED PUTTING HIM ON A POSTAGE STAMP.)
ALUCARD
HE'S BEEN THROUGH A LOT OF CRAP, LIKE BEING SODOMIZED BY AN ARAB, ETC.
HE SUCKS BLOOD AND WHATNOT.
KILL.
MAXWELL
AFTER HE GOT THE WEIRD SCARF THING WITH THE PATTERN ON IT, HE WENT TOO HARDCORE AND WOUND UP DEAD. HIS TRUE FORM WAS PROBABLY PART OF THE SCARF.
THE GERMANS
PISSED OFF AT AMERICA'S "HEART OF IRON" STRENGTH. WATCH OUT FOR AN ATTACK.
ANDERSON
HE POKES HIMSELF WITH NAILS. THAT LOOKS LIKE IT HURTS.
RIP VAN
SHE'S A GIRL WITH GLASSES SO SHE CAME BACK TO LIFE. HOW NICE.

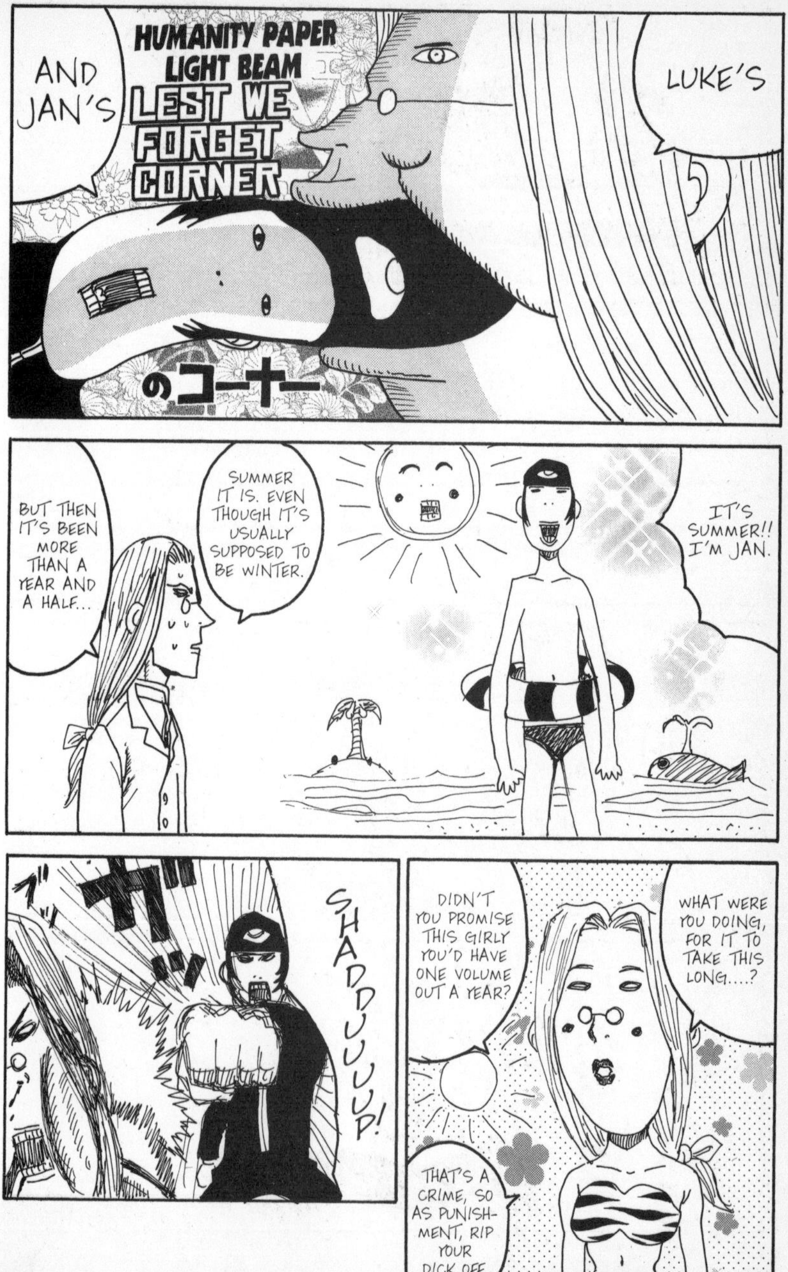
LUKE'S
HUMANITY PAPER LIGHT BEAM
LEST WE FORGET CORNER
のコーナー
AND JAN'S
IT'S SUMMER!! I'M JAN.
SUMMER IT IS. EVEN THOUGH IT'S USUALLY SUPPOSED TO BE WINTER.
BUT THEN IT'S BEEN MORE THAN A YEAR AND A HALF...
WHAT WERE YOU DOING, FOR IT TO TAKE THIS LONG....?
DIDN'T YOU PROMISE THIS GIRLY YOU'D HAVE ONE VOLUME OUT A YEAR?
THAT'S A CRIME, SO AS PUNISHMENT, RIP YOUR DICK OFF.
SHADDUUUUUP!

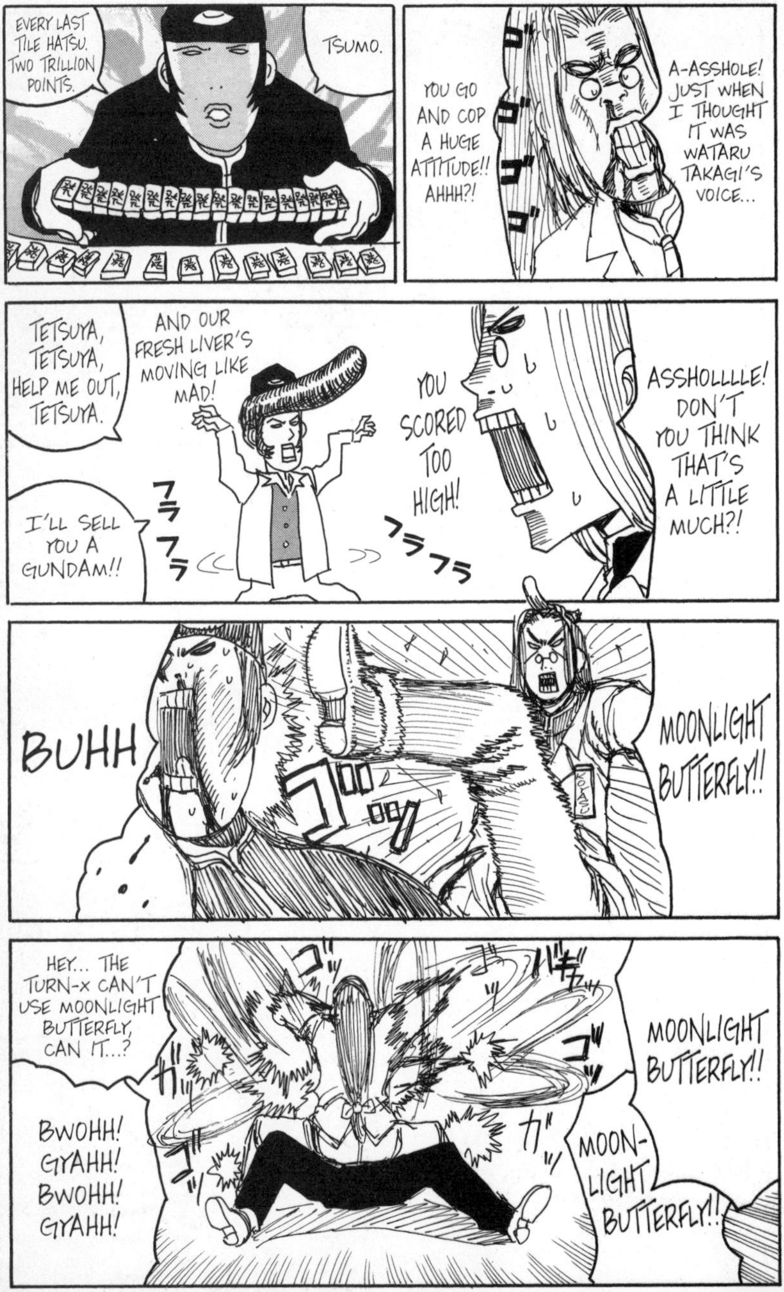
A-ASSHOLE! JUST WHEN I THOUGHT IT WAS WATARU TAKAGI'S VOICE...
ゴゴゴゴ
YOU GO AND COP A HUGE ATTITUDE!! AHHH?!
TSUMO.
EVERY LAST TILE HATSU. TWO TRILLION POINTS.
ASSHOLLLLE! DON'T YOU THINK THAT'S A LITTLE MUCH?!
YOU SCORED TOO HIGH!
AND OUR FRESH LIVER'S MOVING LIKE MAD!
TETSUYA, TETSUYA, HELP ME OUT, TETSUYA.
フラフラ
I'LL SELL YOU A GUNDAM!!
フラフラ
MOONLIGHT BUTTERFLY!!
BUHH
MOONLIGHT BUTTERFLY!!
MOON-LIGHT BUTTERFLY!!
HEY... THE TURN-X CAN'T USE MOONLIGHT BUTTERFLY, CAN IT...?
BWOHH! GYAHH! BWOHH! GYAHH!

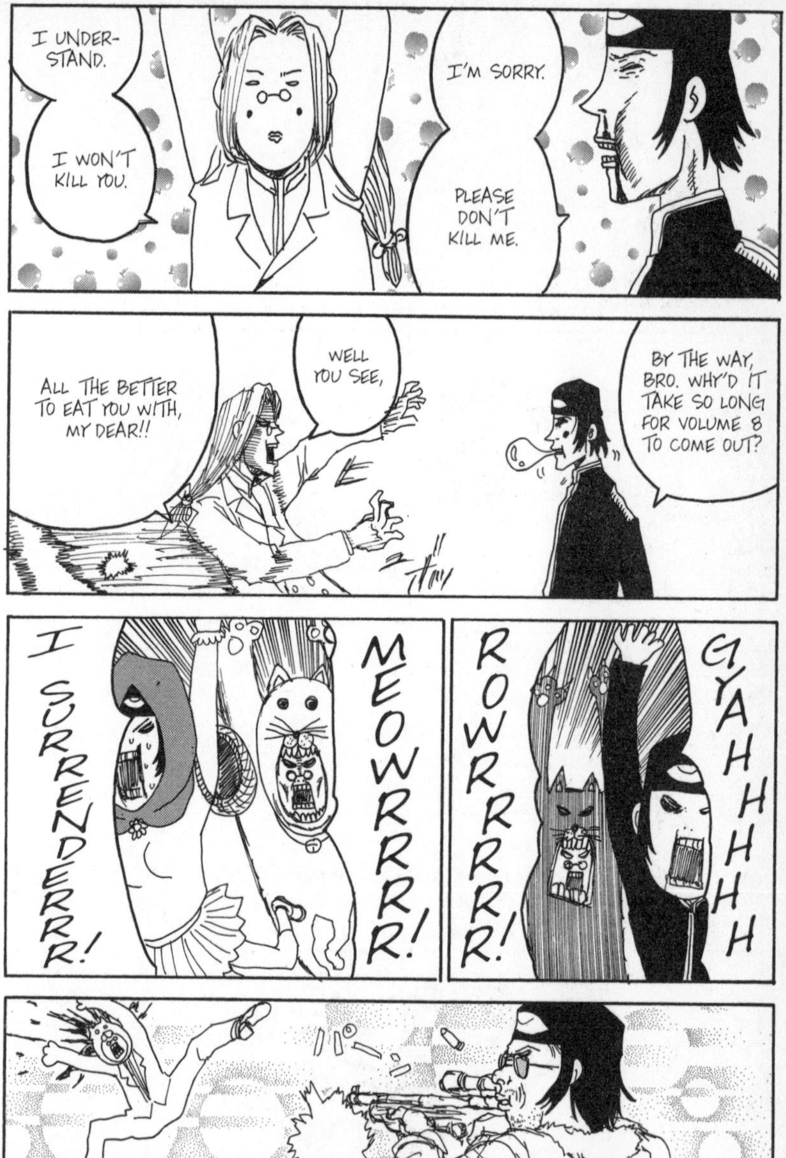
I'M SORRY.
PLEASE DON'T KILL ME.
I UNDER-STAND.
I WON'T KILL YOU.
BY THE WAY, BRO. WHY'D IT TAKE SO LONG FOR VOLUME 8 TO COME OUT?
WELL YOU SEE,
ALL THE BETTER TO EAT YOU WITH, MY DEAR!!
GYAHHHHHH
ROWRRRRR!
MEOWRRRRR!
I SURRENDERRR!
CROSS-ENGLAND HUNTING TOUR

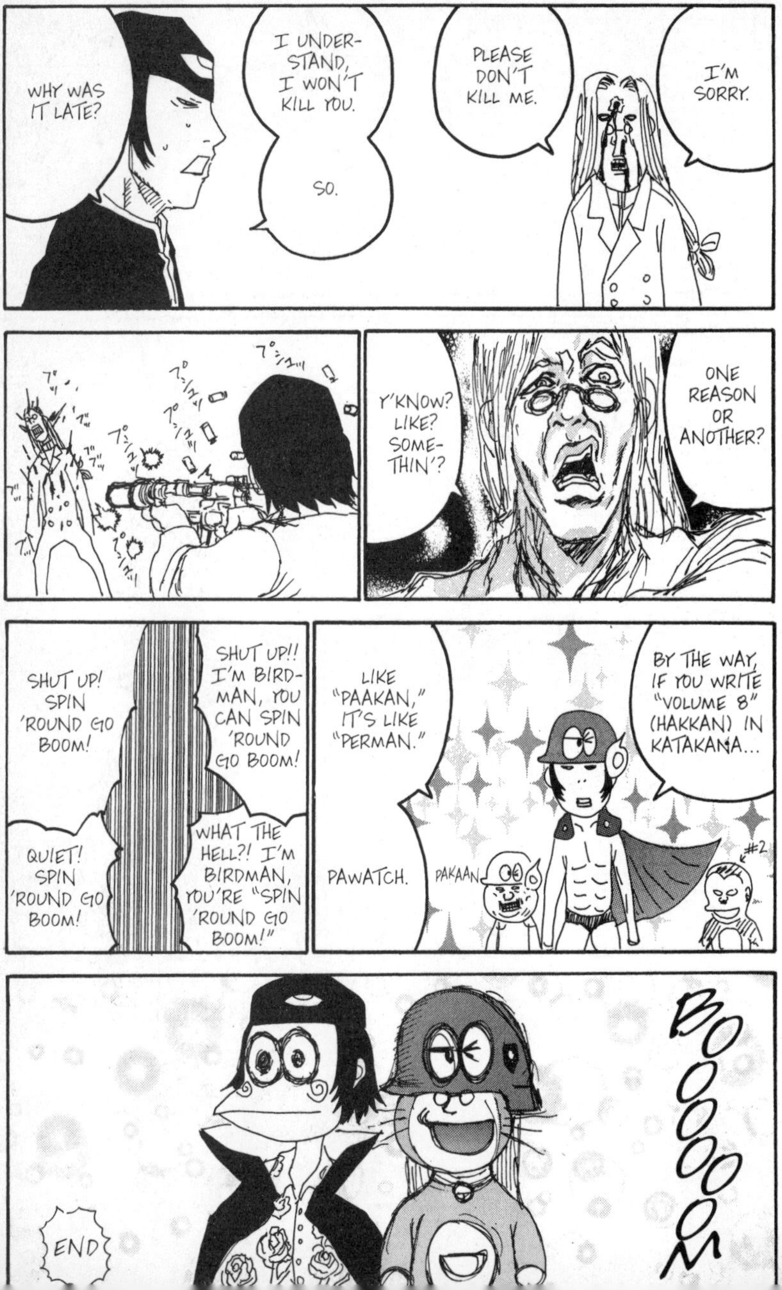
I'M SORRY.
PLEASE DON'T KILL ME.
I UNDER-STAND, I WON'T KILL YOU.
SO.
WHY WAS IT LATE?
ONE REASON OR ANOTHER?
Y'KNOW? LIKE? SOME-THIN'?
BY THE WAY, IF YOU WRITE "VOLUME 8" (HAKKAN) IN KATAKANA...
LIKE "PAAKAN," IT'S LIKE "PERMAN."
#2
PAKAAN
PAWATCH.
SHUT UP!! I'M BIRD-MAN, YOU CAN SPIN 'ROUND GO BOOM!
SHUT UP! SPIN 'ROUND GO BOOM!
WHAT THE HELL?! I'M BIRDMAN, YOU'RE "SPIN 'ROUND GO BOOM!"
QUIET! SPIN 'ROUND GO BOOM!
BOOOOOOOM
END

STOP

This is the back of the book!

This manga collection is translated into English but oriented in right-to-left reading format at the creator's request, maintaining the artwork's visual orientation as originally published in Japan. If you've never read manga in this way before, take a look at the diagram below to give yourself an idea of how to go about it. Basically, you'll be starting in the upper right corner and will read each balloon and panel moving right to left. It may take some getting used to, but you should get the hang of it very quickly. Have fun!

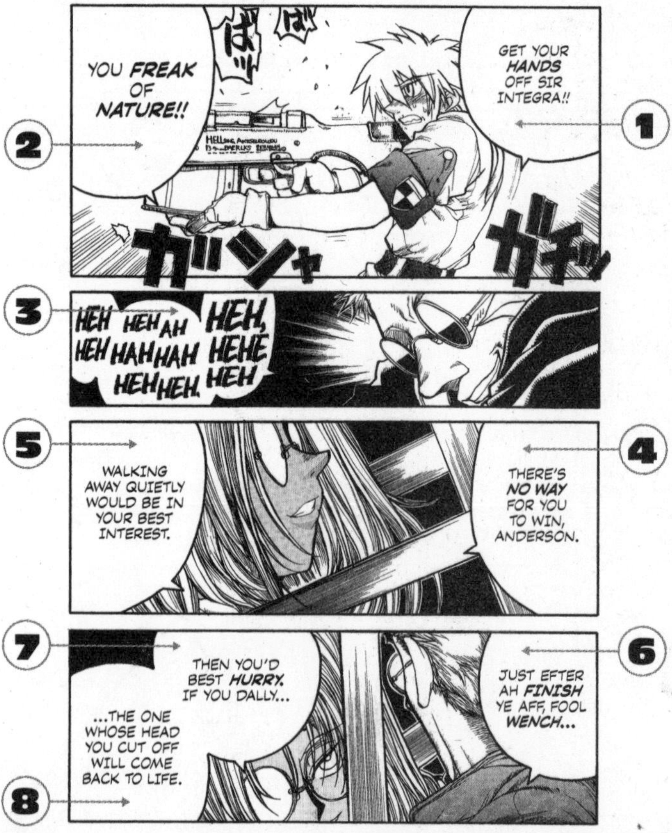
1
GET YOUR HANDS OFF SIR INTEGRA!!
2
YOU FREAK OF NATURE!!
ガチッ
ガシャ
3
HEH, HEHE HEH
HEH AH HAH HAH HEH HEH.
HEH HEH
4
THERE'S NO WAY FOR YOU TO WIN, ANDERSON.
5
WALKING AWAY QUIETLY WOULD BE IN YOUR BEST INTEREST.
6
JUST EFTER AH FINISH YE AFF, FOOL WENCH...
7
THEN YOU'D BEST HURRY. IF YOU DALLY...
8
...THE ONE WHOSE HEAD YOU CUT OFF WILL COME BACK TO LIFE.